Bow Tie

The First Manuscript of the Richards' Trust

Second Edition

By

W.J. Cherf

The front cover's reversing clock image is adapted from the apple.com's time machine logo. The back cover contains a monumental image of the Pharaoh Akhenaten taken from the Luxor Museum, Luxor, Egypt.

ALSO BY W.J. CHERF

The Manuscripts of the Richards' Trust

Bow Tie
Recovery
Children of Ptah
Imhotep
Maat-ka-re. Memoirs of a Time Traveler
Iron from the Sky

The Adventures of J.J. Stone

The First Soul
The Lictor of Magic
I Am the Storm
Dark Blade

Adventures in Paranormal Archaeology

The Magician's Tomb
Netherworld's Gate
Dhampirica
Hallowed Promises

Twenty-Forth Century Mercenaries

I Am Jonathan
I Am Gregory
I Am Krait
I Am Peter

This book is dedicated to those intrepid souls who slugged their way through its many revisions.

Consequently, I have many to thank. The initial victims were Bruce, Karen, John, and Bob. Then Kristin, Kate, Bill, James, Gary, Kalin, Jim and Jan, who offered their kind suggestions and sometimes much-needed blunt observations.

Bless you all.

But Sue gets the biggest blessing for her loving patience and support.

ABOUT THIS EDITION

Author's despise revisiting their former works and this writer is no exception. This new edition may at first blush seem a worthless expenditure of effort for a work of fiction, but in this case, it is justified for several reasons.

First of all, this book and its five subsequent volumes are works of historical science fiction. And as a card-carrying historian, the author takes historical and scientific accuracy quite seriously.

Secondly, horrors of horrors, a good colleague discovered serious factual flaws. The author admits, in all humility, that he blundered. And so those issues have been addressed.

The author would like to thank his good friend Professor Dr. Manfred Gerhard Schmidt for his encouraging words regarding the updating of this book. Manny, you were so right in so many ways!

Additionally, the field of genetic research has moved forward in quantum leaps since this book's inception in 2011. So with this edition, the author took the opportunity to update and make several revisions to reflect those advances. Other than that, the book's plot and characters remain intact.

Despite the original book's length and heft, the type set of this edition has been increased to 12-point for better readability. While the mass of this work was a bona fide bedside counterweight, it now should be a registered weapon.

And finally, I must thank my Sweet Sue for her laser-sharp eyes and discerning perspectives. Love you girl.

"If one accepts the principle of complete revelation, that the gods created a universe which has been essentially static from the beginning, and if one is able to account for any phenomenon as effected by divine agency and therefore not open to human questioning, then there will be little occasion to seek out impersonal causes for our effects, and there will be no interest in the movement of time."

John Albert Wilson

FOREWORD

The realm of fiction allows extraordinary personalities the ability to mold the very landscape of their age; whereas history is that crucible wherein individuals are shaped by their times.

Without question this is a work of historical science fiction. As a consequence, it represents a blending of the above sentiment. While extraordinary personalities indeed populate its pages, they are not the dominating element; rather it is the story itself that really matters and its message.

As one might expect within such a genre much contained within this book is without question factual in every respect. Much is also the product of the author's imagination. As with any work of historical writing, actual events and personalities are described, do appear, and are referred to by name. As with any work of fiction any similarity either to events or individuals, either living or dead, is purely coincidental.

J.W. Richards

Editor's Note

My name is Paul Silas. I am both the editor and executor of the so-called Richards' Trust. So-called because the name behind the trust is a fiction. Nonetheless, I can assure you that the dynamic personality that lurks behind the *nom de plume* of Professor Joseph William Richards is, or at least was, a living and breathing individual of considerable capacity. You can accept this judgment based upon some twenty-nine-odd years of my association with the man.

Per the instructions of the Richards' Trust, three manuscripts are to be published. It is my task, as editor, to make sure that this ardent desire of my colleague comes to fruition. As an editor of a university press, I do have some connections; however, due to the subject matter of these manuscripts I cannot justify their publication under our house banner. So I sought out the good graces of a non-academic publishing house. As a result of that collaboration you now hold the first manuscript of the series.

The Richards' Trust was quite specific regarding the publication of these manuscripts, the schedule to be followed, and what would set the entire process into motion. Put simply, Professor Richards wished, in the event that he could not be contacted after a continuous period of six months, that I, as his executor, was to begin the publication process of the first manuscript on his behalf. Additionally, I have been granted full power of attorney in all matters legal. Once the first manuscript is available in print, then the clock begins for the remainder of the manuscripts.

As of this printing, my client has been missing for some fifteen months. Naturally, out of concern, I immediately instituted an informal and subsequent formal investigation after my loss of contact. His brownstone flat near the university was searched and nothing was found amiss. The requisite layer of dust was present evenly everywhere and without blemish. The perishables of his refrigerator had, and I quote from the Chicago Police report, "grown legs."

As in any such disappearance a domestic trace of his credit card statements indicated that one of his last transactions included a roundtrip ticket to Egypt. An inquiry with the State Department has confirmed that Richards was processed by passport control at Cairo International Airport and admitted into that country. A missing tourist investigation undertaken by the Egyptian Government at the behest of our State Department uncovered that Richards had checked into the Mena House on August 30th. Here, with his splendid accommodations overlooking the Giza Plateau left untouched, the trail of Professor Joseph William Richards ends.

To date, Richards' whereabouts remain unknown; his remains unfound. Consequently, and after the passing of the stipulated period, I, his executor, executed the literary trust.

All advances and royalties from the publication of the manuscripts are to be deposited into the Richards' Trust, where they will be divided equally among several designated funding instruments. Once any of these instruments reaches a specified threshold, then that threshold is to be reduced by seventy-five percent and the apportioned amount is to be distributed equally in the following manner: to a pre-existing offshore bank account, as seed funding for an endowed chair in Egyptian philology at Richards' home institution of higher learning, and as grant funding to a West Coast prostate cancer research institute. Once the specified thresholds are again reached, then the cycle is to begin anew. Once the copyright limitation has expired on the publications, then all instruments are to clear their accounts to the above mentioned entities in final, lump sum deposits, and the Richards' Trust extinguished.

The why behind all of these details is frankly beyond me, while others less so, but these are nonetheless the precise wishes of "Joseph William Richards" to whom I am legally bound as his executor and colleague.

*   *   *

On a personal note, I have already had the privilege to edit and publish several of Richards' academic works, notably his immensely successful ancient Egyptian grammar, *The Scribe's Way*, which appeared under our press' banner. On the basis of these works I thought that I knew the man; in retrospect, I could not have been more wrong. While the narrative style of the manuscripts holds true and recognizable in every respect to Richards' literary persona that I thought that I knew, it is their content that so deeply troubles me. The whole left me wondering, unsatisfied, and with a myriad of unanswerable questions. While I have been vaguely aware through a colleague of the rumors emanating from Wright-Patterson Air Force Base, especially regarding the quantum mechanics research underway there, I was nonetheless totally unprepared for the scientific aspects of the tale told here, their ramifications, implications, and of course the purported true purpose of our university's Philology Annex itself. Additionally, due to my close ties with our university's Near Eastern Institute and its staff, I am cognizant of many of the archaeological and historical details contained within – all that are completely verifiable if not common knowledge. Still, the manuscripts describe far more that in no respect could be squared against the known historical and archaeological record. To be frank, I am left in a bit of a bind and quandary – the mix of the scientific with the historical. In the end, Richards' story left me breathless. Consequently, his manuscripts should be regarded as fiction, as I have absolutely no way of verifying their content.

PROLOGUE
Year 28 (*ca.* 1389 BC)

Looking down upon his remarkably even stump that was once a right hand, Meryptah, high priest of Amen Re, remembered all too well how it happened. But that was not enough, for he did not know why, or for what purpose – only that the Great God had tested his strength and had found it wanting. This personal judgment greatly impressed this man of extraordinary influence, second only to pharaoh himself. The stump was his source of deep selfless introspection that verged upon what others would recognize millennia later as the Christian virtue of humility.

It all had begun while Meryptah was a young acolyte, who was nearing the final completion of his priestly training during an early morning vigil, which had been predetermined by lot, at an hour that was the least desired among his fellow priestly candidates. But that did not matter to the young man of fifteen inundations. The sheer fact that he had even achieved this moment of arduous guardianship deep within the recesses of the Great One's shrine, now before the image of the Hidden One, the greatest god of gods, Amen Re himself, Meryptah counted this as a personal privilege beyond price. With a stiffly rigid back, and knelling on his left knee with his right extended seemingly striding forward, he silently prayed. He held out his arms from his sides, elbows bent, palms facing the life-size golden image of sublime divinity.

By his own reckoning, he was nearing the end of his prayerful guardianship. Still he had not received any sign of the god's awareness to his heartfelt pleas for admittance into his service. Having taken his bodily preparations and precursory vows with absolute care and seriousness, this ascetically-minded acolyte even had eschewed a pad for his left knee. It now ached and burned as it seemed to grind itself into the smooth limestone flooring.

Ever patient, ever hopeful, Meryptah awaited his divine portent within a stagnant cloud of heavy myrrh incense that filled his nostrils with every breath. His never-wavering eyes remained transfixed upon his god's well-proportioned heroic image that was so deftly illuminated by dozens of oil lamps and tapers. It seemed to actually breathe. The flickering flames cast a myriad of shadows across the

1

chamber's golden walls. The image's of the inscribed sacred of texts seemed to move of their own accord.

Then it all began with the appearance of a brilliant pinpoint of light directly above and before Meryptah's head. A growing and luminescent disk began to form. Before incredulous eyes the disk quickly grew in size to a width wide enough for Meryptah's broad shoulders to pass through. Open mouthed and filled with religious rapture and a tinge of fear, Meryptah watched a strange, ivory-white hand and arm emerged from within the disk's glare. To his amazement, it extended down toward the kneeling supplicant. Speechless and not knowing what to do, Meryptah did the obvious. He took hold of the divinely proffered hand with his right and was immediately surprised by its strength. Now in physical contact with the very hand of Amen Re himself, the appendage shook him mightily at first. Meryptah believed it to be a test. But for what purpose he did not know. Then as the god appeared satisfied with the strength of his grasp, the god's hand began to draw Meryptah toward the divinely bright disk. But the acolyte resisted. Refusing to let go of the divine three-fingered hand, Meryptah slowly was drawn to his feet and toward the light by the Great God, who proved to be infinitely stronger than he. To the young man's surprise his right hand was drawn fully within the divine light of the disk. While so immersed in that light, Meryptah felt no pain, just the tension of his tight grip and the stretching of his forearm's muscles. Like a determined crocodile clamped onto the leg of a sickly cow, the acolyte refused to let go.

In retrospect, the last thing the acolyte consciously remembered was the sudden release, the falling back in a heap, and the shock wave that was accompanied by a great clap of thunder that roared in his ears. Meryptah was rendered unconscious, having been stunned by the reverberating concussion within the shrine's confines. It was not long after that three high-ranking *sem*-priests appeared. Bursting through the double-leaved portal of the holy of holies, they wore grim faces set on investigating what the noisy ruckus was all about.

What they found, however, stopped them dead in their tracks, as chaos reigned everywhere within the darkened chamber. Oil lamps spilled their contents when their heavy stands overturned. Glowing red cedar charcoal from the incense burners lay scattered across the floor. Tapers were snuffed out and toppled, spilling their precious bee's wax into rapidly cooling pools. An unidentifiable but distinctive reek of something invaded their nostrils. And in the shrine's center sprawled an unmoving form on the pavement before the god's own image. That Meryptah lay there was not clear until freshly lit oil lamps were summoned. Their mellow yellow light revealed the still smoldering front of the acolyte's white linen kilt that had been singed brown. His naked chest, freshly shaven head, and sides of his arms seemed to glow a bright and painful red. His lips were found blistered and cracked. His eyebrows and lashes were no more and upon closer inspection, the young man's right hand from mid-wrist was no more as well.

While it seemed like an eternity to the priests, in reality it was only a few minutes until the freshly awoken, disoriented, and clearly disheveled high priest hurriedly arrived at the sanctuary. With a deeply furrowed brow, the first servant of the Great God surveyed the scene. At his approach the three *sem*-priests withdrew with respectfully bowed heads.

Going directly to the fallen acolyte and dropping to one knee, the elderly high priest of the Great God carefully lowered his head to listen to Meryptah's battered but well-muscled body. Satisfied that he was still breathing and among the living, he next noted several old and well-healed scars earned during the young man's brief but exciting glider career – brave injuries that he himself had personally attended to. Ignoring the reddened expanses of skin that would be treated with a mixture of palm and olive oils, he noted that Meryptah's lips would heal in time with sufficient honey. But upon seeing Meryptah's missing right hand, the former physician tilted his head in curious clinical wonder.

Lifting the injured limb, he thought, *such a fresh and even mid-wrist amputation. I see absolutely no sign of blood anywhere nor charring of skin – just skin melted and joined as if made of bee's wax.*

Slowly shaking his head in 1 disbelief, the high priest continued his observations. *Never have I ever seen the like before.*

Then snatching a quick glance up at the image of the Great God, he piously reconsidered the potential heresy of that thought.

Sitting back on his heels, the former physician turned and barked at his nearby audience, perhaps too harshly, to fetch the temple's chief physician along with his bandages. Wisely, he wanted a second opinion as to Meryptah's condition. No, he needed desperately another set of eyes to confirm what he was seeing.

Jarred into reality by the high priest's sharp words, all three *sem*-priests scattered like a clutch of doves, leaving the high priest alone with his patient and his thoughts.

Looking up and again acknowledging the golden image before him, Amenemhet, high priest of Amen Re, gently sighed and with suddenly moist eyes quietly said, "Great One, you know how long I have prayed to you for a sign. Some hint as to who you would wish to be my successor. But why did you have to do so in such a cruel way, and especially to one so young, so strong, and so brave in your service?"

The troubled first servant of the Great Hidden One began unconsciously mumbling to himself and shaking his head as he returned to gaze upon his traumatized charge.

"My son, it is now clear to me that the wish of the Great Hidden One is for you to succeed me after I have gone West. This lofty position will be a heavy burden for you. Yet, this thing you will do. Knowing your strong will, just as you bravely succeeded as the first falcon flyer. So too will you serve the Great One far better than any man with two sound hands."

CHAPTER I
Early Fourteenth Century BC

"EQUATORIAL ORBIT ESTABLISHED."

So confirmed the ship to its lone and very aware occupant.

"On that glorious day, oh how I had rejoiced!

"How I savored the delicious feeling of that announcement so pregnant with meaning. I had a hunger, no lust, to breathe again an unfiltered, unrecycled atmosphere. I dreamed with heady anticipation of being able to look up and see stars and not be counted as one of them. But above all, I yearned for that supreme ecstasy of feeling the warm blush of a sun's rays through an organic nervous system, to relish the casual caress of a gentle breeze against newly acquired flesh."

So went the anticipated erotica of this millennium star traveler, a being who had grown weary of its cramped confines, an old and near primordial scout surveyor of the genus *Quimbly*.

"I mention this last only as a point of convenient reference, for not all scout surveyors are of my kind – indeed far from it. For many of my far-flung colleagues are non-organics. The majority are silicate-based of one sort or another with a memory capacity far beyond mine, even rivaling that of my surveyor pod's own storage. Then again there is that remarkable ability of theirs to remain dormant for, well, hundreds of cycles until their craft reawakes them.

"But to return to my kind, the Quimbly, our distinct advantage over the silicates is that as messy and fussy organics, we possess an uncanny ability to adapt, blend in, observe, and even interact with other organics, undetected and with surprising intimacy. Such is our advantage. Such is our curse.

"Yes, it is true that to encounter experiences first-hand and at such a root level presents challenges to our very being and identity. A certain amount of remove at an intellectual level must always be in force. To proceed otherwise would be folly. Would mean potential immersion. Could portend going native. Might risk turning one's back on what a scout surveyor stands for – a gatherer of knowledge, ultimately, a seeker of the First Source.

"But I am getting ahead of myself.

"The ability to traverse broad tracks of the great void of space is one thing. But to actually arrive somewhere has always been far, far more special, not to mention satisfying. During such a crossing, most organics repose in deep stasis, much as do the silicates, choosing not to dream at all, wishing instead to drift through that vast remoteness in unconscious oblivion, ever trusting in the sensor capabilities of their interstellar cocoon. But not I, for consciousness has always granted me the time to reflect upon those places that I have already seen, to ponder what I have already learned, and to speculate upon – no dream – of those places yet to come. In many respects, some would say that my chosen state of alertness is merely yet another curse, all the more so as this one is self-inflicted. In truth, at times it is indeed nearly maddening, with the beginnings of relief gained only at the approach of a planetary system possessing the barest minimums of life sustaining parameters. But as old and experienced as I am, I have always prided myself with my patience, my watchfulness, for I am the first of the galactic scout surveyors.

"Even now, as I find myself in orbit, I gaze down, and as always, I discover myself transfixed in absolute wonder at the miracle that is creation. Despite the many times that I have stumbled across such worlds, I am continuously amazed at the universe's diversity. Its clever ingenuity. But here, above this temperate blue jewel, this thriving womb of life abundant, I am overcome with its raw, natural beauty, its many habitats. I note the orb below is teeming with terrestrial, aquatic and even aerial life. Could it be that chance has decreed for me to find that most elusive of a galactic scout surveyor's goals—the First Source—that place from which all life began?"

Admittedly, those were my first jejune thoughts upon viewing that tempting virgin biosphere, blessedly free of any trace of artificial particulate whatsoever. As always after a long journey, I tend to be a bit too exuberant, a bit too poetic for my own good, verging on the dramatic, even daring the prophetic.

The fact is that the planet below is indeed a fine and intriguing specimen, does justify investigation, and from all of its preliminary signatures, is dominated on a global scale by an intelligent terrestrial species. This data is neither poetic nor dramatic. Rather, it is simply a matter of record.

"Consequently, and on the explicit and implicit precepts of the Galactic Survey Charter to which I am bound, I will investigate this system's third satellite. I will chronicle what I have found. I will act upon that data as is deemed appropriate. Then, I will gather, transmit, and then continue on with my wanderings."

This declaration of intent I then composed and sent to The Survey Institute located deep within the galactic center. Contained within that highly compressed energy pulse were all the usual bureaucratic and scientific details – coordinates, star craft maintenance status, my state of physiological fitness, and the preliminary orbital scans that justify the subject's investigation. Even though I know that this message travels at the speed of light, it would take, in local relativistic terms, approximately 1680 years to reach its destination and the attention of my bound editors. But for me, the trail-blazing first scout, such remove has become my trademark, so very typical of my signature.

CHAPTER II

AD 1871. Deir el-Bahri

It was a magnificent sunrise and the sheer three-hundred-foot limestone cliffs glowed with a warm, rosy red blush. Secreted into the cliffs' half-moon shape were the many rich tombs of the ancient ones, hewn with care and prayer. There also were the many windswept ruins carved with blasphemous images that the silly foreign infidels would hover about excitedly like so many bees, gladly paying to see and draw them.

Over the last several generations, the family of el-Rassul had made a handsome living in these arid parts. A living based on the traffic of local lore, the sale of black market antiquities, and the manufacture of trinkets. It was simply amazing how the gut juices of a goose could artificially age a crudely formed lump of clay into an authentic artifact. Even more remarkable was that someone would actually buy one.

So it goes.

So it always has.

Defiantly standing with his hands on his hips and feet splayed at the very brink of these eastern cliffs of the pyramid-shaped mountain known as El-Qurn, young Ahmed looked toward the verdant river far below. As the self-appointed master of all he surveyed, Ahmed took in the immense majesty of this timeless scene with all the ho-hum emotion of one born accustomed to it. Just then a gusting thermal pulled at the light cotton of his calf-length *ghalabiya*. This temporarily broke his proud posture, forcing him to reposition his tanned, dusty, and leathery feet along the wind-scoured rock. Sensing another thermal beginning to build, the young man again stepped forward to the edge and actually leaned into it, thrusting his chest ahead of his feet, with arms outstretched and sleeves billowing like twin sails. It was a glorious feeling, even if extremely dangerous, but glorious nonetheless. Then he saw that he was not alone in this dare-deviltry, for a soaring falcon hovered before him, watching, not twenty feet beyond his reach. With its outstretched pinion feathers moving fractionally and eyes blinking occasionally, the pair stared at one another, and for a moment in time, became one. One tied to the earth, the other to the sky.

Sensing the air pressure drop more than feeling the waning of the wind, the falcon slowly began to yaw and drifted off, leaving Ahmed yearning for the powers of flight, imagining what it must be like to glide so effortlessly. Little did he know, however, that his distant ancestors had done just that, and from this very spot, many, many times.

Although Ahmed had seen the sun rise from this high place countless times, today was somehow special. Maybe it was the way the Nile sparkled as the first rays of the sun struck it, transforming it from a slithering streak of inky black into its more familiar muddy brown. Or, maybe it was the exceptional clarity of the still cool valley air. He could easily pinpoint with his young gray eyes the glinting blue-glazed tiles of the Luxor mosque some three miles away.

Later chroniclers of this day's importance for modern Egyptology and the pride of the Egyptian Nation would do so in error. For Ahmed's presence atop the cliffs was not because of a missing goat or lost lamb. No. It was the young man's curiosity about a particularly deep crevice in the cliff's face and Ahmed's uncanny knack for locating ancient monuments. His discerning eyes, his lanky frame, his spider-like climbing ability, totaled up to a formidable package even within his own family of tomb robbers – purveyors of illegal antiquities all.

Ultimately, what led to Ahmed's dramatic discovery was not what he saw, but rather what he heard. An strong thermal, which collected before the eastern-facing cliffs, had created a freak updraft that alternately whistled and whispered over the cliff's edge. While it ruffled Ahmed's shaggy head of hair and tugged at his *ghalabiya*, the wind moaned in a strangely unfamiliar way among the rocks. At first hearing and then listening from which direction the strange tones of heated air were coming from, Ahmed went to his right to investigate. They seemed to be issuing from a dark crevice before him that he had never before searched. This immediately alerted his instincts, as well as some primal fears.

Peeking over the edge and looking for handholds, Ahmed, without another thought, began to inch his way down between the narrow sides of the fissure. He slowed the descent by pressing his back against one surface and straining his hands and feet against another. About halfway down, Ahmed stopped to rest and looked up to see how far down he was. He half considered how hard the return ascent would be, and, if he should slip, how no one would ever find him alive. Now wedged securely within the fissure and breathing hard, the young man began to have second thoughts.

Indeed, my ever-inquisitive and adventuresome self, just what am I getting myself into?

Pause.

Surely, it will be a struggle of a climb out.

Or am I just slipping down into a tomb of my own making?

After some more deliberation, Ahmed continued on into the deepening shadows of the crevice. Upon reaching its bottom, which took a good fifteen minutes of slow exertion from his resting place, Ahmed breathed a sigh of relief. As his eyes adjusted to the gloom, he began to slowly look around. On this side, the lower side, here and there, were the dried remains of small animals – some naturally mummified, others just scattered bones. Reflexively wrinkling his nose, Ahmed turned to the other side whose bottom gently sloped up to fill in a gap in the crevice's shattered collection of rocky debris. Then something struck Ahmed as odd about the material of the upward side's sloped flooring. It was made up of small, limestone chips! His heart jumped with excitement, but just as quickly crashed when he realized that the chips could just as easily be the result of natural fills instead of man's industry.

Get control of yourself! He commanded.

Don't go leaping to wild conclusions.

First, calm yourself. Think and consider as your father and uncles have taught you. Look for something out of place. Something that's not just right. Something odd.

So Ahmed began by pacing off the suspicious area. About eight feet wide by twenty-two feet long.

Well, that's certainly big enough for a tomb's entrance. He reasoned.

Next, he scanned the upper walls of the gap with a slowly swiveling head, looking for chisel marks.

None to the left.

None to the right.

None forward . . . but, but what's that?

Directly before the boy was a broken potsherd. Stooping over, Ahmed gently wriggled it out from beneath several limestone chips. It was a rim and handle fragment of a small, tan, coarse-ware storage jar with a triangular piece of its body still attached. His practiced eye immediately judged it to be ancient. Brushing off the pumice-fine dust on it at first stung his eyes to tears. But when his eyes cleared, he was rewarded with a series of curious pictures. Although Ahmed did not know it, he was gazing at a royal cartouche that had been painted on the vessel's handle near its rim.

At this discovery, Ahmed leaned against the crevasse's left wall and slid down until he was sitting on his heels.

Now think, clever one, as you have never thought before. A nearly inaccessible rock cut located high in the sacred cliffs of the ancient ones. A suspicious pile of limestone chips that slope down from a narrow side crack. Where did they all come from? And then this broken piece of a pot with the ancient ones' writing.

Getting up and gently placing the potsherd near where he had first descended into the crevice, Ahmed returned to the suspicious fissure. Heedless of the sharp limestone chips, he began to dig dog-style with his heavily callused fingers where he had found the ceramic fragment. After about five minutes of effort, a small depression had been dug out along the facing wall. Once the dust had cleared, Ahmed found what he had been looking for – chisel marks!

Standing with a mixture of intellectual satisfaction and ebullient chest-bursting elation, Ahmed returned to pick up the potsherd, carefully tied it to the yarn-like belt around his waist, and began his slow ascent out of the crevice. Again using his hands and feet as leverage, Ahmed emerged from the fissure's gloom some thirty minutes later covered with dust, streaked with sweat, and wearing a broad grin.

"I've made it out!" He gasped.

"I must immediately tell my family of what I have found! What I suspect. My family must know!"

Know indeed. For the next ten years the family of el-Rassul would enjoy the financial fruits of this find and live handsomely – and as fate would have it – perhaps too much so. What young Ahmed had discovered had been a carefully guarded secret, nothing less than a cache of royal mummies. Dating from the Eighteenth, Nineteenth, and Twentieth Dynasties, these ancient dignitaries had been piously relocated in this narrow crevice tomb by the priesthood of Amen Re. They had done so because of rampant tomb robbing during the Late Empire. There they had remained undisturbed for three millennia until young Ahmed had stumbled across them.

By 1881, the rumors of fine and rare Egyptian antiquities showing up in the European black market had finally reached the horrified ears of the Egyptian Antiquities Service. The service's agent put feelers out and after the canny exchange of several hundred Egyptian pounds, a probable source had been narrowed down. The leads pointed the service's agents to Western Thebes and its extensive necropolis.

In the end it was an informant's greed and Ahmed's family's obvious prosperity that caused the Antiquities Service's assistant Director, Émile Brugsch, to journey south from Cairo to the household threshold of the el-Rassul. Brugsch, who until this moment had stood squarely in the shadow of his older brother Heinrich's professional career, now was granted his own claim to fame.

After some gentle and not-so-gently applied persuasion from the regional constabulary, Brugsch was led by the el-Rassul to the lofty tomb site, which today is known as Deir el-Bahri No. 320. Upon emerging from its darkness with eyes still glazed, Brugsch at once cordoned off the area.

With block and tackle he removed its royal cache of forty mummies and almost 6000 other antiquities to the safety of Cairo. All of this labor occurred during the oppressive heat of early July 1881. With that act of preservation was established the nucleus of the Cairo National Museum's now world-famous royal mummy collection.

*   *   *

As often happens in science, breakthroughs occur as the result of a frank accident or blithe serendipity. The decisive role that chance plays is difficult to quantify, but it is there nonetheless. It always has. Providence is a force that the ancients recognized as either divine favor or mischievous whimsy. The hubris of agnostic modern scholars reduces luck to either numbers, theory, or sheer inevitability. A fine example of this phenomenon is the case of the dreadfully ill research bacteriologist, who happened to accidentally sneeze over some of his unprotected petri dish cultures. In the course of events the researcher later discovered to his surprise that it was his own nasal mucous – caused by a defeated bacterium, that contained the elements needed to defeat his bacteriological foe.

In short, chance events sometimes feed off of one another, leading one to wonder where one begins and the other truly ends. So while the news of the Deir el-Bahri cache was being trumpeted across the front pages of the world's major newspapers, that very discovery made another possible. For within the clutch of Ahmed's sensational find were included several royal mummies that hailed from the Late Eighteenth Dynasty, individuals who had quite a story to tell. Not surprisingly, the unraveling of that story would take some time. It would once again require a chance jaw-dropping impetuous, before it inspired the concerted resolve of two rivaling national scientific communities.

Chapter III
AD 1941. The Hourglass Seminar

As early as 1939 the Soviet Union had become scientifically aware. Its Secret Service, the NKVD, reported that a massive effort was being made by the West in the realm of high-energy physics and quantum mechanics.

By 1940 the evidence continued to mount. The names of the associated scientists alone were cause for alarm: Enrico Fermi, Vannevar Bush, James B. Conant, and Ernest O. Lawrence. The political and military heavyweights associated with the effort included George B. Pegram, Leo Szilard, Eugene P. Wigner, Chief of Staff George C. Marshall, Secretary of War Henry L. Stimson, and Brigadier General Leslie R. Groves. The lists of notables seemed to go on and on. Clearly, the Soviets reasoned, something truly big was afoot. The signs were undeniable. But what was going on?

The Russians' big break arrived from an unexpected source. A field operative working at the Princeton, New Jersey, post office managed to intercept and photograph a personal letter addressed to the White House. Authored by none other than Albert Einstein, the letter argued cogently for a high-energy physics project, which would investigate the practical feasibility of atomic weaponry. This windfall caused an understandable sensation and was immediately brought to the attention of Joseph Stalin himself. With it, the race was on for the development of a Soviet atomic bomb.

During the ensuing period of frenetic government sponsored science in the Soviet Union, a modest feasibility study was proposed in late 1941, to which a modest amount of funding was received. At Leningrad State University, a select group of three theoretical mathematicians, an engineer, and two humanists – a token philosopher and an historian – convened a seminar on the advancement of worldwide socialism. Given the blandly-titled subject and the advertised 10:00 p.m. starting time, none outside this small clique bothered to take notice much less attend.

The actual agenda for this gathering of eagles, however, proved to be far headier. Christened Hourglass, the aim was to discuss the theoretical feasibility and practical ramifications of time travel.

Advancement of world socialism indeed! And so Russia's most secret and ambitious feasibility study began in full view.

The seminar began with all due academic decorum. Its youngest member, a precocious eighteen-year-old named Dr. Pyotr Borov, had dared to tread a new frontier at the intersection of quantum mechanics and theoretical engineering. This skinny, sandy blond-haired, White Russian, with shocking cobalt blue eyes and porcelain skin, was nominated as the seminar's secretary by its chairman. The rest of the seminar immediately approved. Borov, ever prone to a quick blush, did so on cue. His round Slavic face glowed as angelic as it was guiltless.

So as he took pen in hand at the honor of being the scribe to such an august Scipionic Circle, Borov privately resented the task. He bridled at being shunted to such a menial duty.

After all, Borov reasoned, *wasn't my dissertation the reason for this gathering? My careful reading of Einstein's unified field theory, while everyone else waited for an authorized translation of it? Buried in that man's convoluted German prose I had found the key. Or, at least I think I have. But there is so much to do and consider. My head just hurts to start!*

While this intellectual firestorm was raging within Borov's head, he began tugging on the sleeves of his ill-fitting suit coat and clenching his hands.

To his colleagues, it appeared the young man wished to hide his excitement at his new assignment. That Borov was trying to compose himself. That he even was at a loss as to what to do with his hands. With his young golden crown bowed before them, Borov studied in great detail those clenched appendages in an attempt to avoid all eye contact. In actual fact, the young PhD's mind was racing far ahead, considering, examining, wondering, and hoping for an opportunity to test and put his novel theories into action.

The seminar's founder and chairman, the self-absorbed philosopher Gregor Suvurov, proceeded to prevent unnecessary competition among the overfed egos of the three theoretical mathematicians. Besides, his word was absolute law as he had the right ear of Stalin and as such controlled the source of the seminar's funding. (As to who held Stalin's left ear, is anyone's guess, but some have speculated that Felix Dzerzhinsky's successor, the head of the secret police, owned it outright.)

Suvurov was lean of build, but unlike Borov, he had a swarthy complexion with gracefully graying black hair – both traits of his Black Sea heritage. This soft-spoken and neatly dressed man, while a good listener, did not tolerate nor suffer fools gladly. This seminar was his own personal coup – one that he calculated would place him squarely within the inner circle of the Russian scientific community. While some had smirked behind their hands, Suvurov vowed he would have his day in the sun and young Borov was his to command. This he had made abundantly clear when he moved his two aging parents, both academics, from Leningrad to Moscow.

The third member of the seminar was a plain man of medium build and modest dress. Victor Latysev, an aging but well-preserved papyrologist, was an internationally recognized star. His prominent features were his thick wire-rimmed glasses and hawk-like nose, all of which conspired to grant him an almost gaunt, owlish look. A brilliant and intuitive philologist, Latysev was one of those rare individuals who could sight-read a sixth-century Byzantine papyrus as if it had been this morning's edition of the *London Times*. He took on discolored, worm-riddled, and fragmentary papyri as very special challenges to understand. To him, they were orphaned children who needed his personal attention, a determination of their rightful historical context, and above all, their translation. Latysev's contribution to the seminar would be his open, unfettered mind, and an uncanny ability to make intellectual leaps based on scant, fragmentary data, like his beloved papyri. This last trait had been evinced time after time to such a degree that some believed the papyrologist had prescient powers.

As for the theoretical mathematicians who closed the circle, the Terrible Three – Alexandr Koslov, Nikolai Fedorov, and Dmitry Giga – no triad of minds was as brilliant, nor more discordant. Casual words of civility did not pass between these egotistical and highly competitive men of science. What dialogue did occur was usually couched in the freezingly polite, third person, or worse, with the sneering use of the Russian last name prefaced with "Comrade." As a result, Chairman Suvurov's challenge was to excite, incite, or bludgeon these three academic prima donnas into moments of cooperation before one colleague's fingers found another's throat. The driven Suvurov needed these men, for they were the very best. Unfortunately, they all knew that as well.

Ever prepared, Suvurov made sure he possessed a velvet hammer for them as well. Whether the trio chose to acknowledge it or not, they were made aware that the welfare of their families depended upon their cooperation. While this reality was never explicitly stated, Suvurov's demeanor and well-known connections made that implication a chilling fact of life. As for the seminar's newly appointed secretary, Borov realized only too well this cold reality. He silently scolded himself in utter dismay and guilt as he had been the one who had recommended them all. As Suvurov's much-prized *Wunderkind*, Borov, single, already knew all too well the limits of his gilded cage.

Given these personal undercurrents, another grim uneasiness permeated the oak-paneled seminar room on that snowy night in late December of 1940. The news of the dark presence of Soviet Russia's most recent ally brought an air of urgency and earnestness to the gathering, which unexpectedly astounded and delighted its chairman.

For the papyrologist Latysev, several of his close colleagues in Berlin already had written him coded messages of the changes taking place and of those who had already fled to Switzerland and England. He had heard unthinkable tales of some who were incarcerated without warning or who had just disappeared off the street. His old friend and colleague Felix Jacoby, himself of Jewish heritage, had confirmed these rumors from the safe remove of his self-imposed exile in Great Britain.

Similarly, the Terrible Three had all felt palpably diminished by the defection of Albert Einstein to the New World. One of their own had left them, had abandoned them to face the full force of the Teutonic madness alone.

In such a charged atmosphere, Suvurov surveyed the group as a lion would his pride. He privately gloated about this masterfully orchestrated seminar and his arachnidian manipulation of its participants. But Suvurov could not see everything, for he had failed to notice that the youngest member was having a difficult time containing his excitement. For Borov, he labored to appear absorbed in his secretarial duties.

Could it really be that they were taking me serious about all of this?

Would I actually have a chance to build what my audacious dissertation concluded was possible?

Could theoretical mathematics indeed describe the precise conditions necessary to produce a permeable window into other temporal dimensions?

And if so, can I find some way to bridge from the purely theoretical to the practical?

This rapid concatenation of thoughts blurred through Borov's mind during the space of one silent gulp of air.

Suvurov returned to his agenda after having made Borov secretary. After a long, indeterminate pause while studying his own hands, the chair began by polling the group for theoretical hurdles, dangerous implications, and possible solutions for them.

Latysev was the first to speak. He surprised the group with his carefully expressed concern for what he referred to as "the preservation of the delicate fabric of reality." The papyrologist then proceeded to outline what he truly believed was essential.

"If time travel is practical, then what indeed is reality? For example, what would happen if I ventured back into time and met myself? Or, what would happen if I chose to kill my own grandfather? Would I continue to exist? Could I even return to the present after having done such a monstrous deed?"

Suvurov was stunned. Latysev, true to his legendary suppleness of mind, had leapt far ahead, and tacitly accepted the practicality of time travel. He did not care one whit about the theoretical and technical challenges to be overcome. His first concern was that of a historian – a practitioner of time, a caretaker of chronology.

To Latysev's remarks arose the Terrible Three. Like so many bull frogs floating around a lily pad, they all blurted out in unison the word "paradox." The shock on their faces was comical, for their spoken agreement had been total.

But Suvurov was in for another surprise, for it was the mathematician Koslov who offered a clarification of the concept and the import of what the three were driving at. An introspective man, this savant as a child had struggled with a pronounced stutter and consequently had suffered an unmerciful amount of teasing.

Accordingly, as an adult he rarely, if ever, said anything if he could avoid it. Instead, he preferred to allow his elegant mathematical equations, or a dismissive wave of his hand, to speak for him. Still, it was he who provided the needed explanation, speaking to the ceiling in order to avoid direct eye contact and thus his stutter.

"My dear Professor Dr. Latysev, you have described the conditions of what physicists and philosophers have long referred to as a classical paradox. It is an unimaginable situation where time begins to loop upon itself in an endless cycle of no beginning and no end. I am sure that my distinguished colleagues would agree."

At once both Sidorov and Giga nodded their silent assent. To Suvurov, this exchange was remarkable. The Terrible Three actually had again agreed on something. What's more, the Terrible Three had been somewhat unnerved by Latysev's first concern: reality itself. "The delicate fabric of reality" was after all a rather meaty subject. One that could not be explained away with a typically academic, circuitous theoretical diatribe designed either to belittle or hopelessly confuse.

Then something occurred quite innocently. Giga, his perpetually half-closed eyelids gazing slowly around the seminar table, formally proposed it.

"Comrade Academicians. I wish to say that before continuing any further, I believe the Professor Dr. Latysev has pointed out something extremely seminal. I propose that we first draft a set of rules for time travel before continuing any further in our deliberations."

With that said Giga, a former national wrestler who had recently participated in the 1936 Berlin Olympics, sat back in his chair, and crossed his thick arms across his broad chest in finality. While so doing he dared his chair's two back legs to support his formidable mass. Standing six-two and weighing some 290 pounds, Giga was as much a giant of a man as was his ego and intellectual capacity. He had never been successfully challenged in person and rarely so in print. He was accustomed to having his own way, and with this group he became their initial tiller man.

Silent until this moment, Fedorov had to say something. In fact, he desperately wanted to say something profound in order to establish his place within the group. Fedorov, an unfortunate who traversed life's course in a perpetual state of nervousness, wore a thin sheen of perspiration layered across his prematurely balding head. Priest-like, for as a youth he had been educated in a Russian Orthodox seminary, Fedorov began by taking his typical pose with his hands gracefully folded before him as if in prayer. Then with a deep breath, he began, "Comrade Academicians. I must agree with the colleague to my right."

Swallow.

That action alone reminded Suvurov of a crane gulping down a fish whole.

Fedorov continued.

"It is one thing to discuss transiting into some unimaginable *somewhen*. It is another to do so without all due care."

Again, another one of those agonizing swallows.

And so it all began with an egotistical philosopher chairman, a thoughtful historian, three mathematicians, and young Borov.

Writing furiously, Borov could not believe his ears. Two hours later, hand numb from his scribal duties, the first draft of what would become one of most classified documents in Soviet history had been outlined. As with all government and scientific documents, it would carry its own acronym that stood for *Rukovodnie Ukazania dlya Temporalnogo Isledovaniya*, which translates into English as *The Guidelines for Temporal Exploration*.

Although the Hourglass Seminar took place within the Soviet Union and its funding sponsor was the same, any mention of that political entity was curiously absent throughout the *RUTI*. In fact, the document made no provision and was devoid of any reference to any political or governmental body or bodies whatsoever. Instead, what the *RUTI* did specifically state was that all temporal decisions were to occur within the framework of an international scientific forum free from any religious, political, or ideological influence.

Despite their many personal differences, the four senior members of the Hourglass Seminar remained firm on this issue much to Suvurov's dismay. Such a weighty topic could not become the toy of any particular political or religious ideology. Politicians and politically motivated decisions, they rightly believed, had no place within the *RUTI*. There was just too much at stake to recklessly "roll the dice" in an attempt to please or appease any one particular party chairman, Führer, president, pope or politician. Without question, this apolitical and neutrally positioned ideological clause was the seminar's greatest achievement. It would also become its greatest liability.

Although none of them knew it at the time, once the content of the *RUTI* had become known to their government, that clause would nix any chance for the construction of a prototype device within the confines of the Soviet Union. Subsequent developments would make their mark. As for of the authors of this temporal manifesto, only two would survive the coming holocaust, and only one would succeed at building the near impossible.

During a lengthening silence, Borov glanced up from his hastily written notes to discover that all eyes were now turned to him. The papyrologist, Latysev, gently reached across the worn panels of the seminar table and took the fountain pen from Borov's crabbed and ink-stained left hand. With the other, he deftly slid the notebook over to himself, spinning it around to his seated orientation.

After pausing briefly over Borov's notes the philologist said, "Dr. Borov your script is clear, even, and exact. Your sentence structure is organized, accurate, and direct. This is precisely what I would have expected from such a fine young mind."

Then leaning over the seminar table and taking on a conspiratorial, fatherly tone.

"My dear Pyotr, you have been silent for far, far too long. You have patiently listened, accurately recorded, and successfully made sense of the meandering babble of five old men long enough. Now, my son, tell us precisely, what do you need in order to build the temporal mechanism? After all, it was your dissertation that has brought us all together this evening. Is that not so?"

With flushed cheeks and a suddenly dry throat, Borov haltingly began, while the old papyrologist now wrote. He paused the young engineer's building rush of pent-up enthusiasm only for the spelling of a technical term here, the clarification of a concept there, for he wanted to record it all just so.

The Terrible Three, now getting used to speaking full sentences before one another, murmured among themselves, seeing the youthful physicist and engineer with a growing respect with each passing word. Only Fedorov himself held back from what he considered the fawning of his two colleagues.

Just who was this mere child? Who, for all appearances, could be easily mistaken for a poster child of the Hitler Youth Movement, a prime example of the perfect Aryan race?

There is something about him that eludes me, troubles me.

What is it?

At that moment, Borov's energized narration broke in on Fedorov's train of thought as he laid it all before them. At issue was not the theoretical viability of the concept, to which the Terrible Three each grunted their assents. Far more daunting to the seminar's youngest member were the technical and engineering hurdles before them. He worried over the proper construction materials, a reliable power source, and the critical instrumentation. In Borov's mind, these last might be attainable given the appropriate funding and research.

Again, his listeners nodded silently. Then, Borov brought them all back to reality by sharing with them the young man's deepest concern, a detail that troubled him to the core. Once the temporal device was constructed, how could one calibrate it? For without calibration the device would be worthless. An interesting theoretical and engineering exercise to be sure, but a worthless device nonetheless if you could not predict the *somewhen* you were going.

With this announcement, Borov's gaze was greeted with bleary-eyed stares and slack jaws. Chairman Suvurov was stunned by this revelation, which he believed had not been touched upon in Borov's dissertation. Borov's face predictably turned bright crimson, as he suddenly felt as if he were caught stark naked before the entire world. The young man bowed his head in a personal shame and self-inflicted bruising of ego. Only academics seem to so acutely experience this whenever they fail to entirely solve a problem and then have to rely on the help of others.

Latysev then chose this moment to loudly clear his throat. His sharp eye caught Borov's furtive glance toward Suvurov at the mention of the calibration issue and absolutely recognized the chairman's near apoplectic shock.

So that was it!

Suvurov had not fully grasped the magnitude of what Borov was struggling with, and, to top it off, had most likely read only the abstract of Borov's dissertation. If he had read it through from cover to cover, then he would not have been so shocked at Borov's admission.

And here we sit.

With that insight, Latysev carefully laid the capped secretary's fountain pen length-wise along the notebook's inner binding crease. The old papyrologist then gracefully folded his hands on the notebook before him.

Slowly looking around, he took everyone in, and then said, "Well. At long last comrades, one of us has finally admitted to being merely human. What's more, only one of us truly grasps the enormity of what we have been discussing. Since the time is so early, I suggest that we adjourn and focus our minds on this very issue of calibration at our next gathering."

The papyrologist's timing could not have been better. For at that moment the first weak rays of sunlight that announced the beginning of the next day had begun to penetrate the loft windows of the seminar room. As a block, the group grunted themselves to their feet and shuffled out. All were physically stiff, mentally exhausted. Yet all remained intellectually in high gear. None would sleep before noon that day. When sleep did finally mercifully arrive, all slept like the dead.

The following week they met again. Again they talked all night long, sharing their thoughts, their objections. Again each experienced the same physical weight of intellectual effort. Again all slept the sleep of the dead. For the next five and a half months the vampire seminar, as it came to be known among its membership, continued on. Much was accomplished as the *RUTI* reached its final edit and several theoretical issues were flushed out and clarified. With the outbreak of collegiality, grudging friendships were actually in the process of formation.

Then the shocking news arrived of the German offensive that had begun on June 22, 1941, a diplomatically duplicitous and militarily disastrous adventure – the invasion of Mother Russia, the *Rodina* herself. As Leningrad was the goal of one of the three swiftly advancing columns, its fortification began in earnest to blunt a siege that would begin by mid-August and would last seven hundred days. As for the weekly regularity of the Hourglass Seminar, it was now shattered. All were to be immediately relocated east to the presumed safety of a quiet academic suburb near Moscow where the seminar would reconvene. Or, at least, that was the plan.

CHAPTER IV

AD 1973. Deir el-Bahri

Once again it was a magnificent sunrise. The sheer three hundred-foot limestone cliffs glowed with a warm, rosy red blush. Into the cliffs' half-moon shaped grotto more than three hundred private burials were secreted, many of them made famous by their exquisite wall decorations. But three grand mortuary complexes overawed these splendid tombs of the once powerful and proud.

Standing at the cliff's edge and looking down over worn and dusty boots, young Sergei Anatol took in the majesty of this timeless scene. The earliest of the mortuary complexes lay to the right, sited just off his right little toe. There stood the ruins of a once small limestone pyramid, itself surrounded by the remains of a surprisingly delicate and airy colonnade, the whole fronted by a broad ramp that ran due east toward the Nile and the rising sun.

Just off his left foot stood the magnificent, multi-leveled, multi-ramped, and colonnaded mortuary terraces of Hatshepsut, Egypt's most successful female pharaoh. From this vantage, Senmut, her architect-lover, had been influenced by the former monument's ramp and colonnades. Perhaps even by a consciously pious desire to compliment through imitation. Regardless, the Polish expedition's extensive restorations of that tiered site was breathtaking, down to the subtle dimpled impressions of where the myrrh tree-lined entrance boulevard once coursed.

Finally, directly in front of him, framed between his feet, stood the tall and ruined terrace complex of the Pharaoh Thutmose III, the step-son and successor of Hatshepsut. Perhaps in time, Thutmose's mortuary temple will also take on more form. For when Anatol had begun as a mere sketch assistant, the structure was still buried under a massive pile of limestone clips. After years of careful clearing and sifting, a terrace had slowly emerged that easily eclipsed in size the ancient pyramid and colonnade to its right.

While glancing about and taking in the scene below, Sergei's thoughts began to drift.

Come to think of it, just off to the right is located that famous fissure that once camouflaged the Royal Cache of mummies. Some forty in all, as I recall, many of them kings from the Eighteenth Dynasty, some of the Nineteenth and Twentieth. All discovered some, let's see, some ninety-two years ago. Now that find must really have been something!

So the young archaeologist continued to daydream.

With a sigh of envy, Anatol scratched at his sun-bleached scalp, and recounted that he had labored for five seasons to help clear that central terrace. He had loved the work. The excitement that came with each new day. The experience of being in Lower Egypt: the cloudless, powder blue sky, the dry heat, and the ever-present sunshine that blurred days into weeks into months. What a welcome change from the dreariness of Warsaw's university life. But time was fleeting and Anatol knew that his time was almost up. He could tell by the wondering looks on his colleagues' faces back home that he caught when they thought he was not aware. The quiet conversations behind his back.

To be sure, Anatol was a seasoned archaeologist destined to be one of the best. Yes, Anatol had co-authored several solid articles in well-placed professional journals in the East and West. And yes again, he was slated to write several chapters in the final field publication. But Anatol, biting his lower lip in thought, had not yet been hooded. Here was an intelligent and linguistically gifted graduate student in Egyptology, with publications to his credit and field experience, but without a PhD behind his name. His first love and future career were doomed if he did not find a dissertation topic and soon.

Then a strange thing occurred to him. Taking the coiled length of climbing rope from his left shoulder, Anatol casually looked over to his right where the entrance of the Royal Cache was concealed at the fissure's bottom. Without a conscious thought, he sat down on the wind-blown rock, dangled his size nine feet over the lip of that deep recess, and judged its depth. When later asked what he had in mind, Anatol did not know, but his practiced hands formed a stout timber hitch around the neck of his hand pick that he then wedged into a crack in the cliff's surface. First having tested the hand pick's purchase to his satisfaction, the young Pole backed over the edge and began to lower and walk himself down the fissure's right wall with the aid of his heavily-gloved hands. His brief tour in the compulsory Polish military had taught him a few useful things, but only a few, he reminded himself.

Once his eyes had grown accustomed to the fissure's shadows, he easily made out the passage into the rock cut tomb known officially as Deir el-Bahri No. 320. Letting go of the rope and pocketing his gloves, he walked up and bent his tallish frame slightly over within the tomb's rectangular entrance. The interior beyond was a black hole, but just visible inside and lying in the corner among some wind-blown trash was a discarded two-inch candle stub. Fumbling in his breast pocket past his wrinkled and near-empty pack of unfiltered Camel cigarettes, he found his matches. Once lit, the candlelight transformed the limestone walls of the entrance passage into a golden corridor. As he strode forth, the sand crunching on the bottoms of his boots seemed to echo against the dark silence. With the slowly burning candle in hand and seemingly transported to another time, Anatol's imagination came alive.

"So many royal mummies, so little time," he whispered out of pious deference, as he remembered how the priests of Amen Re had hastily crammed them all into these tight confines in a helter-skelter manner. He recalled the confusion of who was really whom, of the academic arguments, the crudely performed autopsies. And then an idea occurred to him.

What if I had found that cache? What would I have done? What would I have done to figure out who was who? Or, even better, who was even related?

At this point in his ruminations, he reached the right turn in this L-shaped excavation. The candle was nearing its end, but not his racing imagination. Turning around, Anatol blew it out and slowly made his way back toward the dim light that framed the tomb's entrance, gently dragging a hand along the smooth right-hand wall as a guide.

Exertion is a curious phenomenon. Oxygen engorges stressed muscles and invigorates the brain. With sweat streaming from his lean frame, Anatol made his way back up and out of the fissure, walking up the wall as he had descended hand-over-hand. Once atop the mouth of the fissure, he now wore a broad, relaxed smile as his sweaty body briefly sent shivers up his spine as it cooled in the cliff's wind. While he broke free and retrieved his hand pick, recoiled the rope, and looped it back over his left shoulder, Sergei knew what his dissertation topic would be.

*   *   *

In the time that it had taken Anatol to walk down from atop the cliffs above to the tented archaeological base below, he had worked out his thesis topic and had a good idea of its outline. Anatol's habit was that he organized first in his mind and then formalized on paper. Still deep in thought, he absentmindedly acknowledged the morning greetings from his workmen with a wave. His charges immediately took notice. When Anatol was in such a distant mood, it invariably meant good luck. Today the six were sure that they would find something special that would earn them a special reward of *baksheesh*. Just as consciously, each began thinking about what they would do with that newfound wealth.

Entering his wall tent with its neatly rolled up sides, Anatol sat down before his portable desk and began to write. Gently rocking in his canvas chair as he wrote, its hinges squeaked. So deep was Anatol's concentration that when he next looked up, dusk was only an hour away.

All the while none of his archaeological crew had dared to disturb the young Pole. Instead, they kept a silent guard outside his tent, sitting cross-legged side by side, so as to be ready at a moment's notice. In truth, none of them would have dreamed of disturbing the young archaeologist from his labors, because each considered him either their beloved brother or son. Here was a foreigner who spoke their desert mother tongue, who treated them with a profound respect and elegant dignity. Here was a man who had shared water from his own canteen. Each wished that he would someday embrace the Prophet. That he would wed a sister or daughter. To the six, he was extended family. Besides, they were paid their daily wage whether they lifted a shovel or not.

*   *   *

The site's field director, Professor Jerzy Jannicka, had noticed Anatol's absence as well. The heavily-tanned, quiet, and all-seeing director first missed the animated Anatol and his lively crew at their assigned work zone around seven that morning. Checking again later, he saw the young man's six colleagues silently waiting in his tent's shadow. Sheer curiosity getting the better of him, the director raised his field glasses and peered into the tent's cool darkness. He saw Sergei bent over his desk, writing furiously. Putting down his binoculars, Jannicka's first thought was to traipse over and demand an explanation. But then a thought occurred to him. Anatol was never late for anything. If anything, he and his crew were always the first on the terrace. An excited glimmer of a much-hoped-for expectation sparkled in his eyes. He would be sure to ask during the evening meal.

*   *   *

Anatol, upon reemerging into the real world, panicked.

An entire day's labor was lost!

Whipping around in his camp chair he saw that his six faithful workmen were sitting in a row outside his tent. Although their faces were obscured in the shadows of their native headgear, their eyes were filled with a mixture of curiosity and pent-up energy.

Tipping over his tent chair as he rose, Anatol staggered to the seated figures on stiff knees and cramped legs. He fell to his knees in the sand before them as if in a Christian act of submission and looked into their each of their eyes. Then he smiled and thanked each for their silent vigil. He then promised each a full next day, full pay for today's patience, and wished each a peaceful and uneventful return to their village. Without a word, each of the six nodded, rose to their feet, and shuffled off.

*   *   *

Mustafa, the eldest of the group, stole a peek over his left shoulder after about twenty-five paces and noted Anatol was still kneeing in the sand with his hands on his knees. The young Pole's face was a blank slate. Catching the eyes of the others, a wordless exchange was made. The young foreigner had come down from atop El-Qurn, dazed. To them, it was clear. He had had a vision and had attempted to write it down. Perhaps this gentle soul would soon indeed embrace the words of the Prophet.

* * *

Anatol knelt in the sand and noted Mustafa's fatherly glance. He was still groggy and disoriented from the effects of his intellectual whirlwind. For the first time in months Anatol felt complete, directed as if a missing and intimate part had been found. Just as suddenly, his throat almost croaked at its parched dryness. His stomach growled at the delicious scent wafting from the direction of the mess tent. Staggering too quickly to his feet and feeling woozy, Anatol straightened his shirt, ran his hands through his sun-bleached hair, and wandered off to the latrine to wash up.

The conversation around the wooden picnic tables hummed along about the day's events. As Anatol entered the mess tent, he felt guiltily out of touch and so took the empty place at the end. He furtively filled his plate from the family-style servings of food. Almost no one seemed to notice his presence.

The current topic that held everyone's attention was a discussion about a black basalt statue of a seated dignitary that was uncovered the previous day. The figure depicted was none other than Senmut, the most powerful court and administrative official during the reign of the Pharaoh Hatshepsut. At issue was why was this statue was found amidst the debris of Thutmose III's terrace. While hypotheses flew thickly through the air, Anatol gorged himself, his mind still very focused and preoccupied.

Director Jannicka, who had finished eating and already started his post-meal pipe, got up from his place and sat down directly opposite the young man. The director waited, pretending not to notice his assistant's total absorption. Besides, he commiserated with himself, the lad was famished, as he had skipped lunch.

During a lull in the lively debate from the adjoining table, Jannicka put down his ivory pipe and extracted a fresh pipe cleaner from his breast pocket. As he began to ream out the pipe's stem, he casually leaned across the picnic table and in a soft voice pitched to Anatol's ears alone he asked.

"And Anatol, what kind of day did you have today?"

Any other time, Anatol would have choked at such a question, but behind Jannicka's sweat-smudged wire glasses, his twinkling blue eyes gave him away. Clearing his throat, Anatol also leaned forward and whispered that he was in need of the director's professional advice. Sitting back, Jannicka narrowed his eyes and tilted his head to the right, an action that told Anatol that he had Jannicka's full attention and his good, left ear. Then the words began to flow.

While Anatol spoke, the director refilled his newly cleaned pipe, and began to puff away excitedly. It did not take long before the rest of the mess tent noted the director was being held spellbound by his assistant. Occasionally, Jannicka would make a point here, ask for a clarification there. But to all of those assembled, Anatol held sway. The graying middle-aged director with his arms folded across his chest listened contentedly, while slowly rocking in place. When Anatol finished, he replied with a soft, "Bravo," through his pipe-clenched teeth.

Jannicka's next words startled the rest of assembled.

"So, Mr. Anatol, when do you leave for Cairo?"

"Upon the close of the excavation's season."

"Nonsense, I want you at the Cairo National Museum by week's end. An intellectual firestorm is raging inside you Sergei, and I don't want it to go out. Gregor here can supervise your area as well as his own. And don't worry. You are to remain a member of my staff. It is just that now is your time."

With these words of blessing, a hearty round of clapping broke out, backslapping, and after a quick sweep of the area for locals, the ceremonial seal-breaking of the expedition's lone bottle of vodka. It was time for a celebration.

*　　*　　*

The very next day, the six workmen arrived at dawn before Anatol's tent as they had done so for the past five seasons. As had become their custom, Anatol greeted them as if each had just arrived from a long and arduous journey. Then Anatol told them he was leaving on the noon train for Cairo. All shed genuine tears at the news.

CHAPTER V

Borov and the West

While the Hourglass Seminar was flushing out the theoretical particulars and considerable temporal and ethical ramifications of Borov's dissertation, the United States was engaged in two top secret, high-energy physics projects. The best known was the Manhattan Project. Orchestrated from Washington, DC, it involved, in some way or another, the scientific resources of nearly all of America's leading universities. Its first field test took place in the wastes of New Mexico on July 16th, 1945, amid nervous concerns that the device's detonation might precipitate an apocalyptic chain-reaction throughout the earth's atmosphere. While that dreadful scenario did not occur, the atomic bomb's practical application did culminate in the total obliteration of Hiroshima and Nagasaki and initiated the surrender of Imperial Japan.

America's lesser-known high-energy physics project was the ill-fated Philadelphia Experiment. Based on Albert Einstein's Unified Field Theory, the intent was to camouflage a naval ship by bending light around it by means of a powerful electromagnetic field. Initially, the experiment had been a success for the U.S. Navy and its special research department. With the flip of a switch, a naval destroyer docked in the Philadelphia harbor yard had indeed disappeared, betrayed only by an outline and depression of the ship's hull in the water. Despite the fact the technicians thought that "the quiet hole in the water" looked downright eerie, the technology worked.

In essence, a U.S. warship could disappear and reappear at the flip of a switch and all sound was muffled to boot! The only remaining item that troubled the U.S. Navy was how to camouflage the ship's wake while underway, or develop a propulsion system that did not leave one.

But there was one minor hitch. When the ship reappeared, the crew was found suffering from a variety of maladies: severe disorientation, insanity, and some horribly immolated by what looked like spontaneous combustion. The human body, an electro-chemical engine, proved to be incapable of withstanding prolonged exposure within a powerful electro-magnetic field.

Those who had been wearing helmets and body armor suffered the most. In addition, several of the crew went missing and were nowhere to be found. It was reported that under the stress of the electromagnetic field, they had jumped overboard in an attempt to escape their derangement. Just where they went was anyone's guess, but a few of the project's research staff had a theoretical inkling. For when they jumped overboard, they did not go somewhere, but rather might have gone *somewhen*. The fact of the matter was no one knew for sure. So when America first got wind of the Soviet Union's Hourglass Seminar in early April of 1942, the Soviet project naturally generated considerable interest among those attached to the Philadelphia Experiment.

*   *   *

As the German *Wehrmacht* approached Leningrad, the members of the Hourglass Seminar were ordered to close up shop and resume their work in a secluded university suburb of Moscow. During that hurried evacuation one research associate, Dr. Pyotr Borov, turned up missing. At that precise moment Borov chose to defect to the West.

What reason or reasons motivated Borov to abandon his parents, homeland, and risk life and limb while crossing through the German lines, is to this day unclear. What is certain is Borov's sense of timing and uncanny resourcefulness. A gifted linguist, Borov was fluent in German, English, and French, as well as his native Russian. While these languages were necessary to keep current with the leading scientific journals, Borov, who had mastered them fully, now was going to put them to a far more practical use.

Ignoring conventional wisdom, Borov fled west on foot and into the teeth of the advancing Teutonic invasion. During the initial German assault on Leningrad's outskirts, Borov found himself betwixt and between the onrushing Germans and his defending countrymen. Determined to somehow survive, the young Russian reasoned he needed a safe place to hide while the German onslaught surged past. Otherwise, he reckoned his chances of making it through to the German rear and beyond were very slim.

Finding a narrow brick sewage culvert, Borov crawled in without a thought and spent the next thirty-eight hours shivering in the damp and praying, while the roar of war took place all around him.

During a lull in the fighting and when he felt it was safe enough to emerge, he found the immediate neighborhood had been transformed into a smoking ruin reeking of the sweet smell of bloated death. In the dark on his first foray from that vermin's den, Borov tripped over the grotesque corpse of a German officer. It was then an idea came to him. Remembering the famous phrase of the nineteenth century Prussian military officer Carl Clausewitz that "during the fog of battle much is left to chance," Borov decided to use the current battlefield situation to his best advantage.

Borov, now dressed in the tattered and much-bloodied uniform stripped off of the dead German officer, managed to bluff his way through to the German rear as a mumbling and shell-shocked husk of a soldier. Making his way west and south among lines of walking wounded, Borov finally made it to Poland, but only after having crossed through the conquered territories of Estonia, Latvia, and Lithuania. From there, he broke away from the main logistics column and managed his way through Czechoslovakia and Austria all the way to Switzerland. Remarkably, throughout this amazing overland trek of some seventy-two days, Borov's only close brush was from the pitchfork of an irate Swiss farmer, who had found him snoring in his barn's hayloft.

Upon reaching Zurich in mid-November, Borov telephoned a family friend in the United States, Professor Karl Voigt of the University of Pennsylvania's Department of Physics. Fortified with the necessary funds that were wired to him also came a lengthy list of stern instructions. Among them Voigt mentioned friendly academic contacts that included a contact at the U.S. embassy.

Within days, Borov carried a hastily-produced Swiss passport. His instructions outlined a daring itinerary that began with a train ride to Venice and a brief voyage from there to the southern Italian port city of Brindisi. Once there, he was to book passage to the Sicilian port of Catania located beneath the volcanic heights of

Mount Etna. At that point, Borov was to get to the British-held island of Malta by any means possible. And that he did as the sole passenger of a low slung fishing sloop that often made the short trip. He later learned that its quiet, dark-haired captain had been handsomely paid for both the black market goods and information that he so freely provided. As for Borov's passage, that was just a bonus to an already agreed upon bottom line.

Now in Allied hands, Borov's final instruction was to seek out a certain captain of the intelligence corps, the son of a former university colleague of Voigt's, and a trusted friend. At that point, Borov was in British hands, who "by hook or by crook" got him to the States.

On the Ides of March, 1942, an intrepid and barely twenty-year-old Russian immigrant arrived at the naval harbor of Philadelphia aboard a returning Liberty ship from Liverpool. Happy beyond words to be finally on American soil, Borov one day later presented himself on the sunny springtime doorstep of the Voigt's, wearing a Navy pea coat, the uniform of a British corporal, and incongruously bearing Swiss papers. In all, it had been 212 days since he had left his mother country.

After allowing for a week to pass for Pyotr's, now Peter Borov, cultural readjustment, and frankly to "fatten him up," Professor Voigt arranged for a select group of American scientists to meet with him. What they then learned about the Hourglass Seminar left them with glazed and astonished eyes. The possibility that Borov was right stunned them and represented a theoretical confirmation of what his interviewers had already suspected, especially given the four missing sailors of the Philadelphia Experiment.

Just as surprising to the Americans were the authors of the *RUTI* document, the document itself, and the thrust of its apolitical tone. To a man, they were flabbergasted that a project funded by the Soviet Union had dared to philosophically turn its back upon its patron. But it was Borov's own concerns over calibration that left his interviewers scratching their heads in dismay.

One month after that fateful first conversation, more interviews took place in mid-May of 1942. Concerned the Russians had a head start on Hourglass and pushed by Voigt's own influence, Washington expeditiously processed Borov's naturalization papers, which allowed him to move about on his own and outside the care of the Voigt household. But the government suits needed time to think about Borov, Hourglass, and how they could fit him and it into their current plans.

Now a naturalized political refugee, officially a D.P. or "displaced person," it was time for Borov to get to work. Before doing so, Voigt had thought it best for the young Borov to spend some time among his peers, primarily "to catch up on his reading and bone up on current developments in his fields of interest," as he so gently put it. So Voigt sponsored his candidacy for a semester of study and research at the Institute for Advanced Studies in Princeton, New Jersey. He deliberately addressed his letter of introduction not to the institute's administration, but rather to the first permanent member of that remarkable think tank, Albert Einstein, who enthusiastically endorsed Borov's candidacy. So while the government thought about what to do with him, Borov "caught up on his fields of interest" and finished out 1942 amid the idyllic Princeton canopy of blooming springtime honeysuckle, the summer heat and mottled shade of elm and locus trees, and the crisp fall smells of burning leaves and Saturday afternoon football games.

Early during the next year, the precise date was never recorded, Borov, now rejuvenated in body and spirit, became the government's first choice to drive the American temporal project. Placed under the established cover of the Manhattan Project, his project was quietly insinuated into several budgets associated with the Institute for Nuclear Studies at the University of Chicago. Next came the requisition of a modest Quonset hut inside the White Sands, New Mexico, research community. Everything had come together so quickly that the project had not even been given an official code name. Among the project's enthusiastic underwriters, the calibration issue notwithstanding, there remained some hope for finding, and perhaps rescuing, the lost seamen of the Philadelphia Experiment.

Once settled in White Sands, Borov and America's new project began in earnest under the relentless summer heat of New Mexico. As an established budgetary footnote buried within the Manhattan Project, Borov found himself within a thriving intellectual environment that accepted him and his credentials without a thought, especially given his recent stint at Princeton. He was truly within his element. Besides, young Borov had a likable, smiling personality. In short, he was a social hit. Even the Manhattan Project's dour lead, Robert Oppenheimer, had taken a liking to him. However, the Hungarian Edward Teller was not so sure about the lad and considered him a soviet plant. So when the word got out that Borov was to head up a small research team, a line of hopefuls quickly formed at the door of his small office.

What the Soviets had brilliantly outlined in theory, the Americans, standing on their shoulders, now built with their greater physical resources and unfettered technical ingenuity. After sixteen months' hard work, as success began to follow upon success, a working prototype was spawned on the eve of Thanksgiving 1944.

The design of the American device was simplicity itself, a tribute to mathematical and engineering elegance. This early temporal prototype, the American Mark I, resembled nothing more than a loop of bare wire coat hanger suspended by magnets. When the electro-magnetic field and ion emitter were turned on, however, the field that resulted within the loop took on a soft flat sheen, sometimes opaque as milk and sometimes reflective as aluminum. Only six inches in diameter, one researcher remarked that the device and its field looked like a child's bubble blowing wand and hence came the origin of the project's name: Soap Bubble. It stuck.

Proving what the device did, however, remained problematic to Borov and his small team, and in many respects, presented a far greater challenge than its construction. Only after extensive equipment testing and the establishment of rigorous containment provisions, did Borov allow a non-conducting, eleven-inch long, paper soda straw to first probe the field. Just as naturally, it was the exuberant Borov who was the first to do so.

In a highly classified black and white photograph, famous only to the few who were cleared to see it, is depicted the scientist holding a paper straw between the thumb and forefinger of a heavily gloved right hand. Borov grinned back at the camera through his heavily-shielded goggles as he stuck the straw half way into the device's field. The photograph managed to capture the slight electromagnetic eddy surrounding the straw at its intersection with the field, while another photograph showed the smooth, undisturbed backside of the field.

When Borov removed the straw from the field, it came away intact and undamaged. With a stroke, Borov decisively had demonstrated that the field worked. The date was February 4th, 1945. Clearly the soda straw went somewhere, maybe even *somewhen*, but answers to these questions remained obscured.

Precisely where?

Precisely when?

No one knew.

The issue of when fell to Willard Frank Libby, a promising chemist at the Columbia War Research Division and research scholar with clearances with the Manhattan Project. Borov, always on the lookout for a promising approach that might help solve his outstanding calibration problem, heard about Libby and his research interests through several of his White Sands colleagues who had interviewed him in early 1945. Intrigued by what Libby was on to, Borov made some quiet inquiries and received some very favorable assessments. On the basis of those positive appraisals, Borov decided to decisively act and secretly backed Libby's research. While Borov knew that he was supporting a promising scientist with a very reasonable proposal, Borov also realized that he was taking quite a chance by placing so many eggs in one basket. Nonetheless, his gut said it was the right thing to do and so he did it. Besides, he reasoned, had not the Americans already taken quite a chance on him?

Although Libby did not know it, he owed much to his secret patron Borov for the encouragement he received to toy with his pet project: the calibration of free atmospheric radiocarbon. Libby never understood why he had been so generously funded to pursue his radiocarbon research, for he could not see any connection between it, the war effort, or the Manhattan Project for that matter. Simply put, there was plenty of interest by the secretive and hopeful Borov.

By 1947, Libby perfected the technique of analyzing carbon-14 that allowed him to yield the absolute date of when an organism stopped its radiocarbon absorption, give or take several hundred years. Libby's research had blazed an important trail and one that is actively continued today. All that Borov could bank on was that Libby's technique would represent a reasonable calibration approach that he could eventually use for his Soap Bubble device.

Eager to try out Libby's radiocarbon technique, Borov's team began in the following year to take atmospheric radiocarbon samples directly from the enlarged field of their new and improved Mark II Soap Bubble. Using a long, syringe-like probe made entirely of non-conductive tempered Corning glass, the New Mexican research staff began their tests by extending the probe through the now twelve-inch field to take air samples of what they hoped would prove to be other time periods.

At first the experimental technique was a bit hit-and-miss. A given field strength and ion flow level were noted and an accompanying air sample taken. Initially fifteen samples were made. As one might expect, more than just air returned when the atmospheric probe was retracted: volcanic ash, seawater with oceanic flora, and some insects of identifiable genera. Quickly it became apparent that Little Bubble, as the twelve-inch diameter prototype was affectionately called, was one sensitive critter. With the field testing taking place at the White Sands lab, it became abundantly clear that vast sweeps of time were being traversed with every click of the dials on the Mark II's power source and ion emitter.

It turned out that the volcanic ash and seawater samples were far too old for measurement using Libby's carbon-14 technique. Instead, tried and true relative chronological methods and direct observation of these samples, based on the known geology of New Mexico and the archaic microscopic sea life itself, suggested dates in the neighborhood of sixty-three million years before the present. In other words, the samples dated to the age of the dinosaurs. While Libby's methodology had failed to calibrate these samples, an approximate calibration was nonetheless possible through more traditional, relativistic means.

If one considers the first two sample results as representative of the vast swings in time that the Little Bubble was capable of, then the results gleaned from the remaining thirteen samples made no sense whatsoever. They were all modern. Given Little Bubble's differing power and emitter settings for each sample, such results were difficult to understand much less believe. Initially, a fair amount of panic broke out through the lab and considerable soul-searching with these unexpected results.

Instead, Borov challenged his research staff. "Look," he said to them, "Look at the data again for something, anything that looks odd about the thirteen samples. Find for me something, anything, that might indicate a quantifiable element, which can differentiate them."

After a hectic three weeks of investigation, Borov had his answer. Libby had assumed wrongly that the amount of available atmospheric carbon-14 was a constant over time, for Borov's widely divergent samples clearly proved otherwise. In fact, when the carbon-14 levels were plotted, they did not cluster into a straight line constant. Instead, they were scattered all over the graph whose x and y axis were indexed to Little Bubble's power and ion emission settings. The short of it was Borov's team had discovered an important calibration variable that when taken into account would be very beneficial to Libby's radiocarbon technique, but was useless for the calibration of the Soap Bubble. Nonetheless, Borov remained committed to Libby and his research.

As he so eloquently put it to his staff: "Well, darn it all, if the carbon-14 levels aren't a constant. Then just what the hell are they? What's their pattern?"

So was initiated a minor, but very important tangent to the calibration of Soap Bubble device and for the development of Libby's radiocarbon method – the rigorous recording of the levels of free atmospheric carbon-14. For the next ten years, spanning the period from 1948 through 1958, Borov's lab undertook the processing of literally thousands of such radiocarbon levels. Such industry began slowly and only took off once much-needed improvements were made in power management and the monitoring of the ion flow. While they did not know from what eras they were sampling, they did know the sample's related power and ion emitter parameters. By carefully balancing these parameters, Borov's people could state beyond a shadow of a doubt that the radiocarbon levels of the eras that they were sampling were not a constant represented by a straight line. Instead, they appeared cyclical and looked like a sine wave. When all was said and done, and only when all parties were sure about this phenomenon, did Borov leak the possibility to a few interested colleagues.

It took some time for this novel sine wave notion to take hold among the academic community. The question was how to test for the variability of the free carbon-14 levels and where would such data reside. The answer came from an unexpected source – tree rings, and tree rings from the long-lived and slow-growing trees, like elm, oak, and especially the bristlecone pine. The challenge was to build a continuous lineage of tree ring data that went as far back in time as possible. When then tested for their carbon-14 content, the research ran its course and in the process "discovered" the sine wave phenomenon in the amounts of free atmospheric radiocarbon. It had taken some thirteen years to finally see it in print, but the newly-established field of dendrochronology was off and running. By doing so, Borov in his own quiet way had again assisted Libby's research and aided his own as well.

These early setbacks regarding the Soap Bubble's calibration dismayed and frustrated Borov's team to the core. No longer was their project just an experiment that could be pursued with all the confidence and enthusiasm that was typical of victorious, post-war America. Instead, caution and extreme care became the order of the day. The playful photographs of half-disappearing soda straws continued, but the team began to wonder how long it would be before someone unwittingly poked someone, or something, in the eye.

So along with the calibration effort, the post-war years for Soap Bubble were marked by continuous technical development coupled with an overarching concern for safety. Early on, the project staff noted that the enlarged metallic loop that defined the electromagnetic field tended to heat up during extended periods of radiocarbon harvesting. When it did, the loop would first glow, then warp and deform. As it did, the integrity of the field within it would abruptly break down with a sizzling snap and reek of ozone. On one memorable occasion, the field broke down while the glass atmospheric probe still pierced it. The result was dramatic. The probe had been severed as if it had been made of butter, its remaining edge made molten rather than sheared. Fortunately, the research assistant had been wearing heavily shielded gloves and goggles, but all of his exposed skin and hair was singed from the flash. Here a very dangerous lesson had been learned about the Soap Bubble: any breakdown in its field while in use could prove injurious to the careless. Thereafter, flash protective clothing became the order of the day for anyone working near or directly with the device's field.

Another direct result of this experimental "accident" was that the Soap Bubble's development took a new course: the assurance of loop integrity. After considerable experimentation, the project team decided that a loop of a highly refined ferric alloy conducted the electromagnetic field the best. To maintain the necessary uniform shape of the ferric loop under the stress of ever-mounting power applications and prolonged durations, a thick, one-inch ceramic coating was applied over the ferric ring as a supporting exoskeleton. Then a precise five-millimeter groove was carefully milled through the ceramic along the loop's inside diameter in order to expose its ferric core. This marriage of a conductive core with the supportive and heat dissipating characteristics of a ceramic worked remarkably well. So well, in fact, that it allowed for the enlargement of the electromagnetic field's loop to a full two and a half feet across. This improved Soap Bubble, officially christened the Mark III, which would soon earn a nickname as well.

Powering up and maintaining a steady and surge-free source of energy through a Soap Bubble apparatus presented another intriguing engineering challenge. Electricity was the power source of choice, but early on sufficient and reliable amounts of it were in relatively short supply in post-WW II New Mexico. Accordingly, the early tests of the Soap Bubble were scheduled late at night or early in the morning to avoid attracting the public's attention and the ire of their research colleagues to the drain on the local power grid. Still, the flow of the current was oftentimes irregular and fluctuated, which created unexpected and dangerous surges. Added to this was the empirical fact that any expansion of the loop's diameter meant an increase in power by a necessary factor to maintain field strength. A plentiful and surge-free source of power was needed if the Soap Bubble was ever to realize its true potential. Fortunately, help was soon on the way.

Unnoticed by the public, an additional overhead power line was strung from the Hoover Dam across the entire state of Arizona. At a point in that overhead power network, one line broke away along its own tower system to nowhere in particular, but somewhere heading across the Arizona-New Mexico state line toward the San Andres

Mountains. Along that range's western slopes at the opening of a canyon, the power line ended at a modest gypsum and cement plant serviced by a broad and well-used dirt road. The plant and its road, while decoys, did indeed function as advertised in the telephone directory of the nearby town of Truth or Consequences and employment opportunities regularly appeared in that town's daily newspaper. Not advertised, however, was the fact that the plant was federally owned and run and that it played a significant role in the supply of construction material for several secret government installations scattered throughout the region.

The power line from the plant then continued on as an underground cable heading toward the south-southeast. It was from this dedicated line that Borov's Soap Bubble team was provided a nearly unlimited power supply available on an Alpha One priority basis. That meant the Mark III Soap Bubble, or Hoover Bubble, had priority over the electrical needs of nearby Fort Bliss and even the hospital in Alamogordo. For the first time, the Soap Bubble's tests could take place in the light of day. The infamous all-nighters of testing became a thing of the past. The research staff was positively gleeful.

The Mark IV Roscoe Soap Bubble had a short-lived existence. It tested the inevitable question: could a healthy, living organism could pass through a temporal field and return unharmed. At issue and unspoken on everyone's mind were the unexpected and horrible consequences that had occurred to the ill-fated ship's crew of the Philadelphia Experiment, and in particular the whereabouts of those who had abandoned ship while in extremis. While microscopic sea life and flies had been plucked from their environments, to date no one had dared "a round trip from this side."

That changed on February 14th, 1962. A fully goggled, flash-cladded, and shielded Borov passed a freshly cut long-stemmed rose through the field and back without injury. Next was a lab worker's frisky pet tarantula named Magilla, and it too came back without any ill effects. But such was not the case with the pet hamster named Roscoe.

In preparation for the Roscoe Experiment, a four-foot long herpetologist's snake stick was constructed of glass and ceramic that could hold in its grasping tongs a small laboratory animal. The plan was to extend the tongs with the wriggling test subject fully into the field and then bring it back. The task seemed simple and straightforward enough. It was a procedure that had been done countless times during the Soap Bubble's calibration sampling. Why would this time be any different?

In the annals of high-energy physics and experimental quantum mechanics, Dr. Peter Borov's name will never appear. But because of him, the temporal security of our world is a far better, safer place. At the last minute before the Roscoe Experiment took place, Borov, in a moment of far-sighted prudence, had the laboratory totally sealed off. Only he and two heavily armed and protected sentries remained in the lab with their weapons at the ready and their eyes peeled.

The Mark IV powered up. Ion flow was nominal. The temporal field integrity held stable. Borov plunged the probe and Roscoe into the field. As the seconds ticked off nothing remarkable happened. Only the field rippled minutely around the probe's shaft. Then, suddenly, the prong was almost yanked from Borov's grasp, because something had sharply jerked on it from the other side the field! Wide-eyed, the scientist found himself in a wrestling match that he was in danger of losing, himself being slowly dragged toward the field! Clearly, someone or something had latched on to the other end of the probe!

Upon seeing what was happening through the observation window, a panicked member of the research staff shut down the field just as the wiry Borov and one of the sentries had wrenched the probe back through the field. At the flash of its abrupt cutoff, Borov and Corporal Charles Cartwright were thrown back onto the floor. Both men sat stunned on the lab's floor looking like two bobsledders with their legs spread out before them. The corporal still had his arms tightly wrapped around Borov's waist. In any other venue, this scene would have been considered comical, if not one right out of the Three Stooges.

As for Borov, he still held the probe before him in his shielded gloves. The hamster Roscoe was still there, but was squirming quite a bit since its fur was smoking from the flash. But what really caught Borov's eye was that firmly attached to the probe's tongs was a still quivering, massive set of raptor talons neatly cauterized at the midleg! Borov, seeing the sight, threw up into his lap and over Cartwright's arms, all the time still holding aloft the probe, its quivering captive, and the still gripping talons.

The abrupt shut down of the Roscoe Mark IV had turned its internal workings into a running stream of melted elements and acrid smoke. Nonetheless, two-way transit through the field by a living organism had been successful. And that running lab joke about poking out someone's eye on the other side had been proven to be all too possible.

It was around the time of the Roscoe debacle that the Borov team received good news from the public sector with the publication of two long-awaited studies. The first was undertaken by two scholars from prominent East Coast academic institutions. This article brought together a continuous series of oak tree rings that dated from the present back to eleventh century AD. To quote these scholars, "The exceptional value of dendro-chronology as a dating tool is its capacity to establish dates exact to the year for the growth of tree ring sequences."

Of even more importance to Borov and his team was that each one of these tree rings held vital information that related directly to a given atmospheric radiocarbon level. This important linkage was made in the second publication that appeared almost coincident with the first, where "Radiocarbon ages of dendrochronologically dated wood samples are reported back to 2500 BC." Finally, Borov and his team possessed a tool, a benchmark, in which to convert all of their own atmospheric radiocarbon samples into solid chronological dates. The elation was extreme, morale soared. The computers hummed as their atmospheric data was submitted to processing and the reams of green bar paper began to slowly chug its way out of the dot matrix printers.

To the wonder of all, the team discovered that their early horse fly sample dated back, albeit via extrapolation, to about seventy thousand years before the present. Their engorged state was probably on Mastodon blood! Others, however, were of greater age, actually beyond the capability of the extrapolation program to even offer a sober guess. But the vast majority of the atmospheric samples, especially those of the series that began with the Little Bubble and

Hoover Bubble, possessed correlations that were assignable to a specific year.

At present, the Mark V represents the latest iteration of the Soap Bubble series. Extending fully three and a half feet in diameter and resembling a horizontally suspended hula-hoop, the Mark V's power needs are fully one half that of the Hoover Bubble. This dramatic reduction in needed through-put power is due to the use of advanced, super-conducting materials, the extensive use of exotic metalloceramic components, and a carbon-fiber framework pirated from a scrapped B-1 Bomber.

The best feature of the Mark V is its dedicated mini-computer. Constructed of ultra-fast molecular wafer circuitry, the unit's MOSFETs or metal oxide semiconductor field-effect transistors, possess shorter gate lengths that are more efficient than the current 65 nanometer standard, shortened to less than 15 nanometers. In addition, Little Beast, as the Mark V's computer is affectionately called, enjoys layered parallel processors that can theoretically tune the Soap Bubble's temporal field and ion flow to a horizon within any day of a calendrical year. As with all of its predecessors, however, issues still revolve around calibration. Although a daring plan is underway that finally will put to bed that issue and finally address the other – where.

Even more importantly, the Mark V-A version is the first of the Soap Bubble series that can claim portability. Its mini-nuclear power pack, a modified version of the same Radioisotope Thermal Generator or RTG power pack that went to the Moon with Apollo XII, provides a maximum of forty minutes of surge-free run time. No bigger than a backpack frame, the heavily shielded nuclear power pack nonetheless needs a strong back to heft it, or better two to carry it on a litter. To date, the Mark V and portable V-A have yet to earn a nickname, but the fulfillment of that tradition too, given time, will come.

CHAPTER VI
AD 1973. Royal Hair Samples

The living conditions in Cairo are oppressive by any modern standard: overpopulation, filth, poor sanitation, poverty, shaky to non-existent plumbing and electricity, overwhelming traffic snarls, and horrendous air pollution. As Anatol dismounted the overnight train at the main station at Ramses Square, he girded himself for that assault. At the same time, he caught himself reflecting upon how hard it was to return to Cairo, especially after having spent time in the pristine upriver ecology of Luxor – ancient Thebes.

After shouldering his way through the waves of beggars and hawkers of manufactured "authentic" antiquities, he hailed a cab and checked into the Cairo Nile Hilton. While Anatol preferred the older Shepherd Hotel, Jannicka had insisted on the Hilton, reasoning that it was located directly across the street from the Cairo National Museum itself. When asked how the expedition could cover his stay at the expensive American hotel, Jannicka had cryptically replied, "God will provide."

That afternoon Anatol, refreshed from a long shower, walked over to the museum. Strolling past the line of improperly dressed western tourists waiting to enter Egypt's national and cultural holy of holies, Anatol found himself shaking his head in disgust.

How in the world could any tourist agency allow women to dress themselves in such a fashion within such a devoutly Muslim country? It's a miracle that they haven't already caused a riot or have been stoned to death!

Still in shock about the French tourists, Anatol stole around to the eastern side entrance and ceremonially showed his identification papers to the stocky armed guard wearing a crisply creased tan uniform. His nametag read: S. Hassan. An old acquaintance, Hassan offered and the pair shared a quick cigarette. Hassan, himself a student of Egyptology, longed to be attached to an academic field excavation, but both knew that such pairings were granted on far, far more than the luck of the draw. Politics was the coin of such appointments. As Hassan did not have an influential mentor, he fell back on the old and time-honored tradition of developing personal relationships with anyone and everybody. Anatol, for his part, knew how to play this game and promised he would see what he could do. After all, Hassan himself might one day become the Director of the Egyptian Archaeological Service.

Finished with their traditional conversation about a topic that both knew they could do nothing about, Anatol then crushed out his butt into the ashtray on Salim's small desktop. Salim smiled, slapped Anatol on the back, and said, "My brother, oh how I wish that we could work together in the field."

To which Anatol, with a wistful sort of grin, replied, "We both know that it would be Allah's will if we were allowed."

With those words of farewell, Anatol entered the cool shade of the massive pink building. Once alone, he closed his eyes and took a deep breath. He imaged that he could smell the musty and aromatic essence of antiquity itself. As he thread his way through the overcrowded and poorly displayed artifacts of the museum's ground level, Anatol wondered whether he would ever discover something worthy of this institution's public display.

Probably not, he sadly concluded.

Jannicka had arranged for him to speak with the director of the museum. Anatol's stomach was full of butterflies by the time he reached the museum's administration corridor. As he stood before the milky glass door of the museum director's suite, his hands were moist with perspiration. To Anatol, the only thing going for him was that Jannicka and the museum director treated one another as respected colleagues. Anatol felt as if he was an unknown beggar asking a great king for a considerable favor.

The human body, while under stress, can exhibit curiously opposite reactions. And so with a dry throat and sweating hands, Anatol turned the cool brass doorknob. While doing so, he noticed the gold lettering in French on the glass pane was beginning to flake away. What he next beheld took away his nervousness and replaced it with a confused emotion that he could not identify. He wondered. Perhaps I have been in the field too long?

The source of his agitation was the museum director's receptionist. Sitting behind a massive desk as big as a stone sarcophagus, she was flanked by two transom office doors identical to the one he had just entered. Silently Anatol prayed he had caught himself before he had been spotted gaping like an adolescent teenager at his first dance.

She was exquisite. Automatically, Anatol lapsed into the practiced descriptive mode of an archaeologist when first gazing upon a rare find. Clear, smooth olive complexion, dark green almond-shaped eyes, regally high cheekbones, a strong chin and elegant nose, and shiny blue-black hair cut in short bangs with longish side wings that enveloped the ears. Her teeth were perfect and white. She was young, ripe, and full of life.

At the sound of her voice Anatol finally came to. She addressed him in Arabic with a soft and cultured lilt. In response, he hoarsely introduced himself and announced his business. Upon review, he imagined that he had been awkward in an attempt to mask his feelings. Now looking away from the secretary and pretending to examine the Islamic tapestry that hung behind her, Anatol reprimanded himself.

Rein yourself in!

Focus!

After all, my dear Sergei, this is a rather important interview!

After the receptionist deciphered Anatol's curiously stated reply, she smiled her best professional smile and said that she would inform the director of his arrival. Lifting the heavy black receiver of the desk's telephone, she waited. On the second ring, which was easily heard through the door's open transom above the reception area, it was answered by the office's occupant to Anatol's left. After a brief conversation, the secretary turned to him and said.

"Mr. Anatol, the director will see you shortly. In the meantime, my I offer you some tea?"

A bit surprised and also relieved at his momentary reprieve, Anatol's dry throat spoke for him.

"Why, yes. That would be most kind."

Again lifting the telephone, the receptionist did so and suggested that Anatol take a seat in the nearby chair. She then returned to her reading.

Anatol, turning around, parked himself in the proffered chair and steeled himself for what could be a long wait as such was the Near Eastern cultural sense of time.

Again, for the umpteenth time, he started to rehearse in his mind what he wished to say, but his train of thought was short lived, as he realized that the young woman was speaking to him.

"Mr. Anatol?" She said for the second time.

"Yes."

"Is it true that you are part of the Polish Expedition at Deir el-Bahri?"

"Why, why yes. Yes indeed."

"I hope that you do not find my questions inappropriate, but it is just that I am curious as to what it is like working in the field, living in the open desert. I imagine it as being quite interesting, even exciting, and not at all like what the books describe."

Happy to tell of his adventures, Anatol did. And while relating what it all was like, Anatol relaxed and unconsciously fell back upon his flowing literary Arabic that enriched his descriptions of his work crew, the site, his Director Dr. Jannicka, and his visit to the cliff tomb of the mummy cache. Throughout his storytelling, the receptionist noted with some surprise the amazing command that this European had of her native tongue. She found herself amused at one moment by his occasional mixing of classical literary vocabulary with the local jargon of provincial Luxor, and spellbound the next with his vividly conjured imagery. At one point, he even managed to produce from her a genuine smile and a brief, chime-like giggle that thrilled Anatol's heart and tickled his spine. Then the tea arrived, shattering forever that fragile moment.

Half way through his cup of tea, the office door to Anatol's left opened. A huge Egyptian filled the frame. Broad shouldered, almost six-five, a full head of dark hair, clean-shaven, but wearing a well-trimmed, walrus-like moustache. His large eyes took in the scene.

Anatol carefully put down his teacup in its delicate saucer and slowly rose. The secretary, also rising, formally announced who Anatol was and his business.

For Anatol's part, his eyes never strayed from the large Egyptian, while his peripheral vision took in the lithe profile of the now standing receptionist. The large Egyptian noted this remarkable restraint and decided to end the silence.

Striding forward and extending a hand the size of a tennis racket, the Egyptian greeted Anatol with a heavily accented, but clearly Polish, greeting. Anatol smiled in pleasure at the attempt, and formally answered in his best Arabic. That earned him a smile and a rumbling chuckle from the large Egyptian, who then immediately turned and went back into his office. At first frozen in place, Anatol then quickly recovered and realized that he was meant to follow.

Sitting behind a desk even more massive than his secretary's, the large Egyptian watched as Anatol took in his office's expanse. With his practiced surveyor's eye, Anatol thought that it must have been thirty feet on a side, with every inch of the wall space – except for the filing cabinets, doorway, and window behind the desk, covered with book shelves from the floor to its twelve-foot ceiling. Momentarily forgetting who was waiting for him to speak, Anatol noted the wheeled library ladder and its track that circled the room. The filing cabinet tops were covered with unsorted paperwork. As for the desk, it looked to have accumulated several years of assorted bureaucratic stratigraphy itself.

Following his eyes, the large Egyptian shrugged, and said in Arabic, "Yes, this fine desk is a mess. In fact, I cannot even remember what color its top is."

Then the Egyptian shifted in his seat and leaned forward on his massive forearms, carelessly crushing reams of administrative clutter amid crinkles of sound.

"Please sit down, Mr. Anatol, and tell me how my friend Professor Jannicka is doing at Deir el-Bahri."

As commanded, Anatol spoke. The large Egyptian listened politely and with interest, all the while also taking note of the Pole's command of his native language. At the end of Anatol's summary, the large Egyptian then said, "Yes, it is as I expected. Professor Jannicka is doing just fine."

"But Mr. Anatol, what about you? Why did my good friend Jerzy send you to speak with me?"

For this question, Anatol silently thanked God, for he had been rehearsing this moment for what seemed to be weeks, but was only about a day and a half.

"Mr. Director, at the suggestion of Professor Jannicka, I am here to request permission of the Egyptian Antiquities Service, the Egyptian Government, and the Egyptian Nation to gather minute hair samples from several of the mummies of the Royal Cache. I know that this is an odd request, and one that requires the greatest cultural sensitivity, but I wish to undertake a genealogical study of the royal gene pool of the Eighteenth Dynasty. As you well know, several royal mummies from that dynasty were recovered from the Royal Cache. In addition, I seek permission to take similar hair samples from the noble pair of Yuya and Tuya as well, given their obvious importance within the dynasty. My purpose for taking these samples is to subject them to DNA analysis in order to shed new light upon that dynasty's genealogy, and in particular upon the royal personalities from the reign of Amenhotep III onward. I realize . . ."

At this point the director raised his right forefinger to interrupt Anatol's recitation. Anatol's heart promptly stopped beating.

"Mr. Anatol, you are obviously an educated man and one who speaks my language as if born to it. I must therefore assume you are also well aware of my nation's sensibilities regarding the desecration of our royal dead."

Again leaning over his desk, the director then asked, "Allow me to ask you this. If you take such a hair sample, can you return it?"

Looking down at his brand new dress shoes, Anatol said softly.

"*La*" – no in Arabic.

That answer earned the Pole a noncommittal grunt. Sitting back into his chair with a squeak, the Director eyes bored through Anatol as if he were not there. The silence lasted fifteen seconds.

Then, another fifteen.

Finally, with a deep sigh, the large Egyptian said, "My colleague Professor Jannicka sometimes asks too much of me. I will have to speak with him further about this matter. As for you, Mr. Anatol, you do not look like a dangerous barber to me. Now, tell me more about this D-N-A."

As Anatol began to numbly explain the revolutionary findings of the Nobel Prize winning team of Watson and Crick, the significance of DNA, the dawn broke as the director was seriously considering his research proposal and might even approve it. Elation exploded in Anatol's heart. His description of the basic biology, the scientific methodology involved, and the facilities at the Warsaw University's genetic laboratory where the samples would be processed, all these details flowed from of his lips . . .

Again, the finger of the director's hand rose, and again Anatol's heart stopped.

"Mr. Anatol, I am sorry and I must apologize for my ignorance, but all of these scientific details behind your project are, frankly, beyond me. Jerzy told me that I could trust you. And now having met you and having listened to what you wish to do, I do indeed. Now, please go and see my receptionist, who is also my personal secretary, Miss Moussa, whom I believe that you have already met. Tell her to fill out Form Number 375. Dictate to her what you propose to do, what you need. When you are finished, knock on my door, and allow me read the copy to sign. Again I apologize for being so abrupt, but, as you can see, I have a desk to clean up."

With that, the Director returned to his reading, sorting, and stacking of the myriad pages on his desk. Anatol stood on unsure legs, softly thanked the Egyptian again, turned, and quietly closed the door behind him.

As before, the receptionist looked up from what she had been doing. Her doe-like eyes again shocked Anatol's nervous system. Awkwardly looking around, he again found the lone chair, pulled it over to near her desk, sat, and delivered the museum director's orders.

When he recited the number of the administrative form, and what she was to do, the receptionist now secretary transformed into an efficient machine, but one that smelled not of engine oil and diesel, but instead of a delicate blending of jasmine and lotus fragrances.

During the dictation, Anatol was granted a legitimate opportunity for undivided observation. Dark green eyes outlined in delicate black lines, eye lashes that could sweep a floor, a broad and generous mouth, a graceful neck, and again that haunting fragrance. Anatol allowed the thought she could have easily sat for the statues and tomb murals of both Queens Nefertiti and Nefertari.

Through it all, Anatol did manage to control his composure, only to almost lose it whenever she would occasionally smile, look at him, or just move.

By afternoon's end, Anatol had in his possession two of the most precious things in his young life: a signed permit for his scientific project and two hours of bliss with the museum director's personal secretary. To his surprise, the director read the first version carefully and edited it to expand the project under the guise of a museum preservation effort, whose object was all the museum's mummies that dated to the Eighteenth Dynasty.

Once this revision had been carefully retyped, the large Egyptian read it once more, then signed it and handed it to a quivering Anatol saying, "Mr. Anatol, look here."

Anatol's eyes followed the huge man's hand as it gestured at the burgundy surface. He saw the rich patina of well-used leather – the director had managed to clear a portion of his desktop.

"I am told that this desk once belonged to the Director General himself, M. Gaston Maspero. As you know, he and his assistant Émile Brugsch, who first saved the Royal Cache from the antiquities market, brought Egypt's ancient royalty here to Cairo. If I can rediscover the color of M. Maspero's desktop, then I trust you can unravel the mysterious royal lineage of the Eighteenth Dynasty."

The director then continued with a more serious tone.

"Now, Mr. Anatol, do not disappoint me nor embarrass your future *Doktor Vater* and my good friend Jerzy Jannicka."

That said the director promptly sat down and went back to work. Anatol, thanked him again, and left the director's office.

As Anatol closed the door behind him, he turned and gratefully thanked the receptionist for the tea and her secretarial assistance. In surprise at his politeness, she broadly smiled saying, "Mr. Anatol, I wish you much good luck with your most interesting project."

Anatol, realizing that was about as much as any educated Egyptian woman could say to him, gave a slight bow, and replied also with a smile.

"Thank you. But truly, I must thank you, for your assistance with the permit has been," and Anatol paused, full knowing how far he was pushing the cultural limit, "most helpful."

With that he departed, feeling her eyes on him and wishing that he had been born an Egyptian.

By five that evening, Anatol had returned to the Hilton with his copy of the permit, had showered, and was lying naked atop his queen-size bed lazily luxuriating in the plentiful air conditioning. As he stretched, he moaned.

"Such glorious decadence!"

Tomorrow he would run the bureaucratic gauntlet again. It would be a full day, maybe two, but this time he would just wait for all of the appropriate authorization stamps, seals, and signatures to be affixed to his newly-minted permit.

Emotionally, he was on top of the world in a world-class hotel in a most ancient land, but all he could think about was the museum director's secretary.

* * *

Unknown to Anatol, the museum director's personal secretary was thinking the same about him and about how interesting it must be to work in the field. She missed her younger years washing pottery at her father's side, looking for ostraka until her finger tips wrinkled, or sight reading inscriptions to the total amazement of foreign scholars, while earning her father's quietly expressed praise.

On the other hand, accompanying her father on diplomatic and political site inspections were tiresome exercises in smiling smiles that were meaningless. The Germans tended to see right through her and treated her with cool regard. The Austrians were slightly warmer, more concerned about form, but more politically volatile. As for the French, well, she simply dismissed them as the French. But the Americans were the most confusing, for they thought her cute one moment and then confided with her as a total equal the next. But the Pole Anatol she found interesting, intriguing, and the first archaeologist she had ever met that was even close to her age. She had even dared to mention him to her father, which earned only a non-committal grunt.

* * *

While hardly insensitive to Egyptian sensibilities, Anatol was surprised at the emotional hornet's nest his genetic sampling project had created. All the fuss and feathers was not about the samples or the science behind the samples per se, but rather about the subjects of the sampling. The museum director's instincts about any tampering with the Royals had been astute. Despite his camouflaging the project's original intent with that of a preservation study, Anatol met resistance at every turn and the museum director's telephone line sizzled for the next two days.

In the end it was agreed that the genetic samples should be gathered without fanfare, certainly without the notice of the press, and during hours when the museum was closed to the public. On his third day in Cairo, a Thursday, Anatol sat patiently in Gallery 52 between Rooms 46 and 47 on the museum's second floor. There, surrounded by Egypt's ancient royalty, he awaited for the arrival of dusk in the hushed museum. As the end of the evening prayer approached, his jumpy knees betrayed his nervous excitement. Located directly across from him was the blond-haired Yuya, the nobleman father of Queen Nefertiti. Anatol could hardly contain himself before the first glass case was opened.

*   *   *

All concerned had agreed that an Egyptian should be responsible for removing the samples. A young medical internist was selected. At the ready, in a freshly starched white examination coat, Dr. Muhammed Sahfir sat next to the young Pole. Next to him was his examination bag, filled with sterilized test tubes already labeled and capped. The bag also held his rubber gloves, probe, tweezers, and suturing scissors. Once he had been let in on what the sampling project was really all about, he would have gladly paid just to watch, much less perform "the surgery." Educated in Britain, Sahfir saw Anatol as a sincere enough scholar, who spoke his native language surprisingly well, but a nervous chap and one that seemed a bit rough around the edges. Upon reflection, however, Sahfir remembered back to his first research lecture at Oxford and wondered what his colleagues had made of his hesitant, self-conscious grammar. With an inner smile, the internist, now measuring himself against the Pole, could only conclude indeed how far he had come. And now it was this man's turn.

*   *   *

Finally, the appointed time arrived. The chief of security appeared with a massive brass ring of keys jingling from the worn ring of his wide leather belt. At his side was Anatol's old friend Hassan, the museum guard, who for this proud moment had volunteered for duty. Taking a serious mood to his otherwise cheerful countenance, Hassan tried to look grave. He was not all together successful, however, for his sense of history and excitement beamed through undiminished.

Finally, Hassan thought. *I am part of an academic enterprise!*

*   *   *

The physical sample gathering process, after all the excitement, the tension and negotiation, struck Anatol nonetheless as somewhat of a letdown. If any drama occurred that early evening, it had to do with the cabinet locks themselves. Old and gummed up with dust from disuse, several of them required an injection of lubricant in order to coax their stubborn tumblers to fall. After fifty-five minutes of careful work, all the samples were collected. The actual process of snipping the minute hair fragments and placing them in their labeled test tubes took less than thirty seconds each.

In all, the following Egyptian notables were sampled: the noble couple of Yuya and Tuya, the Pharaohs Amosis, Amenhotep I, Thutmose I, Thutmose II, Hatshepsut, and Thutmose III, the Princesses Meretaten and Sitamen, and finally, the Queens Tetisheri and Tiye. At its conclusion, Anatol and Sahfir shook hands and wished one another well. As for the chief of security, he muttered to Hassan that all this sampling was a dirty sacrilegious business, but at least he had the opportunity to fix some locks.

That night in his hotel room, Anatol held up the hand-sewn cloth bandoleer that Dr. Sahfir's wife had thoughtfully stitched up for the occasion. Into each of its soft cotton folds, Sahfir had carefully slipped in one of the twelve test tubes samples. Anatol noted that they were so light, so seemingly insignificant.

With that, the young man pulled out from beneath his bed a steel coffee can and its lid that the hotel's kitchen staff had kindly provided. He then spread the bandoleer atop the bed and began to layer across it shredded strips of cotton batting that he had bought at a nearby pharmacy. When he finished, Anatol rolled up the bandoleer into a tight cylinder and secured it with several large rubber bands. Placing the precious roll into the coffee can, he packed cotton into any gaps he could find. Satisfied his bundle was secure, Anatol placed a small handwritten note on the top of the bundle that inventoried which numbered sample belonged to whom. Sealing up the can with its steel top, he finally affixed a terse identification label squarely on the outside of the can with two generous pieces of packing tape just so.

ROYAL HAIR SAMPLES – (12)
CAIRO NATIONAL MUSEUM
OCTOBER 1973
SERGEI ANATOL

There, that should do it. He thought.

As far as the young Pole was concerned that was the best that he could do.

The day after tomorrow he would fly back to his native land and Warsaw University. Professor Jannicka, who had already telephoned from the field his hearty congratulations, then gave him stern instructions to get to work on his dissertation.

Anatol thought, *I owe a lot to both those men who stuck their necks out for me.*

In preparation for his trip home, Anatol packed his lone travel bag with the coffee can, his field journals, and laid out his clothing. All was in order: airline tickets, passport, and money for the cab. That Friday night being more weary and exhausted then he had ever expected, Anatol slept deeply.

While the future Egyptologist slept, the Egyptian military did not. The date was October 5th, 1973, the day before the joint Egyptian-Arab surprise attack on Israel, the beginning of the Yom Kippur War.

While his airline would later arrange to return Anatol's baggage to Warsaw University, Anatol would never come back to Poland. His thesis outline, field notebooks, and coffee can with its precious genetic contents eventually were placed on an empty shelf in the archive of that institution's Oriental Institute and there they sat, undisturbed, for the next two decades.

What happened to Anatol was a simple tragedy of war, as if anything in war could be declared simple. During the opening chaos of the conflict, the Cairo airport had become a prime target of opportunity for any aircraft with a remaining bomb load that brandished a light blue, six-pointed star.

Salim Hassan, Anatol's museum guard friend and Air Force reservist, was hurriedly refueling an Egyptian Mirage fighter on the tarmac in full view of the civilian concourse of the airport. Anatol, standing before an airport plate glass picture window, was watching with interest that refueling process oblivious to the fact that his friend was down there before him.

The Israeli attack jet did not care, for its pilot saw only opportunity – a parked military jet and a fuel truck. Quickly lining up his aircraft, the pilot pickled his last munitions from his starboard pylon and tore away at treetop level for his home base in the Beer Sheva Desert.

Anatol saw from the corner of his left eye the hurtling silver blur of the attack jet, the descent of something from its underside, and the transformation of the tarmac before him into a fiery inferno. He felt the concussive explosion before the sound caught up, for the parked Mirage was fully armed. Maybe the sound never caught up at all, because the blast's concussion wave reached the windows first, which in turn disintegrated into splinters that shredded flesh and bone. The Pole's remains would never be recovered nor would those of his friend Salim Hassan.

*　　*　　*

The next morning, as the Polish mission hurriedly packed up, the aged workman Mustafa arrived at the archaeological site breathing hard and bearing a great burden. As the familiar faces of the work crews had been absent since the conflict's beginning, Mustafa's sudden presence caused all to stop what they were doing. Looking around as if he had lost an article of great value, the venerable Egyptian finally settled before the standing and curious figure of the dig's director.

Gasping.

"Dr. Jannicka, may Allah be with you."

"And with you as well, Mustafa," Jannicka replied with a gentle bow of greeting and deference to the ancient man.

"What brings you here in such times of turmoil?"

"I bring troubling news. For the village has just learned that a vicious attack by the godless ones occurred yesterday on the Cairo Airport. Several Europeans were reported killed. I fear that my kindly brother Anatol was one of them. Oh, how I wanted that saintly man to be the husband to my grand-daughter!"

"How do you know this?" Jannicka suddenly blurted out.

"Here."

The Egyptian removed from his *ghalabiya* a neatly folded newspaper that he gave to the disbelieving Pole.

"Please read it to me, as I cannot."

Quickly scanning the front page news, Jannicka did not have to speak aloud the import of what he had found. Mustafa's source was right. An Israeli aircraft had indeed attacked the Cairo Airport. Some twenty-odd Europeans had been killed. As he scanned halfway through their names, tears began to stream freely down his face.

Looking up, Mustafa's eyes widened in recognition of his greatest fear and his heart simultaneously hardened in pure hate. Spreading his arms wide, what that frail man then unleashed was a truly soulless, primal wailing scream that first filled, then repeatedly echoed off the surrounding cliffs of Deir el-Bahri.

Several millennia had passed since such an anguished sound last reverberated against those most sacred of funerary cliffs.

CHAPTER VII
Some Photogenic Royals

"Great minds think alike." This common axiom has no better proof than in 1973, the very year of young Sergei Anatol's unfortunate demise. For in that year a human tissue bank was founded in England devoted entirely to the study of Egyptian mummies of all kinds from all eras. At a prominent and well-funded museum, mummies were non-evasively studied using the most up-to-date techniques in radiology, histopathology, serology, and DNA finger-printing. Out of such cutting edge scientific approaches, genetic studies were undertaken and even facial reconstructions attempted. But, it must be said, these studies did not include any of the royal personages of the Royal Cache, or any of the royalty of the Cairo National Museum. Even as this tissue bank was being established, a gifted scientist, respected in the fields of genetics and physical anthropology, began a similar quest in December of 1974.

Working in the heartland of the United States as a member of a major research institution, Professor Harvey James wanted to use the non-invasive technique of radiology to determine royal family relationships between fathers and their sons. While his project was centered upon the precise measurement of the craniofacial morphology of a series of supposedly related mummies, it also included full body x-rays as well. On the basis of such a rigorous radiological examination, James hoped to plot and establish family relationships based on facial skeletal structure and the expression of common and shared genetic factors. Only secondarily was he interested in the results of the full body scans.

Unlike the tissue bank group, some thought James had the extraordinary luck of being granted permission by the Egyptian Antiquities Service to radiograph the entire male membership of the Royal Cache and many others resident at the Cairo National Museum. He was even allowed to x-ray the Pharaohs Amenhotep II and Tutankhamen, both of whom still rested in their royal tombs within the Valley of the Kings. Others knew better, however, that the Director of the Cairo National Museum appeared to be the driving force that had sponsored James' research. But the truth of the matter was that his daughter was behind it all. Shattered as she was at the tragic loss of a young Polish archaeologist, she believed that his brilliant thesis should live in some form or another and might possibly even come to fruition. Consequently, throughout James' labors, the scholar began to notice his project never found itself lacking for any assistance.

On the other hand, James was further blessed with the collegial international assistance of two key players and the cooperation of sympathetic museum personnel. The Egyptian forensic scientist, Dr. Hussein Kamal, and the crack Russian geneticist, Professor Dr. Pavel Norsk, rounded out his project team. Although each was the product of differing cultural, religious, and political experience, each contributed mightily to the whole. On top of that, the trio became so inseparable, so close-knit, that the Cairo National Museum's staff referred to them as the Three Wise Men. This honorific was well deserved as this dedicated team of investigators treated each and every one of their "patients" with extraordinary respect and tender loving care. These actions did not go unnoticed, and as a consequence, the museum's professional staff and its many guards felt a kindred with them and with what they were attempting to do. Therefore, no request made of them, no matter how slight or strange, went unfulfilled.

With all such cutting-edge scientific undertakings, James and his team were in for several surprises. The first had to do with the historical record itself. After a careful comparison of the cephalometric information that the x-rays produced, the data strongly suggested several pharaohs were misidentified, despite that their associated funerary paraphernalia suggested otherwise. In other words, when the cross-sectional tracings of supposedly related individuals were overlaid one upon the other, "strange deviations in craniofacial morphologies" were observed between royal mummies previously believed to be father and son. In particular, the Pharaoh Amenhotep III, long believed to be the natural father of both the Pharaohs Smenkhkare and Tutankhamen, prompted one of the team to actually remark in print: "It is worth noting that the mummy of Amenhotep III shows absolutely no sign of the physical attributes manifested by his sons Smenkhkare and Tutankhamen."

The implication was clear. Their father had to be someone else. But there was far more about the x-rays of the Pharaohs Smenkhkare and Tutankhamen that never reached the printed page, for they were the source of a second, far darker surprise, which had come from left field. The cranial and skeletal makeup of these two biologically related individuals exhibited phenomena unique to the otherwise male characteristics of the dynasty. Specifically, Tutankhamen and the mummy of his older brother Smenkhkare, who originally was recovered from Tomb 55 within the Valley of the Kings, both exhibited exactly the same uniquely uncommon cranial and soft tissue morphologies – morphologies that manifested themselves nowhere else throughout the entire Cairo National Museum x-ray project. In addition, as if the bizarre cranial morphologies were not enough, the full-body x-rays of the pair revealed they were missing their floating ribs, and most peculiar, these males shared a common, but very oddly-shaped pelvic girdle. In life, such traits would have exhibited themselves as an exaggerated tendency toward a wasp-waist and broad hips. Such attributes, although much sought after but seldom achieved on a modern modeling runway, were totally anomalous to the traits of the preceding males of the dynasty, all who manifested clearly mesomorphic traits. Also, James and his team strongly suspected, at least privately, that what they had captured on the x-ray film was so odd, so atypical, that it could well be unique to the human genome.

These physiological data were found to be so unexpected, and so isolated within the Eighteenth Dynasty, that any explanation offered for their presence seemed to these researchers based more on imaginative speculation than firmly grounded fact. Privately, the data suggested to the team that the Pharaoh Amenhotep IV, also known as Akhenaten, was the true father of Smenkhkare and Tutankhamen. But since the mummy of Akhenaten himself was not available, such a speculation seemed a rash extrapolation, representing no more than an explanation based upon negative evidence. Not exactly sound scientific method, the trio rightly concluded. In the final analysis, the three were stumped at the data. No matter how many times they re-evaluated their findings, all they encountered was further evidence that supported their convictions.

They were looking at a biological phenomenon unlike anything seen before in modern science.

Although these truly anomalous cranial and skeletal features were carefully noted and recorded in the team's laboratory documentation, they, nonetheless, never appeared in the scientific literature nor saw the light of day. To be blunt, the three researchers were so profoundly disturbed about the anomalous skeletal phenomena that they decided to drop the entire issue, rather than cast a pall upon the validity of their joint international undertaking, not to mention jeopardize their academic careers.

But unknown to the rest of his team, Norsk was not quite so reticent, for he did append to the full and annotated copy of the team's findings a three-page cover letter that he sent to a nondescript department of the Russian Academy of Science. It arrived in October of 1977. Little did he suspect the quiet furor those anomalous biological observations would cause and what formidable resources would be brought to bear.

Chapter VIII

The Norsk Report

The arrival of winter's first snow had gently blanketed the city in virgin white. To the shuffling middle-aged man it was grand. All seemed so pristine, so pure, but to this careful scientist and meticulous bureaucrat. Even the trailing evidence of his early morning passage seemed to irrevocably break this momentary spell as he began to mount the well-worn stone steps of the ministry building.

Having brushed the remaining snow from the broad shoulders of his heavy wool greatcoat, the last vestige of his lost youth devoted to the defense of his motherland, Professor Dr. Vasily Alexandrovich Ostrogorsky, Director of the prestigious Institute of Theoretical Biology, finally settled himself behind his desk mounded high in unread correspondence.

A deep sigh.

Another lost morning devoted to chasing one's tail, he grimaced as he methodically sorted the unruly mound into piles of important, interesting, and trash.

Half way through this daily chore, however, one large and weighty manila envelope caught Vasily's eye. It bore several large denomination airmail stamps, Egyptian in origin, and on one a portrait of President Anwar Sadat. Noting the upper left corner, the sender was Professor Dr. Pavel Norsk, a former student, colleague in human genetics, and rapidly rising star.

Smiling about warm memories and intrigued by this unexpected correspondence, Ostrogorsky broke his habitual rhythm. Impulsively he opened the envelope, carefully tearing off the envelope's corner with its precious and exotic stamps. These he squirreled away into a folder from the left-hand drawer for his philatelist wife's later pleasure. Pitching the now raped envelope into the circular file, he leaned forward heavily onto his felt green blotter, placed the included photocopied manuscript to one side, and began reading the cover letter's three densely typed, single-spaced pages.

After a third reading, Ostrogorsky sat back deeply into his wooden chair with a creak, took off his wire-rimmed glasses to rub thoughtfully at the bridge of his nose, and for a second time that morning, sighed. The importance of what he just read, and reread several times, the scientist considered curious. In fact, he was taken aback at the rise in his pulse and his visceral excitement. He sensed, quite rightly, that his career was about to take a dramatic turn.

CHAPTER IX
The Philology Annex

At first the property wasn't much, just a well-weathered urban three-story brownstone. Located on a corner, nestled within a heavily-treed university neighborhood on Chicago's south side, the structure shared a windowless narrow gangway with its neighbor to the east. Its seven worn and settled concrete steps were all uniformly cracked at the corners of their treads. The twin industrial strength steel pipe railings were scarred with flaking craters of paint that marked the seasons like the tree rings of the ancient elms and oaks that shaded them.

A fresh coat of brown paint was sorely needed, but that did not bother the elderly but spry visitor who had come to inquire about the property. Glancing up, he noted that while the shaded windows needed a wash, they were at least intact against the weather. That good sign brought forth a smile and a mental nod. Seeing the fine European woodwork of the front doorway brought back a rush of unbidden recollections of his university days at Leningrad State University. The thickly painted black doorknob turned smoothly enough in his hand, and the fine patina of scratches on the green-edged brass kick plate made him smile in another pleasurable rush of memories past.

Going to have to polish that up, thought the visitor.

Once inside from the wind and biting chill, the visitor was greeted with the heavy humid warmth that only cast iron steam radiators provide. Looking around the bare entrance foyer with its peeling lead-based paint, fine wooden moldings, and floor, he quietly murmured, "Just perfect."

Some fourteen years later, the outside of the place now looks much the same except for some subtle details and one addition. The railings are kept scraped and painted. The entrance door's kick plate glows a quiet, inviting greeting to all. The sparkling, near-invisible window glass now display delicate drapes of gossamer lace hung just so in neat gatherings. Along the short entrance sidewalk stands a low institutional sign, which announces in brass roman letters, The Philology Annex.

While the structure had been quietly purchased from the university administration, its renovation and extensive modification, especially to its several sublevels, remained a closely guarded secret as was the tenant's true purpose. Still, the Philology Annex's presence to the community was anything but a secret as it rapidly became, by design, a natural hive of campus activity, a nexus both for research scholars and eager students alike. Its low-key atmosphere provided a warm, cozy, womb-like environment, liberally seasoned with the rich smells of pipe tobacco, freshly brewed coffee, and above all, books. Its many reading rooms resembled archive-like, monkish cells with their gently slanted oak tables, flat central perches, and low reading lights that emitted soft bands of illumination beneath one's eye level.

There were nine such book-bulging rooms in all, three per floor, each supported by its own adjoining seminar room, kitchenette, and bathrooms. Each of these intellectual nests was devoted to the philology and literature of long dead, ancient languages of the Near East and Western Asia: Akkadian, Hittite, Hurrian, Egyptian, Sumerian, Persian, Aramaic, Coptic, and Phoenician. Those in the know realized that the time span for each represented vast universes with each often subdivided into early, middle, and late. Each of these sub-periods often were characterized by divergent grammars, dialects, and subtly different ligatures.

Visitation rights during the academic year were granted at the founder's insistence for the pittance of fifty cents that just barely covered the cost of the laminated identification card. Shoes were left in the entrance way's foyer in orderly nooks on the left and one's personal slippers were similarly stored on the right. Disposable hospital versions were available at the receptionist's desk for, yes— you guessed it, fifty cents. Padding about in slippers was a noisy enough affair, as one would soon discover from the groaning old wooden floors of the halls and stairways. But as the founder had calculated, the enforced slipper requirement made for shuffled, muffled movements and a psychological transformation that engendered a calming effect upon the institution's patrons.

To the casual observer, the sole sentinel of this philological holy of holies was the receptionist's desk, which sat squarely in the center of the entrance foyer in a perfect place of greeting. Behind that desk opened a single, full-length, milky-glassed paneled office door with transom. Painted at eye-level on its frosted surface in tasteful gold letters were the words: HEAD LIBRARIAN. To the right ascended a banister and carpeted flight of oiled wooden stairs to the second and third floors, to the left the entrance archway led to the Phoenician, Aramaic, and Persian carrels.

The aging founder of this philological retreat of research and study, Dr. Peter Borov, had established it for two reasons: the final calibration of the Soap Bubble, and as the training site for those who were to gather that data. Having finally found that Libby's radiocarbon dating methodology was of limited practical use, Borov began to toy with the idea of calibrating his device against well-understood celestial positions and historical milestones. To do so meant sending some brave soul back to an approximate *somewhen*, where the possibility of shooting a star's position in the night's sky or finding a precise chronological date had a high degree of probability. To Borov that meant he had to choose a region that in antiquity was both literate and at the same time well understood by modern specialists, historians, and archaeologists. That, at least in his mind, was a relatively easy decision.

So it was decided that the ancient Near East would provide Borov and his team with the best opportunity for the Soap Bubble's final calibration. But whoever went back to gather the calibration data had to strictly adhere to the *RUTI – The Guidelines for Temporal Exploration*. Borov recognized that meant extensive preparation and training in the script of a language long dead, historical briefings, and intensive cultural immersion before such a hazardous undertaking could be authorized, not to mention the transit to and from. Such study was necessary if a temporal field agent was to be given a ghost of a chance of fitting in, going about their chronological observations undetected, and of course, just surviving. And again, at least in Borov's mind, that too was a relatively easy decision. Ancient Egypt would provide him with his much-needed calibration data. But the real question was, who would become the Philology Annex's first temporal field operative?

CHAPTER X
AD 2000. Chicago

Late Fall in Chicago was notable for its gray and cloudy overcast, biting cold winds that bluster in from Lake Michigan, and a dampness that permeated the joints and made old bodies ache. This was one such day, about a week before Thanksgiving break. The thinning campus population was already in mid-migration to all points of the compass. Meanwhile, a bundled up professor trudged along a sidewalk and turned toward a cold and icy slick pedestrian gangway. Located between the apparently blank, backside walls of two three-story, brick buildings, the professor, changing hands with his old Samsonite briefcase, now fumbled in his pocket and removed an overly large set of keys. Fumbling again with the keys and looking both ways up and down the shadowed alley, he saw that he was safely alone and unobserved. With his free hand full of keys he appeared to lean on the right-side wall. Then with the toe of his shoe, he kicked at a worn, low brick of the same building's wall. With that, an unlighted passage opened inward. Holding the passage open with his right hand on the "stall" brick, he looked around again and then quickly stepped inside as the passage-way's entrance silently closed behind him. If noticed by a passerby, it would have looked as if a man had just walked into a wall and disappeared.

Once inside and with the secret brick façade closed, Professor Ernst Jung waited patiently in the dark while the hidden sensors swept him, and his weight recorded by the pressure plate that he was standing on. Having passed his physical, a solitary red light bulb flashed on overhead, and a disembodied voice remarked,

"Professor Jung, you have lost six pounds. What's her name?"

With a smile, Jung threw his head back and fearlessly answered his tormentor, "She is a first-year physics major from the Sorbonne."

"In your dreams," was the reply and a dark sliding door opened before him.

Already deep in thought, Jung detested the required cloak and dagger, the false entrance, the ever-changing passwords, the sophomoric counter-challenges. Hell, the entire setup reminded him of a popular and trendy spy bar up in Milwaukee that he had once visited as a graduate student. It was all so ludicrous. Why couldn't he just walk in the front door of the Philology Annex whenever someone called a special operations meeting?

To Jung's mind, the most obvious always was the least noticed.

After all, hadn't old Borov himself proven that fact long ago, when he had described how the Hourglass Seminar had been conducted? Right there out in the open and in plain sight? And if I remember rightly, the seminar was even posted outside the Philosophy Department's door!

What balls!

But then again, perhaps they were right as he continued to commiserate with himself.

What would a physicist, and a well-known, Nobel Prize runner-up in quantum mechanics at that, be doing visiting a privately held organization that specializes in languages, especially long dead ancient Near Eastern ones?

First established near and then later allied with the blessings of this south side university, that was the Philology Annex's official public image. But Jung knew better. He understood its hidden side all too well.

But this time the frustration of the high security was banished by Jung's intense curiosity as to why a special operations meeting had been so hastily convened. Unlike in his own department, where he knew every rumor, was privy to every tremor, this meeting engulfed him as a complete surprise.

Well, what's up? And in particular, who screwed up this time?

His thoughts and instincts naturally turned to the secretive and aging Borov, who years ago had recruited him. A wistful smile briefly appeared at the thought of that warming handful of memories. He quietly remarked to himself, "What a fine human being."

Entering the Philology Annex through this particular portal placed Jung rather unceremoniously in the first floor's coatroom. There, he hung up his bulky green Bavarian wool coat, stuffing his brimmed wool hat into one sleeve, his scarf in the other, and his gloves into one of the outside pockets. That Chicago weather ritual completed, Jung peeked blearily into the two-way security mirror

71

provided and noted that he needed to trim his bushy, rapidly graying moustache. The bleary part was fixed with a quick wipe of the lenses of his favorite gold wire-rimmed glasses, a legacy of a research visit to one of Munich's many Max Planck institutes. Finally, now moving into the foyer he removed a stray piece of lint from his tweed wool jacket, slipped off his shoes, and removed his favorite bright orange Tigger slippers from his personal nook. That ritual completed, Jung left for what would be the most memorable meeting of his middle-aged life.

CHAPTER XI
AD 1997. An Old Coffee Can

It had become a tiring climb for the seventy-one-year old. The stone steps seemed more like an endless treadmill instead of a path leading to an actual destination. The banisters he clung to seemed to laugh at his frailty. *Jerzy. You can do better.* He thought.

Six two-story flights of stairs will do that.

Then Jerzy ruefully remembered how he had been able as a youngster of fifty to carry non-stop a full box of artifacts up to the attic annex room, and that from his then basement office to boot!

In truth, the archaeologist had to admit that it had been some time since he, Dr. Jerzy Jannicka, emeritus professor of Egyptology and former chair of the Department of Oriental Studies, had visited this storage room, officially designated his archaeological field annex. In reality it was the aging professor's personal treasure trove of moldy memories, faded and dusty mementoes forgotten. But now it had to be thoroughly inventoried, cleaned out, and swept clean.

Imagine. The venerable old attic niche was to be taken over by a classical archaeologist, who had successfully lobbied the university's administration for it.

Politics, politics! The white-haired head thought as his jaw clenched and teeth ground down savagely onto the worn pipe stem. Stopping before the wooden door and catching his breath, he fumbled in his pocket for the appropriate key. Finding it by feel, he then opened the door and reached around by rote into the gloom at the right to twist an ancient porcelain electric switch. While so doing, a wave of dry, stale air perfumed with the distinctive scent of decaying books and dust breathed forth. Now under the pale yellow glare of several naked bulbs, the archaeologist surveyed the cramped narrow aisle between the shelving that still was, for the moment, his private domain.

Jerzy, this is going to take at least a week of digging, sorting, and compiling!

Or so the old archaeologist thought. And in many respects he was right, already organizing the task in his mind as if it were a fresh excavation, instead of a helter-skelter of memorabilia of far distant and ancient lands.

I'm going to need some help moving all of this stuff about.
Jannicka considered while he pinched his lower lip between thumb
and forefinger.

At that moment a shiny surface caught his eye from an elevated
shelf to his left. Momentarily forgetting his train of thought and
wondering what it was that looked so familiar, Jannicka waded into,
around and among the dusty crates and precariously stacked piles of
yellowed, curling manila files and field journals in his path.

After some contortions and carefully placed steps, he finally
stood before his goal sitting on the fourth shelf up. It was a tarnished
steel coffee can with a bordered shiny square in its center. Behind it
several field diaries were neatly stacked along with a bound
notebook, their top edges all generously covered with a layer of
fluffy, gray dust.

So that's what it was.

Looking closer, the archaeologist noted lying before the can was
its detached label with two sides bordered in dried, curled, and
yellowed tape.

Ah. So that's why the shiny square!

Natural curiosity caused him to pick up the fallen label. He
adjusted his tri-focal glasses and tilted his head back to read the find
in the poor light. Gently holding the paper scrap as if it were made of
fairy dust, he began to read its neat, precisely handwritten message,
inscribed with a fountain pen, the black block lettering now long
since faded to brown.

ROYAL HAIR SAMPLES – (12)
CAIRO NATIONAL MUSEUM
OCTOBER 1973
SERGEI ANATOL

Upon reading the label, instantly a flood of memories and
emotions gushed forth, a faraway and winsome smile creased
Jannicka's cheeks, and unbidden tears began to form.

Yes, my dear, dear Anatol. What a tragic loss!
And how could I have forgotten you after all these years?
You of all people!
What a tragic end for such a young and brilliant mind.

A pause ensued. Then, back stiffening, the professor emeritus of Egyptian archaeology made a private decision on the spot, fueled in part by an imagined sense of personal guilt.

I will have my staff clear this annex. It will be an excavation of sorts indeed and with full documentation. Just let them dare to bitch!

Now reaching out with a quavering grasp he reverently removed the coffee can from its perch along with its associated diaries and notebook. Jannicka then whispered to the shade of his long lost student, "And as for you, my dear Anatol, I will personally see to it that your samples are processed and published."

With moist eyes tightly shut and pressing the coffee can and journals tightly to his chest, he completed the vow.

"I will be honored indeed to write it up myself in memoriam. And come to think of it, I just met a bright young Russian scientist, who gave that fascinating paper on genetic fingerprinting. Now what was his name? Pavel? Pasel? Sasel? Yes, that's it, Pavel Sasel! I must contact him immediately!"

With a chest still heaving from his sobs, the old archaeologist began to compose himself. Putting down his burden, he daubed his eyes with a worn handkerchief of Egyptian cotton from a time long past as the old guilt began to simmer down somewhat. After all, had it not been he who so recklessly kicked his prize student out of the nest and smack dab into the center of that goddamn Arab-Israeli war?

CHAPTER XII

AD 1998. Athens

He was a middle-aged Mediterranean male. Short in stature, a once thick wealth of black hair that had surrendered to a receding hairline, wisps of gray making their appearance at the temples, olive-colored skin, a strong heavily bearded jaw line, all dominated by large black eyes and lashes. The vein that coursed across this left temple bulged and throbbed as he tried to focus in on the sample before him.

Thinking, for the umpteenth-time. *Zacharias, you old goat! When are you going to break down and find time to get an eye exam!*

Looking up from the electron microscope's green screen, he closed his eyes to rest them, causing minute tears to form in their corners.

Ah, that's better.

Then, suddenly opening them up, he removed the sample and reached for the next of the series. Carefully aligning it in the tower, his practiced fingers rapidly recalibrated the machine. And there it was, a classic bow tie mutation on the fourth gene site of the *Drosophila*'s fifth salivary chromosome.

Zacharias Athenasius Philopedes, an internationally-recognized microbiologist at the Athenian Institute of Biology and Genetics, and the world's authority on this particular type of mutation within the fruit fly genera, was not surprised at all at the bow tie's presence. He had been responsible for artificially encouraging its formation. As a young man, he had discovered this mutational curiosity. Ever since then, he had carefully and painstaking chronicled how the bow tie was formed, the conditions necessary for the double loop formation, and, to a certain degree, ways to predict its outward effects.

The revelations gained from Philopedes' research were astounding. Here was a DNA strand that literally looped away from its usual, partnering constituent building blocks. By inciting the mutation at specific locations of a gene, Philopedes had dramatically demonstrated the functionality of gene sites by literally turning them on and off. In essence, he had pioneered the field of gene expression analysis.

His deep concentration was dashed to bits, however, when he heard the inner lab door open, and then gently swish closed. What followed was the dainty sound of new patent leather shoes as they softly scuffed their way around to his fatherly ears.

That must be little Irene coming to surprise me, he thought with a warmth that surprised even him.

Peeking around a nearby lab counter.

"There you are, Daddy!" Said a little girl with large dark pools for eyes and a glossy black curly mop of hair.

"Mommy says that it is time for dinner."

Smiling down at her, Philopedes noted her big broad grin and cheeks and how much he and she were father and daughter. "So how is Daddy's little pride and joy?"

"Hungry!"

"Okay, then let's go."

With that, he shut down the electron microscope's internal system, plucked the sample from it, and slipped it into its labeled sleeve. Looking down again at the breath-taking six-year-old, a chilly tremor coursed through his bones as he thought, *She's so young. She looks so much like me. Lord God, help us if one of her precious genes had a bow tie!*

Lifting Irene up with a rush and placing her on his shoulders, the pair marched off, winding and ducking their way through several corridors to the institute's lone elevator. Riding down, Irene giggled as her father bounced her up and down the entire way. On the walk home, really just around the short block, Zach put his little girl down and the pair walked hand-in-hand the rest of the way.

It was a typical Athenian late afternoon with a hazy blue sky. Yes, it was a Saturday, but Zacharias always took advantage of any free time that he could wrangle on the massive electron microscope.

Perhaps, he thought to himself, *we will all go out for a Volta after dinner this fine evening. Go out for a sweet off of Syntagma Square. Yes. Yes, we will!* He finally decided.

Having mounted the steel and white marble stairs to their third floor apartment, Irene, who loved to be held like an airplane above her father's head, signaled her wish with outstretched arms. Philopedes, smiling with a grimace, grunted her up and so they made their entrance. As they whizzed into the apartment's kitchen, Philopedes' stomach ached as the first rich kitchen smells registered.

How typically Pavlovian, he thought.

His wife, Elena, gave him their private scolding look. At first stumped, Zacharias then remembered his wife's concern about his back and the preferred flying antics of Irene.

Putting her down with a four-point landing, he then rose with a wince that, try as he might, he could not conceal from the penetrating gaze of his loving wife.

Oh boy. I'm dead meat now, he murmured to himself.

Then the telephone rang. Reflexively going to it and picking it up, Philopedes immediately recognized the distinctive hiss of a long distance call. He had no reason to know, but the connection he was now listening to was a heavily shielded, near tamper-proof line. At the other end was a foreign colleague of his, Pavel Sasel, a fellow microbiologist at the University of St. Petersburg.

"Zach. Is that you?" Sasel said over the white noise of the background hiss.

"Sasel, you lusty goat! What a wonderful surprise to hear from you. How are you doing? Where are you anyway?"

"Simply wonderful. I'm at home in St. Petersburg. But Zach, I have a question, I am going to be in Athens tomorrow. Are you free for dinner on the Plaka? Perhaps a little ouzo? Maybe talk some shop?"

"But of course! But the Plaka? That's for tourists. Let me take you someplace special. I have this friend with a wonderful little place on Observation Hill that overlooks the entire city. At sundown, the Acropolis glows a deep ruddy red as if the Persians had just set it afire. It's breath-taking. What do you say?"

"Zach, as always, you romantic, I am totally overwhelmed!"

The content of the rest of the conversation was entirely logistical, when was he arriving, which airline, the usual.

By the time Zacharias had gotten off the phone, little Irene was already concentrating on her vegetables. Elena, ever patient, was holding dinner for the two of them. The wine had already been poured.

Beaming, Zacharias proudly announced to them,

"Tomorrow I will dine at Skiphos' with the world's second most important genetic microbiologist!"

Elena, with a sly grin said, "And who, may I ask, is the first most important gene cracker?"

Feigning total astonishment, Zacharias reared back and roared pounding his thick chest like a simian.

"Why Zacharias Athenasius Philopedes himself!" and then catching himself, more quietly, "of course."

Irene giggled because she thought her Daddy was doing his Lion King impression for her.

Elena rolled her eyes and looked heavenward in a long-suffering look universal to all academic wives.

That said, Zacharias plopped himself down at the table and began to dig in with gusto. Elena's baked red potatoes, lamb, fried zucchini, dried tomatoes, and feta were to die for.

Chapter XIII

AD 1998. Engelhardt Institute

Professor Dr. Pavel Ivanovitch Sasel, a distinguished member of the science faculty at the University of St. Petersburg, was a unremarkable man. Average Central European height and weight, brown hair and eyes, and wire rim glasses. His unreadable and placid face was a round Slavic visage with no prominent characteristics. His complexion was white in winter and lightly tanned during the summer. Sasel worked hard at maintaining this outward plainness in order to easily blend into any European crowd. That was the outer Sasel.

While the outer Sasel was a plain Jane, the inner Sasel was a different sort of creature. Possessing a powerful intellect and a talent for mathematics and biology, he had been identified by the state early on for a scientific career. Sasel also possessed a compact and powerful physique, one that he camouflaged with loose-fitting clothing. This remarkable mixture of brains and brawn was noticed by the Russian secret service, which sponsored his education. By the time Sasel had reached his twentieth year, he held two diplomas, one in mathematics and the other in biology. In short, he was a brilliant mind with a body taut as a bowstring.

Within the Russian secret service, Sasel was part of a very special cadre of placed academicians, who in turn worked with and watched their colleagues. He was second generation of an elite intellectual unit formed to stop the defection of scientists to the West. In fact, Sasel was a member of a special, compartmentalized commission of the Russian Academy of Science, who in turn reported to the Russian Minister of Science and Technology. With such clout behind them, Sasel and his contemporaries were tasked to join and infiltrate the most secret of the *Rodina*'s projects and participate in them as best they could. In some cases, these academician-agents were making their own honest contributions as well, while providing their quiet, internal security.

Sasel was proud of his dual contribution to his country. Unlike some of his other colleagues, Sasel wrote his own articles, delivered his own papers, and managed to publish two recognized scientific works. In the course of events, he had prevented one defection and alerted the secret service to one foreign infiltration. To date, he had not been required to kill, but was fully prepared for that eventuality.

His flight from St. Petersburg to Athens had been uneventful. Taking a cab to his hotel, he settled in, and immediately went to Observation Hill, arriving purposely an hour early. Alighting from the cab a full block away from the restaurant where Philopedes was to meet him, Sasel spent the time taking in the neighborhood, noting the traffic, breathing in the smells, and watching people. After about thirty minutes of such reconnaissance, Sasel, satisfied that all was right with the world, began to saunter over to a coffee shop that was located across the street from the restaurant. There he would set up camp and wait for Philopedes to arrive.

To Sasel's amazement, Philopedes arrived five minutes early. This was a good sign. Old Zacharias was eager for a night out. Having already settled his tab with the waiter, Sasel got up and walked over.

The interior of the restaurant was dark and cool, decorated with simple white-washed walls and the air textured with a hint of ouzo and tobacco. The décor was simple Greek island fare with small square wooden tables and wicker-woven chairs. While adjusting his eyes to this low light environment, Sasel saw Philopedes sitting over in the corner waving at him.

"Pavel! You wild man! How are you doing?" Philopedes exclaimed as he rose and brutally hugged his foreign colleague.

"Not bad Zach, at least up until you squeezed me like a Greek olive."

"Nonsense. Sit. I have already ordered a bottle of ouzo, some extra ice, and a small tomato and cucumber salad to munch on."

Sitting down, Sasel noted something else in Philopedes' eyes.

"My dear colleague, you are not wearing your glasses, how come?"

"Ah, you noticed. Bifocal contact lenses, they are just wonderful, but very expensive. At university I should have gone into optometry if I had had half a brain."

"But my dear colleague, if you do have half a brain, then what about the rest of us poor morons who attempt to understand your magnificent research?"

To this rather syrupy compliment, Philopedes bent over the table and with slit eyes said, "Okay, my dear colleague, what's up, and why all the sudden candy and flowers?"

At first, Sasel did not know what to make of the expression, "candy and flowers," but he could guess.

"It's very simple Zach, I need your help."

So the conversation innocently began. According to Sasel, a young Polish Egyptologist had been tragically killed during the Yom Kippur War at the Cairo Airport. His baggage had survived, however, and ultimately ended up at his academic address at the Oriental Institute in Warsaw. Of all things, a coffee can with a label dating to 1973 was filled with hair samples destined for forensic DNA analysis. The young archaeologist's notebook described what was to be his dissertation topic, a genealogical description of an ancient Egyptian royal family via DNA fingerprinting – a process that while envisioned had not been fully perfected at the time – a fact that the Polish Egyptologist apparently had not been aware. Regardless, the hair samples themselves were from the Cairo National Museum's own royal mummy collection! This last detail alone raised Philopedes' eyebrows several inches and his interest even more.

"But my dear Sasel, where in this interesting tale do you need the help of a Greek fruit fly expert?"

"Excellent point. My colleagues at the Engelhardt Institute in Moscow were curious to know whether you would like to become a member of the Anatol Project."

"Anatol Project? Who's that?"

"Sergei Anatol was the Polish graduate student in Egyptology who first thought of, arranged to get, and secured the royal hair samples."

"Oh, but why me? Why not ask instead that team who worked up the mitrochondrial DNA studies on the Romanov remains? You know, your countrymen Ivanov and that Brit, what was his name, oh, yes – Peter Gill?"

"Because Zach, they are not available. Besides, you are the best gene cracker I know."

Philopedes wore a confused, yet curious frown.

"Yes, yes, Pavel, I know I am. But I'm a *Drosophilae* expert, fruit flies, remember? Pesky little bugs with wings that you find in your salad. Not an expert of the genus *Homo* with its three billion genetic bits of information."

To this anticipated dodge, Sasel played his trump card.

"Yes, that is true, but that madman gene splitter in Heidelberg has declared that he is indefinitely unavailable as well."

At this reminder of Heidelberg, Zach flushed in anger. That choice individual had made life miserable for Zach early on in his scientific career. Any opportunity to show up that ingrate from Heidelberg would be irresistible for the Greek, and Sasel knew this. As for the compliment on his reputation, Zach glowed. The result was one very excited Greek microbiologist.

Shifting in his seat, Philopedes said.

"What's the time frame for the start of this Anatoli Project?"

"The Anatol Project," Sasel corrected, "is scheduled to begin whenever you are available."

Stunned, Zach sat back in his chair and wondered again out loud, "But why me?"

"Because you're the best."

At that moment and precisely on time the waiter arrived with the second bottle of ouzo. Like two inebriated partners in crime, Sasel and Philopedes then made a toast to run the hair analysis. After all, the dream of the tragically killed Anatol needed fulfillment.

For Philopedes, this Anatol Project was a windfall opportunity of a lifetime.

For Sasel, it had been all too easy.

*　　*　　*

A tired and disheveled Zacharias Philopedes looked up from the electron microscope with tearing, bloodshot eyes. Reaching for an eye tissue and his medicated drops, he tilted his head back, dribbled in the eye drops for each, and gently blotted his overworked orbits. Resting his eyes, his mind was anything but at rest, for his eyes just could not comprehend what they were seeing. Here, at the Engelhardt Institute in Moscow, Zach had labored for the past two weeks on this Anatol Project. At first, it had been a grand sort of quest, befitting Don Quixote. The lab work ups of the mitochondrial DNA from the royal hair samples had all proceeded in a straightforward and customary fashion, but when the nuclear DNA gelatin strips were drawn, all hell broke out.

Young Anatol would have no doubt been excited about the gel strips, Philopedes thought. Here was incontrovertible evidence for a genetic break in the gene pool near the end of the Eighteenth Dynasty. While the mitochondrial DNA from the maternal side of the dynasty remained constant, the nuclear DNA was wildly different. To explain these scientific results and put them in a meaningful historical perspective, an expert on the Eighteenth Dynasty was invited from Poland to give a private lecture to the ever-curious Philopedes, Sasel, and his hard-working laboratory staff.

His name was Professor Dr. Jerzy Jannicka. As Philopedes was soon to discover, Jannicka had a very special and vested interest in the Anatol Project, for Sergei Anatol had been his graduate student and archaeological field assistant. As a result of Jannicka's informative talk, his down-to-earth approach, and obvious motivation, Philopedes and he had really hit it off. As best as Philopedes and Jannicka could tell, the narrowing down of the culprit source or first vector for the genetic break appeared to have occurred within the immediate family of the Pharaoh Amenhotep IV. Up to that point, the gelatin nuclear DNA smears of the Royals had a definite and predictable pattern.

After Amenhotep IV, however, a brand new element had appeared that disrupted the family's pattern and Philopedes knew that he had seen something like it before. It troubled him. Nonetheless, until he undertook further analysis, he decided to keep this last curious tidbit to himself. He decided he would not even share it with Sasel until he was absolutely sure. It was that incredible.

That was three days ago.

Jannicka, meanwhile, had returned to Poland and his university a fulfilled man, for he had promised to publish the results as soon as possible in an article dedicated to Anatol. Meanwhile, the gene lab's research staff were in the process of submitting their own joint article to the journal *Science*. But all the while Philopedes continued to toil over the royal's nuclear chromosome smears and slides.

This industry by the dynamic Greek was not lost on Sasel, who remained out of sight. Sasel knew when to leave a scholar well enough alone. He also intuitively sensed something else, and unbeknownst to Philopedes, Sasel had the lab watched and bugged. His friend couldn't fart without Sasel knowing about it. It was clear to him that old Zach was keyed in to something. Over the last three days alone, his face had taken on a gaunt and haunted look. Sleep came and went at odd moments. It wasn't only the fact that Zacharias, a veritable Greek Dionysios, wasn't eating regularly. It was the fact that he was driven. Something was eating at him and his scientific curiosity had taken control.

Now, opening his eyes, Philopedes rolled his tired neck and heard it snap and pop several times. Looking down on the sample, he whispered in his mother tongue, "I know that you are there, somewhere, but where?"

These words were caught by the hidden microphone that had been planted in Philopedes' observation console. While the recorded remark was not clear to the agent at that ungodly hour, she nonetheless and without hesitation rang up Sasel.

Taking a deep breath and letting it out slowly, "I have to quit soon and get some real sleep," the Greek said. Then he removed the sample from the tower and replaced it with the next of the series in a reflex motion that he had done so many times. With his relatively refreshed set of eyes, Philopedes peered once again into the electron microscope's green screen and refocused the image.

"Malaka!" exploded from his lips.

Sitting back with a start, Philopedes was at first elated at the confirmation of his suspicions, then horribly confused, and finally disoriented enough to fall off of his stool with a crash.

Spread-eagled and looking up from the floor like a drooling baby, he whispered again. "I don't believe it. Is it possible? Why yes. Yes, it must be! They have indeed come. Even left a calling card of sorts. To let us know that we are not alone – alone in this universe."

Those words too were recorded by Sasel's team. The meaning of them, however, was translated only later, but for now, their importance remained remarkable only because Philopedes had spoken them. As for the crashing sounds of both the scientist and his stool, well, two delicate eardrums had been bruised.

Slowly regaining his feet, Philopedes retrieved his stool. Again he sat down before the electron microscope's console to reconfirm what he had seen. Philopedes, an expert in fruit fly DNA, their mutations, and in particular the bow tie mutation, saw to his everlasting dismay bow tie formations on several of the nuclear gene sites of the Princess Meretaten. She was one of the six daughters of Amenhotep IV – and he had only just begun looking!

Silently, his mind screamed an insane scream.

What was an artificially laboratory induced fruit fly mutation doing on a set of human genes? And genes that originated from humanity's distant past to boot?

To this silent question, Zacharias could only reply again in a soft, almost reverential tone.

"Indeed, they have not only come, but here is evidence they have tampered with us. That can be the only answer, the only explanation. This is proof of some sort of alien genetic hybridization."

This third statement Sasel had heard himself live over the microphone. Knowing Philopedes the way he did, he knew that his previous findings, as revolutionary as they were, had now been positively confirmed. Now the issue that troubled Sasel was what to do with his old friend Zach?

*　　*　　*

It was past midnight when Sasel chose to make a visit to the lab where Philopedes had holed up. Wearing a comfortable outfit of oversized blue jeans and a baggy pullover, Sasel walked into the darkness of the lab. At first wondering where Philopedes was, Sasel saw a glow from around the corner of the room. Following this trail of photons, Sasel found his subject's balding head nestled in his crossed arms fast asleep.

Standing above the Greek he thought, *Yes, my curious and hard working Zacharias, sleep the innocent sleep of babes.*

Looking around for a chair, Sasel quietly found one and maneuvered it near Philopedes. Sitting down, he then pondered again what next to do with him. Watching the gentle rise and fall of the Greek's slow and shallow breathing pattern, Sasel began to consider his options. Killing Philopedes, while possible, was not an option that he would endorse. Buying his silence would not work either. Enlisting him, however, may well be the best of both worlds: silence and compliance.

After another few moments, Sasel decided on the latter course and no other. He was after all a colleague and a brilliant one at that. His combined insights and experience represented a definite asset. With his mind made up, Sasel reached over and gently jostled Philopedes' shoulder, which earned him a grunt, a quick snorting intake of air, and the rise of Philopedes' head.

Bleary eyed, the sleepy Greek rasped, "Jesus, is that you Sasel? Oh, I'm sorry, I must have dozed off. What time is it anyway? I'm starved."

This last remark brought a smile to Sasel. *Yes indeed, my old Zach is back.*

Now answering him, "Well, my friend, it is well past midnight, but I know a place where a bowl of soup and fresh bread is waiting on you. What do you say?"

"Great, but I have to wash my face and brush my teeth first. I taste of yak."

Laughing with him, Sasel helped his Greek compatriot to his feet. Together, wordlessly, they left the lab. As they did, Sasel saw Zach steal a glance back, hesitate, and then go back to pick up his notebook. Sasel said nothing and just waited at the door, holding it open.

Yes, my sleepy friend, even with one foot out of bed and one in the grave you still have your wits about you. You will indeed make a good and careful recruit.

Once at the institute's commissary that Sasel had kept open no matter what the hour, the two trudged in. Zach disappeared into the john, while Sasel went directly for the soup and fresh black bread that was there under a plastic dome.

Sitting down, the Russian was shortly joined by his colleague and both began to greedily gorge themselves on the fresh potato soup and huge hunks of bread smeared with soft butter. Sated and now wiping his bowl clean with a piece of bread, Zacharias, looking down into the bowl, startled his host by announcing, "You know Sasel, those hair samples that I was working with were not complete."

Slowly looking up the Greek continued. "What I mean is, what I was working with were not the entire, original samples."

Seconds passed and Sasel could only return his stare.

Finally, he said. "Yes, you're quite right. I ran the first analysis myself."

"And?"

"And I found something most peculiar that I had hoped you would find as well."

The Greek now taking on a cagey look. "Perhaps something odd about the nuclear DNA of Princess Meretaten?"

"Exactly, my friend. Tell me your thoughts."

With those words, Philopedes had found his father confessor and the floodgates opened.

"Well, I really don't know where to begin. In my experience, the bow tie mutation is an artificially induced phenomenon known only to occur within the genus *Drosophilae*. But, then again, no one that I know of has ever tried to reproduce such an effect in another species, much less that of *Homo*, at least not until now."

Sasel was pleased with this detached narrative. It was time now to prime the pump.

"So, in your opinion, Princess Meretaten, a daughter of Amenhotep IV, exhibits this trait, this bow tie mutation?"

"No, what I am saying is that she is a carrier. I have no idea whether or not such a mutation would be expressed or not, and if expressed, how. But we can check that easily enough. Surely your medical library has a copy of the *Genome Directory*. All we have to do is match which chromosomes and approximately which gene sites the bow tie formations are found, cross-reference that information with the *Directory*, and then extrapolate from there."

Sasel immediately got up from his chair and ran for the door yelling over his shoulder,

"Zach, quick get back to the lab, I'll meet you there."

Now rising with a full stomach, Zacharias, ever resourceful, filled an insulated stainless steel pitcher with fresh black coffee. Thinking. *Now let's really get down to work!*

*   *   *

Once back at the lab, Philopedes was amazed that Sasel was already deep within an online search.

Carrying two heavy ceramic coffee mugs and the stainless steel pitcher, the invigorated Greek crashed them down on the lab bench and began to pour. The racket shook Sasel from his thoughts, but as soon as he heard who, and smelled what it was, he only smiled and continued peering at the screen before him.

Noting his industry and not wanting to be left out, Zacharias began checking again, counting Meretaten's gelatin nuclear chromosome smears.

"Well," the Greek said, "what I can tell at this point, is that Meretaten possessed four different chromosome patterns that do not appear in her predecessors. I propose that we focus our efforts on these four as I have visually confirmed the presence of the bow tie gene mutation on one of them. Naturally, further study may, no probably will, reveal more. But for the moment, chromosomes 2, 5, 11, and X are the suspicious ones."

Sasel looking up. "Chromosomes 2, 5, 11, and X. That's not good enough. I need at least some approximate gene sites for each."

Away they went into the early to mid-morning hours with Philopedes approximately identifying the gene sites cumulatively affected by the bow tie mutations. Sasel furiously thumped on the keyboard and took notes from the *Directory* as to how the multiple bow tie mutations may have been expressed in the long dead princess.

To appreciate what these two were up against, is to recognize that the human genome, or genetic makeup, is composed of forty-six diploid chromosomes. They contain about twenty-five to thirty-five thousand genes, constructed of about three billion base paired, chemical elements: adenine, thiamine, guanine, and cytosine. Unfortunately, the human genome also contains "a huge amount of so-called junk or non-coding DNA." The accumulation of this "junk" DNA seems to be the result of man's evolution. It was once estimated that thirty, one thousand page telephone books could express a human's unique genomic pattern. Fortunately for Sasel, his computer had a CD drive carrousel that could simultaneously handle the six CD laser disks of the entire *Genome Directory*, its many updates, and supporting commentary.

By noon the next day, a preliminary list of bow tie mutational sites on the four chromosomes had been drawn up by the two exhausted researchers. It was understood that further study across Meretaten's other chromosomes would have to be undertaken. Even so, the possibilities were stunning, for the chromosomes and gene bundles tentatively identified suggested a multiplicity of soft and bone tissue impacts.

The mutation's presence on the X chromosome – the female human sex chromosome – alone suggested its potential for generational transmission. But the total outward expression of such a combination of mutations was a complete unknown within the human species. The possibility, however, that one formation could potentially cancel out another was always there, especially given the remarkable redundancy of the human genome, but neither researcher seriously believed that for a minute.

Calling a halt to their personal marathon, and after each had slept almost twenty hours, the two were at it again, but this time with twelve research assistants who were hand-picked by Sasel. Theirs was a quest, an intellectual race, to discover the extent of Princess Meretaten's gene mutations, and from there to extrapolate all of the possible gene expressions.

At the end of two continuous weeks of an all-out sprint, Philopedes and Sasel called a halt to assess the situation. Indeed, the Greek's sharp eyes and experience had identified the four chromosomes that carried the bow tie gene mutations, 2, 5, 11, and X. No others were found.

But what was now recognized was that consistently only one side of the diploid chromosomal pairs was so affected. This evidence suggested that the bow tie gene mutations originated from only one side of a single mating pair—the Pharaoh Amenhotep IV himself. He had to be the first vector. His nuclear DNA possessed the bow tie mutations, while the mitochondrial DNA had none. This realization led Philopedes to voice a simple question, "Sasel, we must confirm this. What other progeny of the late Eighteen Dynasty we can take a sample from?"

To that question all that Sasel could muster was a blank stare. Then, Philopedes remembered his doodled notes that he had taken during Jannicka's private lecture on the dynasty. Hurrying over to his briefcase, he unceremoniously dumped it out atop a vacant lab bench. Then, like a raccoon, began to sort through the pile as if hot on a scent. With a victorious grunt, he extracted a page.

"Who is Smenkhkare? Is there a mummy to sample?"

"I do not know," replied Sasel.

Philopedes returning to his notes then queried.

"What about a Tutakamen?"

"That's Tutankhamen, Zach. But yes, yes, I know that his mummy has been found!"

"Now, is Tutankhamen a he or a she?"

"He's quite definitely a he. Why?"

"Even though all the bow tie mutations seem to reside in the nuclear DNA, I am curious to know whether they are inheritable by the males, or by different sexes, as was the case with the Princess Meretaten, as it appears she inherited it from her father. And if so, are the same chromosomal sites affected or not?"

"Where are you going with this Zach?"

"Oh, just thinking. Right now it seems that Amenhotep IV is the first vector. I was hoping to find another way that we could positively confirm that. That's all."

With that last train of thought fully absorbed, Sasel announced, "I have a phone call to make. I'll be right back."

Forty-five minutes later Sasel returned to the again humming lab. As usual, Philopedes was glued to the green screen of his electron microscope, his hands performing various sample sorting tasks and minute focus adjustments simultaneously as if each had a mind of its own. Sasel, amazed at the sight, stopped himself short to witness this feat of ambidextrousness on the part of the Greek. Then, rousing himself, he cleared his throat.

"Yes?" said Philopedes. "I have been wondering why it took you so long to find your tongue. What's up?"

"Well, yes. I just got off the phone with Dr. Jannicka."

"You mean you just talked to Jerzy! How's he doing?"

Ignoring Zach's concern about his newfound friend, he cut directly to the point. "Zach, I have good news, bad news, and impossible news.

"First the good news, Jannicka thinks it would be a great idea to sample both Smenkhkare and Tutankhamen to establish whether there is any family connection. No, I know what you're thinking. I didn't tell him what we were really after.

"But now for the bad news, the Pharaoh Smenkhkare, or better, a mummy that we think is Smenkhkare, is in the Cairo National Museum. The fact is that the mummy's precise identity is a bit controversial among Egyptologists. It all has something to do about reused coffins and scratched-off inscriptions. All they know for sure is that the mummy is a male in his mid-twenties, who bears a very strong cranial resemblance to Tutankhamen. Some have even dared to say that they are brothers on that basis, not to mention of the same blood group."

"Really? Blood group analysis. What a brilliant approach! What else did Jerzy say?"

"Well, as for Tutankhamen's mummy, that has been positively identified, but it still resides in his rock-cut tomb within the Valley of the Kings."

Sasel then took a really deep breath of air and slowly let it out.

"Now for the impossible news. At present, Egyptian sensibilities make it impossible for us to even view that royal mummy, much less to get permission to take a sample."

With his head bowed over, all that Philopedes could say was, "I just knew that I should have stuck with my non-royal fruit flies."

What Philopedes did not know was that during his forty-five minute absence Sasel had in fact made two phone calls, one to Jannicka and another to his superiors at the Russian Academy of Science. Their interest was indeed high on the progress of the Anatol Project.

Twenty-four hours later, Sasel would have both his hair samples. Neither he nor Philopedes knew how such arcane items could have been procured, much less who could have procured them, and so fast. But when an armed and escorted courier arrived the next day, that was when Sasel truly realized how important the Anatol Project was to the Russian Academy of Science, and proportionately, how insignificant he had become in comparison. Intellectually, Sasel knew that this moment would someday arrive, but emotionally he was blindsided by the revelation.

CHAPTER XIV

AD 1998. Russian Academy of Science

It was considered one of the most secure vaults in Moscow; surely it was one of the dreariest, even by former Soviet standards. The air was stale and tinged with acrid cigarette smoke that the overworked and poorly-maintained ventilators never seemed capable to remove. It was a visual wasteland. No windows, no artwork, no framed party paraphernalia broke the monotony of its crude plasterwork and dirty tan walls. Only several dirty shadowed squares remained where the party paraphernalia had used to hang. The corner lighting that emanated from very special halogen pedestal lamps was appropriately dimmed for this meeting, but even that diminished harsh halogen glare seemed only to highlight the ceiling's near-wavy surface imperfections, poorly repaired cracks, smudges, and chance cobwebs. Nonetheless, the lamps served their purpose as each gave off a different, barely audible harmonic. When taken together, each so precisely located, their overlapping coverage focused on the centrally located table in such a way as to effectively muffle any and all conversion, should the room be somehow, someway, bugged.

At the room's center, the focus of the aural dampening, was a round table surrounded by six generously padded chairs. Today only three were occupied. Before one lay two purple-colored file folders that indicated their ultra-level security status. One was thick, dog-eared, with an outer cover that possessed the shiny patina of a well-read book. The other was thin, dull in color, and obviously brand new. This secure vault, located deep within the Russian Academy of Science, was a convenient nexus for the three as they all represented different interests, but interests that were concerned about the same matter, the breath-taking and alarming results of the Anatol Project.

"My dear colleagues," the first speaker began with his hand resting on the thin folder for emphasis.

"I have just received another communication from Dr. Sasel regarding the Anatol Project. What began as a gesture of good will to our Polish colleagues has developed along its own lines. Dr. Sasel informs me that he and an outside consultant have identified what Sasel believes to be a watershed event."

The knowledge of, much less mention of that coded expression raised the eyebrows of the other two impassive faces. Within their respective communities of black scientific projects, advanced and theoretical technological undertakings, and theoretical biological research, the enunciation of a watershed event was startling news.

"Does this Dr. Sasel have a clear understanding as to what he has declared? Does he appreciate the enormity of the consequences triggered by such a declaration?" Said carefully and precisely the second speaker.

"In part, absolutely. In part, no. He is a molecular biologist of international standing. His decision to have a fellow expert confirm his suspicions is decisive. I have no doubts about what Sasel has stumbled onto. As to the consequences of his declaration that is for us to decide."

"Excuse me if I appear paranoid, but who is this outsider that Sasel unilaterally decided to bring in for confirmation, and is he a risk?" Emphatically stated the balding third speaker.

"According to Sasel," the first speaker answered, "the outsider is secure. And Sasel's word is all I need."

"Such trust in the judgment of a subordinate is admirable, but given the circumstances does Sasel grasp the wide-ranging magnitude of what he has declared, of the resources that can be brought to bear?"

"Again, only in part."

"Well then," the balding third speaker said, "from where does the data come?"

The first speaker at a momentary loss for words opened his hands as if in supplication. Then with a slight shrug said, "My dear colleagues, from our distant past, from the time of the Egyptian Eighteenth Dynasty."

To this revelation, speakers two and three did not immediately react. Instead, the eyes of each glazed over in thought, and in an instant, they returned to the present. The balding third speaker, a Hungarian, asked with his hands folded as if in an attitude of prayer.

"And who or whom from that dynasty does your good Dr. Sasel think may be the carrier of the suspected extraterrestrial DNA?"

"Of that, he is not sure, although he strongly suspects a pharaoh by the name of Amenhotep IV."

The second speaker then spoke to the first looking at him squarely in the eye.

"My dear Karlov, two items come to mind."

Gesturing to the thick, worn folder the first speaker began.

"First, the Norsk Report we all have read and reread several times. Did not Norsk guardedly suggest the same possibility back in the mid-70s?"

"Indeed he had, Vasily," said the first speaker nodding. "But I might add that he did so with all due care. And, I would also like to point out that the James-led mummy study was only of the royal males. Now, with Sasel's preliminary report, it appears that the genes of at least one female offspring may have been similarly affected."

In reply, "Now Karlov, we have known each other far too long for such gamesmanship. My second question to you is, now that we have an independent confirmation of the Norsk Report, what does Dr. Sasel want done that requires our immediate attention?"

Knowing that he was caught and feeling a certain growing tightness in his chest, Drazinzka, the first speaker, let out a deep sigh.

"As always, Vasily, you and you alone seem to know what is in my heart. And as always, I will tell you. Dr. Sasel has suggested that it would be 'convenient' if a genetic sample could be gathered directly from the period in order to absolutely identify the vector."

At Karlov's use of the word "convenient," "directly," and "period," the bald-headed third speaker, the aging Nikolai Fedorov, Director of Advanced and Theoretical Technological Research, could only snort at Karlov Drazinzka, himself the Head of the Special Projects Directorate.

"And Karlov, let me guess," Fedorov said with words dripping like formic acid.

"I suppose your next words would be to talk to the Americans. Perhaps convince them into letting us use their temporal device? The device that . . . that thieving, bastard, Nazi whelp, Borov first stole from us and sold to them! Over my dead body! I won't have it!"

"And it may indeed come to that," said the first speaker.

While casually looking down and inspecting the fingernails of his left hand, Karlov then dryly quipped. "Let me see if I recall correctly. You know Dr. Pyotr Borov quite well, Nikolai, is that not so? After all, the two of you, no, five of you made up that Hourglass Seminar in old Leningrad. Is that not so? Again, if my memory serves me well, it was you who somehow lost track of him during the fascist assault on that fair jewel of a city. Then just as suddenly, Borov somehow turns up in America, and not Nazi Berlin, where he takes command of the Soap Bubble Project himself. If I might borrow an appropriate American phrase, 'where's the beef?'"

At this point, with Karlov needling Nikolai and Nikolai staring cold, poison daggers in return, Vasily Alexandrovich Ostrogorsky, himself the Director of Theoretical Biology for the Russian Academy of Science, with cool finality stated with a granite conviction, "Gentlemen, we do not need to discuss this, please excuse the expression, this ancient history. What I want from each of you, however, is your undivided attention and support, for I intend to immediately contact the Americans about this matter myself."

With that said, the meeting ended.

CHAPTER XV
AD 1998. Engelhardt Institute (Cont.)

Looking away from his electron microscope with a tired, yet triumphant grin on his face, Philopedes quietly announced that both Smenkhkare and Tutankhamen possessed the same distinctive bow tie mutations, at precisely the same chromosomal gene locations as had Princess Meretaten. Concluding, he said, "Sasel, if I had to bet my life on a hypothesis, it would be that these two males are siblings."

Sasel, exhausted from lack of sleep, wired from too much caffeine, and drained from the stress and sheer excitement of the moment, and what he must now reveal, could only sadly reply to his Greek colleague, "No bet. Believe it or not my friend, I have just learned we are only confirming what others have already long suspected."

At first Philopedes did not move at the revelation. Not even his staring, bloodshot eyes, which now took on an altogether dreamy aspect. He was deep in thought, searching his internal memory banks for a clue to Sasel's surprising news. Then, having found nothing anywhere, he shook his head as if he were waking up.

"So," Philopedes pondered, "All of this rush, rush research is clearly hush, hush. Isn't it?"

Ten seconds passed.

Then continuing his thought, but this time with a certain sarcastic bite, "And now my Russian colleague and dear Russian friend can you share with me what you have been told? Or am I just a highly educated hired gun of a gene cracker, and now come to think of it, have I just become a high security risk as well?"

Noting Philopedes' tone and emphasis on his national heritage, Sasel had dreaded this moment. As with all such relationships when one has discovered that they have been used, Sasel now had to choose between regrouping and turning the situation around or breaking off entirely the relationship. To turn this collaboration around could only be accomplished with full disclosure. Full disclosure would mean the worse for Philopedes. So Sasel made his choice.

"Professor Dr. Zacharias Philopedes, I am sorry to inform you, but the Russian Academy of Science is no longer in need of your services. Furthermore, your travel and research visa has just been revoked. Consequently, you must immediately leave the sovereign territory of the Russian State."

Philopedes was slack jawed at this cold, mechanical, and legalistic pronouncement from one so close.

Then Sasel continued, "In addition, the Russian State has declared you *persona non grata*. Henceforth, all travel within the Russian State and/or any of its territories will not be permitted. Please slowly rise and put on your coat. I will personally escort you out of the lab. Once outside, you will be placed in a diplomatic staff car, which will deposit you and your already packed personal effects at the airport. Be advised that your personal laboratory notes are now also the property of the Russian Academy of Science. Once you arrive at the airport, you will be escorted and accompanied by members of the Internal State Security Force to make sure that you depart on this flight back to Athens."

With that, Sasel formally handed over to his former colleague a confirmed, first class Aeroflot airplane ticket, seat 1A. Destination: Athens.

As the pair walked out of the lab building and into the brisk night air, Sasel chanced one whispered message into the Philopedes' ear, while he entered the awaiting staff car.

"Take care my friend. For if I had told you anything more this evening, you would have surely died tonight in your sleep."

Closing the car's rear passenger door and stepping away from the curb, all Sasel could do was slowly shake his head in negation to Philopedes' haunted look through the partially frosted window as the car pulled away.

"I am getting to old and soft for this business." Sasel sighed as he slowly turned and shuffled up the worn limestone steps that led to the gene lab's entrance.

An entrance, as it turns out, that he would never reach, for the sound of a second approaching car and the honk of its horn stopped him dead in his tracks. Turning around, two men from the car approached him. After a brief conversation, Sasel joined them in the black sedan, which sped off.

*   *   *

"Are you Katarina Sasel, the wife of one Professor Dr. Pavel Ivanovitch Sasel?"

After a brief silence passed over the oddly chilling emphasis of the word "one" and then followed by a hesitant answer of "yes," the inspector continued.

"I am Inspector Jepevich of the Internal State Security Bureau. I wish to inform you that your husband was found dead this evening in his laboratory."

Sasel had been right all along. The Anatol Project was far, far bigger than he.

CHAPTER XVI

AD 1998. Russian Academy of Science

Once again the trio met in the secure vault of the Russian Academy of Science. It was both a somber and angry meeting for the first speaker, the Head of the Special Projects Directorate, Karlov Drazinzka. Somber he was, for he had ordered the sacrifice of one of his best operatives on the altar of maximum security. Angry he was as well, almost beyond words, for he had been outvoted by the second and third speakers on the ultimate fate of the outside consultant Philopedes, who had been allowed to return to his homeland scot-free.

Holding his hands together in a tight, overlapping grip as if to crush a walnut or somehow create a pocket of natural vacuum between them, the first speaker gritted out between his teeth, "Well, my dear colleagues. I wish to inform you that I have followed and carried out your asinine and insane directives to the very letter. The Greek has arrived in Athens unharmed per your wishes and now one of my best operatives is so much planting mulch."

And with an ever-increasing volume, he sneered, "And to what purpose, may I ask? What security risk did Dr. Sasel represent? For the love of my sweet mother, tell me that!

"And if you want to discuss security risks, have you looked at that Greek's security jacket? Damnation! He's a drunk. Has a mistress. And he's in debt up to his eyeballs!

"In fact, I wouldn't be surprised if the entire Anatol Project finds its way onto the front page of some British or American tabloid!"

While Drazinzka ranted and raved, both the second and third speakers remained wisely silent. They knew what they had asked for and the risks involved. They had known what a firestorm the execution of those decisions would cause. Now, it was their time to wait out the verbal thrashing that was their due.

The florid and spitting first speaker paused to gulp some air like a beached catfish and then continued, "And, my dear colleagues, and when that titanic leak occurs, which of you is prepared to face the Western press on the true significance of the Anatol Project? Eh?

Hah! I thought so. I just knew it! You had never even considered that possibility have you? You total assholes!

"And as if that weren't bad enough, have either of you considered in your small, pea-brained, and sheltered minds what the international impact will be on the rest of the world? When it finds out that our very own gene pool, our very being, has been tampered with by an alien life form? That we are really hybrids? Well. 'Hello? Is anybody home?' as the Americans are so fond of saying?

"I will tell you in two words, total anarchy. In short, the end of society as we know it."

With that said the first speaker slammed his fist on the table, suddenly rose upsetting his chair, and stormed out of the vault an embittered man.

After several moments of silence, the third speaker said in a quiet and cracking voice.

"I hope to God that Karlov is wrong. Unfortunately, that does not occur very often."

CHAPTER XVII

AD 2000. Chicago

As Jung looked around it was abundantly clear that all the biggies had been summoned to this special operations meeting. It was also abundantly clear that he was late as fourteen pairs of silent and accusing eyes told him. Properly chastised, Jung meekly took the remaining empty seat in the back row. Once Jung seated himself, the chair who had called this meeting, a high-ranking university administrator, Dr. Paul Young, cleared his throat and began with his distinct Oxford accent.

"Dear colleagues, now that we finally are all here, I have an announcement to make. Evidence is building that may require us to again field test the Mark V Soap Bubble. The temporal horizons under study are reasonably close together, but the operation this time may necessitate the need of multiple insertions, multiple participants."

Jung, as with the others in the room, experienced various levels of shock. The buzz subsequent to Young's opening remarks confirmed it. Jung, ever the one to evaluate, replayed Young's brief and coded words in his mind.

First, something very big of a temporal nature that can be substantiated is causing quite a stir. Second, that big something is important enough to field the Mark V yet again. Third, "horizons under study" means that we have or did have at least one agent already in the field. No surprise there. I'm willing to bet that this is probably connected to that Russian fellow Piankoff. Fourth, the big something requires more field agents. It's getting crowded. That means that the something is so big that we're willing to take on more risk. Fifth, field agents will be deployed several times. Perhaps that means in some sort of retrieval or maybe even a cleanup operation. And sixth and unstated, the big something is serious enough to jeopardize our present reality.

With the initial buzz subsiding, Young dropped his second bombshell.

"My dear colleagues, I wish to introduce Mr. Alexander Andreovich Piankoff, who will brief you further on the situation."

Jung smugly thought. *I knew it! It does have something to do with that Russian! And that means Egypt! This is indeed going to be good, very good.*

Then, almost reflexively as if Jung was conducting his own personal argument he continued the thought, *but in another sense, this is indeed odd. Rarely did Young yield the floor to anyone. And then to introduce a briefing for them to boot! Truly something very big is afoot.*

As if in immediate response to Jung's curiosity the Russian, who had been sitting before the lectern, stood up and stepped forward from the front row of the small auditorium. At first glance he appeared to Jung vaguely exotic in some indescribable erotic way. Although he wore a finely tailored, probably Italian, business suit, his manner and carriage demanded uncommon attention. Then Jung remembered the official scuttlebutt. The first ever temporal operative and a crack one at that. The first ever deployed and wildly successful at the harvesting of critical data for the final calibration effort. And last but not least, the namesake grandson of the famous Russian Egyptologist, Alexandre Piankoff.

*   *   *

Facing his audience with his head slightly bowed, Piankoff's narrow, but well-shaped shaved head, appeared so shiny that it seemed polished. His skin was darkly tanned a deep reddish brown. It possessed almost a henna-like hue to it. To Jung, the evenness of it almost suggested the use of a body cosmetic. But as the Russian slowly and dramatically lifted his head to address his audience, it was his eyes that made Jung doubt the gender of this clearly well-muscled, lean, masculine presence. With eyes perfectly outlined in black, Jung felt that he was looking into the face of a long-dead pharaoh with eyelids colored with the greenish-blue hue of malachite.

In a voice and syntax that revealed even more than the ear could perceive, Piankoff, gripping the sides of the lectern, began to address the gathering in the tones, cadence, and guttural stops of a long dead ancient language. To Jung, it was both beautiful, exotic, and hypnotic. The presentation was a vindication of what the Philology Annex was all about, but it had also meant that Piankoff had just returned from *somewhen* where he had employed those words. Jung again wondered why.

At just that point in Jung's mental meanderings, Piankoff finished his utterances. The silence of the room was deafening. All were thinking much the same as Jung. All were impressed by this most theatrical demonstration and then wondered the why of it. Then, one among their number stood. A short, white-haired man haltingly addressed Piankoff in his acquired ancient tongue. Piankoff smirked and repeated the question in a corrective manner, much the way a first-year language teacher would correct a freshman, not a revered professor emeritus in Egyptian philology. To this rebuke, the Egyptian philologist simply nodded and sat down. As he did so, several of his neighbors heard him muttering contentedly that at long last he finally grasped the correct oral use of the *sedjemef* verbal form.

At this point, Young, who had remained standing off to the side, again cleared his throat, "Dear colleagues, I believe that Mr. Piankoff has sufficiently established his credentials. And most impressively, I might add. But the reason for his presence today is not to demonstrate his superb mastery of the ancient Egyptian tongue. Rather, it is to announce that Mr. Piankoff and his colleagues have requested our help in a certain matter."

Piankoff then paused a moment, looked down as his notes, and spoke in a remarkably neutral voice devoid of any accent. His tone, however, which he could not totally conceal, was thick with controlled emotion.

"Distinguished colleagues, we are all familiar with Euclidean geometry and how two points in space define a unique line. Much the same can be said of a line of scientific inquiry formed by its data. But what happens when the lines of two independent scientific inquiries intersect? The notion that comes to mind is a point of mutual interest beneficial to both parties. In this regard, the Russian Academy of Science believes that it has found such a point of intersection, such a point of mutual benefit. Sadly, I do not believe the data, which I will shortly share, will make anyone in this room very comfortable. Simply put, I truly do not know how else to announce a watershed event otherwise."

With those words the intake of air within the room had almost created a vacuum. Those who had not instantly recognized the import of the coded phrase reacted late, after a heartbeat, for a watershed event within this tight group of experts was one pregnant with meaning. Such a declaration meant that there existed evidence for the presence of extraterrestrial intervention. Piankoff, seeing he had everyone's complete attention, continued.

"The data in our possession suggests the mingling of extraterrestrial DNA with our own. In essence, alien-human hybridization. However, to absolutely confirm this suspicion, I have been charged by the Russian Academy of Science to request this body's assistance.

"First of all, the information that I will share with you today is considered to be of the utmost seriousness and gravity by your counterparts within the Russian Academy of Science. Second, I have personally seen the individual in question, observed him, and his slowly multiplying offspring. Third, indirect genetic analysis suggests that this individual may be the one common source of the alien DNA, the first vector. Fourth, your Russian counterparts would like to make the following collegial suggestion. That a direct genetic sample is taken from the suspected individual. Such an undertaking would positively identify whether or not the individual in question is indeed the first vector. Finally, given the individual and his historical significance, if the genetic sample proves to be positive, then some manner of direct intervention should be considered."

In response to the Russian's measured words, a curious mixture of wonder, horror, and adventurism ebbed through the assembled. Again a buzz of quiet conversation began.

Undaunted, the white-haired emeritus professor of Egyptology, John Milson, again rose and this time asked, "Mr. Piankoff, to declare a watershed event is not a thing to be taken lightly. I, speaking for the assembled here, wish to thank our Russian colleagues for sharing their suspicions on this weighty matter. But who, specifically, is your suspected candidate for first vector?"

Without blinking, Piankoff offhandedly stated, "Why, sir, none other than the Pharaoh Neferkheperure Amenhotep."

While not everyone in the audience knew who this personality was or what he represented in Egypt's historical past, all distinctly heard the title pharaoh. Put quite simply, eyes bulged. Heads shook from side to side in disbelief. Hands nervously clutched at things, and Piankoff was pleased for a second time that he had gotten their undivided attention. The historical implications were indeed beyond imagination.

As for Professor Milson, who knew precisely who this pharaoh was and what he represented, his eyes took on a distinctly dreamy look, his brow slightly furrowed in thought. His lips scarcely moved, while they enumerated those thoughts. As for his head, it slowly, almost imperceptibly, moved from side to side.

"My colleagues in Moscow have proposed," Piankoff began again, "that I should led the genetic sampling team."

At this point, a nondescript member of the university's biochemistry department found his feet and asked Piankoff directly what sort of sample did his colleagues have in mind. To this question, Piankoff shrugged, "I am told that almost anything would suffice: skin scrapings, hair, nail fragments, even feces. But whatever it is, it should be of a significant mass. But by far the very best would be a semen sample."

At this point, this distinguished gathering had found itself enthralled—no trans-fixed—by the magnitude and audacity of the Russian proposal. In essence, the Philology Annex was being asked to go beyond its current chronological calibration studies, to go fully online, fully operational. The organization was being asked to venture far beyond its carefully chosen present path of quiet research and observation as espoused by *RUTI*, itself the product of Russian genius, sobriety, and clear-headed vision.

Following the Russian's last remarks, a free-for-all discussion on the proposal began in earnest. That such a stunt, as one in the audience put it, could successfully be pulled off, he calculated as an outright crapshoot. Then there was the recruitment issue of the genetic gatherers, as one scientist so delicately put it. Questions flew fast and furious.

How many?

How long?

Security clearances?

Personality and intellectual makeup?

An orphan or no?

A million tiny issues had to be explainable if a modern personality was somehow stranded or lost in the distant past. To which another feared that if such an event occurred a potential paradox would result.

Again, Piankoff was pleased and even allowed himself a guarded smile. *Indeed all is going far better than I had ever imagined. My superiors will no doubt be pleased. Such a liberated and uninhibited group this is. And how different they are from my own colleagues! The use of the Mark V Soap Bubble, what a ridiculous name, is to them an assumed given. What this rabble is more concerned about is the establishment of the sampling team's base qualifications and their field training. Just, simply, remarkable.*

* * *

With muddy water flooding his eyes and nose, Joey Richards raised his helmeted head from the rain-sodden field, snorting water, snot, and gasping for air. Pinned as he was under the pile up of entangled offensive and defensive linemen, it would be a while before he got back to the huddle. It was time to take a brief, if soggy, rest. Once free, Richards levered up his half implanted halfback's form with a sucking sound. Blessedly the coach's whistle then blew, sounding the end of another day's grueling practice.

Heading for the locker room in search of a long, hot shower, Richards scraped off the larger pieces of mud and turf from the soaked uniform that clung to his well-muscled frame. Along the way, the defensive nose tackle of the Crimson, a towering and lumbering behemoth of a man, threw a friendly arm around Richards' shoulder pads and shook him like a rag doll. In his highly distinctive accent, the native of Fort Smith, Arkansas, drawled, "That there was one hell of a block you threw back there, Joey. It actually slowed me down some. But for a tiny bit there, I thought you might have needed a snorkel out there."

Richards, looking up into Big Bill's grin that seemed half again as broad as the center gap in his front teeth, try as he might could not get mad at the gentle giant.

"So what y'all doin' after practice?"

"I'll be up in the NEI archives cramming."

"What's with you boy? Always studying around them dead folks all the time. It just gives me the willies thinkin' about it!"

"Billy, 'them dead folks' are just Egyptian mummies. And besides, there are only a couple of them, and they are on the first floor. And I think I can handle them on my own if I have to."

Giving Richards a look of quiet disbelief, "Joey, do you really believe that there is anythin' to all them there mummy curses and such like in the movies? Is that stuff really, like, for real?"

At this point Richards sat down in front of his locker and began peeling away the tape from around his right ankle.

Looking up at Big Bill, "Naw Billy, that's all garbage and you can take that to the bank."

Satisfied and relieved, Big Bill lumbered off to the john to fully contemplate in blissful peace the wisdom just imparted upon him. As for Richards, that right ankle was sore as the devil, but a hot shower, a fresh wrap that he could perform better than the student trainers, and several aspirins would do the trick. He would also keep it elevated while he studied tonight.

Following a wolfed down dinner at the dorm cafeteria, Joseph Richards half walked, half hobbled over to the second floor archives of the university's Near Eastern Institute. Richards liked studying here. It was quiet, off the beaten path, felt oddly homey, and he was forever thankful that he had discovered this scholarly womb during this sophomore year.

Unknown to Big Bill and even the football coach, Richards, now in his senior year, was enrolled in his third graduate language course in ancient Middle Egyptian. No one on the team or coaching staff knew, because he had paid for all the classes out of his own pocket. Besides, he was considered an egghead enough by most of the team with his business major. As it was, Big Bill thought that he was a flat out genius. Needless to say, if news about these Egyptian language courses ever got out, he would be finished and they would never let him forget it. So initially, Richards had feared that Big Bill's questions after today's practice had meant that the jig was up. That someone had found out, but apparently not, at least not yet. For the time being, his secret academic alter ego remained safe and undetected.

*   *   *

It never failed. Whenever Richards entered the archive his heart lifted. His aches and pains vanished. It must have been the combination of the smell of books, the many stained glass windows and their sacrosanct impact, the two-story high Gothic arch of the ceiling, and the rows of sturdy study tables each alight with two shaded brass lamps. Richards found it remarkable how each luminary shed its own distinct pattern of golden illumination, which created inviting blobs of reading space.

A warm and inviting intellectual womb, he thought as he softly treaded into and sought refuge within this academic sanctuary.

In the shadowed darkness of an early Midwestern evening, Richards found that his favorite spot was unoccupied. Sitting down, he first carefully propped up his injured ankle on an adjacent chair and pulled out from his backpack his two lists of Egyptian bi- and tri-laterals. With these in hand, he drilled himself by writing them in simple sentences that he made up.

So deep was his concentration that Richards had not heard the soft and considerate footfalls of the white-haired figure's approach. So immersed was he in his world of hieroglyphs that when Professor Milson softly said, "Hello." Richards jerked, banging his sore ankle in the process against the bottom of the massive reading table that hadn't budged. This knee-jerk reaction made quite an echoing racket within the cathedral-like room. Ignoring all the looks of disapproval at the shattered silence and gritting his teeth in an exquisite spike of pain, Richards whirled, stalled in shock, and then gritted out between his teeth a heavily controlled whisper, "Ah, Dr. Milson! Hello to you too, sir."

Bending over and whispering in a conspiratorial manner, Milson said, "Mr. Richards, may I have a moment of your time in private?"

"Yeah, sure. I mean, certainly. Where?"

"How about in my office down the hall. Second on the right. Please follow me."

*   *   *

After Richards carefully extricating his banged foot from the neighboring chair, gathered up his notes and backpack, the pair quietly left.

As they walked, or in Richards' case hobbled, Milson caught himself thinking, *This is most certainly no mere jock. My colleagues were correct. He studies and does so with depth and discipline. He is clearly well-mannered. Although he clearly has a temper, he has it firmly under control. And by his polite tone, he maybe even hails from a military family.*

I just wonder . . .

Once within Milson's cramped office of overflowing, floor to ceiling bookshelves, which to Richards was nothing short of hallowed ground, the professor settled himself down behind his desk, folded his hands, and said, "Mr. Richards, your presence in my department's Egyptian philology classes has been noted and deemed a bit unusual. Frankly you have tickled my curiosity. So would you mind telling me a little bit about yourself?"

Stunned at the professor's interest in him, Richards began in a croaky dry-throated, nervous sort of way.

"Well, sir, my education is a mish-mash of several European and American private schools. The American ones actually of the military base sort. My father is now US Air Force retired, but when he was active, we moved around quite a lot. Because of that, ever since I can remember, learning languages was a practical tool. How else can you make friends?" He finished with a natural shrug.

Milson gestured that he should continue.

"Well, first it was German, then French, and most recently Arabic. Wherever Dad was based was interesting if not unusual, and so I developed an appreciation for the history of whatever region we happened to be in. First it was World War II. Then it was the French Revolution and Napoleon. But while we were stationed in Egypt, I was totally blown away by the history of that ancient land. Ever since then, anything about ancient Egypt became almost an obsession."

At Richards' mention of languages, Milson curiosity got the better of him and so he asked his visitor in Arabic, a tongue in that the professor was fairly proficient, what he thought of the pyramids.

With a surprised look, Richards replied smoothly in kind with a sure and relaxed manner as was his deft use of colloquial expressions.

Now really fascinated at this football player's hidden gifts, Milson next asked, this time in German, a language that he had mastered during a post-doc research visit, what he missed most of that country's many cultural monuments. Richards, now realizing that he was being sized up, at first faltered a bit at this challenging linguistic gear shift, but after first pausing to unconsciously bite his lower lip, Teutonic word-images began to flow all to the delight of his listener.

As Richards spoke, Milson sat back deeply into his chair, one arm tucked under the other while slowly and gently stroking his clean-shaven chin.

My, he mused, *what a marvelous grasp of the spoken idiom this young man has! Clearly, his control of these two vastly different and difficult languages had been gained through aural means. No classroom instruction could produce such a natural richness, verging almost on a poetic quality. And although some of his expressions are cleared dated, they were nonetheless accurate and dead-on. And I'll wager that after two weeks submergence back into either language, he would no doubt replace them with their current cousins. And then the dawn broke.*

This lad is a natural linguistic chameleon!

What an opportunity we have here.

Richards immediately caught the far away, almost misty look in his eyes.

"Sir, does this mean that I have to drop your course?"

Suddenly roused from his deep thoughts by his student's question, Milson replied, "Oh my no, nonsense, young man, quite the opposite. I was just wondering. Why did you choose to attend this university? If you were so interested in things Egyptian, why didn't you go to Brown or Johns Hopkins or even with your German mastery to Tübingen or Munich for that matter? They all have fine ancient Near Eastern departments."

"Dr. Milson, I thought about it, but this school offered me a full athletic scholarship. So I grabbed it full knowing that the Near Eastern Institute was here."

"So why did you then go out of your way to pay for all of my department's courses out of your own pocket? Would not have your athletic department's scholarship covered the cost of these?"

Shocked that the professor had found out, Richards blurted out, "Dr. Milson, please don't tell the coach! It will get out that I am taking more than the allowed twelve credits. And besides, I am already considered the egghead of the team. It'll ruin me!"

At this interesting revelation, the professor just nodded with twinkling eyes and said with two waving hands of calm, "Have no fear young man. Your secret is safe with me. But I have another question. During last weekend's game against Harvard, tell me what was running through your mind during that screen pass during the third quarter. And tell me the truth. It's important."

Now it was Richards' turn to nod with twinkling eyes.

"Well, sir, frankly, I was just running for my life."

That comment earned Richards a quiet chuckle from the professor.

"Oh, young man, aren't you being just a bit too modest? A sixty-three yard gain? And what about the way you needled that defensive back into spearing you out of bounds, eh?"

Richards had to admit that he was impressed with the professor's grasp of the game, and the game within the game.

"You caught that, huh? Alright, since you want to know, our scouts had pegged that cornerback as a hothead. We all were told to work on him and I had already gotten in several nice opportunities. When he speared me out of bounds and he got the penalty, that was just the cumulative result of a team effort."

As Richards spoke, Milson relived that dramatic play, where an undersized halfback ran, darted, and feinted among his slower, lumbering linemen, making them all look good by setting up their blocks. When he finally broke into the clear, he had the presence of mind to attack the hot-headed cornerback and draw an additional fifteen yards onto an already impressive gain. The professor concluded: discipline, patience, extreme mental agility, calculated cunning, analysis under pressure, and above all, a team player.

The professor then took a different tack.

"Mr. Richards, what is your paper topic going to be for my class?"

Surprised and perplexed, the student gulped and blurted out his reply.

"I didn't know this class required a paper. In fact, I don't remember you ever mentioning it, nor do I remember seeing it on the course syllabus."

"That is all true, Mr. Richards, for the other students, but not for you. May I suggest a topic? It will not be easy, but I think that you will find it, well, useful."

Richards could only numbly nod. How many undergraduates, invading a graduate course, were singled out like this?

Sitting forward and leaning the elbows of his tweed jacket on the desk's leather writing pad, the professor now intoned. "I see that you are a business major. So, I want you to write for me an executive business brief, not a formal paper. Think of it as a sort of scouting report. It is to be without bibliography or footnotes and no longer than five single-sided, double-spaced pages with proper one inch margins. In this case, less is better. Think concise, compact, and coherent. I want it written in layman's terms, as if you were writing for one of your teammates. The topic is as follows. The context is the late Eighteenth Dynasty. The specific subject is the childhood and early years of the Pharaoh Neferkheperure Amenhotep, better known as Akhenaten. What do you say?"

All that Richards could reply was a guarded, "Sure."

"Fine, I will be looking forward to reading it."

Milson then quietly said, "My son, I am getting old and I see something of myself in you. Eventually, someone has to take my place and I detest departmental search committees. I would prefer, no, I want to personally groom my own successor. Mr. Richards, how much thought have you given to becoming an Egyptologist? Perhaps I am getting a bit ahead of myself, do you even want to be an Egyptologist?"

Richards could not reply. With eyes wide and a slack jaw, all he could do was bob his head in the affirmative. It was all he could do not to drool.

"Mr. Richards, and I suspect you know this already, the way in academe is extremely arduous. In a field as narrow as Egyptology, perhaps only thirty-five full-time academic positions currently exist worldwide. Central is a strong sense and understanding of language.

This is a talent you possess. But the knowledge and appreciation of geography, culture, and humanity are just as important. That typically is the result of years in the field. Regardless, I want you to think about this long and hard."

In obvious closing the professor then added, "By the way, I want your thoughts on my desk in two weeks time."

"Yes sir," was Richards' automatic reply, while his head was awhirl.

Leaving Dr. Milson's office, Joseph William Richards had never before in his entire existence been so intellectually pumped, so emotionally psyched. He floated back down the hallway toward the archive unthinking, unfeeling, and with a renewed sense of resolve. His decision to take on the ancient Egyptian language had not been a mistake, but rather had become a possible avenue to his own intellectual fulfillment.

After that brief meeting with Professor Milson, he was a man on a two-week mission. His social life abruptly ended, as did any of his previously squandered free time. Sack time too was shortened. Richards was fueled by the challenge, his natural desire to overachieve, to impress the professor, and yes, get his foot firmly wedged in the door of academia. To see what it might all be like. It all was so intoxicating. The vistas imagined seemed endless.

The first couple of nights came and went quickly, while Richards focused on the raw, hard data of his subject. Then, during a late evening, early morning caffeine haze, Richards realized that there was something very odd about the Pharaoh Amenhotep IV, who had during the fifth year of his reign changed his name to Akhenaten. Then there was the extremely scanty amount of evidence regarding his early years and youth. In fact, a noted Canadian scholar of the period had commented the future successor of Amenhotep III, "was conspicuous by his absence from the monuments of his father."

Just where the hell was he?

Professor Milson had been right, something was indeed missing.

Then during another late night, early morning intellectual foray, Richards received what can best be described as an epiphany—an intuitive leap. Having exhausted the departmental archive's formidable resources for evidence on Akhenaten's nearly non-existent childhood and youth, Richards' innate instincts had led him to review the art of the period. From there he wandered into the many artistic interpretations and professional medical opinions about Akhenaten himself. Was he a man, a woman posing as a man, a eunuch, or some sort of genetic hermaphrodite as some scholars had speculated? Was he the victim of an endocrine system gone wild, a malfunctioning pituitary gland, a full-blown case of Fröhlich's Syndrome, or perhaps even Marfan Syndrome? Was the Amarna art style that he inspired merely a stylistic revolution away from the formalism of traditional Egyptian art? Or was it instead a form of camouflage to hide, normalize, or make legitimate the pharaoh's own seemingly grotesque features? And then there was the issue of new capital of Akhetaten itself. Why did the king move away from that comfortable grandeur that was the traditional Theban capital? Why did he go north and establish a brand new capital city in an isolated and barren Nilotic cove encircled by high cliffs? The desire for such remoteness, isolation, and almost leper-like seclusion that housed the new royal court intrigued Richards and set him to thinking again.

Could it be that Akhenaten was some sort of a freak of nature? An embarrassed royal spawn that was the end result of generations of family inbreeding? Was there something to the conjecture that he may have had been a genetic freak, a mutation of some sort or kind? If that was so, he allowed, then that would explain a bunch.

As Richards began to write, he recognized that the hard facts came easily to paper. But as he quickly ran out of them, the role of interpretation, conjecture, and speculation began to weigh heavily on his mind.

Two days prior to Dr. Milson's deadline, Richards had stopped his research and writing. Stalled out between three and four pages of straight text, it was time to let the brief cool and let his mind unwind. It was Thursday night, the traditional first day of the campus social weekend. Taking a deep draught on his frosty beer in his favorite, noisy haunt, several concerned friends had asked him where he had been. Midterms had past and finals were still far off. So why all the booking, they had asked.

Two beers later, Richards had had enough. It was time to get back to work and finish that brief. Furthermore, despite what Dr.

Milson had decreed, he decided to footnote anything that he considered controversial, and most of his conclusions certainly were. And besides, his conscience would feel better for it.

On the way back to the dorm in his slightly inebriated state, his injured and now stiff right ankle made him appear as if he was a totally slobbering drunk. As Richards crossed the campus, he neared two old brick buildings that had a narrow and windowless gangway between them. From the entrance of the passage emerged a figure of medium height, but slight build. Wrapped tightly in a dark wool trench coat with the collar up against the raw wind, the bald and hatless man turned and walked briskly in Richards' general direction. They passed within only six feet of one another. The man nodded, slowly blinked, and briefly smiled. Richards' returned the silent acknowledgment and then after several heartbeats stopped dead in his tracks. Turning around, the back of the figure was already half a block away. But his face! Full Egyptian eye paint and eyelids painted in malachite! And Halloween was three weeks ago!

Piankoff allowed himself a rare smile. He enjoyed shocking people with his presence more than killing them. The gaping look of recognition on that young drunk had been priceless!

*　　*　　*

It was not often that a professor emeritus pays a visit to a university administrator hat in hand. Usually, it is the other way around. But Milson, at least this time, thought that the gesture might be worth it. Although Dr. Paul Allister Young, grandson of an English viscount and university dean, was sometimes an insufferable Brit, he also knew better than look a gift horse in the mouth. Besides, he counseled himself, time, in more ways than one, was fast running out.

He entered the dean's outside office chambers and presented himself before his secretary's desk. There, hiding behind her self-made fortification of a computer flat screen, appropriate reference books, and weeping tendril plants, she disdainfully looked up over her golden chained half glasses through a sprig of salt and pepper hair to acknowledge Milson's presence.

"May I help you?"

"No, but Dr. Young certainly can."

Mildly ruffled by the evasion, "Do you have an appointment with Dr. Young?" the secretary carefully enunciated with a heavy emphasis on the word "Doctor."

"Why, thank you for reminding me. Yes, I do. Would you please be so kind and inform Paul that John is here?"

"I am sorry, I cannot quite do that."

"And why not?" Milson politely queried.

"Because I do not know who you are."

With the gentle and innocent smile of a newborn, Milson replied, "Madam, of that, I am most glad."

With those words, Milson turned and strode purposefully across the lush Persian floor covering, passed the elegant mahogany paneling, entered Young's office unannounced, and quietly closed the heavy mahogany door behind him. As he did so, he stole a peek in the secretary's direction. She was beet-red, shaking in rage, and furiously dialing—no doubt to campus security.

Young's office, as with all administrative dignitaries of old and established universities, was a splendid example of naturally-aged woodwork and paneling, tastefully appropriate period furniture, bookshelves, and the luscious smell of their contents. The desk, the sacred altar of university status and power, was center stage and Young was comfortably ensconced behind his. Let there be no mistake. Each and every executive office and boardroom in the business world, no matter how well appointed, can ape nothing more than a pale reflection of such grounded institutional power. While Milson's mind took note this well-known but little understood fact, he quickly refocused on far weightier matters.

Young, who knew Milson well and his legendary antics even better, just looked up from the green felt blotter of his neat and spotless desk and smiled. Folding his hands like an obedient altar boy before a high cleric, Young said, "Yes, I can see that you and my new secretary Miss Andersen have already hit it off famously! A dollar wager that the campus police are already on their way."

To that Milson replied, "No bet. I saw her dialing."

He stated while settling himself in one of the large, brown leather, high wing-backed chairs before the dean's desk. Crossing his left leg over his right, Milson got immediately to the point of his visit.

"Dr. Young, I believe that I have identified a potential candidate for the collection of the, ah, genetic material that was discussed at our most recent get together at the Annex."

Young perked up at Milson's use of his Oxford title earned in Economics. This further signaled that his visit was serious and not frivolous. What followed only sealed his opinion of why the professor had come a calling, as they like to say in these wayward colonies.

Milson continued.

"But there are strings attached, which I believe will eventually benefit the university."

Ever intrigued by the complex workings and sometimes remarkably naïve academic mind, Young crossing his arms over his chest nodded to the Egyptologist to continue.

But before another word had left Milson's lips, the office's door suddenly burst open and two goggle-helmeted and Kevlar-armored policemen entered the office in full swat gear. Their Glock firearms were drawn. Miss Andersen, standing like an avenging lioness in the doorway behind them, pointed toward where Milson was sitting.

"That's him, officers! That's the terrorist who threatened me and forced his way in to see the dean!"

All Milson could do from laughing was cover his face with one hand. Young, also amused, deadpanned and consulted his wristwatch.

"Hmmm, three minutes flat. Not bad. Not bad at all! Well done gentlemen! You may go."

Confused, the officer nearest to Young asked, "Sir, what's going on here? We were called on a possible terrorist takeover of the administration building."

The other officer, and now with some heat, snorted. "Is this only some kind of sick drill?"

Young, now with utter seriousness in his voice, replied, "No officer, this is not a drill. It's just a simple misunderstanding on the part of my new secretary, Ms. Andersen. This is her first week. If there is any sort of complaint to be filed with your superiors, please inform me of it personally. You may stand down. I can assure you that everything is well under control. As you can see, I am under no sort of danger or coercion whatsoever."

Now thoroughly confused and more than a little angry with the secretary, the two armed men left the office and quietly closed the dean's door behind them.

After about a fifteen-second pause, Young refolded his hands before him, raised his bushy gray and unruly eyebrows for dramatic effect, and drolly asked.

"You were saying?"

Without skipping a beat, Milson answered.

"I have found a perfect recruit for the Philology Annex. He is a dark-haired Caucasian of mildly Mediterranean complexion, medium height, superbly conditioned, well-mannered, and from a military family, a natural aural linguist, bright, intelligent, and makes sound decisions under stress."

"Pray tell. Just who is this superman?"

"An undergraduate Egyptology student of mine, who just so happens to be our football team's star halfback."

"What?"

"His name is Joseph William Richards. He's a bright first semester senior with enough credits to graduate with this coming January's class. And given the necessary time frame for the candidate's training, I would suggest that he be immediately brought aboard. And I would like to bring him in."

"Alright . . ."

Young was clearly pleased, but was instinctively hedging his bets with the rapid course of this discussion.

"Tentatively speaking, he may be the one, but he will have to have his background checked nonetheless. And there are all of those dreadful tests, and then all the training with the Russians."

"Agreed, but I do not see any problem there. I have done some preliminary checking myself. In the meantime, what would you like me to do?"

"Nothing, now what were those strings you mentioned? I haven't forgotten."

Milson first looked down at his hands, paused, took a deep breath and let it out, and then looked Young straight in the eye and said.

"If our dear Mr. Richards passes muster, which I do not doubt one iota, if he is deployed and comes back safe and sound, I want your assurance that he will receive his undergraduate business degree, and, become a tenured member of my department with the rank of associate professor of Egyptian philology."

Dumbstruck and blinking his eyes only once, Young then narrowed them.

"What's up, John? What are you trying to tell me? Just who is this Mr. Richards you are suddenly so fond of?"

Now leaning forward in his chair, Milson said with passion, "Paul, he has the makings to be the next star of modern Egyptology, just as the venerable James Herald Binliff was, who founded our very own Near Eastern Institute."

"If he passes muster, if he completes his collection, and if he returns, then I will definitely consider it."

"No Paul, that is not good enough, and you know it. Before I turn over Richards to those crazies at the Annex, and that character Piankoff, I want your assurances, in writing, notarized, and placed in a safety deposit box of my choosing."

"Alright, John, I know you are serious. But why all the doom and gloom, the cloak and dagger, and this talk of safety deposit boxes?"

"Because Paul, unfortunately, good men are oftentimes the first forgotten."

A few moments of silence passed and then a nod.

"Point taken. Okay. Now let me get this straight. If Richards passes the security screen and the Annex's quals, if he deploys and is successful with the genetic gathering, and naturally if he comes back, then I will agree to his business degree and will fund an additional tenured post in your department. And yes, I will put that in writing. Is that good enough?"

"Deal. When will that document be drafted and signed?"

"You can pick it up tomorrow after ten. Your new best friend outside my office door will have it ready for you. May I suggest that you bring flowers?"

The very next morning at five after ten, a very humble professor emeritus arrived unannounced at the dean's office bearing a bouquet of flowers.

* * *

Richards was very nervous during the day's Egyptian philology class, for he had slid his brief under Dr. Milson's office door the night before—a full day before it was due.

Boy, was that a first! He's sure to have read it by now.

Having finished his point on the correct use of several confusing Egyptian noun formations, Dr. Milson then regaled the class by dovetailing the grammar lesson with a very interesting aside.

"You know folks, beware of what you may consider an inconsistent, foggy, or confusing grammatical usage on the part of the ancient Egyptians. Just imagine what their troubles would be if they had to learn American English! Think of all the clichés we commonly use, all the puns, all the idioms. All the double-speak. Needless to say, when we are confronted with curious Egyptian noun and verbal formations, we too must always consider their context and always the possibility of double meanings. Especially, when you consider that the ancient Egyptians just loved to pun!

"For instance, if you all would be so kind, please turn to page 94."

This command was rewarded with the corporate sounds of opening books and rustling pages.

"As you all know, this reading exercise is a love poem. And translating poetry, making it meaningful, giving the words rhythm and beauty, are without question the most difficult task of any philologist, for such an enterprise requires the translator to have at their fingertips a depth of experience that few ever achieve.

"Now, take for example this reference to the sycamore tree that the two lovers are sitting beneath. What do you think this image would conjure up within an Egyptian's mind, anyone?"

After a pause of some ten seconds a timid hand rose from a thick-glassed, moon-faced male.

"Shade?"

Gentle chuckling resulted.

With a scowling look, Milson admonished the hecklers.

"Yes, Mr. Knowles. Not bad. To be sure, shade in that desert clime was at a premium. And think of the glorious coolness that it provided. No sir, not bad at all."

Knowles' face simply beamed at Milson's kind defense of his rarely vocalized participation.

"Now, any other ideas?"

After a brief silence, a freckle-faced red-head opined, "The sycamore, if I recall, was a fragrant wood. If the tree was in bloom, sitting beneath it would be wonderful, I would think. Sort of like springtime or a visit to the arboretum."

"Very good, Ms. O'Reilly, our olfactory sense is a powerful intellectual and emotional trigger, one surely to be an object within a poetic muse.

"Again I ask of this distinguished crew, any other ideas?"

Richards, forgetting his usual self-imposed reserve, raised his hand from the back of the room and offered, "Fertility, isn't the goddess Isis somehow connected with the tree?"

Smiling despite himself, Milson wondered aloud, "Mr. Richards, just what have you in mind with this image?"

Now several curious students turned around to register who this usually invisible Mr. Richards even was.

"Well, sir, I was just thinking that making out in the shade of a sweet-smelling tree was for the Egyptians what drive-ins used to be for us."

This leaping analogy that struck so squarely at the very essence of college sexuality caused several of the available females in the class, those who were always in heat, or so it seemed to Milson, to bestir themselves, turn around, and check out Richards. Fortunately for him, today he wore a baggy cotton sweat suit, so ensuring for him a modicum of anonymity.

Not used to being noticed in class, Richards turned bright red, looked down, pretended to write something, and silently vowed, *Never, ever again, Joey-boy, open your big, fat, trap in class again! Remember. Low and slow and no one will ever notice you! Nor will they ever report you to the coaching staff.*

Then at this point in the football player's self-flagellation, Milson came to his aid.

"Mr. Richards your apt analogy is really quite to the point of the question and leads me to suspect that you are a closet poet at heart."

More chuckles were generated, but this time of the friendly and more appreciative sort.

"You see, ladies and gentlemen, the Egyptian language, much like our own, is filled with references to sexuality both muted and not. Consequently, to better understand where this poem is going, we must try to grasp what ancient Egyptian sexual mores were. And in so many words, to attempt to see what turned on an Egyptian."

With that statement, Milson had once again had successfully regained the class' undivided attention. As for Richards, his presence was now long forgotten.

"To begin, the ancient Egyptians knew nothing of our Judeo-Christian moral structure. Remember. Their culture in large part flourished before the birth of Judaism itself, much less Christianity. So try to divest yourselves of those biases right away.

"Then, we must ask ourselves, what sources could we mine that would reveal the Egyptian sexual temperament?"

Ticking off with the fingers of his right hand.

"Written sources for sure, artifacts without doubt. But let's not forget the most important source that they were human beings. They shared the same physiology as we do. They suffered with their hormones just as we do today."

Warming to the subject and with his hands behind him in his typical lecture pose.

"As to written sources, we have several father and son *Admonitions* that date back from the Old Kingdom. These are useful in that they give us a glimpse into the mind of the professional bureaucrat and his upbringing. What to say. What not to say. How to act. How not to act. Proper table and social manners. Basically, how to suck up to your superiors.

"A more direct source of information on Egyptian sexuality is contained in a funerary document that we moderns have come to call *The Negative Confession*, which dates from the New Kingdom. Contained within it are some interesting tidbits. For example, the deceased would deny that he was guilty of the following items that were frowned upon by the Egyptian gods: pederasty, masturbation, adultery, and homosexuality. And, as most of you all well know, if the gods frowned upon these acts, then such acts were known to have occurred within Egyptian society. Such is the mechanism of religious and social taboos—the precursors of moral and civil law codes and their supporting legal systems.

"Perhaps the juiciest, but also most perplexing source of Egyptian sexuality is their love poetry. And of these we have only a few preserved examples. Written typically in the first person, the individual literally has a conversation with their heart about the person of their dreams. The language is simple, direct, short, and sweet. Long-winded, complex, erotic descriptions and passages you will not find. The ancient Egyptians cut to the chase and expressed what their hearts felt.

"But what is perplexing about these love poems is the imagery they refer to, something that we cannot fully understand. Add to this our ignorance of their body language that governs the rules of sexuality. Youth and adolescence is the time when we learn this language, however imperfectly, however awkwardly. Sexual communication through body language occurs constantly, whether in movies, on television, or in a social setting like, well, a singles bar. What we do to attract or repel. The sexual advances of another can be endless.

"Since we must accept that sexual body language developed in ancient Egypt, we nonetheless, as philologists, do not know what those queues were, even though they are referred to in a love poem. And so love poems really are the most difficult of all ancient sources to decode. For example, just what the expression 'to dust one's feet' really means we haven't a clue, except that in several contexts the phrase implies some sort of sexual overtone or activity.

"But take heart, some Egyptian illusions are obvious, even to we dull-witted moderns. For example, imagine yourself at a bar, a party, or some sort of social event. Boy sees girl. Boy wants to meet girl. What does boy do?

"Anyone?"

"He buys her a beer." Piped the freckled-face redhead.

"Very appropriate, Ms. O'Reilly, for the Egyptians were indeed lusty beer drinkers!"

Broad, knowing smiles appeared throughout the classroom.

"He walks over and introduces himself."

Purred an exotic and sultry brunette co-ed.

"Yes indeed, Ms. Gérard, but what makes the sale, as it were?"

With a lurid smile Ms. Gérard replied, "Oh, don't worry Dr. Milson, I'd know!"

At this point, the class was howling and Milson, after a time, had to rein them back in.

"Precisely, the young gentleman's behavior and body language sold him. But ladies and gentlemen, don't you see, Ms. Gérard's answer was based on subliminal messages that she, and she alone, could have interpreted. Messages that even today are difficult to describe, must less put to paper in the form of a poem.

"Now in ancient Egypt, it was common practice for people to shave their entire bodies and wash several times a day."

The sagging jaw lines and looks of total disbelief told Milson much about his own class' sense of hygiene.

"Consider. They shaved themselves to prevent troubles with lice and fleas. They washed because of perspiration and the dirt and dust that accumulated on their oiled bodies. They wore wigs both to protect their shaved heads from the sun and of course to make a fashion statement. Both sexes wore light and airy outfits, either kilts or one-shouldered dresses. Bare or partially bare chests for both sexes were the norm (more sagging jaw lines). House servants of both sexes might only wear a wig and a smile."

At this attempt at humor Milson earned some tension relieving smiles and chuckles.

"But to remove your wig before a member of the opposite sex, in the proper social context, constituted a powerful signal for intimacy among the ancient Egyptians.

"How many times have you heard the expression, 'Let your hair down?' To an Egyptian, they took it literally and translated it as, 'Take off your wig.' Taking your wig off was the opening gambit that may led to a sexual encounter.

"As for the sexual act itself, the physical process, we have a wealth of source material available.

At mentioning this topic, Milson noted a palpable straining of the students' ears.

"It has become abundantly clear to me," Milson continued, "that the mounting of the female atop a prone and submissive male was considered the Egyptian divine norm for the act of procreation."

That revelation earned Milson a simply devastating leer of acknowledgment from Ms. Gérard. He then continued, nearly choking, "If you don't believe me, check out all the references to the siring of Horus between Osiris and Isis, or, for that matter, the creation myth between the earth god Geb and his sky goddess wife Nut. Naturally, these ready examples only begin to scratch at the surface.

"But when it comes to exposing Egyptian sexuality with no holds barred, no source can compare with an old and much-faded papyrus that is housed in the Turin Museum. If you are curious, its catalogue number is 55001."

Frantic note taking erupted.

"This Turin Papyrus, lovingly referred to by its devoted fans as the Turin "porno papyrus," in my opinion, is nothing more than an Egyptian how-do-it, pillow book.

"What is interesting about the papyrus is that it was created with two audiences in mind: the literate and non-literate. For the literate are neatly written columns of cursive hieratic script that describe what's going on. For the non-literate are field upon field of cartoon-like images depicting men and women in every possible sexual position you can imagine. In many respects, this papyrus could be considered the Egyptian *Kama Sutra*.

"And because so many different sexual positions are so graphically depicted, one might conclude that the ancient Egyptians were, at least by our prim and guilt-ridden Judeo-Christian standards, a rather adventuresome crowd."

Ms. Gérard grinned her full approval at this last comment.

"But if you asked an ancient Egyptian as to the actual physical mechanics behind procreation, you might be surprised by their answer, because to them, as far as the extant medical papyri tell us, semen must first enter the body. The big question was, however, through which orifice."

Looks of disbelief, flush, curiosity, and disgust now were evident throughout the class. Again, Ms. Gérard seemed to be the only one comfortably at home with the notion.

"Consequently, procreation to an ancient Egyptian could potentially occur via the anus, vaginal tract, mouth, maybe even the nose and ears. Basically all the natural passageways into the female body."

To this last revelation, a collective gasp from this otherwise blasé group threatened to turn the classroom into an evacuated atmospheric vessel. Milson, inwardly pleased with their reaction, then continued his point without batting an eye.

"This is why, I believe, that the Turin Papyrus possessed such a variety of couplings."

Lost as he always was whenever Dr. Milson went off on one of his famous tangents, Richards noticed that everything Dr. Milson had said, every example, every allusion he made, each word he chose to use, was part of some sort of secret, private code. Why, for instance, did this normally dry and staid scholar choose to wander off into such earthy subject matter? Why did he linger so long on topics of pharmacology, environment, metallurgy, priestly castes, medical papyri, fashion, and polite etiquette?

And predictably, after class was over and all the usual hangers-on had left, Ms. Gérard had several pithy questions for the good professor, only the two of them were left.

Silently, Richards followed Milson to his office and remained standing. Milson having sat down noted this polite restraint and motioned Richards to the lone wooden chair.

Once seated, Richards then saw on the desk before Milson his brief with its margins covered with Milson's light and delicately penciled handwriting. Looking up, Milson could only smile.

"Mr. Richards, I see you are a renegade at heart. You employed footnotes when none were required and submitted your thoughts a day early. What have you to say for yourself?"

Taken aback, Richards shrugged.

"Dr. Milson, I only footnoted what I could not either personally trust or independently corroborate. As for the deadline, I was finished. Why wait?"

Taking in the laconic and revealingly terse answer, Milson then decided to level with him.

"Mr. Richards, if becoming an academic Egyptologist is important to you, would you be willing on a moment's notice to quit the football team and temporarily leave the university?"

Visibly shocked, Richards said, "I don't understand. What you're saying makes no sense. Besides, what you're saying makes no economic sense either. I'm here because of the football scholarship. How can I finish my business major without participating in my classes? No sir. I just don't, flat, understand what you are asking me."

"Nor do I expect you to. But I have another question. Do you trust me?"

"I suppose so, but given the rather strange direction that this conversation is going, I'm not sure."

"Good. Being careful and skeptical are good instincts. But what I am asking you Joseph is this. Are you willing to trust me in order to become an Egyptologist?"

Joseph!

Then guardedly, very guardedly, Richards replied, "Perhaps, but I need to know more."

"Fine, a most reasonable position, but first in your own words, what are your true feelings about Akhenaten?"

Finally, the executive brief, Richards was beginning to wonder.

"Well, he was definitely an odd duck, a real individualist to paraphrase Breasted. Perhaps even a religious and social revolutionary. At the heart of it, I think that he had a big secret, a secret so big that he decided to hide it out in the open."

"An intriguing thesis, please go on."

"Professor, I cannot prove it, but I think that Akhenaten was not normal, not like us. Inbreeding can do some mighty strange things. I checked. Down deep, I really think that the entire Amarna movement, culture, call it what you want, was a smokescreen to camouflage Akhenaten's own physical peculiarities."

"And what were those? You only summarize them in your brief."

"Well, it seems all pretty obvious to me: the oversized cranium, especially in the occipital region, the prominent, extended lower jaw, and finally, the large, slightly slanted eyes and overall elongation of his facial features. Then there is the apparent sexual dimorphism: a male with clearly developed breasts, a wasp waist, and a broad hip girdle. All of these characteristics suggest to me that Akhenaten was in fact a genetic freak or some kind of mutant."

With the mention of the words "genetic freak" and "mutant" it was Milson's turn to pale with shock and Richards took note of it. He had clearly struck a nerve, a very deep and sensitive one.

"Is there something wrong, professor?"

Chapter XVIII
1368 BC. Conception of a God

The middle-aged pharaoh, although considered by his nation as their all-powerful, living god on earth, was nonetheless considered by those who knew him best as something of a stubborn clod. And this was precisely one of those moments. Suffering from inflamed gums and several overly-worn and diseased teeth, Nebmare Amenhotep was having trouble eating his food, not that you could tell from his girth or his love of beer. Because of his sensitive and rotting teeth, the Master of Upper and Lower Egypt was reduced to eating mashed fruit and soft foods. As far as his diet was concerned, he was no better off than a six-month-old child. Right now, with a grimace of pain, the king was attempting to chew some soft, overripe fruit, which resulted in tears of pain and streams of juice and drool coursing down his chin. Needless to say, he was not a pretty sight while he ate. Certainly, Egypt's living god was not at his best.

Witness to this latest feeding fiasco was his ever-adoring and persevering wife, herself a commoner and daughter of a foreigner, the Mistress of Upper and Lower Egypt, Chief Wife, Queen Tiye. All she could do was hold a bowl beneath the king's chin, in a vain attempt at preserving his dignity, while he painfully attempted to chew. During times like these, Tiye wished that her otherwise reasonable husband would consider the counsel of the court physician, Neferher. Practical dentistry was far from an unknown skill. In fact, tooth extraction, the drainage of abscesses, and even tooth filings were practical realities. All that was needed were funds and a willing patient. Resources Egypt's living god had in abundance. Courage went unquestioned for this once well-muscled monarch, whether on the battlefield or during the hunt. But when it came to his teeth, well, that was an entirely different matter.

So, during this most painful of moments, both for her husband and herself, Tiye decided to steer the conversation away from the obvious issue of the king's need for a dentist.

"My husband, I am ripe and want to bear you another son."

The subject of sex always brought the living god's attention to sharp acuity. Tiye knew this, for she had to compete for his affections, given the present size of the royal harem. Although she was no longer the lithe maiden of their wedding day, Tiye was still a stunning beauty with brilliant green eyes and a fine form. Although Tiye and Nebmare Amenhotep had married young and were obviously affectionate toward one another, that fact did not slow the lion-like appetite of the king. He could call to his bedside Egyptian mistresses and palace servant girls. He was married to no less than two Syrian princesses, two Mitannian princesses, two Babylonian princesses, and one from Arzawa. One should also count the myriad ladies-in-waiting that accompanied these diplomatic marriages. Opportunities for the Great Bull of Memphis abounded.

Despite the fact that the palace was awash with the harem's spawn, it was only the children of Tiye who mattered—four girls and a boy. Nebmare Amenhotep's oldest daughter, his favorite, was the bright and energetic Sitamen. When she became of age, she had been elevated to share her mother's coveted title of Great King's Wife—a *pro forma* act, but hardly a reality. His son Thutmose, sent to Memphis and schooled by the high priests of Ptah, was the heir apparent.

Now Tiye wanted his affections once again. Experience and her personal physician had told her that her present readiness would result in a son, a second son for her god, pharaoh, life companion, and lover.

To his wife's overture of rabid love-making, for that described Tiye to a tee, the king's eyebrows arched in genuine surprise. His eyes sparkled in anticipation and challenge. Finally, his fruity mush swallowed and gently wiping his still powerful and well-chiseled chin, the king spoke.

"Well, dear Chief Wife, to what do I owe this most welcome pleasure?"

"My love, do I now require a reason to bring pleasure to the Great Bull of Memphis, and in the process, honor him with yet another strong son like his father?"

Such coquettish sparring on the part of his teenage love and first wife always stirred Nebmare's loins. It was their private prelude. His first partner knew well how to purr in his ear, how to stroke his smooth and shaved head, how to move in such a way, how to pulsate her moist womanhood, how to milk him dry as would any herder his favorite goat. And he well knew that she would continue, and continue, until he would reach such a state of total exhaustion that he would gladly grant her anything she desired. But the Chief Wife never asked for anything, for all was hers already.

"And, Chief Wife, what would Egypt do with another son of the living Horus?"

"Why, Great One, to assist his elder brother in every way: in administration, on the battlefield, and even before the gods themselves."

"Are you suggesting joint rule by my sons, a divided land!"

"No, oh Wise Horus, just wise counsel, an opportunity for the younger to gain the experience of the older, and a way to ensure Egypt is prepared against its many enemies."

"I must think about this novel notion of yours, but for now, I do not have a second son. Shouldn't we do something about that first before we decide on the status of a second?"

Thus the early evening's lovemaking began and it did not end until the moon had reached its highest ascent. During the course of that period the Great Bull of Memphis had bellowed no less than five times. The Mistress of the Two Lands had swoon no less than four. In the end, the pair slept deeply entwined in each other's embrace. Each exhausted and satisfied. Each secure in the belief of their private intimacy.

*   *   *

But high above in geocentric, equatorial orbit, the scout surveyor had been observing the intricate comings and goings of his new-found prize for the past eighteen solar cycles. During that period, the Quimbly had become increasingly impressed by the accomplishments and potential of the dominant terrestrial species, for in several disparate locals, independent civilizations were proceeding fast apace along well established paths of development.

It was all so intriguing, all so exhilarating to watch. But at the same time a slowly nagging concern began to creep into the back of the Quimbly's mind, a concern that soon became dread. A dread that verged almost upon a panicky fear. This scout surveyor had several times before witnessed such rapid development and had done nothing about it, but observe and record from afar. True, in rare cases that warranted it, careful and selective intervention was permitted by his guild's charter.

Nonetheless, the Quimbly had seen too often the ephemeral nature of such cyclical inventiveness, had cringed while it crumbled, unraveled, and devolved into interspecies annihilation. Then, after some time of consideration, the scout surveyor came to a decision that this time such would not be the case. The terrestrial species deserved a fair chance at success, an opportunity for survival, the precious gift of a meaningful future.

That decided, now foremost on its mind became the timing of such intervention, where would it occur, and of course how. Added to its ruminations were the many choices to choose among, the many interlocking variables to juggle. Again after some pondering, weighing of facts, and extrapolating outcomes, the Quimbly settled upon a short list. From there it focused upon a single advanced group who were relatively isolated, which made for a promising social and biological laboratory of sorts. Myriads of issues still had to be arranged anew even for this candidate culture, which was hardly hermetically sealed within a closed system. But then again, it reasoned, none ever truly were.

Now satisfied with the where, the questions of when and how had to be decided. And the more it observed, the more the Quimbly recognized that the species indeed was ripe for a bit of highly selective manipulation. Just a gentle push was all that was really needed. And so the Quimbly again began to ponder, and as it did so, an old and rare sensation emerged that it had almost forgotten—anticipation.

*   *   *

Unknown to the dosing royal couple far below, the constituent parts of their recently united *in vivo* gametes were being remotely combined, recombined, and altered in subtle ways, all in careful preparation for the eventual merge of human and Quimbly. In time, the royal pair would indeed have a second son just as they had wished and dreamed.

And in the fullness of time, he would be special, most special indeed.

CHAPTER XIX

The Recruit

Richards left Professor Milson's office with two things: a mystery about why the professor was so shook up about his assessment of Akhenaten, and an appointment for tomorrow at nine sharp at the Philology Annex. Both worried Richards. In many respects, although Richards would never admit it, he was really a creature of habit, regimentation, and structure. The football program provided him with the primal ritualistic side, with its continuous physical toning and emotional release within the close camaraderie of a team. The equally grueling intellectual path that he had carved out for himself demanded similar structure in the coin of time and dedication. Participation in both had made him feel complete, fulfilled, and satisfied. To so arbitrarily leave both as Professor Milson had suggested was a frightening step. Richards doubted he could make those leaps, not to mention the issue of his graduation.

Still remained the carrot of a possible career in Egyptology that forced Richards to weigh and reconsider. While stretched out on his dorm room bed and drifting at the edge of sleep, Richards decided he would honor his appointment at the Philology Annex at least to check out the situation.

Hell, never up, never in. And who knows, maybe Professor Milson's offer will come true. Whadda' ya' got to lose Joey-boy?

The next thing Richards' consciousness registered was the ringing of his alarm clock, which read eight-thirty a.m. Surprised and a bit disoriented by how late it was, Richards quickly stumbled out of bed and hobbled over barefoot to the communal dorm john and shower. Quickly reviving under the hot water of a powerful shower, he practically hacked himself to death while shaving, he was in such a rush. Applying toilet paper bits to all of his still oozing nicks, he quickly dressed and ran across campus through the early morning's freshly fallen snow to make good on his appointment at the Annex. While in mid-gallop, his mind registered he was in the process of cutting his first period chemistry class. Awash in the guilt of one who never misses a class ever, he continued on.

Never up. Never in.

*   *   *

Arriving at the three-story corner brownstone, Richards hurdled over the low signage of the Annex, bounded up its cement stairs three at a time, and entered the humid warmth of the foyer. Overheated, he opened up his winter parka and then decided to just take it off. Witness to this near-flying entrance was a middle-aged secretary, who had the opportunity to look over Richards quite closely as he took off his parka.

Hmmm, she thought. *Quite a hunk. Oh, for an evening between the sheets interrogating this one!*

As Richards walked over to her desk, she said with a smile that offered quite a lot. "Well now, you must be Professor Milson's prize student, Mr. Richards. Is that right?"

Slightly stuttering out with nervous energy.

"Why, why, yes. I guess I am. Am I already late?"

"Well, by my watch, you are right on time. Please have a seat over there and I will announce you."

Turning to take his seat, the secretary's eyes ever so slightly dilated as they literally feasted on Richards.

Seated, Richards noticed that the reddish-blonde secretary, who was not bad-looking for an old lady, was nicely put together. In fact, he kind of liked the way her chest strained against her white silk blouse while she was on the phone, stretching and creating some puckers in the cloth around the buttons.

Forcing himself to look elsewhere other than at the exposed pink flesh, Richards noted that this outer entrance office looked like every other departmental office on campus. Old and faded paint, ancient and out-of-code lighting fixtures, ubiquitous tan filing cabinets, and a couple of leafy plants. Pipe tobacco and coffee scented the room. On the other hand, he found those two nooks with shoes and slippers to be a bit odd. In the end, only the sultry secretary was really worth his notice. When he returned his gaze to her, Richards was rewarded with her bending over while she was picking up some strategically dropped papers from off the floor next to her desk.

Catching his gaze, the secretary looked up, arched her back, and smiled her best, full knowing what she was doing and loving every bit of it.

Yes, this young buck does have appreciative eyes. She thought as she tracked his eyes.

Unfortunately for the mounting hormonal levels of these two on the verge of rut, this tender moment was shattered as the office door, located behind the receptionist, opened. Out walked a man that Richards swore he recognized, but where he could not place.

*   *   *

"Mr. Richards, I presume? I am Mr. Piankoff. How do you do." Now shaking hands with the young man.

"Please come in."

While shaking Piankoff's hand, Richards, noted the lean build, the perfectly shaved head, and the eyes. Yes those eyes. He suddenly went stiff when he recalled where and when he had first seen him.

Upon closing the door to his office, Piankoff, standing with his hands held behind his back in a stiff pose of a lecturer, then remarked offhandedly, "I see that you have already made quite an impression on Ms. Kelly. Be forewarned, Mr. Richards, Ms. Kelly has a rather large, ah, how should I say, a rather demanding appetite."

So that's her name! Ms. Kelly.

"In my own opinion, I find her to be an efficient secretary as well as a less than discrete nymphomaniac. You have been warned."

Lecture over, Piankoff, then turned and took his seat behind his desk. Richards, stunned at the frank announcement, was left standing. After a few moments, he found his wits and sat down in the office's vacant chair.

As the interview began, Richards became more and more aware of Piankoff's choice of words, his odd syntax, his accent, and his odd choice of tonal pitches and cadence. On a whim, he decided to act upon his instincts.

"Habek sesh djedef secherek."

All Piankoff could do was offer a brief, fleeting, and pleased smile at the philological attempt.

"I see that Professor Milson still does not entirely appreciate the delicate nuances of the *sedjemef* verbal form. But your attempt is a good as any."

Then with a slight tilt to his head and an expression of revelation, Piankoff said. "So now I remember you. You were the staggering drunk that I saw several nights ago."

Richards, emboldened, shot back. "Hardly. What you saw was a student-athlete hobbling home on a partially sprained ankle."

Stated with a cool smile that wasn't. "How refreshing, but enough of these pleasantries. Your presence here tells me that Professor Milson has spoken to you. Are you ready to begin, or are you just curious?"

"All that Professor Milson said was that if I quit the football team and left the university, I had a better than average chance at an academic career in Egyptology."

"I see. Is that all he told you?"

Richards nodded.

A thoughtful pause with pursed lips.

"Well. If we are to continue this discussion in any sort of detail, you must first sign several documents, stipulated by several governments, preventing any disclosure whatsoever of what we are about to discuss. Are you prepared to do so?"

Richards was stunned, but his curiosity got the better of him. Before he could appreciate the magnitude and weight of Piankoff's statement, he was already nodding his assent.

"Ah, good, I like decisive minds. Here. Sign your name in full at the three Xs and please initial these four spots."

Having complied, Piankoff continued, "I wish to reiterate before I begin this discussion never occurred, and if you ever disclose what we are about to discuss, then you will at best disappear, at worst be as good as a dead man."

Richards responded to Piankoff's perfunctory manner with heat. "Enough with all this goddamn melodrama, Mr. Piankoff, just what the fuck is all this secrecy stuff all about anyhow? And for a starter, why don't you begin with yourself, Mr. Glitter Lids!"

Smiling at Richards' elevated attitude and snappy questions, Piankoff replied with a definite chill.

"Mr. Richards, I will be happy to explain whatever you want, but let us make one thing perfectly clear from the start.

"First, never, ever again, use profane language in my presence.

"Second, if you decide to join up with me, you will do what I want, when I want, and without any question or questions whatsoever.

"Is that clear?"

What Richards found so compelling about Mr. Piankoff's statement was the quiet, matter-of-fact manner, in which it was delivered. "No nonsense" would not cover it. "Absolute" was a word that began to approach it.

Finding his voice, he replied. "Yes sir. Crystal clear."

"Fine. Good. Enough said."

With his hands folded before him, Mr. Piankoff began.

"Mr. Richards, this building, the Philology Annex, is not what it seems. It's a shell, a front. Yes, the Annex is indeed involved in the research of several ancient Near Eastern languages. Yes, graduate students and faculty come and go. But in actual fact it represents a special agency of the American Academy of Sciences of which I am a collateral member.

"Mr. Richards, until recently, the true and secret mandate of the Philology Annex was one of dogged chronological research devoted to the technology behind successful time travel. But as with so many things, machines can go only so far. Eventually, just as with the American lunar landing, a human eventually had to play a role and make a contribution. That is when I became involved with the Philology Annex and its founder, Dr. Peter Borov.

"You see, Mr. Richards, I am the Annex's first and only time traveler. In particular, I am this organization's, and the Federal Republic of Russia's, first temporal field operative. Initially, I was sent back to do what a machine could not, provide accurate chronological information, actually, critical calibration data. After all, what good is a racing engine if it doesn't have a tachometer? Well, after a short while, several factors naturally pointed to the ancient Near East as a prime place to start these calibration studies. Ancient Egypt in particular. And so I went back, what, four times now, in order to address all of the basic calibration issues.

"Along the way, I naturally came into contact, admittedly on a superficial level, with the native Egyptians and being linguistically gifted, I learned rapidly. I could do so, because I learned to read Middle Kingdom hieroglyphs as a boy. Let us just say that the talent is in the family. But my problem was that I did not know how to vocalize the language correctly. So while pretending to be a mute priest who could read and write, I learned the vocalization of the language in the field."

"Most recently, I have been investigating, on the behalf of the American Academy and Russian Academy of Science, a strong suspicion that our cultural past has been tampered with by an outside influence, potentially an extraterrestrial one.

"My present task is to find, train, and deploy on these organizations' behalf a second temporal field operative. You have been nominated by Professor Milson as a possible candidate, and could be that unique individual. What do you have to say?"

With a sly smile, Richards replied with a voice dripping in disbelief, "Yeah, sure, let's see. This story of yours sounds like a mixture of several B-grade television series, clumsily grafted onto any James Bond plot that you would care to name. What do you expect me to say? What's your proof?"

"You know, Mr. Richards, the very best place to hide a secret is out in the open. Have you ever bothered to notice how Hollywood trends are started, ended, and when? Do you ever get the feeling that much of Hollywood's drivel may have an agenda behind it all?"

Surprised by the calm and reasoned reaction to his derisive reaction, Richards found himself gazing off with a glassy look, which Piankoff immediately saw and exploited.

"Ah, I see that you are beginning to understand. After all, who would believe a tabloid's nonsense about a monumental facial image on Mars, even as NASA and the European Space Agency are gearing up with a series of Mars Landers? Similarly, who would believe the rants of a college student about temporal field agents, time machines, and the like on a Midwestern college campus? Simply put – nobody.

"To continue my point, try to imagine your government's desire to prepare America for earth's first extraterrestrial visitors? Or even better yet, that your government has in fact been in contact with such beings for decades? How would you dampen the initial panic and the fear? How would you quench the outright republican rage surrounding such a disclosure? Perhaps another lame appeal to national security? No, I don't think so. That ploy would never stand up to the pressure of your liberal media. So instead, a far more subtle move would be to use the media, use Hollywood, to soften the blow, pure and simple."

After a few moments of strained silence, Richards followed up with another question.

"Okay, all of your points are well taken, and if I may say, you present an intriguing thesis. But who's supposed to be your extraterrestrial bad guy anyway?"

"Neferkheperure Amenhotep."

Another moment elapsed, but this time of intellectual recognition, and then, Richards uttered a whispered, breathless reply, "Somehow I'm not at all surprised . . ."

Which was quickly followed by an emphatic.

"Yyyeeesss!"

As Richards exclaimed victoriously he pumped his tightly fisted arm as if he had just scored the winning hockey goal in triple overtime. He then continued with emphasis.

"That's perfect! It just has to be him! He's such an odd ball, such a weird duck."

The quick recognition and sudden enthusiasm on the part of Richards totally caught Piankoff by surprise and prompted him to wonder what Richards already knew that he didn't.

Continuing on with the interview.

"Well, Mr. Richards, are you interested?"

From the broad smile on the young man's face, Piankoff already knew the answer.

"You bet!" was the young man's emphatic reply.

"When do I begin?"

* * *

Never before had Richards felt so alone, been so physically exhausted, so mentally depleted. It was if someone had pulled the plug on him and all of his energy had gone down the drain. Thinking back, it had only been three weeks since he had signed up to be Mr.

Piankoff's potential backup in the field. In retrospect that frivolous act of pen and paper had progressively led to this. Fortunately, Richards had been blessed with a well-conditioned body, a disciplined mind, and a strong sense of self and self-preservation. All of these well-engrained attributes had prepared him for what he was going through right now, to a point.

After experiencing a physical that a NASA astronaut might undergo, a battery of inoculations that transformed his two arms and both buttock cheeks into a mass of welts, aches, and pains, he began the physical conditioning evaluations.

These were followed by a trip to Fort Benning, Georgia, and a two-week crash course at its Ranger jump school. That experience had transformed his body into an absolute rock, several pounds lighter despite the additional muscle mass, with four jumps under his belt, and his silver snow cone jump wings fresh, unworn, and still in their velvet carrying case. Richards had picked up at Ranger school other skills as well, skills more directly connected with self-preservation. Skills that if were ever described in the polite company of university academics would no doubt reduce them to puking, fainting, gelatinous masses.

Mr. Piankoff had read the preliminary progress reports and had to admit to himself that his young charge had all the needed stubbornness of a terrier, and now was a potentially dangerous one as well. But wire garroting dummies and watermelons is one thing, killing a live human being was quite another. Regardless, the kid had done very well within the structured environment of the military post.

Now Richards found himself back on campus at the Philology Annex. What Mr. Piankoff wondered was how would Richards perform on his own within a totally alien and unstructured environment? That was the question that truly nagged at the Russian.

Ensconced in one of the Annex's language labs on the secure second sublevel, Richards was trying to get used to learning while sleeping. The technique was first developed back in the 1950s. Back then, the idea was first to fall asleep and listen to taped material, which after a lengthy acclimation period would then be absorbed by the subconscious. But now, assisted by a neurological enhancement drug, Richards found that his recall was exponentially growing with every dosage.

His language lesson tapes turned out to be of Piankoff himself, who was rattling off conversational late Eighteenth Dynasty Egyptian, complete down to its southern dialect of Thebes. To appreciate the challenge Richards was tasked with, is to recognize that Egyptian is a long dead language, one that can only be provisionally vocalized by modern specialists in the field. This uncertainty becomes clear to the layman when one realizes that this language is expressed only as a consonantal skeleton written without vowels or accents. On top of that, Coptic, its most recent philological cousin, ceased as a written language by the eleventh century AD. Consequently, what the ancient Egyptian language of the late Eighteenth Dynasty, of about 1350 BC, sounded like, is at best an educated guess. But Piankoff had lived it and now Richards was learning it.

Three days ago Richards could hardly make heads or tails of the words and grammar being used. But today, he was already picking up Piankoff's use of tonal emphasis, enjoying some of the puns that Piankoff had inserted, and that Egyptian language so delighted in.

Although invigorating in terms of sheer progress and personal satisfaction, the entire process was downright intellectually draining. And now sleep had become grueling work as well. More to the point, Richards was now itching for a conversation partner to sharpen his conscious skills, to exercise, and build his vocabulary. Unbeknownst to Richards, that precise desire was about to happen, for Mr. Piankoff was convinced that he was ready to undertake his last and final test.

Typical of the Russian field operative, he decided to introduce Richards to his final exam while he slept, since his last dinner had been spiked with a sedative.

Mr. Piankoff's devious scheme was purposeful: to place this green field operative in a free-form, unstructured, and potentially dangerous situation as possible, where he could test Richards' resourcefulness and assess his crash, immersion language training.

Initially, Mr. Piankoff had intended to fly Richards out to Horizon Pass and use the Soap Bubble on this purely training exercise. But that ambitious plan was vehemently vetoed by both of the American and Russian oversight committees citing Section 5 of the *RUTI* that the risk involved was just too great for such a green recruit. Fully vexed with the decision of these weak-kneed academicians, Piankoff had to quickly shift gears and so he came up with another scenario for the American, a very ancient one, seduction.

Allowing Richards to sleep off most of the sedative, he first placed within him a subliminal suggestion to mind his secrets, keep his mouth shut, and to speak only in his newly acquired language. Next, the Russian placed Richards in Ms. Kelly's care with orders to do her best to get him to speak in English, to get him to talk about his training, his visit to Benning, in essence, to break his cover.

As Richards slowly began to come to, he found himself totally naked, on his back, in a strangely soft bed that smelled of fresh sheets and a woman's light and airy perfume. He thought that he could sense another person next to him, because he could feel a source of heat. But through the disorienting drug haze of semi-consciousness, all that Richards could focus upon was he was on the receiving end of some seriously tender and delirious affection. All he could do was moan and roll his head from side to side in a giddy, half-conscious, dream-like state as his arms and legs would just not respond.

Wow, what a vivid dream!

Then, just as he felt his body ready to spasm, his privates were bathed in a cold wetness. Then, just as that sensation was about to hurt, the warm and unbridled process began again. For what seemed an undeterminable period of time, all that Richards could remember and feel was this curious cycle of near total ecstasy and slowly chilling pain. Suddenly from his lips came nearly unconscious words begging for final release, begging in the ancient tongue and idiom of his newly acquired late Eighteenth Dynasty Egyptian.

All during this rather bizarre ordeal, Mr. Piankoff had had the room wired and under video surveillance from several points of view. The Russian knew that Ms. Kelly knew she was on camera, on stage. He also knew she quite liked the idea and was getting off on that fact as well. Without question he was positive the presence of the video equipment was improving her performance.

But when Richards began begging in Egyptian Piankoff was more than stunned. His use of imagery, mythic relationships, even his grammar, was incredibly true to life, and he knew that first hand.

"What a sexual poet this American jock is!" he whispered. "Imagine beseeching Isis to allow him release as if he were her dead husband Osiris! Pity that Ms. Kelly doesn't have a clue as to what he is saying."

To his surprise, however, Ms. Kelly's instincts were quite attuned to the true meaning of Richards' plea, for on the next hot therapy cycle she finally granted him what he had been begging for. As for Richards, his pent-up energies, once released, knocked him out. As he drifted toward a much-deserved, natural sleep, Ms. Kelly leaned over close to his ear and whispered her own subliminal implant that the microphones could not pick up.

*　　*　　*

Following his "interview" with Ms. Kelly, Richards was moved back to his assigned training quarters, where for the next eight hours he slept off the sedatives. During that time, the Philology Annex's house physician looked in on him no less than four times. His diagnosis: physical and mental exhaustion exacerbated by dehydration.

When Richards finally awoke, his entire body was stiff and wracked as if he had just finished a bruising football game. His mouth was parched and felt his lips with his tongue half expecting them to be cracked. Sitting up in bed he was greeted with mild vertigo, but nonetheless felt an urge to relieve himself. Upon staggering up out of bed and twice catching his balance, he finally made it to his private john. While urinating through a strangely sore and seemingly chapped member, Richards began to wonder what day it was, was the dream real, and shook his head. He then noticed the druggy after-haze, the strange aftertaste in his mouth, which felt and tasted much the same as when he was in the recovery room after he had had his appendix out.

So that's it! He thought.
That was no dream!
It was all real!

Next, while standing in a hot shower, he began slowly and methodically to piece together what most likely had happened to him.

Let's see. The last thing that I remember was eating dinner.

And that thought was immediately answered by his vigorously growling stomach, which when he looked down was concave.

That means, he reasoned by stomach time, *that I must have last eaten between five to twenty hours ago.*

That's when I was drugged.

Looking at his watch, he received partial confirmation.

Four-thirty p.m., I have almost lost one day, almost twenty-two hours.

And then it hit him like a ton of bricks.

Piankoff! That bastard!

With the thought of Piankoff's name, and the outrage of what he had done to him, the sheer violation of it, Richards cruelly turned on the cold water and stood there until he felt his self control begin to return.

Stepping out of the shower stall now fully alert and as hungry as a bear, Richards quickly shaved, again noting the length of his beard's stubble, as if he needed any further confirmation of his lost time, got dressed, and went out to find something to eat.

No sooner had he opened his small apartment's door, Mr. Piankoff arrived walking up with two still steaming hot pizza boxes and a six pack of cold beer under his arm. With both of his hands so occupied, Richards did not even give him the chance to smile. Nor could he pass up the opportunity either and slugged the Russian square in the face, dropping the crack field operative like a sack of potatoes. Carefully closing and locking the door to his flat behind him, Richards then gingerly stepped over the unconscious body, amid the fallen carnage of pizza and beer, and went out in search of someplace to feed his face.

While walking toward the main campus mess hall, Richards found himself unconsciously walking past the brown stone building of the Philology Annex. On a whim, or perhaps a vaguely remembered implanted whisper, and despite the afternoon hour and his brutal hunger, he took a chance. He bounded up the cement stairs and entered the front office. There, just as he had hoped, was the splendid Ms. Kelly working at her desk. With a sly and knowing grin on his face, he walked right up to and then around her desk. He whispered into her left ear a certain remembered endearing phrase. That earned him first a devastating smile, a home cooked meal, and then much, much more.

Chapter XX
Maturation of a God

On his fifth birthday, young Neferkheperure had prepared a royal surprise for his parents. The gift was a secret and no one had any foreknowledge of what it was, not even pharaoh himself. Despite all the machinations of the king, the queen, his nosy sisters, and snooping of the harem, the young prince had succeeded in keeping something from pharaoh, something that entire nations had failed to do.

In truth, he had not been alone in this enterprise, for a bright acolyte of the Great God Amen Re, a certain Meryptah, had assisted him in ways that only a surrogate big brother and partner-in-crime could. These salt and pepper twins were virtually inseparable. Meryptah, the older by five years, was tall, lean, strong, and possessed a hungry look that was only emphasized by his sharp, clear, and bright eyes. On the other hand, young Neferkheperure, lean as well, was more graceful in his bodily proportions with narrower shoulders and a tendency to be broader at the hip. His countenance, however, was truly exotic with slightly slanted and oversized almond-shaped eyes of great depth and emotion. His lips, and ears too for that matter, seemed overly large. Rounding out the picture was the prince's prepubescent jaw line that seemed too elongated. But no one seemed to notice. After all, he was just a growing boy in an awkward stage, even if a royal one at that.

Needless to say the surprise project was theirs alone and Meryptah's knowledge of the secret recesses, dusty nooks, and many crannies of the Great Temple's complex was seemingly endless. They had plenty of places to hide it from the king's many eyes. In the temple's woodworking shop, the two had constructed the gift, and now it was time to reveal it.

To the dismay of the royal court, young Neferkheperure refused to reveal his birthday surprise in public, insisting on an audience with his two parents—alone. Such a request, delivered more as a decree, from someone so young was in itself cause for pause. Ever since the prince could talk and walk, he had always been an exception to the rule. Not that he was a bad child, or an overly precocious child. He just approached and did things in a surprisingly adult, almost informed manner. And, having rightly calculated that his father and mother would be intrigued with what he and his friend had constructed, little Neferkheperure was granted his wish.

With a strangely shaped object wrapped in fine white linen, pilfered from the textile stores of the temple, the little prince proudly marched into the royal throne room, which was remarkably quiet, owing to the total absence of the court. Immediate family members, bureaucrats, servants, fan-bearers, and even the palace's Nubian Medjay guards had been dismissed.

It was a curious moment in several ways. Here was the most powerful man of Egypt and his queen, held hostage by their curiosity and captivated by their youngest son's sense of drama. They patiently waited for the presentation. Their son, with a dignified and courtly face, diverted eyes, and stiff demeanor, quietly padded his way across the long and broad ceremonial chamber.

Upon reaching the customary distance of foreign dignitaries and ambassadors, young Neferkheperure gently put down his wrapped gift on the floor, prostrated himself before the royal pair, and announced to the highly polished limestone flooring.

"I offer myself as a sacrifice before the Living God and Mistress of the Two Lands."

"What do you, a mere insignificant mortal, wish to say to Us?" His father ritualistically intoned.

"I, an unworthy wretch, merely wish to present a most unique gift to the Living God and his Mistress."

"Hmmm, this had better be a truly unique gift, for We are not accustomed to waiting. You may rise and make your presentation to Us."

With those words from his father, the prince slowly got to his feet and noticed the light layer of fine floor dust that coated his boyish stomach and chest. He then picked up his gift and slowly unwrapped it, but in such a way that the royal pair could not see it. Then, surreptitiously peeking up from behind the linen wrapping to properly judge the twenty-five feet or so between himself and his elevated and seated royal parents, Neferkheperure quite literally threw his gift directly at them!

His father's reaction was immediate and predictable. He stood up and moved in front of his queen in an attempt to block the sailing missile from harming her. All Tiye could do in the moment allotted was put her hand up over her mouth in shock. Instantaneous anger flared in the pharaoh's eyes and his personal dagger was already drawn, his practiced and seasoned warrior instincts having come out in full strength. But all for naught and for no need.

For Neferkheperure's gift did not continue to sail directly at the pair, but began a slow and lazy banking glide to the right that continued around the entire breath of the throne room only to return and gently settle directly before the first step of the royal dais.

To the royal pair, eyes bulging and mouths agape, this feat seemed to be a miracle. To Neferkheperure, the perfect 360-degree flight around the chamber and perfect landing before his parents was a testament to his prior practice and careful, secret measurements of the throne room.

After a silent moment, the king took one step forward toward the gift, which to him looked like a wooden model of a falcon complete with its painted beaked head. His wife, now standing behind him, peeked around to catch a glimpse of the object before them. Then, looking up into the broad and infectious grin of his youngest son, Nebmare choked out,

"What manner of toy is this? Or my audacious son, what manner of weapon?"

Thinking carefully before replying, Neferkheperure was inwardly pleased that his father had not chosen to use the word *hekaw*–magic.

"My father it is only a gift, but as you have seen, it is a very special one befitting a secret and private audience of the living guardian of Egypt. To answer your question directly, yes, this model is only a mere toy. To answer your question in another way, at least potentially, this toy could also represent a most powerful weapon."

Listening to his son's reasoned words, truly words of counsel, and from a five-year-old at that, made the king pause a moment and reconsider his son in an entirely new light. Then, he bent down and gently picked up the light wooden falcon glider. Cradling it in his once callused hands, he weighed it, noted the fine craftsmanship of its streamlined form, and carefully studied each of its three-palm-width wings, and its curiously oriented vertical tail.

Stumped, he then asked, "Well, my ingenious son, tell us how this wooden falcon toy of yours flies so gracefully."

For the next two or so hours, only the gleeful sounds of surprise, laughter, and merriment could be heard booming from the royal throne room. To say the royal court felt left out of all the fun would be an understatement. Clearly, young Neferkheperure's gift had been a success, but what was it, and why were the royal couple so enjoying themselves? Rumor and speculation went rampant. Despite all of their best efforts, those with their ears pressed tightly to that chamber's doors did not have a clue.

*   *   *

Beginning with that fifth birthday, Neferkheperure had made it a point for the next several years to present a special gift to his now-doting parents. His initial decision to make his presentations private had been a stroke of brilliance that even he, now in his majority, was just beginning to comprehend.

On his sixth birthday, the prince presented his parents with a hand-ground, clear white optical reading lens. Once demonstrated, this immediately delighted his father's aging eyes as he could again read the finely written cursive transcriptions that were taken during all meetings with foreign dignitaries and administration officials. No longer did he have to rely on the scribe's oral reading of them. Nor did he have to suspect the scribe's accuracy either. As for his mother, she quickly learned how to focus a beam of sun light to a candlewick to set it ablaze. The first time that Neferkheperure had demonstrated this feat before his parents, both he and his father had traded a dark and meaningful glance that his mother thankfully never saw.

On his seventh birthday, Neferkheperure again made his parents a gift of wood. It was a curious cylindrical object about three feet long with a deep and continuous groove carved throughout its length made deeper with an attached fin or wall that followed its course. At the end of this curious looking contraption was attached a handle crank so the cylinder could be easily turned.

After placing it before the royal pair and standing back, Neferkheperure said not a word of the object's function. Staring down upon it, it was his mother who was the first to grasp its function.

"My clever son, can water pass along that continuous groove?"

"Yes, my mother."

"And the handle at the end, by turning the whole, will your wooden device carry and lift water as well?"

"Yes, my mother."

Still his father was mystified by the gift and now was further confused by the meaning of his wife and son's conversation.

His patience spent, Nebmare said, "My son, can you demonstrate this, this thing's purpose for me, for I cannot follow the cleverness of your mother's mind."

So abruptly did the double-doored gates of the throne room suddenly open. The courtiers, who were attempting to listen in, scattered like dust motes. Neferkheperure then led his parents and the others to the reflection pool of the main courtyard. There he placed the unhandled end of the cylinder into the pool and rested the cylinder itself against an inner corner. Then he began to slowly turn the cylinder with his two thinly muscled arms. To the amazement of his father, the gleeful confirmation of his mother, and the total astonishment of those in audience, little Neferkheperure began to draw up and out the pool's water along the slowly turning groove. When it reached its end, the water dumped carelessly onto the courtyard's pavement stones.

As the young lad turned the cylinder faster, the faster the water was drawn. Quite literally before their very eyes, the level of the reflecting pool was being diminished by one child's efforts. Egypt, a hydro-agrarian civilization, had just witnessed a demonstration of what would later be called an Archimedes Screw. The ramifications of what the pharaoh saw were virtually endless and all he could do was slowly shake his head in awe at this hydraulic lifting demonstration.

On his eighth birthday, the prince's presentation took place in one of the many outer, but secluded, courtyards of the palace. As his father and mother sat in the comfortable shade of a flowering acacia tree, Neferkheperure strode forward leading one of the king's prize chariot horses. The horse in question, and a very spirited one at that the king noted, was nonetheless remarkably docile in the young boy's sure hands. He was impressed already. As he neared the pair seated under the tree, Neferkheperure abruptly turned the horse, exposing its right flank. It was then that the king saw for the first time a rather peculiar leather appliance with appendages hanging down and belted around the horse's girth.

With a broad grin that his parents had long ago learned was one of genuine pride of accomplishment, Neferkheperure placed his foot in a bronze ring at the end of one of the lose hanging appendages, gripped a convenient handhold on the side of the leather appliance, and then leaped onto the horse's back. With the transfer of weight, the horse reared up on it hind legs. Again the pharaoh feared not for himself, but for his queen who he shielded with his body, and then also for his young son. But again, as before, he had acted instinctively but in vain, as the horse immediately settled down, but now with his son on its back, who was riding around before him with his arms freely swinging in the air. Goggle-eyed, the king saw his son then turn the horse around without using his hands.

Then a young temple acolyte appeared who was carrying several chariot javelins, a bow, a quiver of arrows, and a bronze chariot sickle. Riding over to him, Neferkheperure took a javelin, charged the horse toward one of the mature acacia trees in the courtyard, and promptly split its trunk on his first cast! Returning to the acolyte, Neferkheperure now took the bow with an arrow already strung. He then charged the already damaged tree and embedded the arrow a full half of its shaft's length through the tree's trunk. Returning again to what his parents now realized was their son's grinning partner-in-crime, Meryptah, Neferkheperure finally took the bronze sickle, a deadly, heavily weighted chariot weapon. Again charging the acacia, the king and queen of Egypt now witnessed the total destruction of an entire tree by a scrawny eight-year-old wielding a sun-glinting blur.

Having had enough, Neferkheperure wheeled the horse around and dismounted before them. To the king, his son's point had been very clearly made. For Egypt, the saddle and stirrup had been born, but now it was up to Egypt to take advantage of it.

On his ninth birthday, the royal pair was given a genuine article of war, a sword. Unlike the king's own heavy bronze chariot sickle that was curved inward to form a half crescent, this one possessed a long double-gripped ivory pummel with lanyard and a straight, flat backed shank fronted by a slightly curved blade edge. Its color was odd as well, being highly polished with a color like that of the moon reflecting on smooth water. When asked what was special about this gift, Neferkheperure asked his assistant Meryptah to throw a fine linen cloth high into the air. As it gently blossomed open and began to slowly flutter down the young boy took three swipes at it with the sword, each time apparently missing it. At seeing his errant swings, the king said chuckling.

"My youngest lion, I think that the sword is too much for you. You swung three times and missed as many."

Unruffled, the youngster replied with a confidence that challenged his father, "If I have my father, then, pick up the linen."

Angered with his disrespectful demeanor, the king strode briskly down from the raised dais and tugged at the linen, which fell apart as it was cleanly cut into three uneven sections. The shock on his face was total. His mother's face was ashen.

Then Neferkheperure chose to push his advantage.

"Not only does this gift I made for you cut finer than any bronze razor found in Egypt, but it can shatter your bronze chariot sickle with one swing."

The king could only shake his head, so visibly stunned by such bravado from one so young. Returning to his wife's side, the monarch dragged a remnant of the sectioned linen in one hand. As he sat down with a thump, he said, "My son, just how invincible is that sword?"

"My father, you already know the answer to that question. He who wields it."

On his tenth birthday, Neferkheperure announced to his parents that he did not have a present for them. This was a great disappointment. While the royal pair tried to take it in stride, they were succeeding poorly. After all, had not their young son already invented enough? Were not the irrigation fields already being expanded? Was not the king's own nascent cavalry and Medjay royal bodyguard the best armed? Were not several other inventions being perfected under his son's direction and in total secrecy?

In fact throughout his young formative years, Nebmare was immensely impressed with his young son in more ways than one. For example, he was thankful that his youngest was blessed with the intelligence to recognize that some things were not destined for immediate public consumption. More than that, each gift that his son chose to give clearly could be used either for man's benefit or folly. This double-sided nature of Neferkheperure's gifts troubled the king, something that nagged at him, something that raised his hackles. The feeling was just like a dangerous predator that one sees only as a flickering shadow from the corner of one's eye. At times his youngest son could be very genuine, but at others, he had a calculating, cool temper, and strangeness to his disposition that defied explanation. In the end, the king decided to spend more time with his youngest son in order to observe, to either confirm his darkest fears or dispel them. His mother, on the other hand, blind to her husband's concerns, just could not believe the breadth and depth of her son's interests and his sheer creative genius.

"Where do you find such novel ideas?" she would say.

As for his siblings, Neferkheperure's quiet influence, intellectual superiority, and pride of place were made obvious with every passing year. His once dominating and spiteful older sister, Sitamen, now quietly accepted him as an equal. His older brother, Thutmose, long removed from Thebes and now resident as the chief priest of the god Ptah in Memphis, looked on the doings of his younger brother with genuine interest and joy.

As for the royal court, they were in a constant state of turmoil about the young prince. The rumors ranged from the use of black magic granted by evil god Set to the divine inspiration of Great God Amen Re. But most cruelly of all, the court noted that the king's second son never did grow out of his adolescent, ugly stage. If anything, as he matured Neferkheperure had grown more angular in his features, trending toward an uncommonly tall and lean frame with slim shoulders, a narrow waist, and broad hips. These were not the familiar characteristics of a royal dynasty blessed with stocky, well-built, and muscular warriors. The hot gossip went that the Chief Wife Tiye, after all, was a commoner of unknown bloodlines that supposedly originated in Syria. So was easily, quickly, and maliciously explained Neferkheperure's rather awkward appearance. The young royal was devastated by this abhorrence early on that manifested itself in subtle and not so subtle ways. He felt marked as a creature apart. But in time, especially as his majority neared, he knew he would prevail and that the ill-concealed snickers would finally come to an end.

Outside of his parents, only one other knew the real truth of the matter, the truly inquisitive and scientific side of Neferkheperure. That was his close friend and confidant Meryptah, the acolyte who only aspired to become a *wab*-priest, or lowly "cleaner" servant of the Great God. Neferkheperure had often wondered about his exceedingly bright and inquisitive friend, who possessed such a humble sense of place. That situation, however, changed rather suddenly and unexpectedly the day of Meryptah's initiation into the Amen Re priesthood.

As Meryptah would later recount the event to his best friend, and many others thereafter during his long life, he would always begin:

"While kneeling before the golden image of the Great God during my time of watch and guardianship, with my arms upraised in prayer, adoration, and supplication, a blinding light appeared suspended in the air. Out of it came an ivory white hand. I remember very well my silent shock. I remember equally as well my desire to accept the hand of the Great God. I grasped his strangely fingered hand with my right and gently acknowledged his gesture. The Great God, ever more powerful than I, then pulled back and for a moment my hand and wrist disappeared into his divine light.

"Then sounded a deafening crack of thunder that echoed one thousand times one thousand within the confines of the Great God's most sacred chamber. My own ears were numbed with the sound of many drums. And with the sound came a great flash of light, and a most disagreeable smell, much of which was me I later discovered. For all of my bare skin was lightly burned as if I was a burnt offering. My priestly kilt of initiation was singed and ruined. But that was not the worst of what could only be the Great God's displeasure at my weakness, for he had cleanly severed my right hand at mid-wrist. I let out a great and deafening scream and the rest,

156

Neferkheperure, I do not remember. All I do remember was awaking in the arms of the high priest of the Great God Amenemhet, himself freshly aroused from sleep, as he had not properly applied his eyes or his priestly vestments, wearing a mere household kilt.

"I am told that I was quite a sight when first discovered. Lying sprawled before the Great God's golden image, a cloud of burnt smoke hung in the air above me as if the Great God had provided a cloud in which to shade my injured body. My face, chest, and arms were red and blistered. But it was my right hand, or rather, its absence, which evoked the most attention. It was removed as cleanly as if a man drew a line in the sand. The court physicians were mystified, for there was no blood, just my seared closed stump.

"As for myself, as I now gaze down upon it, I remember no immediate pain, just the mental ache of fingers long lost—the agonizing memory of fingers that do not obey their master. When asked what had occurred, all I could mumble was that the Great God had presented me with a gift that I was not strong enough to accept."

From that moment forward, Meryptah's life had changed forever. For the high priest commanded that he was to succeed him.

Meryptah, now recently elevated to the highest station attainable within the priesthood of Amen Re, still remained quite close to the royal heir apparent. After long chariot rides out into the Western Desert, the pair would pitch a tent, sit in its shade, and discuss at length and in total secrecy, the latest and greatest scheme of invention, philosophical item of controversy, or theoretical mystery.

For both Meryptah and Neferkheperure, such unbridled moments were fast becoming too infrequent. The daily responsibilities of each were building to such an extent as to preclude their continued collaboration. For the now high priest of Amen Re, literally "the god's first servant," it had been an exhilarating intellectual ride, filled with wonder, adventure, satisfaction, and hair-raising moments. For the royal heir apparent, he was soon to lose not a true friend, but also the only sharp and truly empirical mind among this horde of what he had come to know as intellectually stunted and superstitious primitives.

Despite recognizing what the future held, each skirted and refused to discuss their past remember when's. Instead, each spoke only future projects, made arrangements for the next meeting, and considered what next to discuss. In another place, another time, each would have held chaired academic faculty positions at a prestigious research institution, but such was not their lot.

Finally, Neferkheperure held inner suspicions about how Meryptah had lost his hand. As a result, even though it was well over a decade ago, Neferkheperure sensed his time as an observer was fast running out. He intuitively knew that someone or something was on his trail, tracking him. If he was to make the needed and necessary impacts upon this world, the young royal knew that henceforth he would have to watch carefully and act swiftly.

Chapter XXI

AD 2001. Russian Academy of Science

Once again the three men met in the hermetically sealed vault of the Russian Academy of Sciences complex. This time the first speaker, Vasily Ostrogorsky, began the discussion.

"I understand the Americans have listened to our concerns, are willing to deploy the Soap Bubble, and are in near agreement about the securing of a genetic sample. I say 'near' agreement because they insist on sending along one of their own with Colonel Piankoff on the mission."

Listening to this, the balding and ancient third speaker, Nikolai Fedorov, the Director of Advanced and Theoretical Technological Research, exploded.

"This is ludicrous! No, it's fucking insane. Those Americans think they can do anything, anytime, anyhow, to anyone. Don't ever forget, they stole our technology as well! Now they wish to supplant our own field agent!"

Temporizing as one would a spoiled child, the first speaker said, "Now Nikolai, from what I have heard about this American field operative, and of course I use the term loosely, I suspect that at the first opportunity Colonel Piankoff will feed his still warm and living parts to a Nile crocodile. So not to worry, I can assure you that he will be removed from the scene at an appropriate time."

At this intriguing tidbit of gossip, the second speaker, Karlov Drazinzka, the Head of Special Projects, could not resist the temptation.

"Please excuse me Vasily, but I am an old man. Could you expand on this American? I know the Colonel well, and anyone who crosses him is usually embraced by mother earth. I have to know, who is this American?"

"Well, Karlov, from what I can tell from the Colonel's reports, he is an adequate linguist. He successfully attended a two-week Ranger course at Fort Benning, and he is a former American college football player. That is all I know about him."

Karlov, leaning back into his chair could not help but smile.

"My dear Vasily, I believe that the Colonel has finally met an alpha male who is capable of challenging him both intellectually and physically. Consider. The grade of 'adequate linguist' is high praise from Piankoff. Let us not forget who his grandfather was, *the* Alexandre Piankoff, a phenomenal Egyptologist in his own right! Adequate indeed! As for the Ranger short course at Fort Benning, one's mere survival is the only requirement necessary to pass. He accomplished that in two weeks no less! And an American football hero to boot. By my estimate, I believe that the Americans have chosen well."

Vasily, really trying to move the meeting along, "Ah yes, thank you Karlov, for that enlightening off the cuff, third hand, and snap analysis of the American operative whom you have never met. But as we discussed before, no matter how good he is, that American must be conveniently eliminated. Nikolai is absolutely correct. We cannot allow the Americans to possess both the Soap Bubble and a qualified temporal field agent. That would upset the delicate balance of things. It would also seriously endanger our presence in the field. Besides, Piankoff understands our position, long term plans, and is in agreement with them. But I really do believe that we have far more important things to discuss than taking sides on whom, is going to gut whom, first."

To this gentle nudge, Karlov could only offer a wry smile and a nod of understanding.

Continuing Vasily said, "Gentlemen, I have news that the team, such as it is, of our Colonel Piankoff and the American football hero, is due to depart on the mission," studying his watch, "well, right about now. The needed clearances from the Egyptian Antiquities Service have been granted via the good offices of one of our Polish allies, a certain Professor Jerzy Jannicka."

"May that American rot in hell."

Was all that Fedorov could sourly muster.

Then Karlov cleared his throat in preamble. "My dear colleagues, do we ever intend to share with the Americans our preliminary results of the Anatol Project or the Norsk Report?"

Nikolai quickly answered for them all. "No, under no circumstances."

Vasily spoke, "I am very sorry, gentlemen, but we must, and in fact we already have. Those results were the currency that paid for the use of the Soap Bubble. The Americans, despite what your hearts believe, are empiricists too."

Karlov just nodded in understanding and said softly. "*Quid pro quo.*"

"Precisely."

Fedorov steamed.

Vasily merely sighed in resignation and relief that this sensitive meeting had finally come to an end without bloodshed.

Chapter XXII

Year 38 of Nebmare Amenhotep

It was a magnificent sunrise and the sheer three hundred-foot limestone cliffs below glowed a warm rosy red. Atop those cliffs stiffly stood the purified and shaven High Priest of Amen Re, himself colored pink by the sun's early morning rays that reflected on his brilliant white, starched linen kilt. With his arms crossed upon his once proudly muscled chest, Meryptah looked down past the exposed navel of his sagging, middle aged stomach. To his left, between his golden sandaled feet, he saw the fluttering and sun-faded banners adorning the three-terraced mortuary temple of the beloved Osiris Makare Hatshepsut's many colonnades. The branches of the fragrant myrrh trees that flanked the processional way to the ramp of the first terrace swayed gently in the early morning breeze. In fact, Meryptah thought he caught a brief whiff of their delicate sweetness from this height. To his right stood the modest but still magnificent limestone colonnade and pyramid of the long dead Osiris Nebhepetre Mentuhotep. Immediately before him, rising from the cliff's base like the primeval mound of Atum, stood the massive terrace of Osiris Menkheperre Thutmose. Banners too fluttered from here as well, fresh and unfaded ones. And well they should, for his priesthood had benefited greatly from the generosity of that great god during his reign.

From this lofty vantage point with the tips of his well-trimmed toes near the cliff's edge, the aging priest's mind easily drifted off to a far, far simpler time. He imagined again what it had been like to soar upon the gentle updrafts of just such an early dawn breeze. Remembering back with pride to his youthful days as an acolyte of Amen Re, when he had been the first to soar from this very spot, part wearing, part carrying, the first bulky falcon gliding frame. How his co-builder and boyhood friend Neferkheperure had encouraged him, helped to stoke his nerve. He harkened back to the absolute terror of stepping off the edge. How he had shamefully soiled himself as he rigidly steeled himself during his initial dive. How he cried tears to Amen Re when the frame's linen wings had finally taken hold of the wind and he began to soar as had all the many weighted gliding models before this first manned flight. How absolutely alive he had felt upon his first landing, badly skinning both his elbows and knees.

That first gliding flight, millennia before Kitty Hawk's, had been only the beginning. Subsequent soaring flights led to a natural progression of structural improvements. Well-lacquered linen, it was quickly discovered, captured more air, improved soaring characteristics, and increased the glider's speed. Once so coated, it was a short step to entirely adorn the glider's undersides with the brightly colored, outstretched wings of a falcon, to even place upon the glider pilot's head a wind-cheating, hawk-headed helmet.

Since his youth, glider soaring was now possible farther and farther away from the cliff's updrafts, to actually flirt with the limits of the thermals themselves. Hard experience too had taught him many lessons, but then again soaring heights also increased and seemed to have no limit.

Shaking his freshly-shaved and wax polished head, Meryptah could not believe what the Great God had allowed him, a mere mortal, to accomplish during his life. How hard he had worked, all the personal sacrifices that he had made to stand here now, as high priest, awaiting the arrival of the burial procession of the newly-created Osiris Nebmare Amenhotep.

Behind Meryptah stood four subordinates and one glider pilot, but other than that, they remained similarly clad and shaven priests. The four were holding a fully-prepped glider between them. All the pilot had to do was bend over at the waist, tie in, and step off the edge. As for the glider acolyte standing there with them, he was young, wiry, well-muscled, and resplendently half-painted, half-clothed in a form-fitting linen falcon suit. With his black and golden painted hawk helmet resting in the crook of his right arm, the priest wore a serious face, for he was to glide today for the new Osiris. His flight had to be well-timed in order to coincide with the ritual release of the dead pharaoh's *ba*, the bird-like soul with a human head, which would then join with the divine Horus and soar together to the West. There could be no room for error. Thousands would witness his flight. Thousands had to be convinced that he was indeed the divine Horus. The pilot would do his absolute best or die in the attempt.

While all of these nervous flight preparations were taking place behind Meryptah, his thoughts again began to drift back to his first glider flight.

That one had been over a decade ago and it had been indeed a grand moment. Those wind conditions were very similar to these this morning.

Musing, he thought. *Perhaps, if this young falcon lives long enough, I will make him my successor as well. Time will tell.*

Again thinking, Meryptah suddenly had a desire to soar again, to show this young pup of a lion how to truly fly. But, as with so many things, all Meryptah had to do was look down upon his aging and scarred body. Then there was the issue of his missing right hand. No falcon glider could ever be controlled with only one hand. How that traumatic realization had truly brought back a sudden flood of emotions!

There I was within the Great God's most holy of holies. A barely initiated wab-priest, praying, and guarding that most awesome of divinities. And my prayers were answered by the Great God himself!

As tears of remembered rapture streamed down Meryptah's cheeks, he recounted the dear price that he had paid for the Great God's notice—his right hand.

An apologetic clearing of a throat then roused Meryptah from his reveries. Turning around to face the courteous source, the glider pilot, he heard, "Great One, I await your command. I am prepared to soar and led West the *ba* of the new Osiris."

Abruptly turning around again, Meryptah looked out into the valley and was amazed how far the funerary procession of the Osiris Nebmare Amenhotep had advanced, the audible murmur of their passage, and parenthetically, was troubled by how long he had been daydreaming.

For the glider pilot's part, he thought the venerable high priest and first falcon glider was going to tumble over the cliff's very edge at any moment, so deep was he in his teary-eyed and pious rapture of prayer.

CHAPTER XXIII

Horizon Pass

The Gulf Stream V flight from Chicago to New Mexico was Richards' first visit to that southwestern Sun State of the Union. As a graduation hazing of sorts, Richards sported a freshly shaven head. As for Piankoff, who sported a fading Class-A black and blue shiner on his left eye, this trip marked his sixth visit to the home state of the Soap Bubble. As for the flight itself, even though the departure took place from the military side of O'Hare International Airport, its flight log would never see the light of day, for its final destination did not officially exist.

Quiet and remote Holloman Air Force Base is located about ten miles as the crow flies sort of west of the New Mexican town of Alamogordo. White Sands, where the Soap Bubble Project was first established, officially and publicly closed down lock, stock, and barrel years ago. Now, only tumbleweeds and tarantulas roam its deserted streets, wooden shacks, and sand blasted Quonset huts. These known facts hardly could refute that an extremely low profile, high-security installation did in fact still exist somewhere in the region. But where, nobody knew, and frankly, nobody cared to mess with the federal powers to be in order to find out. Besides, the territory itself was just too vast, wide open, desolate, rugged, and forbidding.

Although the Gulf Stream would indeed land, refuel, depart from the Holloman, and return to O'Hare, its passengers did not. Nor did they dawdle at the base. Instead, their awaiting Sikorsky H-60 Black Hawk helicopter and its departure from the base could only be described as having headed sort of northwest and toward the setting sun, deep desert, and its backlit, scrub covered mountain range. Its flight record would be described as sort of north and through the vast desert flats of the White Sands Missile Range, sort of south of Lumley Lake, and heading sort of toward the foothills of Strawberry Peak trending in the general direction of the desert metropolis of Truth or Consequences.

Just as the Manhattan Project had once provided a dramatic cover for the early Soap Bubble research project, so also did the notoriety of Arizona's Area 51 successfully obscure any hint that may have led to this remote installation. The name of Soap Bubble's new home and development facilities, Horizon Pass, was Dr. Peter Borov's own. This energetic and youthful-minded engineer and theoretician, now an octogenarian, had created the name as none other than an obvious reference and tribute to the capabilities of the Soap Bubble itself.

As the helicopter zoomed on a WNW beeline of 290 degrees into the late afternoon sun, Richards was first dulled by the sameness of the vacant desert flats. But as those flats began to give way to foothills, he became mesmerized by the rugged beauty and surprising colorfulness of the rising terrain of this southwestern desert. Skimming just south of Strawberry Peak, the chopper rose and fell as it followed the hills and contours of Parson Canyon. Such flying gave Richards the sense of what it might be like as a raptor soaring on the thermals looking for its next scurrying prey. Then, as the canyon opened up at what is locally called Sulphur Pass, Richards became aware of a curious split-fingered rock outcropping surrounded by stands of brush, yucca, and stunted pine that the chopper seemed to be heading toward.

Richards thought. *Trees. Vegetation. That must mean water. There's most likely a natural spring associated with those rocks ahead.*

As the helicopter neared the outcropping, Richards, remembering his brief military training, scanned about trying to find anything that might suggest logistical support: an old rail spur, a dirt road, anything, and was rewarded when he noticed a rough jeep trail partly hidden in the brush and in the natural shade of a low ridgeline that obscured it from above.

That was clever. It probably would not be seen by satellite.

* * *

During the silence of the ride in from the base, Piankoff took in his surroundings, by choosing to observe Richards' every move and note his reactions.

Yes, he mused. *This young lion will do very well. He no doubt noted the local greening effect of Horse Camp Spring and has even spotted the maintenance truck trail for the compound.*

Very good. Very good indeed. What a pity that such young talent must be eventually wasted.

Then the chopper, still flying hell bent for election, suddenly slowed, flared, and began to descend over a dimly lit, cement helicopter pad that had seemed to magically appear out of the shadows of the nearby outcropping. With a jarring jolt they were on the ground. Glancing at his watch, Richards noted that the entire trip from O'Hare to touchdown was about four-and-a-half hours. The chopper segment itself had been a mere breath-taking, fourteen-minute roller coaster ride.

Jumping down from the unmarked and flat dark gray Sikorsky, the pair, bent over, ran out from under the still twirling blades as the pilot immediately throttled his collector, began his ascent, and started off for base. As the dust cleared and the sound of the chopper blades' soft *whoop whooping* faded into the distance, Richards became aware of several things. The distinctive smell of desert sage brush, the crystal clear air of the 5200 foot plus elevation, and the incongruous sight of an elderly white-haired gentleman standing in a bright yellow Nike jogging suit just outside of the pad's sand eroded yellow safety line. Walking over with Piankoff in tow, Richards introduced himself.

"Hello, I'm Joseph Richards and this is Alexander Piankoff. Who are you?"

Flashing a youthful smile full of white and perfect teeth, the elderly man merely said, "Why, young man, I know who you are. I'm the very reason why you're here," he said with mirthful and twinkling cobalt blue eyes. Extending a firm hand in greeting, "I am Dr. Peter Borov."

Drawing the young man in close and in a secretive tone, he added. "Joseph, I am most pleased to have you aboard. We really need some fresh blood around here, if you know what I mean."

Breaking away, he then turned to Piankoff who was standing nearby, nodded in respectful recognition, and simply said, "Welcome back, Colonel."

Colonel? Richards thought furiously with a wrinkled brow. *What's that all about?*

And then catching himself, Borov remarked to the Russian, "And what happened to you? Did you run into a door knob or something?"

Silence.

It didn't take much for Richards to figure out that Dr. Borov also had some misgivings about his mentor. It was something undeniable about his manner, something subliminal, verging on Freudian. But then again, who wouldn't? Richards sure had plenty.

"Well, time's a wasting. Let's quickly get inside and out of the late afternoon chill before that nosy Russian bird flies overhead."

After stealing a quick and wry glance toward Piankoff, he continued, "It's due overhead in about four minutes. Those chopper jockeys really cut your arrival too close for my liking. Let's move."

At Borov's pronouncement the elderly man then turned and broke into a surprisingly fluid and loping jog leading away from the pad.

The complex at Horizon Pass, as are the great majority of government facilities in the southwest, was a subterranean one that took advantage of the native rock formations. In many ways the complex was much like a medieval castle that used nature for its walls, battlements, keep, and towers. Its camouflaged entrance was comprised of a rickety-looking lean-to shack of weathered silver pine that backed up against a sheer two hundred-foot rock face overhang. Once inside the shack, a gray, featureless, and harden steel door greeted the visitor. The shack itself, really a sophisticated x-ray booth, scanned all who stood before the steel door's frame.

Borov just seemed to wave at the entrance and it opened broadly to accept his passage. Piankoff next stoically stood before the gray portal, waved, and it too opened for him. Then Richards stepped forward, smiled, and waved in imitation as the others had, but this time the door did not open for him. Instead, the floor dropped out from beneath him and suddenly, momentarily, he was in free fall. But his newly acquired Ranger parachute training had not been forgotten.

Before Richards could think, his body had relaxed, knees bent, and ankles locked tightly together in anticipation of a landing, which did shortly occur. Richards rolled easily onto his right side. In all the fall was about eight feet. As he regained his feet, which were mildly stung by the landing in the pea gravel pit, Richards immediately assumed a defensive posture in the total darkness while lightly coughing in the stirred up dust. Then, he was blinded by the bright light of an opening door and momentarily deafened by the roar of good-hearted cheering.

Inside, they had all seen his performance on the infrared video monitor, and it was worth a replay.

"This one is definitely a keeper," one salty security guard had decreed.

*   *   *

After hearing those words and seeing the replay, Piankoff allowed himself a brief moment of pride.

They are saying that about my assistant!

As the hidden teacher within him glowed with warm pride, he felt an unbidden tightening in his chest. Then he winced, reminding himself of their reaction when he had been so initiated by the security pit. For he had been caught totally unawares as well, had fallen poorly, badly spraining his ankle. He had emerged from the darkness of the pit madder than a hornet, nearly injuring several of the security guards before they had Tasered him into passive unconsciousness.

Walking carefully toward the light and the open portal, Richards stopped hesitantly about five feet from the threshold and asked the assembled group with a rough voice, "Well? Do you guys have another surprise?"

This challenging statement of bravado was instantly greeted with another round of cheers with a couple of "woof, woofs" mixed in as well. Sensing that everything was indeed as it should be, Richards then backed up and jumped over the remaining five feet and landed on the inside side of the doorway's threshold, clearing it by several feet to the delight of all, including Piankoff.

Wise move, he thought with approval.

At this point, Richards sensed he was becoming part of the team, a member of a fraternity. Until now, he had been unsure of his abilities. But now, having passed this obvious hazing ritual, having seen a glimpse of the resources that were behind the Philology Annex, Fort Benning, this facility, and Dr. Borov himself, well, he was sold. Football suddenly seemed far, far away and almost, in comparison, boring and too predictable.

Piankoff was the first to slap him on the shoulder, muttering softly to him in Egyptian, "Well done, my young lion. May the evil god Set himself shudder at the approach of your shadow."

It had been three days since Richards had said a word to Piankoff. During that time, he had assaulted him, defied his warning about Ms. Kelly, and generally had shunned his existence. It was only now that Richards had noticed that Piankoff was coming to him and not vice-versa. It was only now that Piankoff was treating him as an equal.

With this realization in mind, he replied in kind, in Egyptian as well. "Thank you, my teacher."

The reaction from Piankoff to this respectful and low-key response was a very simple nod of quiet acknowledgement. With it, all grudges between the two appeared to be paid in full. To be completely frank, although Piankoff would have had considerable difficulty admitting it, if Richards had not decked him outside of his flat, Piankoff could never have trusted either his innate intelligence or his physical training. For with that one punch, that one supreme moment of violent rage, Piankoff knew that Richards, when the time came, could, and would have the capacity to kill. Piankoff noted also that the blow, if it had been directed otherwise, could have easily ended his life, and he well knew it. The fact that the Russian still walked among the land of the living also told Piankoff that Richards, even if seething mad, possessed a modicum of control. In short, he concluded, his new assistant would be a formidable one.

Dr. Borov then casually strode over all smiles with his hands buried in the pockets of his baggy windbreaker.

"Gentlemen, enough of this high school high-jinx, tomorrow we begin local training, acclimatization, and technical orientation. May I suggest hot showers, a meal, and some sack time? We begin tomorrow at seven sharp. Don't disappoint me after such an auspicious beginning."

The eighty-year-old genius in quantum mechanics and engineering then turned on his heel and jogged away down a long, comfortably lit corridor, his sneakers squeaking on the highly polished painted flooring.

Richards and Piankoff, at the suggestion of a hot shower and meal both suddenly became very weary from the bone-jarring trip, not to mention somewhat disoriented by the one-hour time change, dutifully followed their escorts to their private quarters.

CHAPTER XXIV
Year 38 of Nebmare Amenhotep (Continued)

Amid a cloud of funerary incense the proud and strong Horus, Neferkheperure Amenhotep, solemnly escorted his mummified father to his final resting place in the West. The procession itself included a snaking multitude of silent, whitely-clothed priests and the sweating strong backs of the former pharaoh's Nubian Medjay bodyguards. They gladly bore his inner golden sarcophagus with a mixture of honor and sadness. The wailing of the family, the royal harem, and its hoard of children echoed off the surrounding cliffs that set up a reverberation that took on a life of its own.

Flanking the length of the procession were thousands of Egyptians who found themselves saddened and terrified at the death of their god. Their sole protector from chaos, benefactor, and personal intermediary with the universe had passed. The whole spectacle was pregnant with imagery, meaning, and emotion quite simply beyond the grasp of a modern mind.

This procession started from the king's mortuary temple on the western side of the river and then coiled its way through the fertile and golden fields of wheat, toward the dead pharaoh's tomb in the Valley of the Kings. In all, the procession stretched over two kilometers long. But before any burial could be undertaken, critical and important religious and magical rites had to be performed at that boundary between the rich mud of the living and the dry desert wastes of the dead.

From where Meryptah stood, the entire scene could be heard because of the remarkable acoustics of the cliffs beneath his feet. As he saw the end of the funerary column pass beyond the massive twin pylons of the mortuary temple and the awaiting *sem*-priests, he nodded his assent to the young falcon glider pilot.

"May you glide as the divine Horus all the way to Re himself," he piously intoned.

With that, securely tied into the glider's frame, the four priests launched the glider over the cliff. Bending down to hide their presence from those below yet peering over the edge, the five priests then held their collective breaths as the falcon pilot sharply dived to build up the necessary speed.

To Meryptah, this was always the most critical time. Too steep a dive meant death, while too shallow also meant death. And while he was proud of the young falcon flyer's courage, he nonetheless prayed for his success.

"Dear father, grant him a strong breath of wind!"

Amen Re heard him, for the falcon had begun its glide early and even now was gaining altitude, surpassing even the height of the cliffs. In mere moments the glider covered the distance between the cliffs and the mortuary temple and had begun to initiate the first of what would be seven sacred aerial circles that subliminally connoted to the Egyptian religious psyche totality, perfection, and completed unity.

To those on the ground, the arrival of the falcon glider created a highly charged religious, twitchingly fearful, and wondrous effect as to stun the senses. The reaction of the population upon seeing the glider was predictable. All stopped, gaped, and fell to the ground in silence. Put simply, for them time stopped. Only the proud and possessive Medjay stood their ground, refusing to abandon their master. Those unburdened with the pharaoh's coffin drew with a deadly hiss their razor-sharp, steel short swords forming a protective circle. Otherwise, not a sound could be heard, except for the distant braying of a blasphemous donkey. The gentle morning breeze and its buzzing insects seemed loud, boisterous, and disrespectful in the presence of such manifest divinity. All silently counted: one, two, three, four, five, six, seven.

To Meryptah, he vividly remembered this reaction when he was first seen soaring high above the fields of western Thebes one early morning. The collective intake of breath was simply deafening.

After making the proscribed seven circuits above the procession, the falcon glider then drifted off back toward the cliffs, heading West, heading toward the Land of the Dead, disappearing over the Mountains of the Dead, leading the dead king's *ba* to its final resting place. The pilot's goal was to eventually land within the Western Valley of the Kings, the final resting place for Egypt's living gods. There, a recovery group of priests would assist the exhausted pilot from his frame, assuming that he survived the impact of landing in that rocky terrain, which was always a doubtful proposition.

Once the glider was out of sight, the multitude audibly, breathed. As for the young royal successor, Neferkheperure Amenhotep, who was in attendance, he pretended to be equally taken in by this marvel, but deep inside was sickened by the entire charade.

Once I ascend the throne of blessed Isis, the Quimbly-made-flesh silently vowed, *my plans for this planet's dominant terrestrial species will finally be put into motion and, as is so oftentimes the case, things will change.*

First Egypt will change.

Then, everything will change.

But I will not change.

Chapter XXV

Horizon Pass

Early mornings in the high desert are simply breathtaking in their peacefulness, tranquility, and natural beauty. The crisp crystalline air was scented with sage and mesquite—the New Mexican sky a cloudless baby blue. For Richards, it was a revelation. Although he had read and reread all of Professor Milson's books on the ancient Egyptian's sense of religion, psychology, and the impact that ecology had had on them, it was only now that all the pieces were finally coming together.

Dr. Milson, he mused. *Just how long ago was it that we had that fateful conversation that ended with me here? Six, seven weeks max?*

At that point while still deep in his personal thoughts, Richards felt, more than heard, the presence behind him. Turning around slowly and taking on a defensive stance, there was Piankoff respectfully waiting his turn for his attention, taking in his student's measure.

"Yes, my teacher," Richards said in Egyptian. "What is it that your heart wishes?"

Taken aback by the deference and smooth cultural transition, Piankoff replied, happy to exercise and use the ancient tongue and its marvelously quaint and archaic ways of expression.

"Today we learn how to fall through the gate of eternity. But first, my student, you must prepare, brown your skin, and keep your head cleanly shaven, if you wish to be accepted as a priest of one of the Great Gods."

Smiling broadly at the wild notion of working on a tan in order to pass for an ancient priest, and after all the crash course effort up to now, Richards threw his head back and laughed.

Allowing the youthful outpouring of humor to run its course, Piankoff then added in a more serious tone, this time in English, "Well, the good Doctor is waiting for us. Shall we go and see what he is up to?"

On that cue, off they went through the desert scrub toward another hidden access into the Horizon Pass' underground lair, which to Richards reminded him of a grade B movie's notion of an underground missile silo. And in truth it was, for the installation had been constructed in the late 1960s. Rough concrete walls painted bright reflective white. Exposed piping and tubes of all kinds, shapes, and colors along the ceiling and walls of every corridor and tunnel. Everywhere emergency phones and lighting fixtures. Fire extinguishers every fifty feet. Exposed overhead fluorescent lighting. Bright yellow painted stripes running down the center of the wide twenty foot wide corridors and tunnels. Not to mention convex traffic mirrors at every intersection.

It would have been very confusing to navigate such a maze if it were not for the fact that each corridor, intersection, and tunnel was named in stenciled letters on the floor. As with so many things, Borov's sense of humor was clearly in evidence everywhere: Yellow Brick Road, Penny Lane, Trafalgar Square, Times Square, Appian Way, and the like. These accesses interconnected the dormitory area that was named "The Swamp" in honor of the *M.A.S.H.* television series, a particular favorite of Borov's. The mess hall, bakery, and kitchen was Betty Crocker's, the gym Venice Beach, the main lab complex was originally Frankenstein's Castle, but over time it was shortened to just Frank's. The high security area devoted to the testing and storage of the Soap Bubble itself was a far more serious place and its name reflected that fact, Tombstone. But even here, Borov's sense of humor was in evidence, as Richards would soon enough find out.

Dutifully following Piankoff through this maze, Richards eventually found himself before a sealed, circular double door that to Richards looked like the entrance to a bank vault, complete with a short, low ramp leading up to it. The black stenciled letters on the floor before them solemnly announced Tombstone.

Well, Richards thought, *this is it!*

Piankoff, ever vigilant, noted the excited look on Richards' face and the fact that he was unconsciously hopping up and down on his toes. That detail caused a sly grin.

*　　*　　*

While the pair of field operatives walked up to the vault's entrance, four security cameras trained on them took in their every move.

Guard One: "Hey, check it out! Here comes that dangerous Russian bastard that almost took my nuts three years ago!"

Guard Two: "Yeah, he is one, mean, S.O.B., but who is the young greenie with him? Christ, look at him bouncing up and down. I'll bet he thinks it's Christmas!"

Guard One: "Yep, and check out his EKG and heat signature! He and the Russkie must be hot for each other."

Guard Two: "Most likely. And they're shaved too. Probably masquerading again as two mascara-eyed faggot Egyptian priests."

Guard One: "Yeah, but did you see the video on the young one's grand entrance into the security pit last night? I wouldn't want to mess around with that dude in a dark alley. That mother is a cat." He whispered in a mixture of respect and fear.

*   *   *

Slowly the double door to Tombstone began to vertically split open and extend out into the corridor gradually driving Richards and Piankoff back several feet.

Up until now, Richards had become accustomed to the claustrophobic eight-foot ceilings of his quarters, the mess hall, corridors, and secondary passageways of Horizon Pass. Stepping through the massively thick doors of Tombstone's entrance, the two now stood on a steel grated landing that stood about fifty feet above floor level. Richards, stunned by the volume of the area, leaned over the railing and took in the view of what once had been a fair-sized cavern. Now it had been transformed into a massive engineering bay with workshop, a climate-controlled computer room, and a generator area. In the center of it stood a curious looking collection of devices connected to thick power cables.

Striding down a long and continuously curving ramp to the floor level, Richards got a slowly revolving look at that most strange and marvelous creation of man—the Mark V Soap Bubble. It represented an evolutionary series of machines that proudly proved their theoretical basis, justified the purpose of cutting-edge engineering and advanced materials research, and provided the very essence of wonder itself.

To Richards, he saw four black rectangular pylons, each about six feet tall arranged symmetrically like the cardinal points of a compass, that outlined a circle about twenty feet in diameter. Each pylon had its own thick power cable and attached at their tops were short, horn-like devices that were oriented inward, each with their own power cables. In the center of this circle of pylons and horns, a thick, white, hula-hoop-like object, about four feet in diameter, floated horizontally and absolutely still about five feet off the ground.

At the bottom of the ramp, Dr. Borov met the pair. He was as excited as a child with a new Christmas toy.

"Gentlemen, I'm so happy that you are here! Come meet the latest version of the Soap Bubble."

Clasping his hands together, the scientist briskly walked over toward the center of the chamber and its Stonehenge-like cluster of equipment. Stopping about four feet from the nearest black pylon, he spun on his heel to face his too slowly following audience.

"Colonel Piankoff," nodding in one direction.

"Mr. Richards," nodding the other.

"Meet the Mark V, our latest and greatest iteration of state-of-the-art technology in temporal exploration."

Again with Colonel Piankoff? Richards thought. *Again that reference. What is Dr. Borov trying to tell me?*

Leaping ahead as if he were a mind reader, Borov went on.

"Mr. Richards, I know you have many questions, but before I give you a quick tour of the Tombstone facility, what do you know about quantum mechanics and particle physics?"

Caught dumbfounded by the subject and directness of the question, Richards gave a sheepish and blushing shrug and said, "Very little, Dr. Borov."

Looking up with an appraising look the scientist replied with a warm smile. "Well, whad-da' ya' know, a no-bullshit, honest answer. I like that."

With Richards now a little more at ease with his ignorance, Borov continued, "Well, brace yourself my boy, for what I am about to tell you just might freak you out. But before I do, I have to ask you another question. Have you ever used a laptop computer?"

Richards, smirking at the seemingly ludicrous question, found himself blurting out.

"Jesus, Doc, everyone does now-a-days."

"And that is precisely my point! Everyone indeed does, yet no one can precisely describe the quantum mechanics behind what takes place within a silicon chip, yet it works, and reliably so. No one can explain how elementary particles can exist in two places at the same time. And yet they do, for every chip that AMD or Intel or Cray or Hitachi designs, they bank on this neat and little understood trick of particle physics. Joseph, we employ in our daily lives quantum mechanics and particle physics in crude and rudimentary ways. In some respects, when it comes to quantum mechanics, we're like ten blind men trying to describe an elephant.

"By the way, have you ever heard of the Standard Model?"

A negative headshake was Richards only response.

"Well, here's the short course. Scientists have described the building blocks of the universe and the forces that influence these building blocks, really atomic and sub-atomic particles, with what is called the Standard Model. But as with all such neat models, it possesses a mathematical flaw. That flaw is the thing or stuff that describes a particle's mass.

"Joseph, do you know what I mean by mass?"

"Sure, mass is the weight of something."

"Yes, that's true, but mass also imparts to a particle the qualities of color, size, hardness, softness, not to mention its chemical and electrical properties as well. In fact, mass, or masslessness, determines a particle's terminal speed, that being just short of the speed of light. In order to go to faster than the speed of light, one would need to lose one's mass—in essence to become mass-less. But to do that would mean that we understood what this remarkable quality was in the first place. What mass is. The truth is Joseph that we have yet to discover the mass particle. Scientists in Switzerland at the CERN LEP facility almost found that quality, known as a Higg's boson, but failed when they fried their instrumentation. The folks at the Stanford Linear Accelerator Center in Menlo Park tried. The Japanese also took a shot at it at the KEK facility in Tuskuba.

Cornell also tried. Finally, and only after some considerable expense, did the folks at Fermi actually prove the existence of the Higg's boson, and when they did, they discovered that the mass particle itself was composed of several more sub-atomic particles."

Now with his arms crossed across his chest, the scientist stood back, beaming a beatific smile to his numbed audience. Then he continued.

"And with that discovery, Joseph, my life's work has now been made complete, for up until that momentous discovery, the true quantum mechanics behind the workings of the Soap Bubble, despite all of its outward sophistication, remained as poorly understood as the inner workings of a computer chip. We now know how a particle, or for that matter, a living organism, can be in two places at the same time.

"Now Joseph, and before I ramble on too much longer, let's go on that tour I had promised. Take a look behind me over there at those four dark columns or pylons, if you will. They represent the most advanced thinking in room temperature, super-conducting field generation. They, like the ring that you see suspended between them, are triumphs in advanced materials science. What controls them is that refrigerated computing chamber over there that monitors and calibrates all four pylons at once, keeping each in as near-perfect synchronization as possible. These thick cables, which run over to the generator barn over there, power up the pylons. Power, by the way, is furnished cleanly and free of charge by Mother Nature herself through the kind mediation of the Hoover Dam. Talk about sheer horsepower!

"As for those funny-looking trumpet-like thingies atop of each pylon, those are ion emitters. Joseph, do you know what an ion is?"

"Well, I think it is a charged particle of some kind. I know that they are used in air purifiers."

"Yep, you're right! But in our case, we are not clearing the air. Rather these emitters stream carbon ions of an average mass into the mouth of the field that is created within that floating hula hoop before you. In fact, you will be riding their stream much the same way a strong eddy carries you along a river. Ever do any white water rafting?"

To the question Borov received another negative head shake.

"Well that's too bad, because that is just what the effect is like. Those trumpets will be producing positively charged ions going out and negatively charged ones coming back. In short, that's how we 'push' you out and 'suck' you back in."

"And now let me tell you about that suspended ring, that hula hoop. That, Joseph my boy, you will drop through."

Ten seconds of silence passed and finally Richards found his tongue to ask the obvious, "Whadda' ya' mean, drop through the ring?"

"Good question. But allow me to ask you one in return. Why do you think that you were sent, at great effort and expense, to the Rangers' jump school?"

"To get into better shape, learn how to protect myself, and to learn how to parachute jump. At least that was why I thought I was sent there."

"Well, right you are on all counts, but primarily, it was to teach you how to fall gracefully."

Then the dawn broke.

The security pit before the main entrance way to the complex, that test had required him to survive an unexpected fall, unharmed. Or, was there more to it? Richards wondered.

"Fine, Dr. Borov, but what does this have to do with the Soap Bubble?"

With a sly smile on his face, Borov turned and called over his shoulder to a man named Felix to roll over the drop tower. Out of the shadows creaked and rolled an eight-foot platform constructed of white PCV pipe. To Richards, it looked like an ancient wheeled siege tower with a short fiberglass diving board attached to its Plexiglas sheeted, surfaced top. Access to the top was a simple and short climb up a series of PCV pipe rungs fixed to one of its four sides.

"Joseph, please notice that the drop tower is constructed of non-conductive materials. All of its parts are made either of plastics, fiberglass, or ceramics.

"Now as to why we sent you to Fort Benning, well, that was Colonel Piankoff's idea."

Again Borov's conscious use of the rank of Colonel in reference to Piankoff. He clearly really wants me to remember that detail, Richards thought. *But why?*

Glancing over and nodding in Piankoff's direction, Borov then acknowledged.

"And a fine suggestion that it was. But my point behind all of this, Joseph, is this. Once the Soap Bubble is energized, the drop tower is rolled in. You climb the tower, and drop through the center of the suspended ring. We suspect the drop on the other side will be only five feet as well, but experience has taught us that that is not always the case. By the way, as you drop through the ring, for a brief moment in time, you will be in two places at once, just like the particles on a computer chip. Your physiological reaction to that event may be significant. Colonel Piankoff's early experiences with the phenomenon, I am told, were memorable."

Richards did not miss Borov's emphasis of the "other side," nor could he possibly the repeated reference to Colonel Piankoff. Now he at least knew why his jump instructor had always singled him out as the demonstration guinea pig for correct landing procedures.

As for experiencing transit through the ring, that detail left Richards curious enough to glance at Piankoff and ask, "Dr. Borov, precisely what do you mean by memorable?"

"Well, we have only Colonel Piankoff's reactions to go by, but we suspect that the transit reaction may be highly variable. We will just have to wait and see. The best I can say is that your reaction to the field may be a temporary reaction much like motion sickness."

That answer did not please or satisfy Richards, but it did prompt another question.

"Okay. Fine. But then how do we get back? Have a trampoline on the other side to jump back up and through the ring?"

Borov, now with a broad smile, answered, "Very clever Joseph, but impractical and potentially a very hazardous temporal intrusion, because once we go through the Soap Bubble, we cannot either take with us or construct anything on the other side that can influence the course of history. So no trampoline. Instead, in order to bring you back, or to pull you back out so to speak, all we do is lower a rope."

Borov pointed toward the ceiling of the chamber and there suspended from a plastic beam truss was tied an old wooden pulley with a long length of curious-looking rope, at the end of which was a simple noose with a slipknot.

Seeing his curious stare, Borov continued.

"Now you see why, Joseph, that this lab facility is called Tombstone. That hangman's noose there is paradoxically your life line between a *somewhen* and the here and now. By the way, the hemp rope itself was hand made by a local native, woven and knotted to old Indian standards. If we lose a piece of it to the other side, we expect little if any temporal damage will occur.

"But again, I have babbled enough. I think you need a demonstration."

Reaching into one of his nylon jacket pockets, Borov retrieved a small cell phone. Quickly entering a code into the device with a practiced thumb, Borov then said, "Mr. Jeffers, would you be so kind and fully power up the Mark V for a four minute test demonstration?"

"Yes. Thank you."

Turning around so that he was now facing the Soap Bubble, Borov spoke, "Gentlemen, please come over, stand on either side of me, and watch."

For Richards, he did not know what to expect. For Piankoff, it was always a treat to see the Soap Bubble field take form. In a way, for him the entire effect was a near religious experience that verged on magic.

The trio, standing between two of the pylons and about four feet outside the twenty-foot circle, then expectantly waited for the miracle to occur.

"Joseph," Borov commanded. "Squat down next to me and focus your eyes on the interior of the suspended ring before you."

It started slowly. Looking up and through the ring it seemed as if the air was heating up with ripples and waves breaking up the image. But then, quite suddenly, you just could no longer see through the ring. Instead, a totally smooth, silvery gray color engulfed the ring's entire interior.

"Oh, Felix," Borov called over his shoulder. "Would you be so kind and lower the extraction rope until the noose just passes through the field?"

Then with a second thought, Borov again raised the cell phone to his lips and with a voice of total command authority said, "Mr. Macky, secure and lockdown the chamber. We are in the process of a brief test."

"Roger, Dr. Borov." Richards could clearly hear in crisp reply.

Five seconds passed and then Borov's cell phone rang.

"Dr. Borov, sir. All is secure."

"Thank you Mr. Mackey."

Again drawing his eyes to the lowering hangman's noose, Richards could feel his eyes bulge in disbelief as if they were distended in a cartoon, for the noose reached the top of the field, entered it about two feet, and then stopped. From his vantage point near and below the ring, the field remained smooth and unaffected. But just as clear, some two feet of rope was penetrating *somewhen*.

It looked like a cheap parlor trick, but as Felix began to reel in the rope at Borov's command, noose took on a wet sheen, and in fact was dripping once it was entirely recoiled. Then with a loud snap and the immediate reek of ozone, the field ceased to be and Richards found that he could again see right through the ring's interior.

Forgetting where he was, Richards then impulsively walked forward, entered the twenty-foot circle of the Soap Bubble's pylons, and reached down and dabbed his fingers into the growing puddle on the floor from the dripping rope. First smelling and then daring to taste the watery substance, he declared with surprise.

"Salt water!"

Smiling broadly at the revelation, Borov answered the obvious question.

"Why sure. It should be. You have just tasted the Jurassic Sea that once covered this very spot."

"How do you know?" was Richards' reply.

"Well, from the archaic diatoms in the sea water, the geological history of New Mexico, and other relative calibration methods. But Joseph, your question leads to something quite critical, something that only an on-the-scene observer could provide—absolute calibration."

Turning to Piankoff, Borov stated with quaver of awe in his voice, "And Colonel Piankoff here is indeed that first observer, the first to drop through the Soap Bubble to the other side. You see,

Joseph, Colonel Piankoff was the first human to experience transit to *somewhen* and has successfully done so on no less than four occasions. Because of his courage, we can now calibrate the Soap Bubble to within any given day of *somewhen* and theoretically to any given moment within an error of plus or minus 37 seconds.

"But as a practical matter, we have chosen not to ever use the Mark V to its theoretical limits whenever human transit is involved. Instead, and for simplicity, we calibrate only in terms of a given calendrical day and year, allowing the actual time of arrival to be approximately the same as the time of departure, again within the range of plus or minus 37 seconds. This plus or minus error is really quite small. It accounts for the gradually reduced spin rate of the earth's rotation over time. For all of these spectacular chronological achievements, Colonel Piankoff received the Lenin Cross for Valor. Unfortunately, this seldom granted honor is a jealously guarded secret of my former homeland."

Throughout this unexpected presentation Richards noted an ever deepening crimson blush appear on Piankoff's face. Richards had from the first known that his teacher was indeed a Russian, but a colonel, a highly decorated and connected Russian military colonel at that, and not to mention a pioneer of the first rank!

Piankoff, glancing over to Richards, saw the questioning look in the young American's eyes. Saw the admiration, but also the growing doubt. All he had striven for, to train, and then gain the trust of this gifted but idealistic American, has now been brought into question, all because Borov had to flap his fat trap.

Shaking his head in disgust, Piankoff said in a sadly defeated voice, "Thank you, Dr. Borov, for those kind words and for totally breaking my cover. Mr. Richards was not to be told of my background. That is the desire of my superiors, who rightly felt that it was not pertinent to this mission, or the business of Mr. Richards to know who I am. Whatever kind intentions were, Dr. Borov, I assure you they are seriously misplaced."

And with that said, Piankoff turned on his heel and left the chamber without ever looking back.

Richards' only reaction was predictable.

"Jesus H. Christ! Just who is this guy anyhow?"

Borov answered. "Joseph, you are looking at the bravest man that I have ever known. Perhaps even the bravest individual in modern history, who just so happens to be the grandson of the late Professor Dr. Alexander Piankoff, the famous Russian Egyptologist. He is also the most cunning and intelligent field operative that the Russian Academy of Science possesses.

"I know for a fact one of his directives is, or at least was, to kill or have me killed. It seems that former colleague of mine wanted Piankoff to bring my severed head back to this Boyar madman on the end of a pike. And despite this minor side issue, Piankoff is still the best man for this mission.

"But truth be told I suggest that you train hard and carefully, and always, always, watch your back. In fact, allow me to make the following observation. I wouldn't be half surprised if our colleagues in Moscow are considerably miffed at your joining Colonel Piankoff. Consequently Joseph, take special care and always remember—trust is a hard-earned commodity."

The next days were proof enough of Borov's words. Piankoff and Richards went on runs around the neighborhood twice a day, during the early morning and late afternoon. Although the terrain was gorgeous, varied, and the smell of the desert mesquite delicious, the five thousand plus foot altitude of the region spelled agony for Richards, a Midwestern flatlander. By week's end, with his endurance rapidly building, the junior field operative had to hand it to Piankoff, who must have easily been ten, maybe fifteen, year's his elder. On they ran together bareheaded, with plastic water bottles in each hand, in sandal-like running shoes, and the briefest of jogging shorts imaginable. The entire point being to get an even tan. And at altitude, their constant and vigorous motion was needed just to keep warm.

It was during their sixth day of two-a-day runs that Richards began to understand what drove his mentor. Both streaked in sweat and covered in a fine layer of desert dust, it was during a brief rest and water break that Richards finally asked the question that had been nagging at him ever since Borov had revealed Piankoff's background.

"My teacher, why is it that you were the one chosen for the gate to eternity?" He queried in Egyptian, by silent agreement the only language that the two would use whenever they were alone together.

Smiling though the sting of salt in his eyes, Piankoff regarded Richards with a thoughtful glance.

"Well, young lion, it took you long enough to ask. But out of my growing respect for you, I will tell you.

"As a young man I was much like you and I wished to do honor to my fraternal grandfather and become an keeper of Kemet's many mysteries."

Richards then blurted out in sudden recognition. "Now I remember! Your grandfather and Rambova translated the inscriptions from Tutankhamen's tomb!"

"Don't forget a sizable corpus of mythological papyri as well young lion! Regardless, you do my grandfather honor. For that I thank you. But as for myself, my land believed that I had a greater calling than to be a scribe of a sacred language."

Despite the apparent barrier of the ancient language being used, Richards could clearly detect a grim sort of bitterness with those words.

"So instead the ways of secrets and arts of war became my life. My present membership within the association of my land's House of Thoth is my present assignment. I was chosen to be the first traveler of the gate of eternity on the basis of my warlike arts and not my childhood mastery of the ancient Egyptian tongue, although, that last has proved to be of great assistance.

"Young lion, beware, I have killed many times. I fully expect to kill again, if necessary. Although I have gained a certain fondness of you, never betray me. Ever."

With that, the two were off again exploring a new desert gully back to the compound. During that run Richards had much to ponder.

*   *   *

At the completion of Borov's dramatic demonstration of the Soap Bubble on the first day of technical familiarization, one thing struck Richards as odd.

If the mission I am training for is in ancient Egypt, then, why is the Soap Bubble located here in no-where's-ville, New Mexico?

That question was finally answered in full on the sixth day of acclimatization and technical training. Sitting in the now familiar briefing room with Piankoff and waiting for the day's agenda to begin, in walked Dr. Borov with his smile and overflowing enthusiasm.

"Gentlemen, I have something grand to show you down the hall. Please follow me."

Quickly leaving as he always did, Borov took off like a shot through the briefing room's door and into the corridor outside. In response and not to be outdone by the infectious energy of Borov, the pair broke into a lopping jog to catch up to the good doctor. Borov then entered a previously sealed off room several doorways down the corridor. Following him in, the field agents came to a quick stop before a hovering Soap Bubble ring suspended between four obviously portable and collapsible posts with their emitters. Powering the temporal transportation unit was a small field generator sitting on the floor with the usual number of connecting cables. What was slightly amusing about the power source was that it was attached to a backpacker's frame.

Following their eyes, Borov impulsively broke in.

"This is my latest tweak, a portable generator good for about forty minutes of uninterrupted run time. Previously, as Colonel Piankoff could tell you, we had only a fourteen-minute window. At that time, we were cutting it a bit too close. As you can see, the generator is now mounted on a common backpacker's frame, instead of the older version carried on a two-man litter. Don't be deceived, however. That generator is still heavy, some ninety-five pounds, but its frame is Kevlar, being light and strong. The poles are portable pylons, the same as the ones before. And like the backpack frame, they are built for strength and lightness as well. But the really neat part of this portable version is that only two people are needed to set it up and run it in the field. So before we deploy to Egypt, do you guys want to take a crack at running it?"

Answering simultaneously they said, "Sure!"

As almost an afterthought, Borov shifted gears.

"And this," Borov said while bending over and picking up an eight-foot long white plastic tube with a claw attachment at one end and a gripping mechanism at the other, "is your own personal temporal probe. Crude as it may seem, with it, you will be able to plumb the depths, so to speak, of the other side before you drop through. It's a bit crude, and trust me, we're working on a slicker approach, but for now it'll do just fine. Also, you can attach a rope to it from the other side so that we can better reel you in if necessary."

For the next two days, Piankoff and Richards constantly traded roles in carrying the generator or the pylons, emitters, and ring, setting up the pylons, firing up the generator, hooking up the power cables, operating the small temporal calibration computer, and playing pickup games with the claws of the eight-foot probe. In the end, each was convinced they could pick the other's pocket with the probe. Each was convinced that the other could run the entire system all by themselves. Unbeknownst to Borov, they could, although that was considered a dangerous taboo. To Richards, this was just another reminder that he was expendable and that Borov's words of warning about Piankoff and his handlers were to be carefully heeded.

* * *

After four and one half weeks of running, daily head shaving, tanning, and training in the esoteric nuances of quantum theory and practical temporal mechanics, Piankoff and Richards were deemed ready by Dr. Borov to go *somewhen*. Never before had two temporal field operatives been so deployed. Never before had the Philology Annex doubled the odds of initiating a paradox. But the threat of the watershed event justified the risk of a gentle warping of the *RUTI*'s ironclad rules.

But one last and final preparatory item took Richards totally by surprise. It all began when Dr. Borov reminded Richards that he had an appointment at the research complex's infirmary at nine the next morning, the very day they were due to depart for Egypt.

At the appointed time, Richards found himself knocking on the doorframe of the infirmary. Nurse Stewart, a pleasant and middle-aged native of northern Minnesota's Boundary Waters, looked up and smiled with the usual folksy warmth so common of that region.

"Well, Mr. Richards, you are surely as punctual as you are handsome. Come right on in. The doc is waiting for you in Room Number Two."

Thanking the nurse, Richards walked over to the room's door, knocked, and heard the deep, throaty voice of Dr. Allen beckon him in.

While standing before the door, Nurse Stewart took the opportunity to take in the view and noted to herself. *What a bod! Oh to be twenty again!*

Entering Room Two, Richards walked over and readily shook the pro-offered, ham-fisted greeting of Dr. Allen, who by Richards' own reckoning must have weighed in around two hundred and twenty pounds on his five-eight frame. Ruddy-faced, balding, freckled, and calling Oklahoma his home, Doc Allen, as he was affectionately called, silently pointed Richards over to the large examination table and said, "Sit."

After the usual pulse and blood pressure check, Doc Allen decreed Richards had the readings of a dead man. Extending a paper cup filled with water, he then asked him to down a rather large, yellow horse pill.

"What's this for Doc?" Richards said. "I've been poked, prodded, and inoculated by the best. What's up?"

Smiling a sort of shy and down home grin, Doc Allen replied, "Son, in case you haven't noticed, you're as virile and fertile as they come. In short, you're a babe magnet. That pill you are about to down is going to change all that, at least temporarily."

He then commanded, "Bottom's up."

Richards, momentarily hesitating as looked down at the pill, popped it into his mouth, chugged the water, and swallowed it whole. As he did so, the amazement on his face that he even could was evident to the doctor.

Wiping his lips with the back of his hand, Richards then asked, "Okay doc. There. It's all gone. Now what's temporary?"

Smiling. "Oh, about a month, and it will be affective in about six to eight hours. But have no fear, you will still get horny, you will still be able to maintain an erection, and you will still ejaculate. It's just you will be shooting blanks. As to what you just swallowed, well, it's kinda secret, but the scientific community has been aware of it for quite some time. It was initially developed back in the late 60s early 70s by a French research team. It's not the latest and greatest, but it will do the trick. A couple of colleagues of mine are working a less invasive method for male contraception using a sugar molecule that can be taken orally too. Well anyways, the female version of what you just swallowed there is a prostaglandin currently available as a prescription. It's called RU486. However, the active agent in your pill is a protein that targets the testes called Eppin. Ever heard of it?"

Shrugging his ignorance, but still confused, Richards again asked, "But why?"

"Well, it's really simple, Joey. We can't risk you making babies when and where they don't belong."

"Oh." was all that a chastened and blushing brightly Richards could softly reply.

CHAPTER XXVI
Graduation

It was a quiet shock for Richards in that the next steps did not include the usual cap and gown, fanfare, diploma, and well wishes for a bright future. He knew he had worked hard. He had been pushed to extremes that even he didn't know that he was capable of. Perhaps he should have seen it coming all along—notice that he was going overseas. While his memories of that ancient land as a military brat were one thing, now he could not believe that he was actually going back there, or more properly, going back there—*somewhen*.

Again, as before, the unmarked and dark gray Sikorsky arrived hot and departed hot with barely enough time in between for the two men to stow the portable Mark V-A gear and buckle in. Again they flew back sort of east toward the Holloman Air Force Base, that base located sort of west of backwater border town of Alamogordo, New Mexico.

Upon arriving at the Air Force base, the two and their priceless scientific gear were hustled aboard the already cranked up hulking presence of a Hercules C 130 J military transport, again bereft of any markings and painted in a similarly dark gray manner. Once aboard, the pair discovered that they were alone within the belly of a whale with only its mandated two-flight crews of four as company. The only in-cabin, transatlantic conveniences provided for were Air Force flight suits, long underwear for the chill, flight boots, and socks, two slung hammocks, several hot-packed meals, a head that they shared with the crews, and two rows of semi-padded jump benches that stretched along the entire length of the transport's fuselage. And yes, some kind soul had thought to provide the pair with ear plugs and flight headsets to dull the ever-deafening roar of the four Rolls-Royce AE 2100 D3 turboprops, each of which spun all-composite six-bladed Dowty Aerospace propellers.

For two very private individuals who were now accustomed to twice daily runs in the great outdoors, the shared, enclosed quarters of the C 130 J presented a test that frankly neither had anticipated. Suffice it to say, that when the near twenty-hour flight was over, both Piankoff and Richards would be stir crazy, itching for hot showers, and longing for a long, lonely run in the desert far away from the constant drone and whine of unbaffled turbines at full military thrust. But those desires, they would discover, would have to take a back seat.

If the nearly seven hour leg from the New Mexican USAF base to Gander, New Foundland, which had been scheduled for refueling and crew change, had been a numbing experience, then the final leg of some eleven and a half hours while transiting the Atlantic and Mediterranean was sheer agony.

By the time they finally arrived at Cairo International Airport, dusk of the next day had arrived. As the tail ramp was lowered and the seemingly sudden and deafening silence of the turbines became apparent, the next thing that Richards noted was the smell of kerosene that seemed to permeate everything he wore.

Parked as they were in a deserted corner of the flight line, Richards noted that there was something else. Reaching the bottom of the ramp, he finally caught the smell of Egypt. Taking a deep breath, it was a curious mixture that defied immediate recognition. Taking another deep breath, he thought it smelled like a blend of dried or burnt grass, dung, and dust. And he wasn't far wrong, for the staple cooking fuel of Egypt's poor was just that, dried, camel dung briquettes.

While the two stretched their stiff and aching bodies at the bottom of the flight ramp, an unremarkable two and a half ton military flatbed pulled up with its canvas top removed. Again, there were no obvious markings on the truck to be seen, just one very dented and rusty rear license plate in Arabic. Backing up to the ramp, the taillights, or at least the one that worked, glowed back at them like a caged animal's eye.

Stopping with a lurch and a squeak from the brakes not twenty feet from where they stood, out jumped from the cab a jaunty six-three figure wearing a black beret and starched desert chocolate chip cammies bloused at the boots. Walking with purpose right past a staring Richards and Piankoff as if they were not even there, he climbed the ramp and promptly disappeared into the flight deck. Moments later he reemerged carrying the Mark V-A's generator on one shoulder and one of the pylons over the other. Passing the pair a second time and without turning his head, he said in a distinctly Texas accent, "Well, I'm glad that you ladies finally made it. Now how about a hand? Or, would that be too much to ask?"

Jumping at the remark, Richards and Piankoff raced up the ramp and grabbed the remainder of their equipment and loaded it onto the truck bed in one trip. Their driver then slammed close the creaking tailgate, latched it, and again, without a word headed back around to the driver's side of the cab. With one foot on the step up, he simply said, "Ladies, are we ready to go? Or, would you-all like me to assist you into the cab?"

Richards and Piankoff jumped into the cab, Richards in the middle next to the driver, Piankoff at the window. Once underway with a flurry of shifting gears, Richards took a closer look at their loquacious driver.

Hmmm. He thought. *A jarhead if I have ever seen one, but a vaguely familiar one at that, which then prompted him to ask just to hear his voice again.*

"Well, sir. What time is it?"

Looking straight ahead and thinking a moment as he was waved through several heavily-guarded security checkpoints, the driver merely said. "Sir, I am not supposed to know who you guys are, what government or governments you work for, or what's the all fire rush. But to tell you the truth, I have been given specific orders not to fraternize with either of you or even remember any part of this little adventure. As for the time, that's clearly no secret. It's around eighteen hundred hours Lima, that's local time if you don't know, and my wife's as pissed off as a polecat in heat that I am not at home at the dinner table right now. Then to beat all, I have also been ordered to come up with some candy-ass story to cover up all of this. And if you knew my wife, she will buy absolutely zero of that!"

So chastised, the next several minutes passed in silence. When Piankoff broke it, he did so in ancient Egyptian.

"Young lion, it seems that our talkative friend does not know how to treat members of a religious order, eh?"

At the sound of Piankoff's offhand comment in Egyptian, Richards noted that the driver's ears perked up.

Without regard to the driver's sensibilities, he replied also in the ancient tongue, "This is true, master, but from the way his donkey ears wagged at our speech, I am willing to wager that he is well-versed in the modern tongue of this land."

To that snap observation, Piankoff merely nodded and rewarded Richards with a wry smile.

"How very true your words are young lion."

On into the growing darkness they drove. For Richards, it wasn't hard to figure that they were heading generally in a southerly direction along the eastern bank of the Nile. After several honking near misses with errant cabs, trucks, half-sleeping donkeys, stray dogs, and the like, it was obvious that they were nearing Cairo.

Once within the outskirts of Cairo, it became obvious again that their driver really knew the local street system. Weaving in and out of the early evening's traffic, the driver turned here and darted there, all the time consistently ignoring any red lights or stop signs encountered, all the time using his horn liberally at any sign of contest. Finally slowing to a halt in the broad back alley of what looked like a vast government building, the truck began to back up to a darkened loading dock. In all, Richards reckoned the journey lasted some forty-five to sixty minutes of exciting, white-knuckled transit.

Coming to a halt, the driver sprang out of the cab and made his way toward the raised dock, which he easily vaulted up. Then, rapping loudly several times on the dirty and dented corrugated pull down door, he stood with his hands on his hips, and waited none too patiently for it to open. After about thirty seconds, however, the overhead dock light, a single naked bulb blinked on and the grating sound of the door slowly rising soon followed.

At this point both Piankoff and Richards got out of the cab and climbed into the truck bed over the passenger side's railings. Not saying a word, they lifted and handed over portions of their gear and scientific equipment to the driver and what looked like an elderly guard of some kind, dressed in a tan uniform. That accomplished, Piankoff and Richards simply leapt from the flatbed onto the dock with the remainder of the gear and followed the other two into the enclosed dock area, all the while inquisitively looking around.

With his head on a swivel, Richards thought this must be some kind of government warehouse because there were boxes and wooden crates of all kinds and sizes strewn all about with no particular logic or reason behind their arrangement. Laying the Mark V-A components down out of sight and behind one particularly large crate with Arabic writing and several official looking stamps affixed to it, the driver counted its six main parts, and then turned and faced his two fares.

"Gentlemen, this is the last stop. Stay put until someone comes looking for you."

With that, as with everything else, he returned to his truck and noisily made his escape. The warehouse security guard or whatever he was just pulled closed the overhead dock door and latched it from within. Then, he sauntered off to a small darkened side office and went in. The creak of a wooden chair was next heard followed within the next thirty seconds by a rather loud snore.

At this point, Richards and Piankoff had gotten the hint: hurry up and wait. So wasting no time each staked out their claim on two large crates, stretched out in the tomb-like quiet and peaceful darkness, and crashed.

*   *   *

Thirteen hours later they were awakened by the echoing approach of a woman's high heels clicking and clacking on the warehouse's concrete flooring. Piankoff, coming to full alert and on guard, suspected who it might be. As for Richards, it took him some time to work past his initial jetlag and sleepy grogginess.

Looking down from their raised perches, the two men observed an exquisite Egyptian woman and real knock out, who was wearing a modest European cut business suit with a long skirt. If someone told them that she was forty-five, they would not have been believed it. Dressed all in black, she stood before them with her shiny dark hair, cut helmet-like in a pharaonic style with bangs and long swooping side wings. Only a tasteful single stranded pearl necklace offered any contrasting accent.

Looking up at the two men atop the crates, the woman's deep green, slightly slanted almond-shaped eyes took them both in. Holding up her face to them, she proudly revealed her mellow olive complexion, regally high cheekbones, strong chin, straight and elegant nose, and long graceful neckline. She addressed them with a soft voice obviously the result of cultured British schooling.

"Good morning, gentlemen. Welcome to the Cairo National Museum. I am Dr. Sharil Moussa, personal secretary to the director of this museum and the Egyptian Antiquities Organization. The director is waiting to meet you both. Please come down from your perches and follow me."

So off they went, two scruffy-looking, unshaven, unbathed men in wrinkled and slept-in blue USAF coveralls led by a stunning vision. The parade was ludicrous in the extreme.

After exiting the dock area of the museum through a locked double doorway, Richards found he was on the first floor of the most extraordinary collection that he had ever seen. In many respects he had to pinch himself for not having ever considered visiting this one-of-a-kind place. Gigantic granite sarcophagi that once easily embraced fully mummified Apis bulls were on display. Royal statuary that measured several stories high stood over them.

The treasures of Tutankhamen's royal tomb were in full view and delighted the eye. Over there behind dusty glass rested the stone tools, ill-fired pottery, and cultural debris of Egypt's distant Predynastic Period. Housed in its library was a vast papyri collection that contained literary works, administrative texts, and even graffiti that spanned millennia. Not to mention the many storerooms closed to the public that housed what was considered too mundane for exhibit, but too historically valuable to sell or discard. Also not on display was a special class of objects that were considered too profane or obscene for the conservative Islamic temperament. In short, Richards found himself confronted with a collection that could take his entire lifetime, and then perhaps even more, to just view, much less study and fully absorb.

On the other hand, if Richards had thought that the dock area was disorganized, chaotic, and ill kept, then the first floor of the museum was not much different. If anything, this fine collection was nothing more than an overcrowded warehouse with aisles. Its glass cases nothing more than one continuous smear of finger and nose prints. Dust was omnipresent and available in various depths depending upon the remoteness of the spot or height of the statue or display case. It was sad.

Through it all, Dr. Moussa conducted them unerringly through this labyrinth without misstep, eventually to a side hallway that led to a suite of offices. Within was a broad and unoccupied reception desk that was located between two milk glass windowed office doors with open transoms, each over eight feet tall. In fact, the entire suite had very high ceilings with closed off electrical fan connections in their centers, clear evidence of the old pre-air conditioning days. Here too, as throughout the rest of the museum, evidence of dust was present everywhere, but not in such abundance.

*　　*　　*

Before the doorway on the left, the secretary stopped, gently rapped twice, and then opened the door and ushered in the pair. Absolutely every square inch of this huge office's walls were covered with overstuffed book shelving. The lone opening was a square window behind the massive desk whose surface area Richards thought would make a fine ping pong table, that is, if he could see its surface, for it was totally covered in neat stacks of paperwork. Also behind the desk stood a tall Egyptian with broad shoulders with only a hint of a middle-aged spare tire. With his hands held behind his back, the graying director minutely bowed at their entrance into his office and said in heavily accented English.

"Gentlemen, welcome. May I offer you a cup of tea?"

At the mere suggestion of sustenance, Richards' stomach growled altogether too noisily and before either he or Piankoff could reply in the affirmative, the museum director chuckled and then added, "And from the sound of it, perhaps I could arrange for something a bit more substantial as well, eh?"

At their quickly nodding heads, the director looked to his secretary still standing in the doorway, who he had unexpectedly caught the hint a smile on her face.

My, she thought, *the young one accompanying Colonel Piankoff is truly a magnificent specimen. In fact, not since my dear Anatol had so tragically died during that hateful Israeli air raid, have I seen another quite so interesting. But shaved as they both are, and so lean and cat-like in their movements, they look so austere, almost priest-like in a very ancient sort of way.*

Upon leaving to arrange a breakfast for the director's two guests, the secretary closed the door. Almost at once, and with a speed and grace uncommon for one so large, the director circled around his desk, reached out, and gave Piankoff a bear hug that fully lifted the Russian from the floor with his feet dangling. Exclaiming in broken, yet very understandable Russian.

"Piankoff, you old war horse! It is again good to see you!"

"And you too!" Piankoff exclaimed as he tried to free himself from the Egyptian's smothering embrace and his culture's two customary kisses of welcome.

Putting him down as if he were a mere rag doll, the director then turned to Richards, who had kept his distance during Piankoff's welcoming ceremony. This time, the director addressed him in his thickly accented English.

"And so, you must be the American, Mr. Richards. Welcome to my country." He said while extending his hand. "But first tell me, how is my dear friend John Milson's health?"

Initially surprised, Richards quickly regained his tongue. "Yes sir, and, thank you. When I last spoke with Dr. Milson, he seemed to be in fine health. And thank you for asking. I will make a point to tell him that you asked when I return home."

To Richards' statement, the director's eyes took on first a surprised, then guarded, far away and misty look.

"Mr. Richards, I can tell that you do not yet know. My good friend John Milson was diagnosed some time ago with cancer. Did you not know this?"

By Richards' look of confusion and panic, it was clear to the director that he had not and so he decided to change the subject.

"Ah, so Mr. Richards, is this not your first time in Egypt? Yes? Well, may I suggest, the next time when you are not so hurried, that you allow my secretary, Dr. Moussa, to be your personal guide to see the sites. I see that she regards you very favorably."

Taken aback again and emotionally beginning to feel a bit like a tennis ball at the Wimbledon Finals, Richards replied as only he knew how. "Why thank you, but I don't know what you mean."

"That, young man, is entirely my point. If you do successfully return with this renegade of a priest here, I am granting you my permission to see her."

With a face of total confusion, all Richards could do was shake his head as if dislodging some butterflies.

Piankoff broke out laughing.

"My young lion," he said in English. "I believe that you Americans have an expression, 'run with it.' The director here has just given you his permission to see his only daughter. Don't disappoint him!"

Then both the director and Piankoff shared a private laugh of their own at Richards' expense and total confusion.

Then on a more serious note and without skipping a beat, the director got down to business.

"Colonel Piankoff, at Karnak all the appropriate preparations have been arranged for your arrival. The entire site will be temporarily closed to the public while you are there. Even the French Epigraphical Survey has been notified that the sanctuary area is closed and off limits. Their absolute outrage at my autocratic behavior has even been communicated to me by their ambassador. Piankoff, you would have loved it. I frankly told that miserable excuse of a man that he and his country do not own the site. If they wished our continued cooperation, then they had better bend to my wishes. Besides, their present research is not even near the sanctuary. And as you well know, over the past twenty years, the French and I have never gotten along."

Turning to Richards, the director then said, "You know, Mr. Richards, I really prefer dealing with anyone who is not French, even Americans." He said with a broad smile and twinkle in his eye.

Knowing that his chain was being pulled, Richards just smiled. "Why thank you, Mr. Director, I will try and not to do anything that would upset that delicate *status quo*."

Pleased at Richards' snappy reply, the director then turned to Piankoff and said. "Before my daughter returns with your breakfasts, would you be so kind and treat my ears again to the sound of my country's ancient tongue?"

Smiling and with a brief nod, Piankoff began to chant and sing a simple melody with words that any ancient farmer would have sung. To the director, closing his eyes and gently swaying with its rhythm, it was like listening to sweet nectar. To Richards, struck by the song's musical cadence and earthy meaning, he realized that it was a song of unrequited love. After a few moments consideration, the young man decided just how appropriately Russian it really, truly was.

When Piankoff had finished, the director, now turning to Richards, quietly said. "And Mr. Richards, what can you offer me?"

So caught unawares, the American began describing in the most poetic of terms his first impressions of the director's daughter, and unconsciously broke into a cadence that also was song-like. Throughout this extemporaneous recital, Piankoff regarded him with a dreamy, almost mystical look that the director did not miss.

Finishing, the director then asked. "Well, you do speak beautifully, but what about? I could catch some of the vocabulary, but your manner is very different from that of your colleague's."

At this point, Piankoff broke in. "My dear friend, I must apologize for my young lion here."

He said as he placed his hand on Richards' shoulder.

"Without question he possesses a poet's heart. As for the subject he chose, well, let us just say that he has just paid your daughter the most kind, courteous, and respectful of compliments."

The director, smiling broadly, was clearly pleased.

Then two respectful raps at the door announced that their breakfast had arrived.

*   *   *

Leaving the director's office and gently closing its massive door behind her, Dr. Sharil Moussa immediately went to her receptionist's desk and efficiently rang up the kitchen of the Nile Hilton Hotel, which was located just across the street. After briefly exchanging traditional morning greetings with the kitchen's assistant chef, and deftly deflecting yet again one of his invitations for dinner, she ordered two full-blown American breakfasts with an urn of coffee and one of strong Egyptian tea. Finishing her pious duty, she then sat back in her leather chair with a creak to listen in on her father and his guests.

Although she suspected that her father knew that his daughter could listen in on his private audiences, he had never let on. In fact, with his office transom opened the way it presently was, all sounds coming from the director's office were bounced, if not focused, into the reception area. Certainly, such an acoustic advantage was a boon to any director's secretary. Sharil just sat back, closed her eyes, and imagined herself as a fly on the wall.

By the time she had so ensconced herself she caught the tail end of her father's endless railings about the French and next heard the distinctive voice of the Russian and his all too adolescent song. She had heard it several times before and almost knew it by heart. That her father liked it was hardly a surprise, even if he could not entirely comprehend some of its more subtle and visceral meaning, his background and understanding of the Russian was all that he needed. While Piankoff serenaded the director, Sharil found herself drifting off, almost day-dreaming, thinking about all the work she had done at Cambridge that now allowed her to understand the ancient farmer song's crude meaning, even if its tempo was quite catchy.

After a brief pause, Sharil heard another voice, a younger, and to her ears, a far more innocent one. She reasoned that it could only be that of the American. This song was not a song, and yet, it contained a poetic quality and rhythm that was a song nonetheless. To her blushing shock, Sharil slowly came to realize that she was the subject of the recitation. She was the focus of those beautifully archaic and yet sonorous tones. To Sharil, the American's voice and the meaning of his words were truly warm honey delicately, deliciously, drizzled.

While her father and the Russian chided the young American about his more than causal interest, Sharil lazily and briefly dozed with a wistful smile on her face. Her silent reverie was suddenly shattered with the arrival of the Hilton's food hot packs complete with a splendid cart of dishes and silverware.

Why is that American hotel so good at what they do! She silently raged at the intrusion and then found herself immediately tempering her words. *Perhaps he will return, and perhaps, Allah will grant me another chance for fulfillment.*

CHAPTER XXVII
Luxor

The four-hour helicopter ride south to Luxor, courtesy of the U.S. Army's Delta Force, went uneventfully. For Richards' benefit, they flew during daylight so that he could familiarize himself with the landscape of that once ancient land. That a daylight flight by an American military chopper was even possible, requires explanation. The U.S. choppers had fast become an Egyptian commonplace with Delta Force training taking place throughout Egypt's deserts and mountains in preparation for a Near Eastern war that no one truly wanted.

During the flight, Richards and Piankoff did not speak to one another. Each was clearly sorting out their own thoughts, making out their private wills, trying to anticipate and counter the unknowable. For Richards, it was like that time before a big game, where you find a quiet place and reflect, review one's assignments, and face your own personal demons, who are always far, far worse than any natural opponent.

For Piankoff, this time enroute to Luxor was a time of immense peace, a time to rest and conserve his energy. After all, he had already been across and back four times and his superiors considered him as seasoned as one could get. Deep inside, however, Piankoff remained a worrier, who deeply believed that one could never be totally prepared. He knew firsthand what could go wrong and what it was like to feel the sense of being homesick and oddly lonely for one's own time. First and foremost, he alone appreciated the many ill-considered variables that could turn this mission into a disaster.

Part of the problem was Richards himself. Piankoff had, sorry to say, come to like the youngster. He had real promise and a creative grasp of the language that even he did not possess. The truly odd thing about that last observation was that Piankoff, for the first time in his life, was comfortable with just that fact.

Slowly shaking his head, Piankoff reflected that he must be getting old. With that last thought in mind, Piankoff leaned against his gently swaying safety harnesses with his hands tucked into his pockets and drifted off into sleep.

Several hours later and just before sundown, the chopper roared into the Theban area. To Richards, the sight was just, simply, magnificent. It was like a home coming. For Piankoff, the shift in the constant, white noise thrum of the helicopter's engine told him all that he needed to know.

As the chopper flared at the edge of the Luxor Airport, a crude-looking, but somehow still mobile truck began to lumber over in their direction. As Richards and Piankoff disembarked through the barn door-sized side exit and the chopper's rotors began their spin-down, a familiar truck tailgate neared. Stopping about ten feet outside of the rotors' sweep, the passengers were dumbfounded when again that jaunty character in a black beret and heavily starched chocolate chip desert cammies trotted around to the back of the truck.

In a look that only could emphasize their disbelief, Richards and Piankoff found themselves again staring at the same highly-efficient and immensely put out military figure. All that they could think about was how royally pissed off his wife must be, and consequently, how much were they going to pay for it.

Instead, they both received a snappy salute once they reached the outer limit of the chopper's twin rotors, a bone-crushing, single-stroked handshake of welcome, and familiar and laconic orders to mount up. Richards, jumping in the cab first as before with Piankoff behind, could not shake his strong sense of déjà vu. And all the while that welcoming ceremony was underway, the helicopter's crew had efficiently emptied and loaded their gear and the Mark V-A from the chopper onto the bed of the truck.

As soon as the crash of the closing tailgate was felt, the ever-efficient driver jammed the truck into gear with a wincing metallic crunch, and with a lurch they were off. Before they knew it they were again being waved right through another airport's series of security checkpoints. Once out of the airport's confines, the truck driver began to expertly maneuver, this time in a westward direction and into the outer urban sprawl of a third world town. Darting through narrow streets and around mud brick hovels, their ride then vaulted over the high mound of a railroad track and then made a sharp right turn onto a heavily rutted road.

After briefly traveling along its deep and dried ruts for about a quarter of a mile, the rickety, weathered truck came to an abrupt dust-choking and gravel-crunching halt next to a chain link fenced gate of a huge enclosure. It seemed to take an eternity for the transiting dust cloud to clear that the truck created by their truck's passage and abrupt stop. Eventually, a figure in a tan uniform slowly emerged from the tiny open air guard shack that was behind the fenced in area. There, he stood waiting for their driver's approach at the chained gate.

Then it happened, for Richards it was the shock of recognition, for Piankoff, almost a magnetic, yearning homecoming. Emerging from the truck's cab, the two stood, stared, and then walked up and peeked through the chain link fence on tiptoe in child-like trances. The pair was filled with an odd sort of wonder, for contained within the fence's circuit was a place totally out of character with the surrounding third world urban blight. Within the fence line was the almost square, park-like campus of the magnificent Karnak temple complex.

When seen from this seldom used eastern gate's perspective, the temple's outer enclosure walls of ruined brown mud brick stood only some twenty meters distant with guard shack situated at a breach in it. Beyond this girdle wall that once divided the profane from the sacred, the pair saw the ruined expanse of a vast, monumental architectural wonder. Indeed, Karnak represented nothing more than a single rambling complex of limestone construction that began as a single core structure that was added to over the millennia. In all, Richards remembered the expanse of this area as being about a quarter of a mile on a side. In fact, the grand First Pylon or entrance to the Great Temple was that distance straight ahead. They were in essence nearest to the temple's back door.

When the Greek poet Homer sang of Egyptian Thebes with its hundred gateways, he was referring to these interconnected structures. In all, modern scholars have identified some ten monumental gateways, or pylons, with numerous side passageways, access points and common doorways. When in its prime, perhaps the blind poet's count wasn't so far wrong after all.

From a bird's eye view high above where the two field operatives stood at the eastern fence line, the east-west orientation of the Great Temple of Amen and its Sacred Lake was obvious. This vast artificial reflecting pool to the south at this time of day acted like a blue mirror for the cloudless sky. Across the lake from this vantage point stood in mute silence a vast and seemingly countless number of waist-high archaeological remains that were connected to the main temple at the mid-point of its southern exposure, which angled off in a direction slightly east of due south. Modern scholars have dubbed these structures the Southern Buildings with their four vast, football-field sized courtyards and their appropriately massive pylons.

In truth, the scene was almost too heady a brew to absorb within the sweep of a mere mortal's glance. Its impact felt disorienting and was palpably so for Piankoff. So much history and so many memories packed into such a confined space. A space now totally overrun with volunteer weeds and desecrated by an odd assortment of wind-blown legacies from the modern world. Here once proudly stood smooth, tall, majestically inscribed and richly painted walls, towering flagpoles from which fluttered bright and colorful pennants waving in the breeze, obelisks exposed to the sky tipped in gleaming electrum. Now, all was reduced to weathered, dusty gray, and injured limestone ruins.

Reverently whispering to Richards, Piankoff crooned in Egyptian, "Young lion, you simply cannot believe what sacrilegious deeds have transformed this most wondrous and beautiful precinct, dedicated to the most powerful force imaginable on earth, into the ruins that your uninitiated eyes see before you. But in a short time, you too will come to know the meaning of my words."

While intellectually Richards understood the impassioned emotion behind the Russian's statement, he could not relate to those deep currents. At least, he told himself, not yet. Instead, all that he could focus upon was their primary goal, the Great Temple itself, which stretched out before him toward the distant setting point of the sun. Deep within its precincts Richards knew that they would find, womb-like, the ultimate holy of holies of the ancient world, the innermost sanctuary of the great god Amen Re. Getting there, however, Richards realized, would have to be done on foot. That meant that their gear and the Mark V-A would have to be lugged into position, set up, system checked, and then they would have to prepare for their transit into the *somewhen*.

Breaking the silent pair out of their momentary reverie was the clatter of chains and the screeching sound of the gate opening on its rusty hinges. Without a word, the threesome began unloading the truck of its precious cargo. Again in what seemed like moments, Richards, their driver, and Piankoff were off, snaking their way through the precinct's ruins with the Russian in the lead.

For Richards, all was a blur. As he struggled under the weight of the backpack's fission power cell, all that he could think of was how little he knew and how unprepared he felt. He was embarrassed that he had never even considered archaeology as a field of legitimate interest. He was embarrassed at his rank ignorance of the subtle nuances and changes in Egyptian architecture over the millennia, really embarrassed that he was treading on ground held sacred long, long before Christ even walked the earth. Now he was to go there, attempt to blend in, somehow eventually secure a viable genetic sample from a living god, and then return. All Richards could do was chuckle at this sudden, personal revelation.

Yeah. Sure. What a near-sighted and gullible turkey I've been.

While this private conversation was raging in Richards' head, they were blithely skirting around the many monumental limestone columns, pylons, and walls of the precinct inscribed with famous deeds, the Royal Records, of the Pharaoh Thutmose III. Directly in line behind those, the group finally arrived at a long, narrow room with rose granite walls, the innermost sanctuary, the holy of holies of the great god himself.

*   *   *

By two in the afternoon the next day, the full heat of the sun punished the town of Luxor, its inhabitants, visitors, and the Great Temple complex. While those shimmering waves of heat beat down, all activity halted. Those who were intelligent took a nap, or at least remained in the shade. Only a few ignorant, or very stubborn, tourists, probably Brits, wandered aimlessly about wondering why all the archaeological sites were closed, why all the usual soda pop vendors were nowhere to be found.

It was during this lull the four portable pylons of the Mark V-A were locked into position with their ion emitters and drop ring, as it had come to be called. Piankoff, with his hands resting on his hips, surveyed the scene and after a cursory inspection, all looked ready for the power up test. Nodding to Richards, who was sitting cross-legged in front of the backpack power unit's control panel, Piankoff signaled him to simultaneously turn two large and very oddly-shaped keys all the way to the left. Soon a low vibration, more of a rhythmic thrumming, began.

After the first twenty seconds of warm up, the drop ring slowly began to stir on the ground as if it were a dried leaf rustled by a breeze. During the next twenty-second interval, the ring had stabilized itself between the pylons four inches off the ground. During the final twenty seconds, the ring had slowly risen to its standard five-foot design elevation and held it. Richards, glancing over all the LED indicators, gave Piankoff a silent thumbs-up sign as they were all in the green. A sudden movement to Richards' left briefly distracted his attention as the military driver was making quite a fuss at swatting at something on the wall.

Probably spooked by a friendly scorpion, Richards surmised with a half smile.

Then after a full two minutes of power up, Piankoff, who had been walking all the while around and inspecting the pylons, merely nodded again. To this command Richards turned the right key, and then four seconds later by the indicator lights before him, the left key one notch to the right to bring Mark V-A into its neutral, stand down mode. As he did so, the drop ring slowly began its descent to the ground.

*   *   *

Having assisted the pair in the erection of the pylons and the hooking up of the power cables, the truck driver now tried to become invisible. He stood casually in the shade in his desert cammies and peered out with tightly slitted eyes from underneath the bill of his canvass fatigue hat. The truck driver surveyed the scene and still could not believe what he was witnessing. From the shade of the sanctuary and out of harm's way, he could only slowly shake his head in silent wonder.

Even though this is your fifth deployment, it is your first nurse-maiding of two droppers, that Russian Colonel spook and now the greenhorn jock Richards. Regardless, this whole notion of time travel still gives me the willies. And now if not one screw up would be bad! Why in the world are they sending two? Jesus! They just do not pay me enough to stay in this man's army!

When the ring had finally settled on the ground, Richards then simultaneously turned both of the keys to the far right notch and the unit shut down entirely. Standing up from his place before the backpack power unit, Richards could only smile in a nervous, pregame sort of anticipation. Piankoff, on the other hand, had carefully positioned the Mark V-A within the sanctuary under some wooden scaffolding temporarily borrowed from the recently evicted French Epigraphical Survey. In many respects the scaffolding was perfect for their purposes, being nothing more than a wooden framework that was lashed together with hemp rope. Totally nonconductive, it was perfect as a drop and retrieval staging point.

As for the Mark V-A's position under the scaffolding, Piankoff had made that determination according to his own precise recollections. As a temple priest while on a previous deployment, he had memorized its floor pavement while sweeping it on his hands and knees. According to those minute calculations and some honest guess work, the Mark V-A now was set up a full two meters before the image of the god and some two and a half meters from the chamber's curtain walls and entranceway. In other words, there was plenty of room to drop into and roll safely away within the heavily-sequestered great god's chamber. It had worked before. It would succeed again. But Piankoff was not one who took any unnecessary chances, and so the next time the Mark V-A was fired up in preparation for the drop the probe was to be employed to confirm his memories.

Now satisfied that all was as it should be, Piankoff, ignoring the truck driver's presence, a clear military presence that he had come to rely upon yet always held suspect, addressed Richards directly in Egyptian.

"Well, the gate of eternity appears to be working. Our next step, young lion, is to confirm our destination, stick the spear, and then prepare ourselves for the journey."

To Piankoff's words, Richards merely nodded in understanding as he went over to get the white, plastic probe.

Noting Richards' quiet acquiescence, Piankoff followed his stiff actions, while he wondered about his colleague's present state of mind. Abruptly, he decided to find out.

"Young lion, how are you feeling right now?"

Richards' looked up, gamely smiled, and stated the obvious.

"Many birds are fluttering in my stomach as I contemplate the gate of eternity."

To such an honest answer Piankoff could only nod in understanding, but cautioned himself.

He had better not flake out on me now. Piankoff thought. *If he does, that will make it far easier for me to put him out of his misery.*

During this latest exchange, the semi-bored and impassive face of the truck driver broke into a brief smile as he thought triumphantly.

Well Tuna, that time you caught "gate of eternity" and "young lion" twice, and that could only be Piankoff's pet name for Richards.

The man shifted his position slightly in the shade.

And who said that this old language specialist first class was all washed up!

Chapter XXVIII

The Mummy's Hand

During the early hours of the following morning, the pair, satisfied with the field power up test of the Soap Bubble Mark V-A earlier the previous day, now input and double checked the temporal coordinates. This delicate procedure both Piankoff and Richards undertook with the greatest of care. As they had worked out during their technical training in New Mexico, Piankoff first entered the data with Richards confirming its accurate entry. That done, then Piankoff reconfirmed the data directly with Horizon Pass via an encrypted satellite phone that the driver had brought along in his truck.

"How did it go?" were the first words out of Borov's mouth following the cessation of the white noise hiss of the encryption.

"Nominal," replied Piankoff, who then thought it politic to add, "It set up and ran like a dream, Doctor Borov. Just as before. You should be proud of your development and technical staff."

Ignoring the obvious compliment, Borov then asked, "And your driver, is he still there?"

"Yes," replied the Russian. "He stays out of the way and is as reliable and efficient as a machine."

"And of the temporal data, please confirm again what you entered?"

"I read: 1363 BPE, January 5th, 2:12 a.m."

"Right on the money, please proceed with the probe and then report in. And, Colonel Piankoff, good luck to you and your team."

"You are very welcome Dr. Borov."

Piankoff reached down, cut off the satellite transmission, and let out an oddly deep sigh. Looking up, he saw Richards already connecting the plastic cables that actuated the probe's claw and had snapped together its six and a half feet of PVC tubing.

As for their driver, he remained in his favorite recess out of the way, trying to look cool, calm, and collected. But Piankoff could tell from the slight tilt of his head, his hand up against his ear, and glassy eyes that he was concerned elsewhere, listening to something through what probably was a tiny ear mic. Even though this was his fifth time in the field with the driver, Piankoff had yet to detect any of the security forces this man commanded. Yet, his sixth sense strongly suspected they were out there, somewhere. While that realization brought the Russian a sense of well-being, it also brought a slippery chill up his spine, for never would his superiors believe that the Americans had a security force as stealthy and cunning as that of the truck driver's.

Most certainly, Piankoff mused. *My young lion here is totally oblivious to the fact that our driver is anything other than that. Much less that he commands such an invisible security force!*

Having snapped the last of the probe's sections together, Richards sat up and also caught the dreamy and glazed look on their driver's face, while he was leaning against the sanctuary's far wall. Looking quickly down so as not to give the man away, he then remembered that one, very special, and highly classified briefing during his two weeks of Hell Week at Fort Benning.

It had been really weird, for he had been the only one in the entire briefing auditorium, sitting front and center in the first row. That was the first time Richards had met Major Charles "Tuna" Abraham Cartwright of the US Army's Special Command Detachment, a group of men who officially did not exist anywhere in anybody's budget.

The briefing was scheduled at seventeen hundred hours, during everyone else's dinner hour. Freshly showered after the day's torturous events and in clean fatigues, Richards had patiently waited. He was starved, dog-tired, thirsty, and half-dozing for fifteen minutes in the silent gloom of the hall. Remembering the rule to wait zero minutes for an assistant professor, five for an associate, and ten for a full prof, Richards, disgusted, stood up to leave. He turned to his left and nearly jumped out of his skin. There sitting in the third chair to his left was a totally blacked-out figure.

"Holy shit!" Were the only words Richards could remember wedging their way past his heart that was clearly lodged in his throat.

The silent figure said, "Well, soldier. It took you long enough to notice me. I've been sitting here for the last three minutes. So that tells me you are not a proper soldier. Therefore, you could only be that pansy-assed-college-football-player-puke, Mr. Richards."

With that announcement, the lights in the hall came up along with the simultaneous chambering of twelve weapons. Spinning on his heels, Richards realized he was surrounded by twelve similarly blacked-out individuals, all who were training short, squat, automatic weapons with silenced barrel extensions directly at him.

Richards' said again, "Holy shit!"

Quickly followed by. "What's going on? Am I some sort of a hostage?"

Before five seconds had past, for Richards an absolute eternity, all thirteen of the blackout figures started laughing uncontrollably. At first Richards could not tell why. Then he sensed it. Besides his ashen face, he was visibly shaking from head to toe. That was all too apparent to his surrounding jury.

So had went Richards' first introduction to Tuna Cartwright and his "school," for from that moment forward, his respect for the man and his team knew no bounds. No way was he going to give away to Piankoff what an elite force surrounded them, who provided their security, and who ensured the Mark V-A did not manage to somehow wander off.

Richards then saw that Piankoff was waiting.

"The hand of god is ready," Richards unwittingly and prophetically said.

Nodding soberly in his direction, Piankoff stiffly said, "Well then, climb up the scaffolding and get ready while I power up the Mark V-A."

Locking his legs together and straddling a rough wooden beam of the scaffolding, Richards sat with the probe resting across his knees. In position, he looked directly down on the stationary loop of the Soap Bubble. Piankoff, noting that he was ready, turned the device's twin keys to the left and the soft thrumming of the power pack began. While the pylons slowly began to build up their charge, the Russian again checked that the temporal data was correct.

For Richards, the next two minutes of power up seemed to drag on, but slowly the ring began to rise up directly beneath him. As it did, the hair on the back of his neck began to rise as well. Was that a static charge or was it just his imagination?

Piankoff then said. "All is in readiness. Slowly extend the probe."

Richards gradually lowered the probe vertically through the mirror-like center of the stabilized ring, claw end first. Slowly the first six inches disappeared, then another six, then another foot, then another. All was going well.

Then suddenly, someone or something on the other side began pulling on the probe!

Fortunately for Richards, who found himself in a vertical tug-of-war, he was well anchored to his perch with his legs wrapped around a beam and hands locked on to the probe. In another place, his struggle would have been humorous and perhaps something directly out of a comedy skit, but not here, not now.

Seeing what was happening, the truck driver flew up the rigged scaffolding and stood above Richards grabbing onto the free end of the probe, lending his support. Piankoff, in a neutral, but extremely firm voice called for the extraction of the probe. Both Richards and Tuna complied with a united grunt as the probe's claw vertically cleared the ring. But it was not alone, for a human hand was firmly clutching one of its claws.

Piankoff, seeing the hand, immediately turned both of the power packs command keys to the far right initiating an emergency shutdown. As a result, both Richards and the driver were bathed in a bright, electric-blue flash followed by an ear-splitting crack of sound that seemed to echo for an eternity within the walls of the sanctuary. With ears ringing and the reek of ozone everywhere, Richards and the driver, both clearly sun burned if not singed, had frozen in position and had not let go of the probe. They still held it in its near vertical position.

With the sudden emergency shutdown, the drop ring fell some five feet to the stone pavement of the sanctuary. There it first bounced, and then bounced again. On its third bounce off the limestone pavement the drop ring shattered into several pieces before all of its fragments finally came to a noisy, tinkling rest. But holding on to one of the probe's tongs was a still quivering human hand that was neatly cauterized at the wrist! Richards, seeing the sight, immediately threw up into his lap, but did not give up his grip on the probe.

All that the driver could do was look in wonder and whisper, "Damn."

Piankoff just stared off in silence and then stated the obvious. "Well gentlemen, it seems that today's departure has been blown. I will immediately ring up Borov and see what he has to say."

With that, Richards crudely wiped off his soiled chin with one hand, while refusing to let go the probe with the other.

The truck driver, meanwhile, had released his white-knuckled grip and swung down to floor level to get a better look at the now stationary hand that still had a death grip on the probe. Taking hold of the probe just above the claw, he gently shook the probe so that Richards would finally let go of it.

The driver's ingrained training then took over as he walked over to a small Styrofoam soda cooler. Emptying it of its beverages, he then gently pried at the death-frozen fingers, loosening them. Then with a reverence that Richards could not imagine from such a man, he packed the hand away in the remaining ice. Having sealed the cooler's lid, he then walked over to a low wall near the corner of the sanctuary, and with great deliberation, began to methodically heave up his last meal. Looking down on his own soiled clothing, Richards did not feel quite so foolish or ashamed.

*   *   *

Piankoff's secure satellite transmission with Borov after the aborted and ill-fated temporal probe did not go well.

"But you were the one who said that no one would be in the great god's inner sanctuary during that time of day!" Borov screamed through the receiver of the portable headset.

"Yes, Dr. Borov, I said that in my experience no one would be."

"But why did you have to cut the power with the hand on our side of the temporal rift, for Christ's sake! Who knows what sort of temporal impact that may have caused! Christ! It could even be the hand of a pharaoh!"

"That is very true, Dr. Borov, but I am still standing here within the great god's' sanctuary, and to my way of thinking, nothing of substance has changed."

With that ill-advised answer, Borov lit off like a Roman candle on the Fourth of July. All that Piankoff could do was sit and take it, while Richards and the truck driver listened in on the most colorful recitation of the *RUTI*'s guidelines.

Finally, having run out of breath, Piankoff then asked Borov the inevitable. "Dr. Borov, do you have another drop ring that you can fly in? And for that matter, suggest another temporal window that we could potentially use?"

Borov, still breathing heavily, but now presented with two tangible, non-emotional issues to chew on, gasped. "Colonel, I can easily scavenge the ring from Tombstone and have it there within twenty-four hours. But as to temporal alternatives, I have four to suggest. But I pray that you choose the last one, for it will calibrate to a date precisely ten years later than the last. Ten years is a long time. I know. I know also that you and Richards will have to reconsider some of your operational strategies. But I believe it to be the best, the safest. What do you think?"

Stunned, Piankoff at first did not know how to reply, for this was the first time Borov had asked his opinion on anything. Up until now, the scientist had treated him like an interesting, but highly dangerous lab rat.

After a moment of consideration, the Russian softly answered in his mother tongue. "Dr. Borov, I think your suggestion to reattempt a crossing ten years hence is most wise."

What followed thereafter could be best stated as a mending of fences between the two Russians. Both knew that the other had done his best given an unprecedented situation. Both at least tacitly understood the other's need for decisive action, the other's theoretical concerns. Both desperately needed the other. Piankoff secretly thanked God that Academician Fedorov had lifted Borov's death sentence, for he had come to admire the scientist's intelligence, enthusiasm, and, for the lack of a better word—guts.

When the conversation reached its conclusion, Borov expressed as intimately as one can over an encrypted line. "Sasha, take care my son. Someday I wish to see you sitting across the table from me wearing a second Lenin's Cross. We will both be roaring drunk. And security be damned, you will tell me why you think you earned it."

"Da, Pyotr, I shall mightily try."

Finally hanging up the satellite unit's receiver, Piankoff stood, briefly shook his head, and smiled. Seeing that Richards and the truck driver were waiting impatiently for an explanation what had just transpired.

"Well gentlemen, it looks as if we will get another ring within twenty-four hours. Thereafter, we will run a system test again. If all is nominal, we go, but this time, we will be moving ahead a full ten years in time. That means young lion that several of our operational plans will have to be reconsidered. I suggest that we get to work."

*   *   *

Meanwhile in New Mexico, Borov had just gotten off the line with his personnel at Tombstone, inquiring on the availability of a replacement drop ring. He found out, as he had expected, that there was one. With a deep sigh, he said, "Well, at least that issue has been quickly solved."

Then after several seconds of harried, but random thoughts, another notion came to mind and it was most welcomed for it caused him to smile. It seems that the Mark V-A has earned a nickname.

"I dub thee, TMH—*The Mummy's Hand*. Besides, I always did like that corny old movie!"

Chapter XXIX
Year 3 of Neferkheperure Amenhotep

Richards' first impressions were of extreme silence and dryness. He had landed on a remarkably smooth and cool stone pavement, which his freshly shaven left cheek pressed against. Next, his senses recorded the heavy and numbing aroma of incense, smoldering cedar wood shavings, candle wax, and of countless subtle, flickering shadows formed by the glow of burning tapers and oil lamps. All this he experienced in mere moments. All this that was so ancient, yet so real.

His first drop through the ring's field could only be described as a slow fall through a humid, sticky, but permeable membrane. Going through it, he had felt somehow slimy, unclean. But that was only a momentary sensation, which had quickly passed. What remained, however, was an unsettling sense of dislocation—not of nausea as Piankoff had warned, but rather of imbalance. Remembering how Dr. Borov had emphasized that the human body was nothing more than an electro-chemical engine, Richards now understood, while he gritted his teeth and waited for the unsettling sensation to pass.

His landing had been Fort Benning perfect and the thump of his relaxed, lean weight had been inaudible against the stone flooring. Now, with his equilibrium settling down and eyes that were rapidly adapting to the flickering gloom, he began to silently creep, crab-like, dressed in only a white kilt and woven grass sandals over to where his partner had moved behind the left door pivot of the sanctuary's entranceway. As Richards moved, he sensed a presence behind him. Allowing himself to take a peek over his shoulder, there sat in the smoky, gloomy haze, the life-sized golden image of the great god Amen Re.

He thought. *From the smooth looks of it, it must be made of solid gold! That thing must weigh a ton!*

Gathering himself and continuing on, Richards quickly reached Piankoff and gave him a thumbs up to let him know that he was okay. But Piankoff was unusually tense, tight-lipped, and with streams of sweat coursing down the sides of his freshly shaven head.

Sensing that something was drastically wrong, his look of concern was enough. Piankoff just slowly shook his head in a mixture of frustration and disgust. He pointed to his right ankle, which had already taken on a bloated and swollen look that was apparent even in the low light. The pain the Russian was silently enduring was considerable. Tears were running down his cheeks smearing his carefully applied eye paint.

Between his clenched teeth, he finally whispered in Egyptian. "Young lion, your schooling is past. I fear the worst. I think that my ankle is broken."

That said, Richards carefully sat back against the wall next to his colleague and began to unconsciously run through his emergency checklists. Their first and earliest retrieval window would be in twenty-four hours. Their field contact, whose mere existence no one knew about except Piankoff, had yet to be met. He, Richards, must make a favorable impression on this contact in order to win their future trust and assistance, and to find help if at all possible.

Breaking this momentary reverie, Piankoff again whispered through clenched teeth in Egyptian, "We must move. Help me up. We must leave as soon as possible. We cannot be discovered here."

Richards stood up and almost stumbled forward, catching himself at the last moment. He had forgotten Piankoff's warning about sudden movements following a temporal drop. The closest thing recognizable about the sensation was the vertigo that one sometimes encounters after doing inverted pushups against a wall. But his reaction was more than just a physiological reaction to the drop, the internal dimensions of the sanctuary seemed, no were, much larger, almost by a factor of two. Then he remembered.

This was the original Eighteenth Dynasty sanctuary chamber, not the later one built of pink granite by the brother of Alexander the Great some one thousand years in the future!

Once his head had cleared and legs steadied themselves, Richards gently reached down, took the Russian's left arm, and lifted it over his right shoulder. Being shorter than Piankoff by some three inches meant that the Russian could now lean on Richards and hobble along on one foot. It would be painful, but it would have to do for now.

Next, just getting out of the sanctuary would be a challenge. Standing before what was obviously a massively heavy set of cedar wood doors, Richards placed his hand against the center fissure of the doors and slowly applied an outward pressure. As he did so, he was astonished by how easily the door leaves moved and boldly whispered open a crack. Peering out, he saw no one. Pushing ever so gently more, both he and Piankoff individually squeezed through a narrow gap just barely wide enough to allow their passage. Momentarily leaving Piankoff unsupported on one foot, Richards then had to carefully nudge both leaves back into their fully closed state. To do so, Richards gripped the two edges with his fingertips, powerfully flexing the muscles of his arms and back, all the while gently coaxing the leaves back to rest.

The why for such care with the opening and closing of the great god's sanctuary doors Piankoff had explained to Richards early on. For the door pivots were connected to two hidden bronze gongs by ropes, ropes that Piankoff had discovered (how, he had never said) were under tremendous tension and as a result were a bit stretched with age. Consequently, any dead slow movement of the near-frictionless doors would not trigger the gongs. Further, the stretch in the alarm ropes was such that one could pass through a narrow opening as they had just done.

Now dripping in sweat from exertion and nervous tension, Richards now understood and appreciated why Piankoff had trained him so hard. Taking hold of the Russian again, the pair began to hobble off to their left. They momentarily rested in the dim lamp light against the sharply cut, beautifully carved, and painted historical reliefs in the Great Hall of Records of the Pharaoh Thutmose III. Hidden in the darkness of a column's shadow, the pair then made their way to a little-used southern side entrance of the hall, which led to the colonnaded Great Festival Hall of the same king. Quickly as they could manage, the pair then moved through its forest of inscribed columns as silently as foggy wisps on little cat's feet. Even Carl Sandberg would have been proud with their progress.

Now zigzagging this way and that, following Piankoff's direction, they finally reached the inner side of a massive wall that appeared to have no exit. Recessed in a cleverly disguised shadow created by a seated black granite statue of the lion-headed goddess

Sekhmet, the Russian indicated the way. Taking it without question, Richards and Piankoff soon found themselves outside of the Great Temple. They took their first breaths of the clear, cool night desert air.

Looking up, his partner's intake of breath caused Piankoff to look himself. As anyone who has ever lived in a desert can tell you, the starlight in such pristine environments is simply overwhelming. Moonlight is such that you can almost read a newspaper. But in the pre-industrial desert environment of the Fourteenth Century BC, it is the very clarity of these phenomena that made them all the more so stunning.

Smiling, Piankoff murmured. "Yes, my young lion, you truly are city bred."

Following that quiet remark, the two instantly froze, for both clearly had heard a noise from a nearby shadow. Unbelievably, it sounded almost like a snicker that was choked off. Out of the shadow came toward them a short, silent, and indistinct form. It was a priest.

The priest said to them in a hushed, sarcastic, yet clearly understandable Egyptian.

"Stargazing are we? How you two do carry on. And here I am supposed to be waiting for pharaoh's own special envoys from a distant land. Could you two somehow be them?"

With a simple nod from Piankoff, the priest turned and began to led them through a maze of low subsidiary, white-washed mud brick buildings. These included granary structures, various gradations of priestly housing, and storage facilities that nourished the Great Temple of Amen Re. During their dizzying meanderings, all that Richards could tell was that they were heading in a roughly southerly direction away from the main temple proper. Once, stealing a glance over his shoulder, he could still see the top crest of the southern outer wall of the Great Temple behind him that confirmed his suspicions.

He had time for only one orientation, for their guide was quick and allusive. They hobbled along as best they could, but Richards began to wonder whether it would be easier if he should just carry the Russian over his shoulder fireman's style, as his chest on fire from exertion and sweating like a proverbial pig. They then suddenly overtook and almost ran over their shadowy priest, who had stopped stock still in a narrow gangway between two low structures.

Whirling around with eyes that flashed with lightning, the whispered voice lashed out at them.

"What's wrong with you two? You are as slow as oxen and as noisy as braying donkeys! Do you wish to awaken even those who have gone West? Now, stand here in absolute silence. I will be right back."

And with that the form vanished around the right corner.

Richards, his chest heaving heavily, tried to get control of his gasping effort, calm his breathing. Piankoff, who had been wincing with every movement, just gently patted his supportive arm and gave him a thumbs-up sign. He too was exhausted from the brief, although serpentine journey. All he could do was hang his head in an attempt to catch his breath for the next sprint, the next excruciating and jarring stabs of pain.

Then the guide reappeared and impatiently motioned the pair back into motion. Richards, not believing how stiff he had become in such a short time, let out a grunt and received another sharp look that would have stopped a Marine drill sergeant cold. On they went around the corner and immediately into a dark open doorway where a strong hand stopped them in their tracks. A quiet rustling behind them announced that the woven reed doorway had been lowered. Richards' stressed senses noted the delicious smell of fresh bread mixed with incense, sweat, and something else, something vaguely moldy. His stomach, right on cue, growled noisily.

Then in the total darkness a distinctly masculine and commanding voice quietly chuckled and said, "I hear that you are hungry. I am honored. But first speak the correct words. For if you do not, prepare yourselves to go West to the Underworld domain of Apophis this very night."

Piankoff, gritting his teeth in sheer agony, carefully formulated the required words.

"We are but strangers in a strange land."

Richards, despite the situation, could not help smiling to himself, in recognition of that famous Ray Bradbury quote.

With a grunt of recognition and a quick command, a single oil lamp began to sputter to life in the far corner of the room.

Before the pair stood a very serious-looking priest dressed much like themselves in a simple white kilt and sandals. In his left hand was a crescent-shaped sword with a wickedly sharp inner edge. The priest's age could not be ascertained, as his head too was cleanly-shaven. Relatively tall for an ancient and of strong build, only some worry lines around his eyes and mouth and the first beginnings of a paunch could suggest the coming of middle age.

As for Piankoff and Richards, this formidable priest could have cut them down where they stood, hanging on to each other as they were, exhausted, thirsty, easy prey. Instead a wry smile formed, and extending his arms he marched forward and hugged, no crushed, the pair together kissing both of their foreheads exclaiming.

"My brothers, welcome to my household."

Richards was relieved at the warm welcome, but was horrified to note the priest's right hand, or, to be more exact, the lack of it! It was missing from the wrist down! In fact he found himself staring at its cleanly formed and tanned stump.

Could this be the same one who just yesterday lost his hand to our probe! Oh please Lord, say it isn't true!

Having finished his welcome the priest stepped back and crossed his arms before him in such a way as to hide his missing hand. He then continued.

"My good and old friend Piankhotep, I see that you are injured. Is it your foot or leg?"

Piankoff, grimacing, simply stated. "It is my foot. I am such a clumsy ox."

Nodding, he turned and beckoned to the now silent priest, who had lighted the oil lamp behind them. "Inform the physician Ankhmes that he will be receiving a patient shortly. And if you receive any rebuke from either him or his household about the hour of this request, tell them beware or they will have to deal directly with me, Meryptah. Now off with you."

In response, the priest quickly bowed and hurriedly slipped out past the drawn reed door.

Even to Richards' relatively green in-country ear, he could tell that this Meryptah was no one to fool with. The accustomed command voice of absolute authority was impossible to miss. In another time and place, Richards could easily imagine this priest would have made one hell of a good football coach or one hell of a general. In either case, he was a natural-born leader. It truly was a good thing that he and Piankoff were such close friends, but from when?

Remind yourself to ask about this guy, Richards noted to himself.

"And now, my dear friend Piankhotep, who is this young lion?" said Meryptah, who now directed his attention squarely upon Richards.

"He is my good and dear friend," Piankoff replied, "and he is my most trusted assistant. And what you have said is not only correct, but prophetic as well. For his name is indeed Mayneken—young lion."

Meryptah merely listened while he held Richards' steady, clear-eyed, and unwavering gaze. Then, breaking the stare-down, he glanced over his lean and powerful body. He then remarked to Piankoff, "He looks as dangerously quick as an angered horned viper. But," and now looking directly at again at Richards, "is he civilized enough to speak our tongue, or is he a mute?"

Richards, who had not ended the stare down, merely replied in a soft voice, "Most noble Meryptah, I first wish to ease the pain of my master. Second, of doing you honor. And only lastly, of filling my belly."

Pleased and a bit surprised by Richards' direct tone, Meryptah then smiled the knowing smile of someone who had finally taken the measure of another.

"Mayneken," he said, "I shall attend to all very soon."

Meryptah gestured to the broad, mud brick bench that surrounded three sides of the interior of the one room structure. This wide shelf was variously decorated and padded with heavy cushions, rugs, gaily-colored tapestries. Here and there were strategically placed oil lamps of which only one was lit. In one corner was a wide and open bowl of what could only be various fruits and dates. Two jugs of water sat closely nearby. Alongside were several still steaming triangular loaves of fresh bread and next to them were no less than three sealed jars. Their clay vintage stamps declared them to be one of wine and two of beer. Both were the produce of the vineyards and breweries of the great god's temple.

Richards guided Piankoff over to the right padded bench or *mastaba*, as a modern Arab would have called it. First easing him down and then carefully elevating his injured limb on several cushions, Richards then quickly filled a common earthenware goblet to the brim with water and held it to Piankoff's lips. The injured man greedily gobbled it down. Next, Richards took a length of linen, quickly tore it into several bandage-like lengths, wetted them down with the cool water and then gently and expertly wrapped Piankoff's swollen ankle in a way recognizable to any modern athletic trainer.

This whole performance was carefully scrutinized by Meryptah, who then logically asked. "Mayneken, are you a physician?"

"No, Great One, it is just that I have been in battle many times and have come to know the way of these things."

"I am pleased to hear that for otherwise your skill in wrapping would have made you a *wab*-priest of Anubis, or even worse."

This reference to the ancient Egyptian embalming priesthood brought a smile and a soft chuckle to Richards' lips, for certain members of that profession had often been accused of necrophilia—hence the "or even worse" comment.

As for Meryptah, he was pleased that Mayneken had caught his attempt at humor. *This so-called young lion may indeed be a special one at that!*

With Piankoff somewhat more comfortable, Richards then surprised Meryptah with a specific request.

"Noble Meryptah, my master requires a thick brew of willow tree bark. Is this possible?"

"Why, why, certainly! But first should you not wait for the opinion of Ankhmes? Besides, does Piankhotep here have a headache from too much beer? I thought his foot was injured?"

Meryptah could not have known that willow bark was a natural source of aspirin. He did not realize that as a mild pain reliever and vasodilator it would also help reduce the foot's swelling as well. Regardless, he was so impressed by Mayneken's take charge attitude that he himself left in quest for a draught of willow bark brew.

Finally alone, the pair merely locked eyes. Richards, then formally addressed his colleague in his Egyptianized name.

"Well, Piankhotep, my teacher, I believe that your ankle is either badly sprained or broken. How do you feel?"

"Like the fresh dung of a sick and dying donkey," rasped Piankoff.

"Why did you send Meryptah on that errand? Don't you realize who he is? He is the High Priest of Amen Re! Besides, why willow bark brew?"

Looking down over his well-muscled, crossed arms and smiling like a dutiful registered nurse, Richards replied. "Willow bark brew is chock-full of good things. It will taste horrible. You will drink it all. It will help to both ease the pain and reduce the ankle's swelling. Is that clear?"

Then he thought to add with a grin. "Please, my teacher."

Smiling despite his precarious situation, Piankoff could only reply, "Physician, I will fully comply."

He caught himself thinking about how the once young and green Richards was now taking care of him, how he was naturally taking command, how well his initial performance had impressed Meryptah, who is one a tough character. He could only smile to himself.

Richards interrupted his reverie.

"Now, Piankhotep, your devoted assistant wishes to know how did you come to know Meryptah? And did you happen to notice his missing right hand? Is his missing hand, ours?"

"As to your last question, unquestionably it is. That dramatic and traumatic event guaranteed his ascension to the highly regarded position that he presently enjoys.

"As for his friendship, he only believes us to be very powerful and special friends of the Great Horus, that is, the former Great Horus, now the recent Osiris Nebmare Amenhotep. As to why I chose him, he was the close childhood friend of our target, who is now the new Great Horus."

Then continuing on after a deep and labored breath.

"Needless to say under his care and with his influence we should be able to meet our goals."

Richards, who was drinking his fill of water and wolfing down several dates, was stunned by his mentor's matter of fact discourse on how he chose, befriended, mutilated, and then manipulated a native's trust.

All he could think was, Russians. They have such a Byzantine mentality and approach to practically everything they do.

At this point, the sound of hurried footsteps arrived before their hideout and Meryptah appeared, a bit winded, but with a stopped and sealed jar in the crook of his right arm. Appearing as he did, Richards could not help but imagine what a splendid fullback he would have made, the way he carried the jar was just like a pig's skin.

Saying not a word, Meryptah handed the jar over to Richards, who immediately broke its seal and began to pour the uncommonly fragrant liquid into Piankoff's cup.

Not wishing to offend Piankoff's standing with Meryptah, Richards couched his next words carefully.

"My teacher, please drink this to ease your pain."

Taking the cup, Piankoff skeptically raised one eyebrow and peered over its lip at Richards before drinking it, giving a look that said, are you sure young lion?

All that Richards could do was nod. Piankoff tilted his head back and downed the contents of the cup in one gulp.

Richards first surprising thought was. *What can he do with vodka?*

For Piankoff, the taste was not bad, in fact, it strongly tasted like a sweet raisin wine, no, a sweet date wine. Handing the cup back to Richards, his arm began to numb, his vision to blur, his head became strangely uncoordinated, his eyelids exceedingly heavy. Then he just sat back, passed out, and began to slumber.

Shocked, Richards first looked at Meryptah, who looked very pleased with himself. Next, he looked at the seal on the jar, which only now he took the time to notice had a particular botanical shape. That drew a very deep and audible breath of dread from him.

Yes, he thought. *I remember Professor Milson's lecture on ancient Egyptian pharmacology. His discussion of the many excavated* bil-bil *jars that looked exactly like this one, and what Tim Scarbourgh's book had said they contained.*

Richards began to slowly rotate the jar in his hands to see if there was any other sort of an identifier, a seal stamp, anything.

There it was!

In disgust and baring his teeth like an enraged animal and with a low growl, Richards' response was deeply ingrained. He spiked the jar into the hard-packed earthen flooring with such force that it shattered and splattered its contents throughout the room on both himself, his master, and of course Meryptah, whose composure, at first surprised, was now angered.

Ignoring the rising blush on Meryptah's face, Richards turned and faced him and in a quiet, but withering tone.

"Noble Meryptah. That was not willow bark brew. Who gave you that sealed jar?"

Now realizing Richards emotional explosion was not directed at him, but his medicinal source, Meryptah cooled his anger slightly, but not much, especially since he was not used to being talked to like a scribe's apprentice, much less a physician's errand boy.

"The medicine was proscribed by the royal court physician, Ankhmes. Given the nature of the injury that I described, he overruled your addled suggestion, as he put it, and gave me that jar instead."

Richards, realizing with what and whom he was competing against, decided that diplomacy was best. Falling to one knee and bowing his head before Meryptah, he then formally stated.

"Noble One, I am sorry for I know that I may have offended you! My only wish was to do the very best for my teacher. Your many and kind efforts on his behalf will be remembered for eternity. Strike me if I have offended you. For your anger I have earned is with me and should not be known to my teacher."

Meryptah took Richards up on his offer, for the lights, as they say, suddenly, painfully, blinked out.

*   *   *

He sensed warmth, the smell of incense, sweet flowers, and then a softness followed by a gentle tickle of a breeze blowing across his chest. Finally came the feeble first conscious attempt to stir.

Ahhggh!

My neck, no, my head feels as if it has caved in! Richards thought. *What a hangover! I won't try that again!*

Then with a mixture of good humor and taunting, a disembodied voice spoke to him in Egyptian.

"Mayneken, I see that you are finally awake. Would you like some willow bark brew for that headache of yours?"

With that verbal needle, Richards first slowly opened one eye and then the other to discover that he had been moved. Slowly sitting up with a grimace of pain, he carefully swung his legs over the edge of the comfortable bed frame that he had been placed upon. Hanging his head and looking down at the floor, he saw his naked feet on smooth limestone paving. Daring to reach around to the back of his head, he found a knot the size of a golf ball.

Ah, the grim evidence that Meryptah had taken me up on my offer! An offer apparently accepted in full, given that I am still alive.

With his arms resting on his knees, Richards finally leveraged his head to look up. Before him he found a smiling Meryptah towering over him again, but this time he extended to him an exquisitely hand-beaten bronze cup.

Rising now to stand to his full height, Richards asked taking the cup, "Where am I?"

"You are within the guest chambers of the royal annex. Both you and your teacher are the honored guests of the Great Horus, although at the moment he is unaware of his generosity.

"Now, Mayneken, drink deeply. This will ease your pain."

Accepting the cup and experimentally taking a sniff of its liquid contents, Richards' nose curled a bit at its sharp odor, which reminded him vaguely of a chemistry lab.

"Willow bark brew?"

"Willow bark brew," Meryptah nodded, smiling back.

Swallowing the entire contents of the cup Richards consciously told his mind not to gag. Wiping his lips with his forearm, Richards then returned the now empty cup with a slightly painful bow of the head in thanks. For Meryptah's part, he only mechanically accepted the returned cup, for he was carefully inspecting every inch of Richards' lean, superbly muscled, and now naked body. Then bending down into a full squat, he began with clinical interest to examine the four arthroscopic scars that surrounded Richards' left knee, probing at them with the forefinger of his left hand. Rising, he gripped Richards' left shoulder and turned him around as if he were a department store mannequin. When Richards' complied, he heard Meryptah's gasp as reverently touched with the fingers of his left hand the four nasty parallel scars that ran from Richards' left shoulder blade across to above the right hip.

Quietly the high priest asked. "Brave and noble Mayneken, how did you receive these marks of battle?"

Gulping and thankful Meryptah could not see his shocked face, Richards furiously invent a story.

He thought, *what can I tell him? That I got those scars because I was a dumb little shit, when I dumped my Uncle Bill's vintage Indian at 73, blew out my knee, and slid on my back for what seemed like forever? Fortunately, I did it on a smooth runway. To this day I will never forget Uncle Bill's face. As tore up he was about the bike, he never mentioned it once. He had totally focused upon me.*

In the end, Richards decided to split the difference between the truth and fiction.

"Noble One, the story of my imperfections is not the result of battle, but rather of my stupidity. When I was a young man on a lion hunt with my uncle, I broke my spear into the chest of a magnificent she-lion. Thinking that I had pierced her strong heart and killed her, I came at her too eagerly with my knife to take her tail. One of the lioness' forepaws, however, was not dead, and in her death throws she marked me so."

Properly stunned and greatly impressed with the tale, Richards' poetic style, and turn of speech, Meryptah could only say, "I now can see Piankhotep has indeed chosen, wisely."

At the mention of Piankoff, Richards replied.

"Thank you again for your many kindnesses, Meryptah. But where is my master? I wish to see him."

"I see you are again of only one mind. But be not concerned about Piankhotep, for he is in good and capable hands.

"But as for you, before you can see him you must first properly dust your feet. You are no longer traveling the river. You are now a house guest of the Great Horus."

Although frustrated by the dismissive response, little did Richards realize the treat that was in store.

* * *

As soon as Meryptah took his leave, Richards began to explore his immediate surroundings. He was in a well appointed high-ceilinged room about twenty by twenty feet square that opened onto a balcony-like porch. Its whitewashed mud brick walls and ceiling were brightly decorated in masculine motifs with painted scenes of lion hunting, hippopotamus spearing, and fowling along the river. Above his comfortably padded bed frame, which stood on narrow but beautifully carved lion's feet about a foot high, he noted an elevated and cleverly gathered bunch of fine linen that no doubt served as mosquito netting. In each corner of the room stood chest-high stone supports with multi-necked oil lamps. Along one wall, hanging from a light and airy wooden framework, were several carefully placed linens and what seemed to be a freshly washed kilt. Finally, next to his bed frame stood an exquisitely carved piece of furniture with intricately carved ivory inlays. Opening its lidded top, Richards immediately smelled the fragrance of cedar wood. Inside he then discovered tiny and delicate ceramic ampoules. Curious, he gently tugged at one's stopper and instantly recognized an intense bouquet of the papyrus flower.

Perfumes, oils, and deodorants. This place is almost a Holiday Inn Express!

Satisfied that he had exhausted his investigation of his quarters and finding himself totally at ease with his nudity, Richards then stepped out onto the veranda surrounded by a low stone railing made up of slats carved as arching cobra and a central set of steps that opened to a marvelous view of the bustling broad highway of Egypt, the Nile. It was then that it dawned upon him that he was now on the western bank of the river. Apparently, both he and Piankoff were secreted across the river during the night.

This place must be the former palace of Amenhotep III, he reasoned. The *Malkata* of modern Egypt, "the place where stuff can be picked up," so numerous and thick were the pottery sherds of that archaeological site.

Again looking up to take in the view, to his left stood the capital city of Thebes, or *Waset*, as the ancient Egyptians' called it. At that very moment, Richards counted no less than twenty-four wooden river craft flying their traditional rectangular sail. No doubt they were shuttling passengers and commerce to and fro in an endless cycle common to all river ferries around the world. Then, he noted another thirteen or so papyrus reed skiffs, which looked like modern surfboards with extremely low gunwales.

How in the world do they keep them from tipping them over? He asked to himself.

Further to his left, he could easily see the expansive temple complex *Ipet-isut*, "the most select of places," dedicated to the Great God Amen Re. Its monumental white limestone gateway was ablaze with bright paints and inlayed precious metals. Before it colorful banners fluttered lazily in the wind atop their electrum-tipped flagpoles. Behind these could be seen the gleam of the gold capped obelisks of the Pharaohs Hatshepsut and Thutmose III protruding into the cobalt blue, cloudless sky.

Marking that site as to where they had dropped into this era, Richards then estimated the distance as being about a mile and a half to two miles away as the crow flies. Not far, he thought, but surely a distant trek for someone with a broken ankle.

Immediately before him across the river stood the Luxor Temple, *Ipet-resyt*, or the "Southern Harem." Smiling to himself, Richards then remembered what Professor Milson had said about the temple. That it was the site of a once-a-year ritual orgy for the Great God and no doubt his priests and priestesses as well.

Ah, these Egyptians, Richards crooned to himself.

Still taking in the scene and leaning forward on the railing of the veranda, Richards' blissful day dreaming came to a screeching halt, when he heard two girlish giggles coming from his room.

Spinning around there stood two lithe, well-proportioned servant girls, each wearing black-plaited wigs, eye-paint, sandals, hip necklaces, and grinning, dimpled smiles.

Wide-eyed, Sia thought. *My! This noble is as hairy as an Apis bull. Meryptah had been correct. He has been on his journey far too long.*

Meanwhile her partner, Tia was thinking. *I have never before seen such broad shoulders! He must be a most powerful warrior, but his head is shaved in the priestly fashion. Could he be both priest and warrior?*

Appearing totally nonplused at Richards' obvious embarrassment, the pair each took him by the hand and led him out of his quarters to an adjoining room of similar size, decoration, and appointments. Once there, they had Richards sit down into a shallow-rimmed mud brick basin, where they began to drizzle and then pour jugs of hot, cedar-scented, sun-warmed water over his head.

This feels good, so soothing, Richards thought as he lifted his still very sore head to face the falling water's soothing stream.

Once wet, the servant girls began to briskly scrub him down with mitten-like hand coverings that they alternately dipped into the basin's water and into an open vessel of extremely fine limestone powder. The effect was a mild abrasive bath that invigorated and sensitized his entire being. Much as with Meryptah's reaction to his scarred back, so too did these marks draw the attention and wide-eyed wonderment from his two beautiful bath attendants, who up to this moment had not said a word to him, but began muttering quietly amongst themselves.

Then they began on his feet and being very ticklish Richards tried to control his squirming, but the girls playfully took advantage of him. The heavy and thick calluses on Richards' feet again attracted their curiosity, for they had never before seen the cumulative effect of modern athletic shoes on the human heel nor had they ever seen before such an arched foot, being far more accustomed to a flatten foot pad. Undaunted by their discoveries, each produced a small conveniently shaped stone and began to gently abrade away the offensive and ugly heel deposits. Again while Richards wriggled. When they were finished with his heels, the charming pair, still armed with their stones, now carefully filed away at his toenails. His fingernails were next, which they quickly formed into smooth and even curves.

After a final rinse, again in the heavenly cedar-scented water, Richards was made to rise and step out of the basin. Looking down he saw that he had left behind a small deltaic deposit of fine limestone, skin, hair, and bone in its bottom. Standing with his legs wide and arms extended, the ever-smiling and giggling pair briskly dried him off with linen towels of the sort that Richards had earlier seen hanging in his room.

So that's what they're for. Richards now realized.

Finished, and again each taking a hand, Richards was then led over to a slightly sloped, flat, wicker bed, where he was told to lay down on his back. With one on each side, they both began to generously slick and massage him with a scented oil.

Probably sesame oil. Richards thought.

Then came the moment of truth as they both began to shave him! Starting at the ankle of each leg, the pair proceeded to shave expertly and rapidly in quick, overlapping strokes.

The mere sensation, Richards thought, was simply to die for.

As they both began to progress up Richards' powerfully muscled legs, a certain tension, no panic, began to build deep within his mind. Again remembering that lecture by Professor Milson on ancient Egyptian hygiene, the point was made that the entire body had to be shaved as a prevention against fleas and lice. Squeezing his eyes tight, he attempted to invoke the god of logic to calm him. Then his curiosity just got the better of him and he peered over to see their highly honed bronze razors. That was a distinct mistake for with that image, he totally lost it, and beads of sweat began to pop out on his forehead.

He silently prayed. *Please don't let one of them slip!*

Expert groomers they were, blessedly, they didn't.

Now with both sides of his body totally shaved foot to neck, the pair had him turn over and the process from ankle on up was repeated. Then Richards was asked to turn over and sit up, while Sia shaved the top and back of his head and Tia his forehead, neck and face.

As for Richards, leaning back on his hands with his head back, he was clearly in la-la land.

His first thought, *This could become habit-forming.*

But as the lovely Tia shaved his face Richards was confronted with her charms up close and personal and as with all flushing and vascular reactions controlled by hormones, he stirred.

Wide-eyed at the priest's reaction to her, Tia did only what seemed to be natural, and so she straddled him with a smile.

This priest is truly an Apis bull! As she groaned in obvious pleasure.

Dr. Milson, you would never believe this! This is what "the dusting of one's feet" means.

*　　*　　*

Now fully composed, refreshed, scented in fresh and woodsy papyrus oil, dressed in a fresh kilt and sandals, his eye-paint expertly applied, and fed a marvelously delicious breakfast of dates, fresh hot bread, honey, dried fish and cheese, Richards was fetched by a somber middle-aged functionary dressed in a simple white kilt and sandals. As they left the confines of his guest area, they crossed an enclosed courtyard with a reflecting pool and several blooming and fragrant trees. Looking up and finding the sun, Richards estimated that it was about eight in the morning. Walking half around the pool, they entered another portal on the courtyard's opposite side. Once within, it became apparent to Richards that this guest area was a mirror of his own and sure enough they soon entered Piankoff's quarters.

Bowing at the waist to his colleague, Richards formally intoned, "Good morning, my teacher."

Looking up at his guests from his breakfast, the very same as what Richards had been treated to, Piankoff said to the accompanying functionary.

"I thank you for the courtesy of guiding my assistant to my quarters. You may now leave."

With the departure of the silent guide, Piankoff got down to business.

"This," pointing to his extended, splinted, and wrapped foot, "I am told is broken in no less than two places. I am also told by the court physician Ankhmes that he was successful in mating the breaks evenly. As for the pain, well, good old Ankhmes has provided me with a jug of this. Do you recognize it, Mayneken?"

Looking over, Richards saw that it was another sealed *bil-bil* jar.

"Do you know what the liquid of that jar contains?" Richards asked.

"Well my dear Mayneken, I can surely tell you that it is not willow bark brew," Piankoff exclaimed with a laugh.

"No, not willow bark brew, Piankhotep, but red poppy resin diluted in sweet raisin wine."

Not grasping the significance of what Richards had just told him, Richards interrupted his mildly sedated mind.

"How much of the sweet wine did you drink?"

"Oh, about a half a cup since I awoke."

Then he began to again ramble on. "Why do you ask me this question Mayneken? And with such a cross and furrowed brow? Ankhmes specifically told me to drink a half a cup whenever the pain returns. So I did as I was told.

"By the way, he wants to meet you. It seems that your demand last night for the willow bark brew constituted some sort of personal affront to him and a breach of professional etiquette. Be advised that as the court physician he also has the ear of pharaoh."

Having listened patiently to his slightly slurred speech, Richards then decided to break through the drug-induced haze and reach his partner. Stepping forward and then squatting down close to be eye-to-eye, Richards whispered slowly in modern English.

"Piankoff. The sweet wine is laced with raw opium. Do not drink any more of it or you will become an opium addict like the Roman Emperor Marcus Aurelius."

To this total breach of security Piankoff's eyes widened in alarm, then blinked several times as the message was clearly received. Gulping several times like a gasping beached fish, he then carefully formulated his reply in the ancient tongue.

"Thank you, Mayneken. I did not realize. In fact, come to think of it, you're right. I haven't been myself lately. I was beginning to wonder why."

Looking down at his slightly trembling hands, he quietly added. "And now I know why."

Piankoff then looked away and stared off into space while unconsciously grasping and rubbing his hands together, trying to somehow regain their control, to calm the trembling. For Richards, this was a good sign, for whenever his mentor was deep in thought he exercised his hands in this way. Richards also knew that Piankoff didn't smoke. In fact, he was a total health nut and in this business had to be for his life depended upon it. Now confronted with the fact that he had raw opium polluting his system Piankoff was shocked by that frightening revelation.

Returning to the present, Piankoff then lucidly asked Richards.

"Will you be able to make our first check in?"

"I do not know how, for I have no clue as to where I have been. But if you wish me to try, I will."

Sitting back in contemplation, Piankoff then decided.

"We will try today if we can, but tomorrow we must. Otherwise, our distant friends will needlessly worry and I do not want that to happen."

Richards then moved on to what was really on his mind.

"How are you going to get around? Have you even tried to stand?"

Piankoff at first frowned a bit at the first question, and then began to lever himself up to answer the second. Richards came over to steady his partner, who, with just the effort of being vertical and standing on one foot had broke a fresh sweat on his head. Breathing hard, Piankoff then nodded for Richards to let him go and then began to slowly hop around the room. Richards could tell that the slight jarring of each hop was causing considerable pain in the Russian's foot even in his semi-drugged state. Finally stopping after five hops, and now dripping wet in perspiration, Piankoff declared, "I think a pair of crutches would do the trick. Then there would not be any bouncing stress. What do you think?"

"Fine, but the crutches will have to be made. I just cannot go out and buy a pair. Perhaps my colleague and physician friend Ankhmes can be of help. Besides, I think it is high time that I paid him a courtesy call."

Richards then said with a wicked grin, "I will return with a pair as soon as I can. In the meantime, stay put, keep the ankle elevated, and by all means, stay away from that sweet wine."

Smiling, Piankoff said, "I think you would make a fine physician, Mayneken."

With that Richards left his partner. As he exited Piankoff's quarters he found that the man who had guided him here had been standing outside the entrance the whole time waiting for him. Suspicious, Richards' made a slight bow to the guide and politely asked whether he knew the present whereabouts of the court physician Ankhmes.

Surprised by the deference that Richards had paid to him, the somber man briefly smiled, regained his composure, and then said,

"Noble Mayneken, it is my desire to assist you in any way that I can. Please follow me."

Off they went through a maze of rooms, chambers, halls, and courtyards that would rival the palace and gardens of Versailles. It did not take long, however, before Richards had become convinced that there had to have been a shorter, more direct route to the physician. His guide was purposely going all around Robin Hood's forest just to confuse him. Richards, as a test of this theory, began noting everything and anything that he could use as a landmark. Sure enough, while crossing an enclosed courtyard there was the very same tree with a drooping branch. When Richards saw it, he stopped immediately, crossed his arms, and took a belligerent stance with feet wide apart. His guide, continuing on a few feet, then recognized that he was no longer being followed. Turning around he saw Richards' demeanor and casually asked.

"Yes, noble Mayneken. What is wrong? The noble court physician Ankhmes is just a few feet away."

"That," Richards began in a very quiet tone, "my dear friend, is very doubtful, for this is the second time that we have passed through this very courtyard and through that portal before us."

Now lowering his voice to barely a whisper, "Now, my dear friend, allow me to be clear. We are now going directly to Ankhmes. No side passages, no detours, directly to the physician, am I understood?"

The guide, throughout this lecture, took it with a straight back and unwavering eyes. The only give away that Richards could note that he had placed him under any stress whatsoever was that he had unconsciously hid his hands behind him. Noting this, Richards softened his speech a grade and then observed.

"My friend, please excuse my brusqueness and total lack of manners. By what name are you called?"

In surprise, the guide stammered out. "Thutmose, Noble One."

"Ah, Thutmose, that is a truly noble name. Please understand. I am more a warrior than a priest. That which I need I go directly after.

"Now, quit hiding your hands. I will not beat them with a rod as if you were a scribal student. Serve my master and me well, and I will never embarrass you or speak ill of you before anyone. I swear this upon my family's memory."

During this mild reprimand, Richards could see that Thutmose went through a series of facial transformations that reflected indifference, smugness, shock, relief, and finally a hint of respect.

Well, Richards observed. *I hope that I finally got through to him. If he works out, perhaps he may be useful.*

After a few seconds past and the words settled in, Richards purposefully relaxed his stance and body language, and in a friendly voice said, "My dear Thutmose, you are my trusted guide, please take me to the court physician, Ankhmes."

With that, Thutmose shared a small smile with Richards and bowed his head saying, "As you wish noble Mayneken."

CHAPTER XXX
The Royal Physician

They arrived at the physician's chamber moments later. The subject of their quest was completely engrossed, sitting cross-legged on the floor, while busily writing upon a low writing desk. Surrounded by twenty thick papyrus rolls, the physician was focused on one before him. Richards could not help but imagine what a treasure trove just one of those rolls would have been to a modern Egyptologist.

Ankhmes, with his bald head bent over close to the writing surface and with the fingers of his right hand heavily stained with ink from his reed pen, reminded Richards of his childhood days and the many story books that his mother had read to him. This scene was precisely what he had imagined a far-sighted wizard's gnome must have looked like.

Having quietly stood before the furiously writing physician for a good twenty seconds, and then another, Richards decided to break the ice, and loudly cleared his throat.

Not even looking up from his writing, Ankhmes in a gruff voice said. "Leave me. I am busy."

And promptly continued to ignore his existence.

Richards, who had had enough to his man's attitude, shifted to the crossed armed stance that had so effectively worked with his guide Thutmose.

Then he said in a quiet, yet confident tone, "I can see now why my orders for willow bark brew were not followed. The listener was far too busy to listen to my command."

Abruptly looking up in a mixture of shock, recognition, and anger, the physician slitted his eyes, pursed his lips, sat up to his full height and said nothing. He didn't have to, or so he thought. After all, should not his full glare be sufficient enough to scare away this minor nuisance?

For Richards, he could only smile and chuckle down at what looked like an Egyptian Budda, for that is precisely what the middle-aged and overweight physician resembled.

Richards' chuckle brought a mild gasp from Thutmose, who was trying his best to now hide behind his charge.

Meanwhile the physician's silent glare continued unabated and now was underscored with an extended lower lip of pouting defiance. Ignoring all of these signals and recognizing them for what they were, a bluff, Richards then stepped forward into the room and squatted down cross-legged before the physician so that he could share the same level eye-to-eye. But even more, Richards wanted to invade his space, to make him uncomfortable, to make him feel assaulted in his own territory, to put the physician under siege. It worked for the pout disappeared, wonder became doubt with a bit of fear tinged the physician's eyes as he leaned back as far as he could go without falling over and overturning his writing desk.

Richards then asked, again in his quiet and confident tone.

"Most noble Ankhmes, chief physician to the royal court and the Master and Mistress of the Two Lands, greetings, I am Mayneken. Now that I have the pleasure of your undivided attention, my teacher, Piankhotep, requires two walking sticks so that he may walk. Where could I find such things?"

Having regained his composure somewhat, Ankhmes responded in a remarkably high and squeaky voice that either betrayed his remaining fear, his anger, or the fact that he was a neutered male. Which, Richards could not ascertain.

"Walking sticks? Are you referring to a walking stick that the old use to support themselves?"

"Yes, exactly, but two, not just one. One for each arm."

"Yes." Said the physician as his eyes glazed over momentary and his voice began to take on more and more the authoritative aspect of his station.

"But would not the use of two walking sticks put too much strain on the shoulders in their attempt to support the body's entire weight?"

"Not if both possessed a hand hold midway down their length to lean upon."

Ankhmes then thought. *Just who is this brash Mayneken? Who knows the workings of willow bark brew and that of the red poppy? And his ideas are so curious!*

And why would an injured noble with a broken foot want to walk when he could be so easily carried instead? And this ingenious use of not one, but two walking sticks, most curious indeed.

"Well, noble Mayneken, what your master requires does not exist."

Richards continued. "Well then, from whom did you get the wooden splints with which you so carefully and expertly mended my master's ankle?"

"Why, why, the splints came from the wood scrap of the royal carpenter, of course!" Ankhmes retorted as if he were conversing with a total fool.

Richards' reaction to his retort surprised him.

"Noble Ankhmes, my teacher and I thank you for that information. In your wisdom, do you think that my fine guide Thutmose here would know where to take me to meet the royal carpenter?"

"By the *ka*s of his ancestors he should, the royal carpenter Kasekhkem is his younger brother!"

Richards, now wearing a surprised smile on his face, turned and looked over his left shoulder at Thutmose, who at his mention was still in a slight bow to the court physician.

Upon turning back around. "Noble Ankhmes, my teacher and I wish to again thank you, but before I leave, may I ask what all of these learned scrolls contain?"

Now, clearly in control of the situation and flattered that Richards had asked, Ankhmes began, "Finally, someone recognizes the great weight of the task before me. Before you over there are three ancient medical treatises that are most useful, but which require additions. Those over there are imperfect copies, but with some valuable additions. Here, before me, I am making a new edition of the old and imperfect, thereby improving them all through my great labors."

"May I read its beginning?" Richards innocently asked.

Now with an enthusiasm that Richards had long recognized as universal among all aspiring academicians, Ankhmes grabbed one of the rolls from the floor and extended it to him thinking.

Now, let's see if this puffed up and clucking muscle-bound rooster can even begin to make heads or tails of it!

Gratefully accepting the thick papyrus roll as if it were the most fragile and precious gift imaginable, Richards then bent over into the typical cross-legged scribal sitting position and began to unroll the papyrus. Carefully curling it back to reveal its first careful vertical columns of writing, he began to slowly read, keeping his place with his left forefinger, his lips silently moving as he read. Then, in near shock of recognition, Richards curled the papyrus scroll forward to jump ahead and confirm his suspicions.

"Instructions concerning a wound at the top of an eyebrow." He read aloud.

"If you examine a man having a wound in the top of his eyebrow, penetrating all the way to the bone, then you should massage his wound, and draw the gash together for him with stitching.

"You should then say concerning his condition: One having a wound in his eyebrow. An ailment which I will treat.

"Now after you have stitched it up, you should bind fresh meat upon it the first day. If you find that the stitching of this wound is lose, you should draw it together for him with two *aiiy*-strips (now just what's that?), and you should treat it with grease and honey every day until he recovers."

My God! Richards thought. *This is a clinical treatment from the famous Papyrus Smith medical papyrus! I wonder whether this is the original or the copy that would ultimately survive into modern times to be translated by James Breasted?*

Simultaneously, Ankhmes sat stunned as he listened to his visitor's fluent reading of the highly specialized medical treatise.

Just who is this so-called warrior Mayneken? Not just anyone can sit down and read such a technical treatise as easy as that! And he is doing it right before me. Is clearly comfortable doing it! And damnation, he has scanned forward and I fear that he has found that scribal copying error in the fifth column. I can just tell. He is frowning over it!

Just as Ankhmes' building anxieties were about to climax, Richards looked up, smiled, and said, "Wise and noble Ankhmes, what you are now doing, be assured, will benefit Egypt for all time. Assembling the correct directions for the healing of the body is a truly divine pursuit. It is, I fear, a far, far better one than mine. Please complete your labors. Eternity demands it."

Richards reverently returned the scroll to Ankhmes with both hands, politely bowed, stood, and left, while tiny rivers of grateful tears began to roll down the overfed cheeks of the court physician. Richards' exit had turned his well-muscled back to the physician and in response Ankhmes could only let out a gentle wheezing sigh as his eyes widened and jaw quivered at its muscular development. Then the physician saw the four massive scars that stretched across it like a sash of honor.

Such a bright mind, such a beautiful body, and clearly the marks of such a warrior!

That was all that the physician's overloaded mind could grasp.

Once outside the physician's chambers, Richards turned and smiled to Thutmose.

"My dear friend, now, I would like to meet the royal carpenter, your younger brother."

And off they went, one with purpose, the other with a growing sense of pride and a growing respect for a young and strangely wise warrior.

* * *

Piankoff lay on his padded bed frame and fumed about his clumsy stupidity. That slip, that misjudgment had put the entire outcome of the mission into serious jeopardy. Despite it all, he had to admit to himself that he had been very lucky. Here, in this primitive enemy territory, or so it seemed, he had broken his ankle. Best of all, it seemed that his green partner was fitting right in. Never before had he met such a cultural chameleon.

Perhaps, he mused, *Richards represented that final, ripe culmination of an American culture where all were destined to become actors.*

Regardless of situation, he had to admit, even to himself, that the young man was very knowledgeable, had a gift for language, remarkable spine, and a sense of presence that demanded, no commanded, attention.

And again his grasp of pharmacology. Where did that come from?

But what were they to do about their scheduled check in? What could they report to Horizon Pass? That I broke my ankle on the insertion drop? Wouldn't that make them want to immediately pull the plug on the mission? Yet, Richards was doing so well, perhaps with me running interference, we can still obtain the required genetic material.

While deep in thought considering these matters, Piankoff felt a slight breeze and the tickling whisper of a presence. Casually rolling his head over to see who was there, all he could do was sit up in shock. For there, standing in the doorway, was none other than the Great Horus himself, the Pharaoh Neferkheperure Amenhotep with Meryptah and Ankhmes in tow.

Without thinking, Piankoff rolled off of his bed frame to prostrate himself before the Living God of Upper and Lower Egypt. As he did so, he could not muffle a grunting moan of painful agony as his splinted ankle bounced on the floor. Nonetheless, he made it, the back of his exposed head and neck facing the pharaoh. His arms outstretched in an act of total submission. With his nose and forehead pressed against the floor, Piankoff next felt the slight pressure of a sandal's sole upon the back of his head.

Oh well, he thought through the waves of declining pain. *This is about par for this course. Either Meryptah is a double agent or I am a very lucky man.*

Feeling the sandal's pressure lifted, a deep baritone and gentle voice spoke to him.

"My subject, I commend your sense of respect for my presence despite your painful injury. I merely wished to see an example of Ankhmes' skill at mending bones. I hope that my appearance and your understood sense of place have not undone his excellent work."

Now with a voice of far more authority he addressed his companions.

"Meryptah, Ankhmes, assist this priest back to his bed frame so that I may better examine what was done."

To this command both men took hold of Piankoff under his arms, straightened him up to his full height, and then laid him carefully back down. Throughout this entire maneuver, Piankoff was careful not to gaze directly upon the pharaoh's continence and instead focused upon his sandaled feet, feet with five toes, all of the same length except for an ever so slightly longer big toe.

Piankoff thought as he was carefully maneuvered into position, *that detail is surely odd. Must remember to add that one to the report.*

Once back on the bed frame, the pharaoh promptly ignored him as if he were a mere lab rat. Instead, he faced the court physician, who was standing at its end, who described his clinical diagnosis of Piankoff's injury, the type of sedative that he had administered to the patient, the actual setting of the ankle, and finally the application of the splint and its careful wrapping. Occasionally, the pharaoh asked a question as to dosage, procedure, what a bone break looked felt like. To these queries, Ankhmes answered as best he could, but Piankoff could tell that as good a physician the man was, he was nervously edgy during the entire interrogation. If he could tell, then no doubt so could the target.

Another thing I must add to the report. The target is very inquisitive about the workings and limitations of the human body and its repair.

During this entire time, all that Piankoff could think of was that this examination reminded him of an experienced hospital ward physician on his rounds with his students. But more than that intellectual observation, this was Piankoff's first close, really close look at the physique of the target. By his best estimate, he stood nearly six foot six, a quite extraordinary height for an Egyptian, weighed about two hundred and twenty pounds, clearly endomorphic in body type, wide at the hip and narrow at the waist and shoulders, with a pronounced and protruding gut. He carried most of his weight in the fatty tissue of his thighs, hips, stomach and chest which sagged as if he had a woman's breasts on the verge of lactation.

But all of this was relatively unremarkable in comparison to the subject's face, jaw line, and cranial morphology. In all his years of applying makeup, witnessing police lineups, and memorizing faces and facial types, never had Piankoff seen such a face that was so uncharacteristic of the human genome. In their particulars, each feature was recognizably human. But in their collective totality, they made up a composite that was far from human-looking.

Armed with this up close encounter, Piankoff began a pre-rehearsed list of clinical benchmarks that he asked himself. Is this a classic clinical case of pituitary dysfunction that resulted in acromegaly? Did the king suffer from a genetic condition known as Marfan's syndrome? Could the subject's apparent sexual dimorphism be the result of a double-X, Y chromosome mutation? Could it be that as a child he was the victim of a vitamin deficiency? Or, could he have been exposed to some mutagenic agent?

All of these possible scenarios, which he had studied in great detail while at the Russian Academy of Science, just didn't ring true, or were even plausibly close. Something more was afoot here.

Then he noted the slow and languid movements of the arms and hands, the extraordinarily large and slanted eyes, overly large mouth and heavy lips, the sheer length of the cranium, the prominence of the jaw, and the length of the nose. None of these features, when seen from such close proximity, in this combination, could be termed normal to Piankoff. As the target exited Piankoff's room, the herky-jerky locomotion of his legs, spine, and swinging of the long arms reminded him more of a cross between a praying mantis and a gibbon than a human being.

Now blessedly alone, a heavy sweat broke out on his forehead. He could hear his heart pound, the blood rushing through his veins. Rationalizing, Piankoff realized that only now did he notice his body was responding to a massive adrenaline rush, triggered by the natural fear and flight reaction.

Smiling to himself, *I must be becoming jaded or else senile. I didn't even shit myself!*

But then he quickly reconsidered. *But nonetheless, do I have some interesting material for the exobiologists back home!*

Breaking his concentration yet again, to his great distraction, was the sudden arrival of Richards with his guide Thutmose in train. To beat all, the pair had with them a set of crude, but serviceable wooden crutches!

Richards' proudly announced for Thutmose's benefit. "Teacher. Behold, the brother of my trusted guide Thutmose has built for you two very special walking sticks so that you may move about on your own and without the aid of a sedan chair. I have been assured that the strength and resiliency of the wood will service you well until your foot mends."

The point of this speech naturally prompted Piankoff to ask.

"Mayneken, my fine assistant, your industry and ingenuity are remarkable, but what kind of wood are these special walking sticks made from?"

"Why, my master, I am pleased that you asked. From the wood of the willow tree. It should reduce your pain."

To the punch line of this revelation, first Piankoff and then Richards were reduced to something akin to laughing hyenas. As for Thutmose, caught unawares and left totally out of the loop, he could only smile out of politeness, while these two nobles made absolute fools of themselves.

And here, I had even begun to respect Mayneken!

CHAPTER XXXI
A Dinner Invitation

Having dismissed Thutmose for the rest of the day, Richards and Piankoff, now with the aid of his crutches, went wandering through the royal annex with a mind to head outside toward the Nile. What the pair was not prepared for, however, were the shocked stares and outright giggles at the sight of Piankoff's new method of locomotion. Both knew it was only a matter of time before the royal physician would hear the news in this small community that was all ears.

"Look," they would say, "an injured priest walking on two sticks! Why doesn't he want to be carried instead?"

Stopping and sitting down to rest near its western bank under the shade of a fragrant acacia tree, the two finally had the opportunity to privately discuss the day's events out of ear shot of anyone. Richards' successes were evident in Piankoff's mobility. But really what took center stage remained the Russian's close up observations of their target.

"Mayneken, the target, Meryptah, and Ankhmes paid me a visit today while you were away and the target's physiology is most strange. And the way he moves, fluid one minute, stiff and almost ungainly the next, it is all most curious. Frankly, I really don't know what to make of him, except now that I have seen him, it becomes all the more imperative that we somehow obtain some sort of genetic material from him."

Listening carefully to what his colleague had to say, Richards then added, "At the very least, we must record your observations and get them through the gate of eternity during tonight's check in. There's no question about it. Do you feel up to attempting it?"

"I will manage, even if it is only to play decoy, while you throw the report through the gate's opening.

"Furthermore, from here on in, and having met that thing, we must assume at all times that we are being watched, followed, and that we will not return. Consequently, our mission's purpose has subtly changed. Not only will we attempt to collect a sample, but also we must assume that each day's report will be our last and best reconnaissance for whoever else may follow in our footsteps."

He then continued in earnest.

"Given the size of the king's head and the surprising resonance and command of his voice, I would not be surprised if it was a latent mind-reader, if not wholly a mind-speaker. While I was in its presence, I purposely mixed my thoughts between observations and frightful things just in case. And if the time comes, I would suggest the same for you as well."

"What you say Piankhotep makes good sense. The notion that the target could be a mind-speaker had never occurred to me. That was a very good observation, which could explain in part why no one else seems even to notice his strange physiology. It's as though they were under some sort of magical spell. And now, you said that both Ankhmes and Meryptah accompanied the target during his visit, correct?"

Piankoff simply nodded.

"What do you say we have dinner with Meryptah and pump him for whatever information he has about the Great Horus? We could well learn something significant that might give us an edge."

Nodding again, the Russian rasped. "It is a fine idea, but we must be careful, for as helpful as Meryptah has been, he could become a liability as well."

Richards then asked the one question that had been on his mind ever since he met Meryptah.

"Piankhotep, when and where did you first make Meryptah your contact?"

Sitting back with a knowing look in his eyes, Piankoff paused to answer. He regarded Richards in a calculating way. Then, finally averting his eyes to watch a farmer plowing with his oxen, he said.

"That, my friend, is my business. But given our present situation, the question is a valid one, and one deserving of an answer, even if in part."

"I first met Meryptah about fifteen years ago when he was a temple acolyte. I remember noticing him because of his bright eyes and intelligent face. At that time I too was a priest. I chose to befriend him because he was and remains the target's only boyhood friend. I know that they used to sneak off every so often into the desert and for what purpose I do not know. Then there is the matter that he wanted very much to be the high priest of the Great God. It was felt that he was more than capable, as you yourself have seen, but only a miracle could absolutely deliver him that wish."

Then Piankoff dropped his bombshell.

"Mayneken, the price of his current high station was his right hand."

"Piankhotep, he knew that he would lose his hand?"

"Not in so many words. But he did know that he had to be aggressive in the pursuit of his desired career. In truth, we had a fifty-fifty chance that he and he alone would be in the sanctuary when we conducted that fateful test probe. And we won. Now you finally know why I shut down the gate to eternity the way I did—to create a miracle."

All Richards could do at this latest revelation was slowly shake his head in disbelief. He then asked, "Yes, he is now the high priest, but how come he is so loyal? How, for instance, did he know when we were arriving?"

"To your second question, that was a matter of simple communication. I dropped a sealed papyrus scroll through the ring during the check test run following the emergency shutdown. It was found on the floor of the great god's sanctuary and was subsequently delivered to him.

"As for your first question, I assisted him several times in what can only be called the development of strategic technologies. About this subject, however, I can say no more. As it is, my people and your people are very fearful that several basic tenets of the *RUTI* have been irrevocably broken. The general opinion of both sides, however, is that what was shared will not be passed on by either Meryptah or our target to damage the time line downstream."

Richards, between gritted teeth, asked, "Why wasn't I briefed in on all of this?"

To which Piankoff replied with a non-answer.

"That is a very good question. I suggest that you ask Dr. Borov and Professor Milson as soon as we get back. After all, it was they who decided on the vast majority of your preparatory curriculum."

To this obviously evasive answer, Richards could do nothing but fume, but instead he decided to probe Piankoff via a different route. So he began in a reasonable voice.

"My teacher, these things that you have shared also tell me that I have finally gained at least a portion of your trust. For this, I am deeply moved. However, if you had broken your neck on your drop through the ring instead of your ankle, then I would have known nothing of these things. My survival and the ultimate success of our mission, at the very least, would have been far more difficult to accomplish, if not totally compromised. And then there is the issue of being lost out of our time. The potentiality for a paradox would have been enormous. Surely you know these things as well as I. And so I ask you again, why wasn't I informed of all these events prior to the mission?"

Piankoff having patiently listened to all that his colleague had said was inwardly pleased that he had not accepted his first answer, but was surprised at the diplomatic tone and logic behind Richards' argument. Finally, he liked the stubborn firmness of being asked again.

This brutish man-child is maturing fast in this environment!

Mentally squaring his shoulders for what he knew would be a painful shock to Richards, Piankoff began.

"My dear Mayneken your progress on this stage of existence has become dizzying. Your mastery of the language, your ability to read people, your sound decisions to be bold and brash, docile and well-mannered, have not missed my gaze or that of our hosts. I consider you now, at this very moment, every bit the equal of myself. The only thing that separates us is experience and experience is a very harsh and unforgiving teacher.

"Mayneken, if I had knew you would have succeeded so well, so fast, I can guarantee you that I would have given you a full briefing prior to our drop. My friend, and now I can sincerely say that with a clear conscience, how was I to know? And so before I end this tender subject between us, let me say that henceforth my knowledge is your knowledge. I will try to teach you every trick that I know. But at the same time be aware that some things I can never tell you. Some things I can never give you a valid reason for why. Sometimes it is something from the gut, but other times it could be an issue of my land's secrets to which I have been sworn my loyalty to for the past fourteen years.

"I tell you this because I remember seeing you turn white when Borov referred to me teasingly as a military officer. It is true of course. I am a high-ranking officer because my security access, training, and my experience requires it. And while I am in the process of confessing all to you like some superstitious old woman, you may as well know that I work directly for a very secretive and powerful man located very high within the great beast's house of secrets.

"Unfortunately, this same man has become old, inflexible, hateful, and is becoming more and more single-minded by the day. Believe it or not, this same man wanted me to kill Dr. Borov. Why you say? Because as a very young man, much as yourself, Borov made a very wise choice and left his homeland to a land in the West. And when he left his homeland for the other, he brought with him the knowledge of the gate of eternity. Now I ask you, Mayneken, what do you think my land of the beast would have done with a gate of eternity?"

Richards sat quietly listening to the hushed words of Piankoff trying with all his might to decide whether or not to believe him. It all sounded so plausible, so reasonable. He even mentioned the aborted hit contracted on Dr. Borov that he had been told about.

Piankoff, noting the averted eyes and slightly furrowed brow of Richards, then followed up.

"Right now, if I were in your sandals," Piankoff added playfully, "I would listen carefully, but withhold all judgment on anything that I have just shared with you. It is a lot to chew. But if there is anything that I do wish you would consider, it is this. You're good. No, you're an extremely fine, but green field operative. The way Thutmose responds to your every word is proof enough of your potential for me. You will become a first rate operative, but only with further experience."

Having said his piece, Piankoff then heard Richards' stomach rumble in hunger. Smiling, all he could do was shake his head at his partner.

Beginning to rise and refusing Richards' help, Piankoff stood up, gripped his crutches, and said. "I see that your stomach and the sun are in tune. The sun is in its last quadrant, which around here means that it is about time for dinner. They prefer to eat early here, just before or during sunset. So let's head back before our absence becomes an eyesore."

Along the way back, the two discussed in some detail just what should be on the day's mission report and how they might get back to the sanctuary in time so that they could deliver it. To Richards it seemed an easy enough process. To Piankoff, however, he all too easily could conjure up a multitude of unfortunate scenarios that could seal their collective doom. Regardless, the pair decided to make their attempt.

The main problem as they saw it was how precisely to calculate 2:12 a.m. Obviously, they couldn't given the present situation and they dared not try to develop a means given the tenets of the *RUTI*. So that fact meant that they had to be in the sanctuary for a prolonged period of time and simply wait for the opening to appear. And the longer that they remained within the sanctuary meant the greater their chances at being detected.

*   *   *

By the time that they arrived back at the royal annex, Thutmose the guide stood faithfully waiting for them at the steps of Richards' veranda. By the worried look on his furrowed brow and the constant twisting and rubbing of his hands, it was clear to them both that they were in hot water.

"I was so concerned," the guide said. "I could not find either of you anywhere within the guest quarters."

Richards decided that it was his responsibility to relieve his faithful guide.

"My dear friend, please accept my apologies for our absence. It was just that my teacher, Piankhotep, wished to go for a short walk to test your brother's two fine walking sticks and to offer a brief prayer of thanksgiving to Hapi, the guardian of the Nile. Then noticing the late time of day, we immediately returned for the evening meal."

Then Richards got to the point.

"But why, my friend, were you looking for us?"

"Why, the High Priest Meryptah wishes you to join him at tonight's meal as his special guests. Perhaps many nobles and high ladies will be there as well. You never, ever, really can tell."

Then looking down in embarrassment, he continued.

"You both should immediately prepare yourselves for this occasion."

Richards now finally getting the point smiled and said, "My good friend are you accusing us of smelling like donkeys or perhaps even a pair of oxen?"

"Oh, no, Noble Ones! It is just that your feet may have become dusty. And as the gods themselves say, one can never be too clean."

"Thank you, Thutmose, we will both attend to our needs immediately. But would you be so kind and later lead us to Meryptah's evening meal?"

"I would indeed be most honored."

Thutmose with a minute bow turned and vanished.

Immediately, Piankoff asked with a wicked grin.

"Mayneken, do you find the bathing arrangements here to be of your liking?"

"Oh yes, my teacher, I find them most stimulating."

"Then, Mayneken, I shall not keep you from that which you must do."

And off toward his quarters he went gracefully swinging one-legged between his two supporting crutches.

Not a moment later, Richards' attention was caught by a pair of quiet giggles. His charming and nubile bath attendants were awaiting his arrival, apparently alerted by the ever helpful Thutmose. Again taking him by the hand, they went to the next door bathing room.

Yes, Thutmose well knew what he was talking about!

Dusty feet indeed!

*   *   *

As the sun's shadows began to lengthen and before its golden rays disappeared behind the western mountains that marked the Land of the Dead, Thutmose appeared to fetch Richards from his chamber. With a quick glance, Richards noted that Thutmose had also shaved, removed the dust from his feet, and was now wearing full-length linen as well.

Hmmm, he thought. *Is this going to be a black tie affair?*

So Richards asked. "My friend Thutmose, I see that you are most splendidly attired. Must I be so as well, so as not to offend our most gracious host?"

With a slight bow and averted eyes, Thutmose said. "Not at all Noble One. Youth has its liberties. Enjoy them."

With that they were off tracing a route through the royal guest annex that Richards did not recognize. Passing through the complex's outer pylon led them toward a worn mud brick path where three open sedan chairs waited with their bearers.

Richards could not hide his surprise.

This is right out of Hollywood!

As they neared, Richards saw that Piankhotep was already seated with his crutches in tow in the center chair. Thutmose took the lead chair leaving the last chair for Richards, which looked like a partially enclosed kiddy roller coaster mounted on two long and stout poles. Once seated, four well-muscled men of similar statures lifted the chairs using only one arm and a leather strap that was cunningly looped around the pole and wrist, eliminating the need to grip with the hand. Walking on the outside of the poles and in lockstep with one another, Richards was amazed at how smooth the initial lift and ride was.

The chairs were constructed of expensive cedar wood imported from the forests of Lebanon. Their decoration included friezes of embossed gold foil and beautifully carved ivory inlays. For Richards, it seemed criminal to be carried in such a priceless conveyance. It rubbed against every democratic fiber of his being, but it did keep his feet from getting dusty. And these chairs definitely reflected the image of great personal wealth and influence that his host Meryptah apparently enjoyed.

As the trio neared the Nile, it became apparent that a sizable river craft was awaiting their arrival. Lifted over its gunwales, chair and all, the dinner guests were set directly on the deck, and then the boat pushed off into the northbound current. All was quiet as the tiller man slowly guided and sculled the craft to the opposite shore's stone and stair-stepped landing, while the twelve bearers stroked in time with their long-handled paddles.

It was a blissful moment plucked out of time. Ducks and ibis alternated between filling the sky with swirls of their colorful plumage or gracefully plummeting as one to land among the lotus and papyrus choked shoreline. The southern upriver breeze was cooling and with it came the rich scents of lotus, river, fresh mud, and cooking fires. The river craft itself must have cost a fortune, for it was entirely built of cedar wood as well as the twelve long and spear-tip bladed paddles.

Gently alighting on the eastern bank, the boat was moored. The three chairs were borne in their turn and the bearers effortlessly climbed the twenty or so steps to the top of the quay's sloping ramp. It was then clear to Richards precisely where they were going—the temple complex of the great god! Pinching himself, Richards then remembered that Meryptah was, after all, the high priest of the great god, thus lived within its enclosure, and enjoyed the resources of that sacred precinct.

Such power, influence, and resources! Richards considered. *Probably as much if not more as the Vatican Vicar himself! Now why did I not think of that before? I must remember again to compliment Piankoff on his foresight.*

*　　*　　*

Having rapidly passed through the Theban marketplace, which was an absolute riot of last-minute commercial activity at this late hour, they were admitted through a modest side entrance in the surrounding white-washed mud brick enclosure wall of the great god's grand temple complex. After snaking their way single file between several mud brick structures, the bearers finally turned into the broad courtyard of a truly grand residence made blindingly brilliant with fresh whitewashing.

As to who lived in such secluded, semi-palatial grandeur within the great god's temple complex there could be no question, for at the entrance to his rambling house Meryptah proudly stood with his feet set wide and powerful arms crossed across his chest. His grinning smile of welcome was broad as the Nile itself.

Thutmose, as the lead chair, jumped out of his sedan chair as soon as it came to rest, politely bowed to the host and then began to assist Piankoff onto his crutches with Richards not far behind. Mildly impatient with himself and all the fuss and feathers being paid him, Piankoff, once firmly standing on his left foot, shooed away Thutmose and his assistant. Then, with his crutches, he slowly and proudly mounted the limestone steps, stopped at the penultimate, bowed his head and said. "Most noble Meryptah, I and my assistant are here in obedience to your wishes."

At the sight of Piankoff moving on his own and up the stone steps to his household, flabbergasted the high priest. It was the first time he had ever seen the use of two walking sticks. While Piankoff fought himself up the steps unassisted, the priest considered this sight.

And here is a man with a freshly broken ankle, not a day old, climbing my household's steps and standing before me. Who then politely pledges his obedience to my invitation to the evening meal!

The Osiris Nebmare Amenhotep had chosen his agents well indeed. And note, Meryptah, how protective of Piankhotep Mayneken is. He follows his every step as if he were his teacher's very sheut, *or double. Such loyalty from a warrior too has its own meaning and significance. The bond between these two must be that of bronze made hard from much beating.*

Then, breaking out of this momentary reverie Meryptah, remembering his manners, proclaimed in the traditional manner.

"Welcome all to my household. My heart is most glad at your safe arrival. May my house be as yours."

Then he thought to add. "And noble Piankhotep, I notice the wet glistening of your head due to your efforts. May I offer you a draught of fresh beer?"

To such an offer, Piankoff only could broadly smile.

Once out of the heat of the setting sun, Richards noted that the cooling shade of their host's rambling house produced a pleasant, almost chilling relief. In terms of its interior decoration, Richards felt remarkably at home, for the house appeared to be furnished with a sparse, if not Spartan, masculine taste. As with the exterior, the interior walls too were whitewashed and unadorned with murals of any kind or the running multicolored borders or friezes as was the case at the royal guest annex. Standing in the main hall, only the six brightly painted, two-story papyrus-form columns provided any colorful opposition. The flooring consisted of smooth limestone paving.

Moving on into the darkening banquet room, the remaining natural light came through the wooden slats of small clerestory windows that were incorporated into three of this room's walls. Their canny opposition allowed for a gentle and cooling breeze to circulate. A low, wooden groaning board table dominated the center of the room, which was surrounded by colored floor coverings, and several pillows. The visual result was of an interior that seemed uncluttered, unusually spacious, cool, and fresh.

Richards reasoned that guests were expected to sit and eat on the floor Japanese style.

The room smelled of several cedar oil lamps and of the largess on the table. It groaned under the weight of fresh breads, fruits, cheeses, and roasted meats, not to mention a variety of unrecognizable cooking spices that were available for dipping. Right on time, the combination of such sights and smells made Richards' flat and well-muscled stomach growl and growl loudly.

Meryptah, upon hearing this bodily complaint turned to Richards and said, "Noble Mayneken, you have paid my household a great compliment, and you have yet to even sample my table!"

Looking him up and down, he exclaimed with resignation. "Oh, to be so young again!"

With that thought behind him, Meryptah then indicated where he wished Piankoff and Richards to sit, one on each side of him. As Piankoff got off of his crutches, Richards helped him down until he was comfortably seated. Richards noticed that Thutmose had politely removed himself to eat elsewhere, probably in the kitchen, and there he would remain until needed.

Again Meryptah took notice.

Mayneken's care for Piankhotep is truly touching. It is as though one is the son of the other. But I know that that simply cannot be.

As the two visitors settled themselves down, Meryptah raised his filled cup in benediction and solemnly intoned.

"My dear guests, I toast to this meal truly for it is made for laughter, and beer only makes it all the more merry!"

At hearing the toast, Richards' ear perked up.

That toast sounds so familiar!

So the meal began with several cups of fresh beer, which Richards found to be remarkably refreshing, delicious, and carbonated, even if it was a bit thick and poorly filtered by his modern tastes.

Never again will I complain about Guinness being too heavy a beer. This is the first time that I have ever drunk beer and had to almost chew it as well.

The table conversation, predictably polite at first, quickly warmed as the beer began to take its effect. What Meryptah was most curious about were Piankoff's dual walking sticks. Once satisfied, his next question was why would a noble such as Piankhotep even bother with them? This, then, led to an involved discussion of needful bodily fitness, which their host, although he politely listened, clearly thought was utter nonsense.

"After all, is that not what the young are for? And for that matter, the very purpose of sedan chairs?" he countered.

Piankoff, realizing the impasse, had to bite his tongue and agree with his host.

With that victory under his belt, Meryptah began to tear away and distribute generous portions of freshly roasted duck, which all greedily ate with their hands, while cleaning their fingers on chunks of bread that were then devoured with gusto. Following that course, they then dived into the fruits, dates, and cheeses with relish.

The entire lot was continuously washed down with numerous cups of cool beer. As is inevitable with the natural carbonation of beer and coupled with its mass consumption, someone had to be the one to burp and Richards, finally, was the first to break lose. Unknown to either of the field operatives, Meryptah himself had been long in dire agony, but it was not considered polite as host to be the first one to do so. Consequently, Richards' gustatory explosion was much appreciated and was quickly followed with a hearty one from Meryptah. Piankoff, suddenly realizing the significance of such a display, then ripped one off himself, which sparked off another round of laughter.

Richards, the youngest of this merry crew, found himself pleasantly inebriated, but still with his wits somewhat about him. Piankoff, who had been since the second course unconsciously shifting himself about due to the slowly returning pain in his ankle, was drinking deeply in an attempt to numb himself without having to resort to the dulling, nightmare producing, poppy-laced raisin wine. With his slight build and strong desire to purge his body of that dreaded narcotic, he was fast succeeding. As for Meryptah, it was clear that he was just getting started. With his greater bulk, he would have succeeded in drinking these two lightweights under the proverbial table, if it were not for one, minor interruption to this fast-becoming, raucous, and memorable evening meal.

In the midst of much laughing, belching, and general tomfoolery, the house steward came rushing in and quietly announced to the master of the house's ear the arrival of someone of apparent importance. This fact both Piankoff and Richards easily divined from the suddenly sobered and glazed eyes of their host once the whispered message had taken hold.

Suddenly, Meryptah heaved himself to his feet, swayed ever so slightly, got his bearings, and loudly commanded, "Abase yourselves, for the Living God of Egypt and Mistress of the Two Lands have arrived!"

Stunned at this sudden order, at first neither Piankoff nor Richards moved. But as soon as they heard the rustling sound of many footsteps behind them, the pair pushed away from the table, rolled over on their stomachs, and faced the entrance to the dining room with the backs of their necks and heads exposed in complete and abject submission.

Although both were somewhat dazed from all the beer and fine food, they nonetheless noted the palpably chilling change in social climate. Fortunately, both had remembered to veil their thoughts, flooding their minds with the overwhelming emotions of fear, dread, and foreboding before the presence of the pharaoh.

With their eyes focused on the floor, each saw within their narrow fields of vision two sets of sandals come into view—one large with equal-length toes, the other with small, delicate, and petite leather sandals decorated with heavy gold foil. The shuffling of other, more distant feet, suggested the presence of the pharaoh's own household guards as well, most likely Nubian Medjay warriors.

Directly, the large pair of sandals strode forward and for the second time that day, Piankoff felt the gentle pressure of the sole of the target's foot on the back of his head. Again he heard that deeply sonorous voice that seemed to quake his very being.

"Ah! For a man with the broken ankle you do get around quite well. Could it be, as I have heard rumored, that you can indeed walk unassisted with the aid of just two walking sticks?"

Removing the pressure from Piankoff's head, the deep voice then intoned. "Truly remarkable, truly remarkable indeed."

Shifting his position, he then placed his foot upon Richards', who unconsciously tensed the powerful muscles of his entire back, shoulders, and outstretched arms.

The deep voice now said, "Ah! My dear Meryptah, and who is his strong young one with what looks like the marks of a lion across his back? It is clear that he rebels against the pressure of my foot. Should I fear him and crush his head like an egg shell, or, should I spare his life?"

Meryptah, now wide-eyed that the supreme Lord of Egypt would say such a thing within his own household, stammered out, "Most Powerful One. You will do what is best for Egypt. But these men are honored guests in my household and agents of your now divine father. To punish them would be to punish me as well."

At which point, Meryptah also fell to the floor before the target.

While still resting the sole of his foot on Richards' head, the Living God, Neferkheperure Amenhotep, considered all that his trusted boyhood friend had said.

Agents of my father are they? Of the long dead Osiris Nebmare? Just who are these men? I sense nothing but fear from them. And this young one, just who is he? Again, I sense nothing but irrational, illogical fear. Why? Why am I the focus of their fear?

At this point, a light, feminine, and melodic voice broke the tension of the moment. With a remarkably calm and diplomatic tone, she said, "My husband. Since when is not the word of your trusted boyhood companion not contain anything but the truest essence of Maat? Are you now suggesting that he cavorts with the likes of common thieves, grave robbers, embalmers, and assassins?"

With this reasonable rebuke, Richards felt the foot's pressure disappear and with it, came relief, and his first notice of an expanding stain of sweat on the floor's pavement that had begun from his dripping nose.

Then in a very deferential tone, "Hmmm, as always, my first wife, you are absolutely correct."

Now musing aloud, he added, "But even here in Thebes, within the sacred circuit of the Great God, I sense a coming disturbance the magnitude of which even I cannot entirely explain."

Breaking from his reverie, the target then again found his authoritative tone.

"Meryptah, arise my old friend, so that you may face me."

In an almost intimate and conversational tone that excluded the presence of all others, the target then said, "Tomorrow I wish to discuss with you my plans for the construction of a new temple, a temple that will be located just outside these very precincts to the east where Re makes his first appearance. Since space for such an undertaking is so dear, I must ask of you, my friend, to make yet another sacrifice."

Said as the pharaoh's eyes briefly flitted over to where his missing right hand should have been.

"A portion of the cultivated lands of your priesthood will be forfeited to provide the space which I require. But have no fear. I will provide you and your priesthood compensation ten times tenfold. Come to my chambers tomorrow only after the life-giving rays of Re have fully appeared."

With that said, the target turned and walked out, but the feminine voice remained.

"My dear husband's trusted companion of youth," she began.

"I know that this must seem a great shock to you. It may even appear as almost a betrayal. But have no fear, despite my husband's wishes, or maybe in spite of them, I will always remain your most trusted guardian. But allow me to warn you, Meryptah. My husband is set on this divine course of action. Little if anything will he allow to stop him. Even I, as his Chief Wife, dare not attempt to dissuade him. Be so forewarned my kind and good friend, and know that you have an ally in the First Mistress of the Two Lands, Nefertiti. I will protect you and yours as long as I hold breath."

At this point, again a pair of feet softly and slowly moved-off into the distance to be followed by the others unseen. Only then, did Piankoff and Richards dare to peek up from their prone positions. When they did, they found the high priest of the great god standing stock-still and facing the room's entranceway with a troubled mixture of anger and sadness on his tear-streaked face. Breaking out of the moment, he turned, returned to his place at his table, sat down, poured himself a full cup of beer, and chugged it down straight. Carefully placing the empty cup down, he then noticed that his two guests were carefully watching him, taking the measure of his mood.

Meeting their eyes, Meryptah said. "Piankhotep, it has begun. Egypt, henceforth, will never be the same. He has already said as much many times before. The terrible heresy that you warned me about those years ago has come to pass. He and I have argued over this issue for the past six years. He believes the influence of my priesthood to be a threat to the throne of Isis. What utter nonsense! He believes that the great god is but a mere aspect of some greater god—some greater truth, a god that he calls the Aten, the sun disk. What heresy! Was it not our guardian father and lord Amen Re who delivered us from those ignorant and godless Hyksos? For the first time in my life, Piankhotep, I feel truly rudderless."

With those words, both Piankoff and Richards looked at one another and a silent message was passed. Fate and the slowly grinding wheels of history had delivered to them a motivated ally.

After about thirty truly pregnant seconds had passed, Piankoff took a deep breath and with a theatric tilt of the head let out an equally deep sigh of shared commiseration. With that eloquent non-verbal preamble completed, he then began, "My dear friend Meryptah, High Priest to the Great God Amen Re, do you wish to discuss how our friendship may assist you in the righteous preservation of Maat?"

What a clever ploy, thought Richards, *to first introduce the issue of what the modern world would later coin the Amarna Revolution as a discussion of a philosophical-religious abstraction that for the ancient Egyptian signified order, stability, and constancy with the gods and the known universe. And once thrashed out at the intellectual level, my dear Byzantine friend will then no doubt subtly shift to a series of operational objectives. Simply brilliant!*

With a glazed and dreamy look in his eyes, the high priest murmured his answer as if reciting an acolyte's catechism long ago committed to rote memory.

"The righteous preservation of Maat is not within my compass, for I am merely the instrument of our Living God. It is he who is responsible for maintaining the all important balance between the divine and profane."

To which Piankoff replied, "That is the perfect answer for a perfect time. But is today, this very moment, one so sublime?"

Again two tiny rivers of tears began to flow down the cheeks of the once most powerful priest of the land.

"No, Piankhotep. This is a far less than sublime moment."

Then with a hardening of the eyes, a dramatic shift in emotion and purpose suddenly took place, and with it, a coarsening of voice.

"Piankhotep, this is the second time in my life that you have offered me your hand. The first time, I was a mere boy and you offered me then wisdom. But now, indeed, this is more a moment to consider, plan, and eventually act to aid, if necessary, our Living God in the righteous preservation of Maat."

Looking down, the deeply hurt and crestfallen priest said, "My dear friend, what have you in your heart?"

"How well do you know the First Wife, Nefertiti?"

With widening eyes and a shrug, Meryptah answered, "Ever since she was a young child of the fine and noble household of Yuya and Tuya. In truth, she has been much like a younger sister to me. I see beyond her great beauty. I know her heart and it is good. But secretly, she fears her husband and more recently even her children, but for reasons that I do not know.

"This I can feel! Yet, she speaks not a word of it, even though she has already given him many daughters.

"And as for his sons, well, while they are not hers, she has cared for them as if they were."

To the high priest's revelation of the king's sons, Richards' eyes bulged in disbelief.

Nowhere in the archaeological record is there any mention of any sons! There is evidence galore for his six daughters, but of no sons.

Could it really be then that Smenkhkare and Tutankhamen were actually the target's sons by a secondary wife?

Unaware of Richards' stunned academic discovery, Piankoff just nodded to their host in understanding, and then pushed on.

"My dear friend, have you ever noticed anything odd about the physical appearance of the Living God?"

To this direct question, Meryptah could only look down in thought at what had once been his two hands and a far, far away look came to his face.

"I have known the Living God ever since he was a young boy, since that time we have been close companions. At that time, as I best recall, the only thing that I remember noticing was the curious evenness in the length of his toes. Other than that, he was an ordinary boy as was I. But he was an extremely bright and inventive one."

At this point, the now reflective priest then regaled his two guests with all the secret projects and inventions that he and the young royal had ever been involved with, acknowledging the occasional assistance that Piankoff had given in their successful completion. During all of this Richards was astounded at what had been accomplished and then wondered how many times his colleague had broken how many laws of the *RUTI* in order to secure the then young man's loyalty.

At the end of this lengthy narrative, another round of beer was poured, during which Piankoff asked, "When, my dear friend, did you, let us say, become uncomfortable with your companionship with the Living God?"

Taking a very deep breath, the priest slowly shaking his head just said, "When my young boyhood friend started to become a man. Strange things occurred that I cannot explain. Our friendship remained as before, but a certain distance came between us. I sensed he was stepping away from his youth, just as we all do, but there was something more, something that I just cannot define.

"And then, as we both matured, instead of growing out of his awkwardness his appearance became worse, he became—odd, strange. I was not the only one to notice this change in him, for no royal heiress was willing to become his consort. After many polite rejections, he went into memorable rages that only his loving mother

Tiye could calm. The result was his betrothal to the fair and beautiful Nefertiti, herself of non-royal blood, being the daughter of foreign nobility.

"But to answer your question, my dear Piankhotep, the boy I once knew was a skinny and ungainly lad that was all arms and legs. But since he has matured, you can see for yourselves what he has become. It is only those from outside the royal court, from outside of Thebes—traders, travelers, foreign emissaries, and those like yourselves that can clearly see what stands before them. It is almost as if those around him, the entire court for that matter, have been made by some magic completely blind to his appearance."

"But to return to his strangeness that you have referred to," Piankoff quietly asked, "is it something that you could describe and share with us?"

Again that dreamy look appeared on the priest's face.

"One thing I can tell you is that even as a young man, when the two of us were busy devising and inventing, we did not speak very often. It was as though we spoke without speaking. And it always happened very fast. It was so effortless and precise in its clarity of meaning. There were not words for what we discussed, described, or imagined. Until this moment, I have not thought much about it. We were so close, and so tight-lipped about our projects, that I do not remembering actually, physically speaking, or holding a conversation. That is not to say that we didn't converse constantly and on a dizzying variety of topics."

To this revealed evidence of a telepathic linkage, if not imprinting, both Richards and Piankoff paled ever so slightly. Then Richards dared to ask his first question.

"My dear Meryptah, when was the last time such a wordless and private conversation took place between yourself and the Living God?"

"Why, this very day, in fact, during his visit this evening. The only reason that I physically spoke was in deference to the First Wife's presence, and to state firmly the obvious, that the two of you were my honored dinner guests in order to hopefully enlist her aid."

Richards now pressed his question a bit further.

"Meryptah, how precisely did that wordless conversation begin? What I mean is, who began it? You or the Living God?"

"It began as soon as I saw him. He was very curious about who you were Mayneken and was especially hopeful to see you, Piankhotep, demonstrate the use of your twin walking sticks.

"Initially, it was a good conversation. A conversation that brought joy to my heart, because it reminded me of our youth filled with the immensity of curiosity. But then I could feel him sense fear. That troubled his heart. I suspect that the fear he felt from you he understood as a reaction to his appearance. That made him angry, aggressive, actually to think hateful things, especially toward you, young Mayneken. And then for a moment, I heard in my mind he thought of you as a mere insect that deserved to be crushed underfoot.

"This shocked me, because as a youth, insects had always fascinated him. We used to discuss them, their organization, and their endless toils and constructions hours on end. But now, he holds them in contempt and thinks of men as such. As I have said, his new opinion of insects worries me.

"And now it is his desire to raise up a new god above all gods, to actually build a temple to this god Aten outside, and overshadow these very sacred precincts. Such an abomination makes me shake my head in disbelief. And if that would not be enough, he has discussed with me the possibility of changing his name to give honor to this other 'god.'

"With so many changes, so many acts against tradition, how can the Goddess Maat be nourished and preserved? To this question I have no answer, Piankhotep. But I must say that my heart is very heavy with dread for what might become of my beloved land."

For such a powerful man as this to so freely pour out his heart this way, Richards thought, *must be a man clearly at an impasse. He had referred to himself as "rudderless."*

How apt!

Piankoff then began thinking in a tactical manner.

"Meryptah, if the future of Egypt is jeopardized, if Maat cannot be nurtured, what then?"

Leaning heavily against the table before him and looking at Piankoff with eyes of stone, a surprisingly quiet yet forceful voice came forth from the priest's lips.

"Egypt may be in for another dark time. It is well known that time of the Hyksos, that time of foreign rule, was a time of desecrated temples, lawlessness, hunger, poverty, division, and above all, godlessness."

Then with darker emphasis.

"I will not allow that to happen again during my lifetime, not while this body still draws the breath of life."

With a tip of his head, Piankoff asked, "Is it permitted that I and Mayneken go now to the sanctuary of the great god, so that we may pray to him concerning this matter?"

Surprised by the request and the change of subject, the priest readily agreed, adding that perhaps he too should accompany them, and pray for guidance in this time of need. To this Piankoff surprised Richards with his assent.

Now what is that crazy Russian up to now! Is he actually thinking of inviting him along to witness our check-in? What a manipulator!

"Good. Then it is agreed. We will all go to ask the great god for guidance. But before we depart, may I suggest that we first attend to some private and necessary issues, namely, my bladder is about to burst!"

*   *   *

The brief journey on foot to the great god's sanctuary went uneventfully. They had only encountered two lowly *wab*-priests, both sound asleep and snoring. In fact, as both Richards and Piankoff had noted, security within the temple complex was virtually non-existent. If they had entered through the southern side passage as they had done on their arrival, they judged they would have seen not a soul.

The timing of their arrival within the sanctuary could not have been better, for after only a few minutes of quiet meditation and prayer a great light did indeed appear before the golden image of the Great God.

So this is what the Mark V-A looks like at the receiving end, Richards thought. *Most impressive!*

Piankoff, too, looking suitably shaken for Meryptah's benefit, expertly palmed the short and weighted papyrus scroll, their field report, in preparation for throwing it into the light.

Meryptah, upon the sudden appearance of the light, could only gasp in a mixture of religious rapture and painful physical memory. Simultaneously crying and praying to his god, the high priest was simply overwhelmed at the return of the vision that had so changed his life.

Pushing himself up from the floor onto his one good foot, Piankoff then addressed the light directly.

"Oh, Great God Amen Re, we seek your wisdom. Accept this prayer for guidance that I now offer to Thee."

With those words, the weighted papyrus roll flew through the air and into the light, whereupon it totally vanished. Richards thought that the whole was a great parlor trick. Meryptah was stunned by the fact that a physical message could be actually given to a god. On the basis of this new phenomenological fact, the high priest promised himself to include in all rites henceforth a prepared written message in the event that this opportunity should happen again. As for Piankoff, he was just pleased that his awkward one-footed throw was accurate for his ankle was troubling him mightily.

CHAPTER XXXII
Special Delivery

As for Major Charlie "Tuna" Cartwright, he did not like surprises. So when he fired up the Mark V-A early that first morning with its new ring installed and barely got it up to nominal operating conditions, he had not planned on spilling his entire cup of coffee all over the front of his fatigue blouse. This mishap occurred, nonetheless, when he had reflexively ducked as a blurred object barely missed hitting him square in the face. Swearing like a sailor at his self-inflicted plight, Corporal Kramer, who was manning the power pack, could just barely stifle down his mirth.

"All right, corporal, stuff it! We have delivery of our package. Now do a standard shut down."

The corporal's fingers flew at his superior's command, stepping down the shutdown procedure as per the numbers, per the book.

Tuna Cartwright, quickly getting himself together, did not take long to find the flying culprit—a bound roll of weighted papyrus.

How quaint he thought as he gently turned and weighed the object in his massive hands.

This precious object has literally traveled nearly three and a half millennia in less than a couple of nanoseconds.

Un-fucking-believable!

Then, ever so carefully, he began to remove the double-wound and overlapping twine that had secured the roll. As he did so the package's throw weight fell out of one end of the cylinder to the floor. This went unnoticed by Cartwright. Sitting where he was, it was Corporal Kramer, who actually saw the greenish stone hit the floor.

"Excuse me, Major, but something green just fell out of the package."

Stopping what he was doing, Tuna stood stock-still, moved down into a squat, and began scanning the paving stones around him. And there it was, big as life. It had rolled over near the base of one of the pylons. Stepping over and picking the object up, all Tuna could do was whistle.

"Boy, what a pretty rock!" was all he could say, for between the thumb and forefinger of his right hand he held a near-perfect fifty-seven caret cabochon of gorgeous blue-green lapis lazuli. As beautiful as the semi-precious stone clearly was, it was, nonetheless, of secondary interest to the soldier, who promptly and absentmindedly pocketed it under the flap of his left breast pocket never having thought of turning it over to examine its flat side.

Returning to the papyrus roll itself, Cartwright continued to remove its twine, unrolled it to its full length, and began to read its contents. In disbelief, he reread the message twice more and then re-rolled it up. Then in a soft and distracted voice he said.

"Corporal Kramer, would you please be so kind and fire up the satellite radio, and while you are at it, make sure that you select the alpha-encrypted link to Horizon Pass."

At the tone of his major's voice, the unusually polite address, and the mention of the rarely if ever used alpha link, Kramer knew that the major was really excited or really scared, the latter which he had never seen. Again his fingers began to fly in earnest.

*　　*　　*

At 4:17 p.m., Dr. Peter Borov was sitting before his desk and typing an email, when Major Cartwright's call on the satellite hookup was routed to his office. Grumbling at being roused from the depth of his meditative composition, Borov tersely answered the ringing phone.

"Borov here."

"Dr. Borov, this is Major Cartwright."

The sound of the hissing encryption link and the major's voice immediately got Borov's attention and spiked his curiosity.

"Sir, I am using the alpha encryption mode. Be advised that I am having three, repeat three, of my men deliver to you personally the first package. Expect them to arrive at Horizon Pass within the next twenty hours. That is all."

With that laconic message delivered, the connection that originated from the other side of the world was severed. Needless to say all of this put Borov to puzzling over what had just occurred. Looking at his left hand, he began to count on his fingers each point that Major Cartwright had made during the brief satellite link.

First, even over the encryption, the usually calm, cool, and collected Major Cartwright sounded rattled.

Second, Cartwright chose to use the alpha encryption module, which has been used only once before and that was during an emergency!

Third, the use of the alpha encryption may also suggest that Cartwright suspects someone may have been trying to listen in.

Fourth, the link was short and sweet, making it even more difficult to get a fix on it if someone had been trying to break in.

Fifth, the contents of the package could have been divulged over the satellite link, but he again chose not to do so, instead relying on its physical transfer by no less than three of his own men.

And finally, he made a point of repeating that three of his men would be delivering the package. Jesus, just what was so balls-o-fire sensitive that Major Cartwright would have felt the necessity to go to such lengths?

After musing on these points, Borov sighed.

Now back to this funding report! Finish it now so that you can be totally free within the next twenty hours.

Now, where was I? Ah, yes . . .

Chapter XXXIII

AD 2001. Russian Academy of Science

Deep within the secure vault of the Russian Academy of Science, the three men of influence met again.

"Gentlemen, thank you for coming so promptly. I will be brief." So began the first speaker.

"Early this morning, at precisely 3:17 a.m. local, one of our reconnaissance satellites over the Near East picked up a short, encrypted, and compressed uplink that was shunted to another satellite, whose ownership happens to be the U.S. Air Force Intelligence Agency. Unfortunately, due to the level of encryption and the briefness of the transmission, we were not able to completely decipher its contents."

Then the first speaker passed out a single sheet of paper to each of his two colleagues.

"However, for what it is worth, this is what we have.

...using...mode
...advised...having
...repeat...you...first
...expect...pass
...twenty...all.

"My dear colleagues, I regret that the gibberish you have before you is the best that we can do at the present. On that you have my assurances.

"What is so interesting about this satellite transmission and why it caught our attention was precisely its brevity and above all its encryption and compression, which to my department's best knowledge are both unique in many respects. I suspect that someday some bright, young, whippersnapper from the mathematics or technology division will eventually duplicate the code and its compression, and in so doing, will no doubt earn a doctorate in cryptography as a result.

"As to why the Americans felt the need to use, no waste, such a unique encryption suggests to me that something very big is going on somewhere in the Near East. And to my best knowledge, and obviously yours as well, that can mean only one thing. Something very big is going on that is connected with the Mark V-A, which is presently deployed in Luxor, Egypt. Fortunately, our very own Colonel Piankoff is already on the scene, as it were. I counsel patience and that we await his report.

"This is all that I have to communicate at this time."

CHAPTER XXXIV
Another Special Delivery

As for Dr. Borov, Cartwright's three men did indeed deliver the package within the specified twenty hours that he had promised. In actual fact, it was more like eighteen, which in itself represented something of a record for international, non-military travel. Sitting on his desk were two priceless objects. The one was a delicate, greenish-yellow roll of freshly manufactured papyrus that still possessed the bouquet of fresh vegetation. Bending over, Borov sniffed at the roll and imagined a lingering spicy scent to it as well.

Ah, the smells of recent antiquity, Borov thought. *Their library and archive collections must have smelled like a fresh hay barn or perhaps even a brewery!*

The other object was this gloriously smooth, blue-green oval stone with veins running through its surface of what appeared to be gold.

Cartwright's men surmised that the stone was included merely as a throw weight, so that the feather-light papyrus roll could be easily thrown through the temporal aperture.

I just wonder about that.

Reverently cradling the stone between his thumb and forefingers, Borov then noticed that the backside of the stone was flat, and turning it over, gasped at the beauty of the intricately carved hieroglyphics that were inlaid in gold in six horizontal fields each separated by a single line.

Strange, Borov thought. *Neither Major Cartwright nor his men even mentioned this inscription. I wonder if the major even took notice of it. Regardless, I must immediately pass this stone on to Professor Milson for his appraisal of it.*

Only after having satisfied his nose and the curious stone that accompanied it, did Borov gently unroll the papyrus and begin to eagerly read.

Target confirmed at close proximity as exhibiting extremely
atypical physical characteristics.

Telepathic contact with people in immediate, line of sight confirmed.

Have successfully made contact with ally.

My assistant is nominal and is performing beyond expectations.

I have a broken ankle, but am mending and comfortable.

Sample will be taken within next two days time.

Daily reports to continue.

Extraction: end of day three, 2:12 a.m. Lima.

Will definitely need sling at extraction!

Borov's immediate reaction to the message was to stop, reread it several times, absorb its contents, and, as was his habit, begin counting on his left fingers all of its salient points. Leaning back in his chair, he took off his wire-rimmed reading glasses, closed his eyes, rubbed at the bridge of his nose, and paused to think.

First, the target is extremely atypical. Such a coldly clinical remark could mean almost anything, but coming from a man like Piankoff, considering his background preparation in physiology and genetics, seeing the target in the flesh must have been a real freak show. Atypical indeed!

Second, telepathic abilities! Now that is a wrinkle that no one before had thought to consider! And given the target's reportedly bizarre cranial morphology, such an innate ability now seems almost too obvious. Now, I wonder how those two rogues managed to mask their thoughts, while they were observing the target at close proximity. I must remind myself to ask them about that one and also prepare for the future.

Third, I see that Piankoff has again found his contact. Good. Now, I just hope to God that they choose not to remember our friendly and helpful operative and mention our heroes somewhere within the historical record!

Fourth, Richards is performing well. And here I was just hoping for his survival! Such laconic praise from Piankoff can only mean the very best – especially given the fact that he admits to an ankle injury. My, my, will Professor Milson be pleased to hear that his star pupil is doing so well!

277

Fifth, it certainly looks as if they have decided upon an ambitious schedule for the sample's procurement. More power to them! And the less exposure in the field, the better! I wonder what they plan to bring back. Nail clippings, a hair sample, or the whole enchilada? If I know Piankoff, probably all of the above just to make sure.

Sixth, a sling for extraction.

Hmmm, is he exaggerating about his injury or is that wily Russian up to something?

With that last thought in mind, Borov picked up his desk phone and arranged for a satellite uplink to Major Cartwright. When he spoke to the Communications shack, he purposely chose not to use the alpha encryption module. Instead, Borov decided to tease those whom he suspected might be listening in. In Borov's mind, sometimes information received in the clear could entrap and confuse as much as that which was mysterious and fragmentary. While he waited listening to the ether hiss of the uplink, Borov carefully composed in his mind what he wanted to say.

After some ten or eleven seconds, a clunking sound announced that the link had been established and the standard encryption program was firing up. A moment later Borov heard over the encryption's hiss.

"Tuna here."

"Ah, Mr. Tuna, I wish to thank you ever so much for the two pounds of sushi you thoughtfully delivered. All was devoured immediately by the various members of my family. Let me just say that we found it delicious."

Tuna Cartwright, still a bit groggy by the arrival of this 4:26 a.m. phone call, still had the wits about him to recognize that Borov was not using the usual alpha encryption module. He also noted that Borov had couched his words in their personal code—one that he knew that Major Cartwright understood and could play along with. Borov knew about Major Cartwright's passion for fishing in the tangled mangrove thickets of Louisiana's bayous back since his days at White Sands. The two of them had enjoyed many an expedition together with a variety of rods and reels. So sure enough and right on cue Tuna Cartwright shifted into his natural Cajun dialect.

"Ah, well, sir, I was kinda' hoping that you and your family would appreciate the fish, seeing as though we just caught 'em fresh."

"Well, on that account, you are absolutely correct. But in the future, you just might want to plan on using a net to see how much more you could catch at once."

"Well sir, that may require that we would need to fetch a boat with a winch. And besides, catchn' fish on a line is far more sportn,' ifn' you-all catch my drift."

"Yes, Mr. Tuna, I do appreciate your fine sense of sporting etiquette, but what would you do if you happened upon a whole school of fish at once?"

Cartwright, for his part, did not miss Borov's emphasis on the use of a net, and clearly got the message, as they say.

"Yessir, I catch yur meanin'."

"By the by," and in the process borrowing a familiar catch phrase of Mark Twain's that indicated to Borov whether he had anything else to say, "would yur family up North have a taste fur any crawdads? They be runnin' as well."

"Nope. That disgusting practice of sucking their heads is not exactly their cup of tea."

"Damn Yankees!"

"Exactly."

With that Borov hung up the phone, sat back in his wheeled chair, and enjoyed a private chuckle. Shaking his head, he thought deliciously. *Just priceless!*

And recruiting him since the old days back in New Mexico was a brilliant stroke of security. Besides, his Louisiana dialect will no doubt cause my dear Russian colleagues no end of distraction. Mark Twain's paraphrase will be analyzed. Damn Yankees will be too and the entire play read and reread for any cross-referential significance.

Let Comrade Fedorov rot in hell!

*　　*　　*

Placing the satellite link's headset back into its cradle, it was all that Tuna Cartwright could do from breaking out into rolling belly laughs. Returning to his field cot, he stretched out his long and lanky frame and tried to compose himself.

Borov is one cagey dude!

First, he transmits with the standard encryption, full knowing that our satellite system has been probably compromised by the bad guys. Then he gets me to carry on in that trash Cajun nonsense that we cooked up years ago. But apparently he takes the Russian's request for a sling extraction real seriously. My only question is just who will need the sling, Piankoff, or is that sneaky little Russian runt planning on hoisting something really heavy duty to our side?

Yeah, the good doctor has always been a real fine piece of work. He must have been a real handful for his Momma.

With those pleasant thoughts still fresh in his mind, Cartwright's head gently turned on his pillow and he began to snore.

CHAPTER XXXV

AD 2001. Russian Academy of Science

Contrary to what had become a tradition as of late, this time it was speaker number two, who had called his other two colleagues together, and had begun the discussion.

"My dear colleagues, you have before you the transcript of the recent satellite transmission between Dr. Borov at Horizon Pass and who we believe to be the field commander of the American Mark V-A in Egypt."

At the mention of the words Borov, American and Mark V-A, the Hungarian Nikolai Fedorov, Director of Advanced and Theoretical Technological Research, noticeably bristled.

"The good news is that this time we have a complete transcript, because its encryption is one that we understand very well. The bad news, although I cannot prove it, is that I believe the transmission to be devoid of any import whatsoever. Furthermore, I believe we are being played for fools. In fact, I detect a tone about the transmission that I can only characterize as playful deceit."

"While I understand, and to some extent, share your intuition regarding the importance of this transcript, I do believe, my dear Vasily, that we should run this conversation through my department's screening committee. Besides its several odd turns of phrase, they just may find something of value." So did Karlov Drazinzka stonily state, the Head of the Special Projects Directorate.

With a sigh, the first speaker, Vasily Alexandrovich Ostrogorsky, the Director of Theoretical Biology, looked down at his hands and nodded in consent.

"I just wish, my dear Karlov, not to perhaps needlessly expend your valuable resources."

"Think not about it, Vasily. Since the fall of that accursed Berlin Wall, they have not been fully utilized, even with all of our recent internal problems. Besides, it will be an amusing exercise for them."

CHAPTER XXXVI
Year 3 of Neferkheperru Amenhotep (Continued)

Richards awoke in the early pre-dawn light to the sound of cooing doves. As he lay on his padded and pillowed bed frame wrapped in a fine linen coverlet, a cool breeze ruffled the draped waterfall of gossamer linen that enshrouded his bed and kept the noisome nocturnal insects at bay. Reliving yesterday in his mind, his first day in the field, Richards shook his head in amazement at all that had happened, all that he had seen and experienced, and soberly, how much was yet to do.

Today, they were to approach and interview the various personal caretakers of the royal household to discover whatever they could about their target, his habits, and any of his eccentricities. They also were scheduled to meet Nefertiti, the Great Wife and First Mistress of the Two Lands, and the long friend and personal confidant of Meryptah. From these sources, Piankoff and Richards would then divine how to get their hands on any form of genetic material, be it fingernail clippings, hair, skin scrapings, or the ultimate Holy Grail.

Without a doubt, many intangibles were aligned against their success. But in all of their considerations, the Great Wife's cooperation remained the key. The how of that question frankly scared Richards to the quick. The entire proposition left him feeling as if he were slowly wading in a mixture of thick molasses. Speed and quickness could not be relied upon. Instead, a careful and plodding plan had to be put into place. It had to be something simple, yet nearly foolproof. Something so easy to say, but so nearly impossible to do. Just considering the negative ramifications brought a light sheen of sweat to his shaved head, a head that he may well lose, but only after a thorough Egyptian examination with a cane.

Suddenly, all those gruesome descriptions by Professor Milson about the examinations from the Ramesside tomb robbery texts came to life in Richards' overactive imagination. So he decided that failure would not be an option. Nor could be their discovery by the target.

Just as these weighty issues began to truly depress Richards, the wind-chime-like sounds of gentle giggles announced that it was time again for his morning toilet.

Smiling, he thought. *What a way to start the day. It sure beats the hell out of staggering into Starbucks for a morning jolt!*

Following his bath and shave, rub down, and breakfast of fruit, bread, and cheeses, Richards then went looking for his trusted guide, Thutmose. He did not have to go far, for just beyond the threshold of his sleeping chamber Thutmose stood faithfully waiting for his noble charge to appear. Upon seeing Richards, he respectfully asked, "Noble Mayneken, I trust that you have slept well?"

"Thank you, Thutmose. Indeed I did. The breezes of the Nile sang me to sleep. And yourself?"

Thutmose, taken aback by his young noble's nearly poetic answer and surprising personal concern, causing him to blush in embarrassment. Finding his tongue, he then stammered out with a minor bow.

"My noble Mayneken, I am honored by your interest. Yes, I too did sleep soundly after last evening's excitement."

At hearing this open ended opportunity so offered, Richards decided to probe a bit, and in a quiet and conspiratorial tone asked.

"My dear Thutmose, may I ask you a question?"

Raising his right hand and forefinger, he added. "But before you answer, I wish you to know that you do not have to answer if you do not wish to. I will take no offense. But if you do answer, I want to know truly what is in your heart."

"Noble Mayneken, what you ask may be a difficult question."

"Yes, I know. Perhaps it would be good if we went for a brief walk before visiting my teacher, Piankhotep. Would that be of help to your tongue?"

Blushing again and now intrigued that a noble was interested in what he actually thought, Thutmose nodded his consent and off the pair went. In what seemed like no time at all the two arrived near the Nile's reedy and lotus-choked western bank overlooking the early morning hubbub of commercial riverine activity.

"Noble Mayneken, I do not know truly what you seek, but I have never before seen the Great God in the flesh, nor have I been privileged to see his Mistress. That the royal pair appeared unannounced at the house of Meryptah I do not find odd. After all, He and She may go wherever They may wish at any time."

"I understand, my dear Thutmose."

Richards continued.

"But I am not of the royal court. My household is in the far north, at holy and sacred Memphis. I am a warrior, Thutmose. I have campaigned as far north as the land with the contrary river that flows in the wrong direction. I have been made cold by falling water from the sky. I have seen beasts beyond imagination. All of these I have been able to face with a strong heart.

"But Thutmose the Great God alone frightens me and perhaps well he should. But what I need to know is am I alone with this mindless fear, or does the entire court share it as well?"

Impressed by the brief narrative of his travels, yet wide-eyed at Richards' open frankness about his fear, Thutmose said with a tense voice, "Noble Mayneken, be assured that you are not alone in your fears. Many share them. Last night, I shared them. But be advised that many who have discussed the Great God and his rather, shall I say, peculiar ways, have either disappeared from court or have had their personalities strangely changed.

"As you are probably aware, Meryptah knows the Great God perhaps the best among those in the Land of the Living. He was His boyhood friend and confidant. But again, as you saw and heard just last night, that relationship is strained. Because of that, I believe that Meryptah's days are numbered."

Placing his hand on Thutmose's left shoulder and giving it a gentle squeeze, Richards, deep in thought, nodded in understanding at his guide's words. Then, in a dry and raspy voice, he said, "Thank you my friend for sharing with me the openness of your heart. Much of what you said has only confirmed what my own heart has been saying to me. In many respects, we are of the same mind. It is just that as a stranger in a strange land, I need the thoughts of others wiser than I."

At this compliment, Richards could swear that Thutmose's stature grew several inches. He was sure that he had totally recruited his guide and earned his confidence.

After another moment of reflection, the pair soundlessly began their trek back to the royal annex and Richards' appointment with his teacher, each deeply engrossed in their own thoughts.

*   *   *

Sitting before a reclining Piankoff in the subservient pose of student to teacher, Richards in a hushed voice shared in precise detail the results of his impromptu morning interview with Thutmose. Throughout it all, Piankoff remained silent, listening intently, and pleased at the uncanny ability of his young colleague to earn the confidence of those he touched. At the conclusion of Richards' summation, all he could do was nod in agreement. Leaning close to Richards' right ear, the Russian said, "Indeed, Mayneken, we are up against a most formidable foe, but one who must be sampled nonetheless. But now for my news, early this morning, before the rising of Re in all of His splendor, I received a most unexpected visitor—the Chief Wife Queen Nefertiti herself."

The shock on Richards' face must have been comical, for Piankoff's usually dour and granite visage broke into a smile of satisfaction.

"Well?"

"Well, she came to me, because our friend Meryptah suggested that she do so."

"On what pretext?"

"That I am a seer of the future and a wizard."

"Of Oz?"

At that, Piankoff chuckled lightly. "At first, I thought that precisely myself."

"But a seer and a wizard, you must be kidding!"

"Not in the least. Have you not noticed the extreme deference shown to us by no less than the high priest of the Great God? Have you not asked yourself who our hosts believe you to be? Must I remind you that you are no less than my assistant? What better cover can you invent? To be brutally honest, both Meryptah and Thutmose would gladly give their souls over to the evil demon Set for a chance to be in your sandals."

"How did you establish yourself as such a seer of the future and wizard without bashing all of the rules of *The Book of Gates*?" Richards asked with a hesitant touch of premonition.

Piankoff inwardly smiled at Richards' turn of idiom as he unconsciously translated *The Guidelines for Temporal Exploration* as the Egyptian religious text *The Book of Gates*.

"Why most predictably my dear colleague, for I broke almost every rule. But what is important is that most of what I revealed will not be passed on into the historical record."

"Most?"

"Well, who really knows for sure? But the glider toy that I helped a young Meryptah to build, I know did eventually appear in the archaeological record. A very crude second century BC copy of it was found in a Sakkaran tomb and is now securely locked away in the Cairo National Museum. The only public record of it is a picture in a display case on the second floor of the Deutsche Museum in Munich, safely lost among their vast aeronautical collection. Other than that, only a false prophet named Erik von Däniken mentioned it in one of his books. All in all, hardly anything to fret about."

Richards, now with an angry burn to his face, then asked, "Again my dear friend, why was I not told of this 'profession' of mine? It would have considerably helped my so-called cultural adjustment in the field."

"There were several good and obvious reasons. First, I wanted you to establish your own personality, your own way, to invent yourself in a plausible and individually comfortable manner within a culture that you were striving to understand. That, by the way, you have succeeded at far beyond all expectations. In fact, your invented military cover was brilliant, especially given your fine physique and your impressive scars, whose import on this culture's psyche somehow managed to escape my notice. But more remarkable is your common touch for one so young. You, in all of your western openness, have managed to disarm even the most severe.

"For example, take the physician Ankhmes, a bureaucratic snob, who knows and fears who I am by profession, was charmed by your gentle and unassuming way, and surprised by your knowledge of pharmacology and medical literacy. Be assured that you more than proved your own intellectual wizardry to him! The open secret is that he wants to know you in other ways that I know you would not approve.

"As for Meryptah, your loyalty, faithfulness, and protectiveness toward me was duly noted, and warmly so, almost immediately. Incidentally, your ingenuity in the procurement of my crutches was proof enough of your own innate sense of practical wizardry, which even drew the unfortunate notice of our target.

"Further, I did not want you unnaturally or inappropriately proving to our hosts your powers as either a seer or wizard. I feared that would have occurred if I had told you up front your true occupation. Instead, throughout, you have naturally proven yourself, established yourself, your own way, as my assistant in ways that no other can hope to match."

Richards slowly nodded as his quick young temper cooled.

"Only now, my Teacher, I see the great wisdom of your decision."

"Good. I am glad you understand. But to return to my early morning visitor, the queen is concerned about her daughters and stepsons."

"How so?"

"She had the usual concerns. Will they survive beyond childhood to become mature men and women? Which one will succeed her husband? Will they marry appropriate to their station? But once we got beyond the typical hocus-pocus and freshman psychology, I learned something very interesting.

"Each of her children, to one extent or another, seems to possess telepathic and telekinetic abilities. As a wizard, Nefertiti asked me about such abilities and whether their manifestations meant that her children were being possessed by demons."

"Demons? Just what are these little monsters up to?"

"She really didn't say directly, but I suspect that her children are teasing her unmercifully by anticipating her every move to her total distraction. And, significantly, her husband encourages this behavior, holding long conversations with them without moving his lips, yet the queen herself can hear the entire dialogue."

Richard then theorized.

"Is it possible that Nefertiti is feeling the cumulative effects of social isolation to such a degree that she can be of use to us?"

With a smile Piankoff nodded.

"And?"

"And later today she will deliver to us whatever she can, how can I say, acquire."

"Again, on what pretext?"

Shrugging his shoulders, Piankoff merely stated the obvious.

"Every wizard needs material to work with."

"And what does she expect in return?"

"Answers as to why her husband is so physically atypical, his obvious telepathic and presumably telekinetic abilities, and how those passed on abilities will affect her children. Down deep, she wants to know whether her husband and children are possessed by demons or merely blessed by the truly divine. In short, I am nothing more than her therapist, her psychiatrist."

All that Richards could do was gulp and then asked what seemed the obvious.

"What did she say about his physique?"

"Well, apparently the king wants more children very much. To say that they try to do so several times a day seems to be the norm. The queen seems not to mind, but she is nonetheless distressed about her inability to satisfy a king who wants more heirs, and quickly."

"But what about his physique?"

"Well, the queen was not very specific, except to say that she must mount him very carefully as he is so massively large. Apparently, the entire act is extremely exhausting for her."

"Okay. But just what is she delivering to you later today, the entire enchilada?"

This last Richards colorfully translated as "spicy stuffed bread roll" much to Piankoff's amusement.

"We will see. I gave her the entire wish list—nail clippings, hair, and semen. We will just have to wait and see what transpires."

At that good news, as Richards sat back his tense back cracked. Unconsciously rolling his head, he then cracked his neck, stretched his shoulders, and suggested, "Perhaps we should go for a walk, my teacher. Get some air. After all, today is a most beautiful one. There is much to see, much to learn, much to understand about this land."

"Agreed. Besides, as you well know, I pride myself in my fitness and I wish to purge myself as soon as possible from any affects of that poppy-laced raisin wine."

"My teacher, if we do go exploring, I must insist on not creating a scene, which means that we take sedan chairs."

Grumbling at the logic of his assistant's arguments, all that Piankoff could do was give in, yet again.

*   *   *

As nightfall began to descend on their second full day in the field, Piankoff and Richards returned to their chambers tired, thirsty, hungry, and covered in a mixture of sweat and dust. Both promised their seemingly tireless sedan chair bearers that they would not be out touring the next day. That announcement had earned them broad smiles and sighs of relief—a promise however that would be promptly broken.

Piankoff noticed that Richards quickly disappeared to "dust his feet." For himself, he fully expected to find something waiting for him in his sleeping chamber and was not disappointed. There, sitting on the exquisite cedar wood table that occupied the center of his room, sat several objects. Hobbling around the table on his crutches, Piankoff silently chided himself for looking for booby-traps. Sitting gently down on a beautifully carved scissors campstool, Piankoff put aside his crutches and gave his entire concentration to the objects before him.

The Russian's first concern was whether any of the objects included any metallic content, and after the first cursory inspection was relieved that none appeared to be so. His concern was real, for never had any metallic object ever passed through the Soap Bubble's ring—either experimentally or by accident. That fact had led to the removal of all of his stainless steel tooth fillings and crowns and their replacement with porcelain, much to the consternation of his country's employers, who could no longer track him with the usual GPS tooth transistor. As for Richards, he was such a healthy specimen that his teeth were perfect.

Perhaps those fluorinated water systems of the West were of some practical use after all, the Russian mused to himself.

Now, for their contents.

Gently lifting a small and smoothly finished, brick red, ceramic stoppered jar, Piankoff slowly turned it in his hands.

My, it's the same size as an old NATO hand grenade!

Opening its stopper and peering in with one eye, the jar contained numerous flecks of bone, no, nail clippings.

Yes! The Russian silently exclaimed.

Carefully twisting the stopper back into the throat of the small jar and placing it back on the table, Piankoff next reached for its identical twin. Weighing a bit heavier, its contents held a heavy, thick, milky, still semi-liquid mucous-like mass at its bottom.

If this is just the result from one coupling, then this is an enormous semen sample!

But just then he remembered Nefertiti's comment about her husband's size and sexual appetite.

Sealing the jar and returning it to the table's top, Piankoff then picked up a miniature ivory inlaid cedar box. Gently lifting off its cover, a full braid of dark hair bound with a short length of yellow twine was nestled at its bottom. No doubt from a child, this represented a cherished future heirloom. Perhaps even lovingly braided by his mother Tiye herself.

The Russian's next thought was one of paranoid security.

Where could I secret these valuables?

Quickly looking around his room, no secure possibilities immediately came to mind. But just to get them out of sight, the Russian decided to hide them within his bed clothing.

How sophomoric! This would be the first place anyone would look—certainly most anyone's mother. But this will just have to do for the moment.

Once out of sight, Piankoff again plopped himself down on his stool with a tired sigh thinking.

Tonight's contact will be critical.

Richards and I must deliver these samples and prepare for extraction a full day early. The sedan bearers will be disappointed, if not furious that we're going back across river!

I just hope that the sling is ready!

CHAPTER XXXVII
Sling Retrieval

Tuna Cartwright waited outside the pylons of the operational Mark V-A, while he and his three subordinates looked ridiculous. All were armed with butterfly nets in anticipation of catching another thrown papyrus package. Instead, they were completely shocked to see Piankoff's shaved head emerge from the smooth surface of the drop ring and grunt out in broken English.

"Ready the sling, immediately!"

Dropping their butterfly nets, Tuna Cartwright and his men shifted gears and swung the makeshift wooden crane's boom and tackle over the ring's aperture, and lowered a crudely formed double-looped sling of hemp rope.

"God, I am glad that we were prepared for this early extraction," Tuna said with pride while playing out the sling.

One jerk on the rope from the other side and the four-man crew all began to reel it in hand over hand. Just like that, Piankoff, a man of slight build, rocketed up through and clear of the ring. The boom swung wide and he was quickly deposited outside the circle of the Mark V-A's portable pylons. Released from the sling, the process was repeated and very shortly Richards stood by his side. He had not bothered with the sling, but chose to hang on to the sling's main tether. The entire extraction had taken less than twenty seconds. Once all were clear, the major ordered the shut down the Mark V-A with a single nodded command to Corporal Kramer.

What followed was a ludicrous scene where two former ancients, one standing on one leg and clutching a parcel against his chest, the other gripping two strangely built crutches. Facing them were three sweating soldiers and their commander. Tuna Cartwright then broke the moment with a firm, but friendly voice.

"Welcome home gentlemen."

Piankoff reacted by slowly sliding down where he stood and sat on the floor with his splinted leg extended. While he did so, he could not help but notice.

I was right all along! The truck driver was the security leader of this mission! And by the look of these three subordinates and the one over there manning the device's power pack, they all are far more than just raw bone and muscle.

As for Richards, he too plopped down, being glad to be back in one piece.

Stepping forward Piankoff, Tuna Cartwright drawled. "Well, Mr. Piankoff, what have you in the parcel?"

"What we came to get."

Was the Russian's answer in thickly pronounced English as he carefully handed over the parcel.

"Fair enough. Would you like our medic to take a look at your leg?"

"Yes. But first I wish to make a personal phone call on your satellite uplink. May I, Commander?"

Taking a few moments to consider the Russian's request, Tuna Cartwright nodded with a smile and said, "Yes, you may. But thank you, Mr. Piankoff, I am only a major."

Then he barked.

"Corporal Kramer, fire up the satellite phone for our honored guest. He wants to call his mommy."

Ignoring the major's sense of humor, Piankoff began to review in his mind what he would say to his superiors, full knowing that the entire world would be listening in.

With Richards helping him up to his feet, he took his crutches and moved over to the nearby satellite phone with its pizza pie-sized dish antenna. Here, he again plopped down, and smiled up at the massive form of Corporal Kramer, who then wandered off to a discreet distance. Taking up the receiver and punching in the international telephone number for the Russian Academy of Science in Moscow, Piankoff then sighed. After a few moments, the connection was made and a thick voice at the other end said.

"Da?"

Shifting into his Russian mother tongue was at first difficult, but nonetheless, he did it.

"Comrade, this is your long lost son."

"Sasha! Is that truly you! You are back early!"

Now shifting from true concern to purely business in the blink of an eye. "My son, do you have anything for me?"

"Absolutely, more than enough for both parties and plenty from the entire shopping list."

"Sasha, such results could mean another Lenin's Cross."

"Yes, but let us wait until the entire mission is successfully completed."

"As usual your sense of duty remains most admirable."

With that the connection was broken in Moscow.

Now exhausted from all the pent-up nervous tension of the delivery, Piankoff softly replaced the hand set back into its cradle. Looking up at Corporal Kramer he smiled and said, "Corporal Kramer, now I am ready to see your medic."

CHAPTER XXXVIII
Burning the Midnight Oil

It was late. The halls of the Near Eastern Institute were long silent from the sounds of treading feet, but Dr. John Milson worked on. Here, in the institute's basement archive and conservatory, Milson sat before a lab table wearing a pair of cotton restoration gloves. Before him he had nestled the striking blue-green oval of lapis lazuli in some cotton batting within a small cardboard jewelry box. Piankoff had used it as the throw weight of the first package. Having arrived by special courier that morning, Milson had wasted no time in acquiring for the object a museum registry number: NEI 734201. Next, he had it carefully measured, weighed, and photographed. Now with all of those preliminaries out of the way, the aging Egyptologist was down to the nitty-gritty of his task, the translation of the stone's inscription.

To his right was his yellow legal pad organized into three vertical columns and covered with penciled notes in his careful and precise handwriting. In the first column he had faithfully copied the engraved and inlaid hieroglyphs. In the second, he had transliterated those many symbols into their Latin-lettered equivalents. In the third, would go its translation.

Now, carefully closing the stone's acquisition box, he rose from the lab stool, while his body let out a creak of stiffness. Slowly walking over and placing the box within drawer Number 3, of the small finds cabinet Number 7, he was now ready to go. With his yellow legal pad and Number 2 pencil again in hand, he went over to the staff elevator and pressed the UP button. When the elevator arrived, his last act was to douse the lights of the lab. His next stop was the institute's archives, two floors above.

Exiting the elevator unto the institute's darkened second floor, Milson ambled over to the archive more on instinct than with his eyes. Entering that vaulted room with its roof of wooden arches he stopped at his favorite table, the first on the left, and turned on a reading light. Putting down his pad and pencil he then wandered over to where the archive shelved its copy of the multi-volume

Ägyptisches Wörterbuch. Removing volumes III, IV and VII, Milson then returned to his table and got down to work.

Working as he did at such a late hour pleased the old Egyptologist. Removed from all the distractions of life, here, now, he could truly think deep thoughts. Regarding the accurate translation of the stone's inscription, Milson already had a good idea what it said. But just to make sure, he was here, deep within the peace and tranquility of his own personal, intellectual womb, just to check up on his legendary memory.

Although the inscription possessed all the earmarks of a formulaic proudly announcing the birth of a royal heir, several of its interdependent clauses, depending on how they were read, could produce dramatically differing interpretations as to the stone's meaning and significance. Without doubt, Milson suspected that was why Piankoff, or Richards for that matter, had included it in the package.

The checking and cross-checking process required patience as it was a slow and tedious process. The institute's copy of the *Wb*, as it was typically referred to, had a page of graph paper bound and interleaved between every page of the dictionary's many volumes. On these facing pages, the faculty and staff of the institute had meticulously recorded next to practically every citation references of grammatical or philological relevance that had appeared after the dictionary's fourth edition in 1982. Making an informed translation of a difficult reading, therefore, meant one had to first consult the *Wb*'s citation, its own internal source referencing, and then check to see what additional notes, if any, had been written upon its facing page.

Blessedly, Milson noted, precious little controversy surrounded the two readings that he was confirming. After about forty-five minutes of careful word-smithing, he had his translation with a minor grammatical commentary. Shaking his head in disbelief, he finally reread the translation.

King of Upper and Lower Egypt
Lord of the Two Lands
Neferkheperure Amenhotep
(To whom) life is given Tutankhaten
Born of my body

May he rule with his intellect (mind?)(And) live for eternity.

For Milson the stone was historically significant in the fact that here was clear-cut evidence that the target was the father of the famous Tutankhamen. That, in and of itself, would shake up many scholars.

But who was his mother?

Was it Nefertiti or some other lady of the harem?

That was not at all made clear from this inscription, Milson thought.

Ah yes, as always, one question answered, but another is posed.

So it goes.

Because of his connection with the Philology Annex, however, it was the last line that had caused him the most concern. Although his conservative bent forced him to bracket the word "mind" as an interpolation, it was in actual fact nothing of the sort. To instead read the phrase as "with his intellect," while more a tradition one, would have been an outright lie. For the Egyptian word here, *sia*, one of the three divine aspects of pharaonic rule, could mean various things depending on context: divine understanding, insight, wisdom, or divine intellect. The dirty fact was the phrase was nothing more than an outright, although coded, reference to the pharaoh's wish that his son would genetically inherit his father's telepathic abilities and rule accordingly.

Sitting there in the darkness of the archive, pad before him, head in hands, Milson suddenly felt totally helpless.

What have I done?

Taking a deep breath and then slowly letting out, Milson, sitting back and with his eyes closed, slowly let a tear run down his sallow face.

John, you have been selfish and recklessly so. You wanted to handpick your successor. Okay, so you did. Now, if only he can return home safe and sound.

CHAPTER XXXIX

AD 2002. The Russian Assessment

Once again within the secure vault of the Russian Academy of Science, the first speaker, Vasily Alexandrovich Ostrogorsky, Director of Theoretical Biology, addressed his two colleagues.

"Gentlemen, as you already know, last month we received our 'cut,' as the Americans put it, of the genetic material that our field operative, Colonel Alexander Piankoff, procured for them. Those samples, which were composed of the target's semen, hair, and nail clippings, have been thoroughly analyzed by my laboratory staff.

"First of all, and perhaps most interesting, the target's DNA revealed a chromosomal makeup that does not include a bona fide Y-chromosome. Instead, as best as we can determine, the target possesses two X-chromosomes and a third sexual chromosome that we have identified tentatively as a neutral. This neutral chromosome appears to be able to act as either an additional X chromosome or, perhaps, as a surrogate Y-chromosome. Within our experience, such a flexible chromosome arrangement is unique within the human genome, although it does have certain parallels within some hermaphroditic genomes, such as snails, worms, and some reptiles. In summary, the target possesses one extra, variable, sexual chromosome.

"This curious situation, however, does raise the interesting question as to whether a male offspring of the target would be fertile or sterile. At present, we do not know for certain, but our people strongly suspect that the males may be sterile, and if they did sire, only females would be produced.

"Additionally, there exist multiple occurrences of the so-called bow tie mutation throughout the target's entire DNA matrix. In fact, every chromosomal body possesses at least one, while in others, multiple instances. The affects of so many mutations, whether in combination or not, and the multiplicity of their possible expression, simply defies calculation.

"Finally, we have positively identified that the bow tie mutations discovered by Sasel and Philopedes among the Anatol samples have a one-to-one correlation with the bow tie locations as expressed by the target.

"Gentlemen, in summary, it is the conclusion of my staff that we have in our possession the genetic material of an organism not of this earth. Furthermore, and principally on the basis of the neutral sex chromosome, we may also posit a strong hypothesis for an organism that can willfully select its own sex.

"As to what other characteristics this organism can display and in what combinations, we have barely scratched the surface. It is the opinion of several of my researchers that the genetic makeup of the target could be best compared to that of a child's set of building blocks. What is unique about this set of blocks is that each in its own way possesses a multiplicity of variables that can express themselves differently when placed in combination.

"In short, the organism is a genetic chameleon."

After listening carefully to what their esteemed colleague had to report, both of his colleagues were stunned.

"What do you mean Vasily?

"Is the target truly an alien?" asked the Head of the Special Projects Directorate, Karlov Drazinzka.

"I cannot but consider that a very, very strong possibility. Not only is this organism flexible in that it can genetically organize itself, at least potentially, but it can also fit itself into its surroundings as needed."

"What sort of powers could such a creature possess, Vasily?"

"I have no idea, and, I believe that it probably has few limitations. Remember, Piankoff did specifically mention that the target was an inline telepath and that its offspring were telepathic and telekinetic."

Finally, the Hungarian Nikolai Fedorov, Director of spoke. "It is my opinion that this organism represents a serious threat to humanity and the course of human events as we understand them. I move to eliminate this threat."

His colleagues agreed.

CHAPTER XL

AD 2002. The American Assessment

Ever since the arrival of the divided genetic sample, the university's state-of-the-art gene laboratory had been humming along twenty-four hours a day. As a rude consequence, all university faculty, staff, and students associated with the lab had found themselves evicted and their personal research halted, while a sizable force of non-university laboratory personnel had taken over. Physical peace and quiet between the two groups was provided by an equally sizable force of university security guards backed up by a government security force led by Major Cartwright and his men, all who were spectacularly armed in full body armor, their heads goggled in Darth Vader-like Kevlar helmets. While their quiet presence was deemed shocking overkill by all those involved, it was deemed a necessary evil that only a potential watershed event could justify.

Before the screams of lab time squandered, delicate experimental results lost, and grant funds wasted, all such complaints were quashed with guarantees of generous, future fiscal support and lavishly upgraded facilities. For some, such openhandedness during a time of quiet, declared emergency was sufficient, even if unappreciated. For others, these accommodations were not enough.

For those hardcore cases, a bureaucrat, who heralded from a darkly powerful but innocently sounding governmental agency, made a brief visit. This tastefully dressed business woman took the more cantankerous aside, patiently explained to these scientific prima donnas the facts of life, how monumentally crucial this work truly was, and what their cooperation would mean to their future careers, come what may. In one extremely vocal case, a vociferous associate professor that was pushing for promotion to a full prof, she vanished on an unscheduled, all expense-paid, two-year sabbatical to map the genotype of the Antarctic snow flea *in situ*. The news of this sudden scientific windfall had spread like wildfire. The message could not have been more clear.

"Don't mess with this lab or its personnel, period."

The project lead of the American mad dash analysis was himself not an American citizen, but rather a Greek, a man who feared for his life and the welfare of his family. Officially, he had been granted an emergency sabbatical from his university post in Athens to care for a close relative in the States with a grave illness.

Unofficially, Zacharias Philopedes' presence in Chicago to led the genetic analysis of the target vector was no chance mistake. His groundbreaking research in the bow tie mutation made him an attractive candidate. His professional contacts and dogged reputation made him a likely candidate. But it was Philopedes' close brush with his late colleague Sasel and the Russian Academy of Science that made him the only candidate to led the American analysis team. Besides, his family members were presently the honored guests of Dr. Peter Borov, and were protected, safe and sound, within the bowels of Horizon Pass itself.

Within the secure auditorium of the Annex's first sublevel, the usual suspects gathered, the same group who had first been informed of the watershed event alarm. True to form, it was that near-Nobel physicist, Dr. Jung, who was again the last to arrive.

As before, Dr. Young convened the proceedings and then introduced Philopedes, who was wearing a white lab coat, his favorite Grateful Dead tee shirt, and half reading glasses propped up on what was left of his curly, graying mane.

"Good morning," the Greek began.

"As you know, the research team has been hard at work around the clock for the past five weeks. To say that we are all fried would be an understatement, but we have discovered much, and with every discovery we make, we are presented with a multiplicity of questions. But today, I wish to present to you what we know, and what we think we know, about the genetic makeup of the target vector. May I have the first slide please?"

The room dimmed appropriately and the far wall became a blaze of light arranged in three vertical columns with identical images in each.

"What you see before you is not a bunch of chopped up Chinese noodles."

Polite chuckles appeared at Philopedes' weak attempt at humor.

"What they are, however, are chromosomes, more properly chromosomal bodies, that are identical throughout all of the genetic samples that we have received. This proves that all the material that was procured came from the same organism.

"Next slide please.

"This schematic diagram shows a typical set of human chromosomes on the right with the target vector's arrayed in comparison on the left. Please note that the target vector possesses two sexual X-chromosomes, and, what we think is an extra sexual chromosomal body as well. Its significance is unknown.

"Next slide.

"What you are now looking at is an electron microscope's view of only a portion of the target vector's extra sexual chromosome. Please notice that just within this narrow sector of this DNA strand that you can see no less than three bow tie mutations. Here, here, and here. I feel compelled to also say that the high incidence of this mutation throughout all of the target vector's chromosomal bodies is dizzying, especially since such mutations have only been produced to date as the direct result of external experimental forces. To my knowledge, the bow tie mutation cannot occur in nature, only in the laboratory, at least until now.

"Can we have the lights please?"

While the lights came up and his audiences' eyes completed their refocusing, Philopedes patiently waited to drop his bombshell.

"In short, my preliminary hypothesis regarding the genetic makeup of the target vector is the following. What we are looking at is an organism that is constituted of a multiplicity of interchangeable puzzle parts, but puzzle parts that have been purposely engineered into the present pattern that we see before us.

"To be blunt, the target vector is an artificially engineered organism that in outward appearance is similar to the human species, but in no respect can claim membership within the human genome.

"Are there any questions?"

Philopedes had calculated this moment. Here, arranged before him was the most powerful brain trust outside of the Russian Republic. The impact of his preliminary findings were, to put it mildly, stunning. The silence of his audience was confirmation of that fact.

After about fifteen seconds of shock and bewilderment, the first squirming began, which begat some scratched scalps, stroking of chins and beards, adjusting and cleaning of glasses, and some pulled ears and noses, all evidence of the typical body language that academics employ while in deep thought. Finally the first hand arose.

"Dr. Philopedes, I am curious, especially given the extra sexual chromosome. In your estimation, what is the sex of the target vector?"

Pleased with the question, Philopedes warmed to the topic.

"Well, at first glance, with two X-chromosomal bodies, one would assume that the target vector is a female. But with the third sexual chromosome available as well, we could have either a triple X chromosomal super-female, or an XXY androgynous male, or, as a third possibility, some as yet to be determined sex or sexes. But my money is on the XXY male on the basis of the first hand, eye-witness account of the operatives in the field. And of course, there was the semen sample."

Then the next question was voiced.

"Dr. Philopedes, in your opinion, is the subject capable of inbreeding within our genome?"

"Most definitely. I have already witnessed in Russia the results of such a coupling via the presence of multiple instances of the bow tie mutation in a human female. But as to how such a transmission would express itself within our genome, much, much more study is required.

"As for genetic transmission, my opinion is that the female sibs will be fertile and fully capable of passing on these mutations. But as for the males, well, I believe them to be nearly sterile, possibly capable only of siring females. But again, I would like to point out the obvious. Much, much more research needs to be done just to substantiate those points.

"But to return to the question of genetic expression, the field reports strongly suggest, no indicate, that the sibs of the target vector all evince telepathic and telekinetic abilities. As to what other expressions such a mating could produce would require years of laboratory research. However, if one of the sibs were available for study, then the entire assessment process would be greatly sped up."

These last words created a predictable storm of righteous indignation and reaction.

"Dr. Philopedes are you proposing that we kidnap a young child and then submit them to laboratory analysis like some lab rat!"

This question was greeted with several approving nods and many more used the body language of cross arms and narrowing eyes to convey their displeasure.

Smiling, Philopedes thought, *I wonder how long it took for the Russians to seriously consider the merits of that proposal.*

Now answering the question.

"In case some of you do not know, my family and my two young daughters are presently in the care and protection of your organization. I merely mention this to underscore that fact that I am a father.

"That said, the fact remains we do not know how multiple bow tie mutations within the human genome could be expressed, or suppressed. The genetic variables and triggers are endless. On the basis of my previous work in St. Petersburg, we identified only a handful such transmitted sites within a long dead individual. Those sites were widely scattered throughout the individual's chromosomes. I have no way of testing whether or not that dead subject was either telepathic or telekinetic within the limitations of a gene lab.

"What I can say, however, is this. Has anyone here considered whether such hybridization will be harmful or beneficial to the human genome? That question is what I am struggling with. We can work for decades in the laboratory, but we will never know what we can learn in mere moments from a living example."

Another question appeared.

"Dr. Philopedes, I appreciate your dilemma, but what about the target vector itself? In your opinion, what should been done about it?"

Pausing, Philopedes gathered his thoughts. "I really do not know. If the target vector improves the human genome, where is the harm? But to intelligently make that decision we need hard data, data that I believe can only be derived from a living subject and not from a long dead one."

Silence again broke out with some more squirming, ear and nose tugging, shin stroking, and head scratching. Then, Philopedes added, "Oftentimes the simplest solution in science is the best. We could just do nothing and have faith in nature to take its course. But I can assure you that our colleagues in the Russian Academy of Science will not tolerate such a passive and optimistic approach.

"As shocking as this may seem to some of you, what if the target vector is indeed harmful to the human genome? What then? Again, I can assure you that our Russian colleagues will be of a very strong and united opinion, even if it betrays some paranoia. And I might add in their defense, some paranoia is quite healthy.

"Regardless, any decision must come down to the study of a living, breathing individual. I am told that we can do this now, today, if we wish. We do not have to remove the individual from its familial unit. We can observe in the field."

This suggestion brought forth another intellectual firestorm. But this time is was about the qualifications of the field operatives, the potential long term effects of their presence on the time line, their judgmental soundness, and their ability to provide accurate data. To these voiced reservations Philopedes could only smile.

"Well, from the sound of your protestations regarding the fitness of the field operatives, one might think that you are unanimously in favor of kidnapping a young child, separating it from its loved ones, and placing it within a sterile psychological environment for observation."

Abrupt silence.

"Or, are you willing to trust the observational abilities, good judgment, and decision-making of your temporal field operatives? The decision is yours, but act quickly for time's-fast-a-wastin'."

With a hurried flourish, Philopedes left the auditorium for his laboratory and far more important things. The final decision as to what should be done about the target vector, did not concern him as much as that promised phone call to his precious Elena.

CHAPTER XLI
Cram Course

Richards found himself again enjoying the New Mexican desert. It wasn't the pristine sand and rock of ancient Egypt, but then again, what could be?

What surprised Richards was how much he needed the four weeks of down time. He hadn't realized how tight he had been, how primed, and how exhausted. Now, back in his own time, his daily schedule was an ever-challenging mixture of physical exertion, cross country jogging, followed by mental stimulation. This last Professor Milson had provided, for Richards was now steeped in writing his PhD thesis on an especially crusty topic of Egyptian philology—and to teach it properly.

"The key my dear man," Milson had said, "is to try to think in terms of the student. What is the best way to grasp a topic? Not as the teacher and how to teach it. Trust your instincts. They are very sound. Above all, you must prove your thesis on the basis of evidence without giving away the benefit of your extraordinary, first-hand experiences."

That last, Richards was soon to discover, was difficult, but Milson had the solution. There was nothing wrong with presenting an alternative solution to a thorny issue through the guise of a speculative footnote. As a result, what Richards discovered was that he would first formulate several vanilla lines of academic text and then compose a well-documented footnote in their defense. After only four weeks of writing, Richards had found that he had written over one hundred and fifty pages of dense and lucid text, which he then emailed to Milson.

That very night, Milson had called informing him he was coming out on the next plane from Chicago. What Milson had not said was that he was coming out on the dedicated company Lear jet. At breakfast the very next day, Milson appeared and sat down across the breakfast table before his young student.

"Well, my dear man, you look marvelously fit and healthy!"

Gulping in shock at the professor's sudden presence, all that Richards could do was nod his head and clear his mouth of oatmeal and milk smothered in brown sugar and raisins.

"Professor Milson! Why, you're already here!"

Suddenly remembering his manners, Richards stood and extended his hand in greeting. "Welcome to Horizon Pass!"

Taking the young man's hand, Milson said, "Ah, yes, thank you. Now sit down and finish your breakfast, while I order my own."

While the professor did so, Richards noticed the not-so-subtle hints of gauntness to his face and frailness in his hands that he had never before noticed. Even his epidermis resembled more a translucent parchment, his underlying veins a delicate, blue tracery mosaic. The whole picture highlighted by a slight tremor. Remembering the concerned words of the Cairo National Museum's Director, his condition must be worsening.

Having finished ordering his breakfast with the steward, the professor again focused on Richards with his intense gray eyes.

"As you know, I received the first draft of your dissertation and I have already read it in its entirety. Right now, I would judge it as about fourth-fifths complete. What do you think?"

"Well, sir, to be frank, I need some serious time in the institute's archive to check my sources and find any other opinions that I may not be aware of. For all I know, some of my readings and opinions that I buried in those alternative footnotes, as you call them, could be off-base."

To this answer Milson could only smile with fatherly pride.

"Mr. Richards, it is time for me be frank. This dissertation of yours does not require you to address every instance of scholarly debate that may or may not support your thesis or your alternative arguments. Rather, your contemporaries must confront your work, your fresh propositions, and your data. And we both know why. Only you and you alone have had the luxury of having been there and done that. As of this moment, you are the authority, not them. Keep that in mind.

"Now as to the manuscript, at least as I see it, once we get beyond some of your more interesting grammatical constructions, you must add a solid conclusion. You will then defend your thesis against two other philologists and myself. When that's done, this work should be gone through by an editor and then immediately submitted to the university press' editor for their consideration. By the way, I will be your editor. As for the press, I have already made some preliminary arrangements. They will be expecting to hear from you after your defense, which, while potentially harrowing, few could hope to defeat. In fact, some good might come from such a thorough discussion. Just remain logical and humble. And always remember, who is really the expert on this topic. That person is squarely you."

At this casually delivered announcement, Richards' jaw sagged. First, the topic was suggested and then tacitly accepted. Second, it only needed some editing. Third, write a conclusion. Fourth, defend it. And Fifth, submit it to the university press three weeks later. Yeah, sure.

To Richards' mixed reaction, Milson asked, "Is there something wrong, Joseph?"

"Why yes, professor, there is. PhDs just do not grow on trees in seven weeks time and thereafter are sent to a university press. What gives?"

Softly blinking and smiling gently with his eyes that sent a passing wave of fine wrinkles to ripple, Milson responded.

"Why Mr. Richards, the fact is that it is really very simple. You possess powerful linguistic gifts. Your entire life has been devoted to them. Further, you possess a brutally logical and sensible mind. You have a marvelous gift for expression and organization. You like puzzles and you solve them effortlessly. And, need I point out that you thoroughly know how to speak a dialect of a long dead ancient language. Furthermore, you're fresh back from then. You're focused, immersed, and to be honest, what else is on your plate?"

Pausing to take a breath, the professor continued.

"Frankly, the next project that you should begin consciously thinking about is a thorough-going grammar for Eighteenth Dynasty Egyptian and its two principal dialects, and when it is completed, begin teaching."

"You have it all figured out, don't you Dr. Milson?" Richards replied.

"Well, yes and no, Joseph. All I know is that you have been granted an unprecedented opportunity in a dusty old field of study that desperately needs someone to shake it up, to breathe fresh life into it.

"And about your thesis, soon to become the leading authoritative classroom text on the ancient Egyptian language, well, if I were tell you that it will be just brilliant, I would be wasting my breath. Instead, let's finish our breakfasts and find someplace quiet where we can talk. I have several questions that I want to ask you about. In particular, this curious expression that you alluded to as 'to dust one's feet.' Now just what is that all about?"

*   *   *

Within the isolated and highly regimented structure provided by Horizon Pass, Richards had found his stride. In fact, it was a tossup as to which he enjoyed most, the early morning run through the breathtakingly vivid colors of the New Mexican landscape, or that deep intellectual challenge that followed the cleansing, post-jog shower.

As for his Russian colleague Piankoff, Richards had not seen him since their extraction in Luxor. Despite his breakneck schedule, Richards had to admit that he missed the man on his runs and especially their conspiratorial conversations in their acquired ancient tongue.

*   *   *

While Richards was half a world away and thinking about Piankoff, the same could be said of the Russian, who, despite his own guarded nature, deeply missed the youthful energy and secure luxury of having the young lion at his side.

"Colonel Piankoff?

"Colonel Piankoff, you seem preoccupied. Should we perhaps reconvene today's debriefing after a short break?"

The lovely interrogator asked with a raised right eyebrow.

Stammering out his answer, the Russian operative replied, "Yes, yes, that would be fine. Perhaps ten minutes."

Yes, my dear Piankoff, I can tell that you miss your young lion, the adrenaline rush, and high adventures you shared in the field. Somehow, the thought of returning to that blessed ancient land makes all of this exhausting, boring, and repetitious debriefing tolerable.

Getting up from the heavy oak seminar table and slowly walking unassisted toward the antiseptic-smelling hallway and its institutionalized tile bathroom, he continued his personal conversation.

As for this ankle, good old Ankhmes truly had known what he was doing. Now, all I have to do is get permission from that incompetent excuse of an orthopod so that I can begin training again, Piankoff thought.

No doubt Mayneken is out running daily through the winding wadis of New Mexico and becoming ever more an untamable wild stallion.

Damn I miss him.

CHAPTER XLII
The First Teleconference

The secure satellite teleconference uplink between the two parties was generously provided for by the United States Air Force. They owned the satellite. Never before has such a thing been done and most likely, thought the Air Force Chief of Staff, never would it again.

As for the two participating parties, the entire event was something of a technological marvel, for this was the first time that simultaneous voice recognition and translation softwares were being used, not to mention that either party had ever before met face-to-face. This last wrinkle was not so much an issue for the Americans. But for the Russian principals, individuals who prided themselves on their faceless anonymity, the presence of the video camera before them represented a considerable concession.

On the American panel sat four individuals. Dr. Zacharias Philopedes, bio-geneticist and project lead of the American's sample analysis, sat to the camera's far left. Professor John Milson, Egyptologist, cultural and historical consultant sat next to him. Professor Ernst Jung, quantum mechanics physicist, sat to the far right. Finally, Dr. Paul Young, economist, university dean, financial liaison, and de facto representative of the Philology Annex on Borov's behalf, sat between Milson and Jung. All unconsciously sat forward in their chairs and leaned heavily on their long conference table. Eager anticipation filled their eyes. Their hands noticeably revealed their excitement. Young's precisely folded hands betrayed the curiosity of a first year freshman. Jung was deeply engrossed in expertly twirling his pen with his left hand. Philopedes nervously arranged, rearranged, and re-rearranged his stack of papers and pen before him. Milson, his chin resting in the palm of his right hand, feigned total boredom, while he rhythmically thrummed the desk with the fingertips.

Opposite the four Americans sat the three enigmas who dwelled within that curious warren that was the Russian Academy of Science. Academician Nikolai Fedorov sat to the left of the camera.

Academician Vasily Alexandrovich Ostrogorsky sat to the camera's right. Lastly, Dr. Karlov Drazinzka sat squarely in the middle. Unlike their colleagues at the other end of the connection, all three Russians were sitting back deeply in their padded chairs, exuding an air of confidence and control.

Needless to say, the gathering of such a rogue's gallery, by anyone's estimate, was genuinely recognized as a truly historic moment. For the Russians, their curiosity about who their American counterparts were left them mildly disappointed with some, but were definitely dismayed at the presence of Philopedes. To the point that Fedorov had stood and rudely dragged Drazinzka off-camera and whispered, "We should have eliminated that Greek with Sasel!"

To which Drazinzka could only nod in approval.

"Especially since who knows what intuitive insights he may have shared with them about Project Anatol, or for that matter, the Norsk Report." Fedorov added.

The American panel members, upon seeing for the first time their counterparts, were not impressed with the ancient and withered trio. But for several American intelligence agencies that were allowed to tune in, courtesy of the U.S. Air Force Intelligence Agency, the telecast was an unprecedented opportunity to study three very influential ghosts, who were known only by name and reputation. To view this triumvirate in the flesh, to study their interaction and body language, was an intelligence coup beyond imagination. Agency heads of several psychology departments had already reallocated their budgets to find the funds necessary to spend weeks, if not months, analyzing their every move, gesture, facial expression. As for the Air Force Chief of Staff, he could swear that he could almost hear the cash register ringing with institutional chits.

At the appointed time, Dr. Young began the meeting with a note of greetings and observed that this momentous face-to-face was long overdue. Several minutes later, he concluded his remarks saying that the participants should endeavor to work hard together in the spirit of international cooperation to find a solution as what to do about the target vector.

Forgetting himself, Fedorov elbowed his neighbor Drazinzka, who had slightly bent his head in his direction, and whispered. "That bombastic fool, the answer is elimination, pure and simple!"

Unfortunately for Fedorov, and unknown to the entire Russian panel, this entire exchange had been clearly picked up, translated, and transmitted to the American panel. The only visual indication from the Russian side that something was amiss were several rather bewildered glances shared among the silent Americans and the now tomato-red complexion of Dr. Young's typically ivory complexion.

Choosing to overlook Fedorov's comment and deciding to address it later, Young paraphrased in the florid Russian dialect of St. Petersburg a famous quote of Lenin.

"Dear academicians, indeed, just what is to be done?"

The linguistic shock of Young's question, and the rather artful way he delivered it, was evident on each of the Russians' faces. Then, slowly they marginally turned to one another and Ostrogorsky spoke in a formal and rehearsed tone.

"Dr. Young, fellow colleagues." He nodded to each half a world away.

"May I say that we too hope that this historic meeting will engender improved cooperation between our respective scientific communities. Indeed, it has been a long time.

"In answer to your most direct question, Dr. Young, there are many variables first to be discussed before any decision can be made as to 'what must be done.' However, my colleagues and I are not accustomed to lengthy diplomatic discussions akin to the historic SALT talks. Instead, we are men of action, who sit squarely at the head of, and in command of, our respective areas of influence."

Cough into a fist.

Sip of water.

Again slowly and carefully folding his hands before him, all the while thinking.

Let that fact sink in, Dr. Young.

"Dr. Young, I will answer your question in the following way. First, our laboratory data to date, and seeing that the esteemed Dr. Zacharias Philopedes is present on your distinguished panel, he knows well what I mean, can only begin to suggest a course of action regarding the target vector and his potential downstream effects upon the development of the Western Asiatic genome."

Milson quickly surmised. *And by Western Asiatic, Ostrogorsky no doubt includes the* Rodina—*Mother Russia!*

312

"What is far more critical to our decision making are the eye-witness accounts of the field operatives, who as you well know have reported telepathic and telekinetic abilities exhibited by the children of the subject and telepathic conversations having been observed between the subject and his children.

"We believe that these new abilities only represent the visible tip of a vast genetic iceberg, an iceberg that will in time threaten and divide the human genome into two, creating two populations in essence: one aristocratic and all-knowing, one subservient and dumb.

"Furthermore, we are also sensitive to the possibility that the subject is just a precursor, a guinea pig, or feasibility study if you will, to an alien colonization effort.

"Consequently, we unanimously propose that the target vector should not be allowed to influence our genome any further, and, should be eliminated at our first opportunity."

Knowing full well the sensitivity of the uplink microphones, the American panel could only stare back in amazement and at one another regarding the bold proposal placed squarely at their feet.

Then, to the Russians' surprise, Philopedes posed the following question.

"Gentlemen, how many of you are grandfathers?"

Ostrogorsky responded with a knowing smile. "I am a grandfather twice and a great-grandfather once."

Both Fedorov and Drazinzka remained silent.

Philopedes, now addressed Ostrogorsky to the exclusion of the others.

"Academician Ostrogorsky, what would you say if our field operatives were allowed to return and observe firsthand the genetic impacts in the children of the target vector, in order to gather evidence with which we may then make an educated decision? It just may be that the target vector is not a fifth columnist, nor a threat to the development of our genome, but rather the source that will allow our species to continue its presently aborted evolution."

Ostrogorsky, listening while looking down at his now open and relaxed hands, visibly sighed as he thought.

This Greek could be correct! Our species has ceased to appreciably evolve or adapt ever since the discovery of fire!

"Dr. Philopedes, I believe that you have posed a very interesting point of view. We will reconvene in five minutes time."

That said, Ostrogorsky signaled to someone off-camera with the universal throat-cutting motion and the video feed from Moscow ended abruptly.

The suddenly snowy video feed from Moscow caught the American panel by surprise. Three of their reactions were typical. Young swore under his breath. Milson found the Russian's sudden desire for privacy typical of their culture. Jung became remarkably hopeful that the Russians indeed had found their long lost hearts. Only Philopedes found himself smiling.

Western Asiatic genome indeed! He thought. *Only the biologist Ostrogorsky would appreciate an appeal to human evolution. Especially since he believed that the Russians would be the benefactors of such evolutionary traits!*

Philopedes' continued reverie was as suddenly shattered with the re-establishment of the Moscow video feed.

For the Russians' part, and although their seating positions had not changed, something nonetheless had. There was a heaviness to their faces that defied words. Again Ostrogorsky began in a solicitous manner with shoulders shrugged, open hands, and looking to each in turn, said, "Drs. Young, Milson, Jung and Philopedes, we wish to first apologize for our potentially impolite behavior. We merely wished to discuss the merits of what Dr. Philopedes had just brought up. As your intelligence agencies have no doubt probably already told you about us, then you know that we represent a close family, and as with all families, we have our own firm opinions."

Young thought. *What a classic instance of Byzantine understatement! Off camera, I bet that those three were probably hacking each other to pieces!*

"That said, Dr. Philopedes, and with some reservations I might add, we have agreed to alter our first position. We have considered your evolutionary proposal and will provisionally support the deployment of an observation team. We are curious, however, just what would such a team look for?"

Stunned at the conciliatory and almost chatty tone of the Russian panel, and of Ostrogorsky in particular, the Greek became wary.

Well now, they took the bait. But is he the only sane one? Or is he only the one who just appears to be so reasonable?

"That is a very good question, Academician Ostrogorsky, and I don't have a satisfactory answer for you at this time. The mere chronicling of odd and out of the ordinary physiological and psychic manifestations would represent a rudimentary baseline. Beyond that, I would hope that both of our groups could put together their own lists. If we both wish to follow this course, we indeed need to discuss this matter fully."

Ostrogorsky then realized, by the look on the other American's faces, Philopedes' proposal was as new to them as it was revolutionary to us.

Just who is this Greek? Only poor Sasel truly understood him. More's the pity.

"Indeed we do, Dr. Philopedes, indeed we do, but not at this time. I think what each of our groups need to do separately is to thoroughly discuss what to look for, a time period for observation, and then a period that would allow for a re-evaluation of the data."

Then Ostrogorsky shifted his gaze and asked, "Dr. Young, when would you wish to reconvene?"

Caught a bit unawares, Young blinked, bit his lower lip, looked around his colleagues, and said without thinking, "Tomorrow, same time, same channel."

Smiling across the void of distance at Young's unconscious wit and momentary confusion, Ostrogorsky decided to pick up on his line and said, "Don't worry, we'll be here ready and waiting."

With another signal off camera, the Moscow feed again ended in a snowy blur.

CHAPTER XLIII
Psychic Blocking

Richards, having already completed his daily run through the desert, a refreshing shower, and some quality time on his nearly-completed dissertation, was starving. Digging vigorously into the compound's daily special of rare roast beef, real mashed potatoes and garlic, fresh corn, peas, and four floured biscuits, Richards then guzzled down four glasses of milk to wash the whole down. Wiping his lips on his napkin, he then began seriously contemplating the demise of some warm apple cobbler.

At this critical juncture in his lunch, the good Dr. Borov appeared at his table and asked if he could join the young field operative. Smiling down at Richards and noting the remains of his gustatory carnage arranged around him, Borov bent over and tied a stray lace on his right Nike and thought, *Ah, youth!*

But Peter, such a finely tuned engine as this, surely requires its fuel as does such a finely tuned mind. Milson chose wisely and should be rightly ecstatic with his progress! And given the current state of his health, it is probably the best possible motivation for a man fighting for his very life.

Breaking from his thoughts, Borov now heard Richards asking him if he wanted anything from the buffet. Glancing over and noting that Richards had yet to attack the apple cobbler, he said, "Why Joseph, how kind of you. How about you grab some of that cobbler over there, and while you're at it, grab some for yourself."

Smiling with his usual infectious energy, Richards bounded out of his chair and returned moments later with two simply huge portions of the dessert. The scientist then quietly mentioned, "Joseph, I have good news for you and Colonel Piankoff. You're scheduled shortly to go back."

Quickly raising his freshly-shaved and heavily-tanned head from his face-plant in the cobbler, Richards sparkling eyes told Borov everything that he needed to know about his young charge's readiness. Clearing his mouth of dessert, Richards sat back, squared his shoulders, and stated the obvious.

"Dr. Borov, I am ready as ever."

"Yes, I know you are."

Then leaning forward across the table in a concerned and fatherly tone, Borov said, "But this time, you and Colonel Piankoff have been tasked with a slightly different, but also more hazardous task. You are being redeployed for a maximum of two weeks, not as gatherers, but this time as historical observers. How long you actually take will be up to the two of you, but no more than two weeks. It seems that the powers that be, both Russian and US, want hard data on the physical and psychic capabilities of both the target and his progeny. No small task, especially given the narrow time frame and the need for the two of you to work in relatively close proximity of the royal family.

"Concern for the preservation of the historical record and required discretion will be absolute. But the biggest danger that you will face will be the telepathic abilities of the target and his children. We do not want to alert or threaten the target in the event that he or his children telepathically rapes or plunders your mind. Yes, Joseph, you heard me correctly, mental plunder, rape, violation. To address that issue, both you and Colonel Piankoff are to undergo, as a safe guard, deep hypnosis in order to block any potentially damning information about from whence you came, not to mention the existence of the Soap Bubble."

To Borov's mention of mental rape, Richards' formerly confident face had turned ashen. He had never, ever considered that before.

Folding his hands, Borov then continued, "Well, I can see by your face that you understand what I'm getting at. As before, Joseph, I am not here to scare the pants off of you, but to warn you to remain alert to your historical context and mission profile. Also, I am told that the necessary hypnotic blocking is far more accepted by the individual if they approach it a relaxed, open mind. Do not fight the process.

"By the way, you are scheduled to see Doc Allen today at two o'clock. Please don't forget."

With that said Borov got up and left the cafeteria. He had not touched his cobbler.

Richards, now alone with his thoughts, couldn't finish his either, and looking down at his watch, he got up and bused the table.

*   *   *

Two hours later, Richards found himself at the infirmary. Nurse Stewart, as usual, looked up and smiled with her usual warmth.

"Well, Mr. Richards, it's good to see you again back safe and sound. The doc's waiting for you in Room No. 2."

Thanking Nurse Stewart with a big grin, Richards went over and walked into the indicated examination room.

Meanwhile Nurse Stewart, just a tad moony-eyed, watched the operative move away, causing her to unconsciously shake her head.

Doc Allen, who was coming down the hallway behind her, noted his nurse's reaction, walked over to her desk, and quietly whispered. "You know, Marge, Joey there has Ephiphedrin-5 running through his bloodstream. I'd say that's a green light, if, of course, that's what's on your mind."

Pretending outrage at what Doc Allen had just suggested, Nurse Stewart could only lecherously smile and then say with a quickly straightening face, "Now, Doctor, wasn't that a breach of the sacred doctor-client relationship?"

"Could be. But remember, I am the doctor for the entire staff of this complex. That means I must be aware of everyone's state of health and mind."

Smiling devilishly and with a quick wink he left for his waiting patient.

Entering the examination room, Doc Allen, pointed the standing Richards over to the large recliner and said, "Make yourself comfortable, Joey."

Obeying the directive, Richards stretched out and allowed his body to sink into the luxurious padding, while Allen gently closed the door and dimmed the room lights to a twilight setting.

"Okay Joey, here's the deal," rumbled the good-natured Dr. Allen.

"First, I suspect Dr. Borov has already given you the general outline of what you might be up against and what we are going to do about it.

"Is that correct?"

"Yes sir."

"Good. Now what I am going to do first is place several deep suggestions in your mind to help protect you and your cover. Once that is over, I am going to turn on and tweak up your natural recall a bit. Then, to fully develop and appreciate that ability, you will have to do some exercises and drills. In some ways, Joey, the brain's a muscle too, and I will show you how to exercise your improved ability to remember.

"For now, however, I just want you to sit back, relax, and close your eyes.

"Good.

"Now, I want you to imagine that your extremities are slowly sinking deeper and deeper into the chair. Imagine yourself sinking right through the chair.

"Falling right through the floor.

"Go ahead, try it, you'll like it."

Richards complied and felt himself relaxing, sinking, and beginning even to almost to drift off, which was real easy given all the blood that was coursing through his stomach trying to digest his lunch. In short, a massive food coma.

Hearing the physician turning in his chair, Richards next felt a comfortable, warm glow across his face and shaved head. Allen had turned on a tightly focused halogen spotlight.

"Joey," he said in a comforting and subdued voice. "Can you see the light through your eyelids?"

"Yes."

"Good. Is the light too bright?"

"No."

"If it is, I can always adjust it.

"Are you comfortable?"

"Yes. The light is just fine."

"All right then. I want you to continue to relax your body and just sort of unconsciously focus on the light. Okay?"

"Sure."

Thirty seconds passed.

"Okay Joey, now I am going to slowly count to ten backwards. As I do, I want you to imagine that you are sinking deeper and deeper into the chair so that by the time that I reach one, you are almost asleep. Okay?"

"Yyyessss," the young man slurred.

"All right, here goes. Ten."

Pause.

"Nine."

Pause.

"Eight."

What Richards was not aware of prior to the countdown, was that the chair in which he was sitting was actually a highly-sensitive cardiac and cephalic recording device. On the computer screen that was embedded in Doc Allen's desktop, the physician was simultaneously observing Richards pulse, heart rate, and several brain wave patterns as he counted.

Given Richards' marvelous physical condition, Allen was not so amazed at how quickly the young man had settled himself out, but given his present level of confidence and well being, Allen was astounded how quickly his brain patterns had fallen in line, and had begun to level out as well.

"Seven."

Pause.

"Six."

Pause.

"Five."

Pause.

"Four."

Pause.

"Three."

Pause.

"Two."

Pause.

"One."

Now Allen paused for a full ten seconds.

"Can you still hear me Joey?"

"Uh-huh."

"Good. Just relax and focus your mind on my voice. We are about to go on an interesting journey."

In the next breath Allen could not help but think as he looked down upon the gently resting figure.

This poor youngster. After I am finished with him he will never again be truly the same. What a pity. Damn those politicians and bureaucrats!

CHAPTER XLIV
Return to Year 3 of Neferkheperure Amenhotep

By the time Piankoff had arrived at the sanctuary of Amen Re, the Mark V-A had already been erected and tested by Cartwright's men and thoroughly inspected by Richards and Tuna himself.

As for Richards, he was looking eager, anxious, and raring-to-go. But there was something new about his assistant that he could not quite place—a sense of purpose, an increased inner strength, a quiet confidence of one no longer an amateur, no longer green.

That must be it, Piankoff thought. *He's no longer a virgin operative anymore.*

Striding over to his partner on his now fully mended ankle, Piankoff greeted him with genuine emotion in their adopted ancient tongue. His reaction at seeing his young lion again even surprised him. Richards also pleased to see his teacher, embracing him.

Both had been thoroughly briefed as to their mission by their respective sides. Both had undergone the necessary hypnotic blocking to prepare them for any potential telepathic assault from either the target or his children. Both were itching to get back.

"Okay, gentlemen," Cartwright bellowed with a smile. "Departure is within the hour. That means that it's time to strip down, gear up, and get your makeup on! Let's get this show on the road!"

So both of the field operatives began their preparations. While Richards would return precisely where he had left off, Piankoff was busily wrapping his now fully healed ankle in what was a remarkably accurate duplication of Ankhmes' original. It was decided that he would miraculously recover on the other side in a calculated move to solidify his place as a true wizard-priest. Thus, his unique crutches would travel back as well.

To the field operatives it seemed only moments from the time of Tuna's good-natured bark to the now familiar mounting of the wooden scaffolding before the energized Mark V-A's levitating drop ring. As they stood at the brink, the two exchanged witticisms in their ancient tongue. Both knew that they were returning after only an absence of approximately one hour's time—just enough for their chanting prayers to the Great God.

When the final launch point was announced, Richards went first—this time in a conscious attempt to prevent the disaster that had previously occurred. Dropping effortlessly through the ticklishly wet sensation of the Soap Bubble's field, Richards landed soft, rolled, and immediately braced himself as best he could under the glaring glow of the field to assist his partner. Dropping his crutches through first, Richards quickly clearing them aside. Three heartbeats later Piankoff arrived with his ankles tightly locked together, landing with bent knees, and rolling in one smoothly performed motion that would have made any Ranger jump master proud. To this performance, Richards, wearing a broad smile, gently helped up his colleague and earned a silent thank you. But before proceeding, they sat there just gathering themselves, allowing their subtle transit disorientation to pass.

With a silent blink, the ring shut down and the pair now squatting together in the dim light and now familiar incense haze of the Great God's sanctuary. Both sincerely hoped that their return had not been somehow observed. Then, taking the traditional Egyptian attitude of prayer before the golden image, kneeling and sitting on their heels with their arms outstretched to either side, they both began a low and sonorous chant-like hymn sung to the notes of a plain song. After several minutes they concluded and left the sanctuary squeezing through the sanctuary's massive doors, again so not to trigger the alarm gongs.

Winding their way through the silent temple and following a path now well understood, and with a relative swiftness that only a healthy man on crutches could achieve, Richards and Piankoff reentered the domestic precincts of Meryptah only to find that their faithful and overworked sedan chair bearers were fast asleep where they had left them only two hours before, relatively speaking.

Entering the household proper, Piankoff on his crutches, passed through its multi-columned entrance. There the pair discovered that the high priest himself was also fast asleep among the pillows of his bedchamber. The household's chief steward and a sleepy Thutmose, no doubt aroused by the thumping of Piankoff's crutches, appeared and asked the pair if they wished to return to the royal annex.

Nodding their assent, he then rushed out to awaken the bearers. During this, the gentle snoring of Meryptah could be heard all the way to the entranceway where they now stood, causing Piankoff to remark, "I do believe we have overstayed our visit."

The three went back outside, mounted their chairs, and to a mixed chorus of yawns, creaking joints, and grunts, they were off back to the still-awaiting river boat. After a non-eventful ferry ride back across the river, the threesome arrived without apparent notice to their respective quarters within the sleeping royal annex.

For Richards, his return had become a deep indescribable pull, a yearning. He missed the star-encrusted night sky, the dazzlingly brilliant sunshine, the entire texture of this ancient environment. Besides, as he began to succumb to a deep and confident sleep, there were always his bath attendants to awaken him.

* * *

Piankoff, now lying comfortably within his darkened bedchamber, suspected that the conclusion of this mission would be his last. It was not that his luck had run out, but he could tell he was losing his edge, his drive, and that the old fire in his belly was just not there. As with any experienced and proven marathon runner, he was becoming more and more aware that he had to hand off the torch. With these thoughts running through his head, the Russian frowned for his young lion was fast coming of age.

What a prodigy that young man is!

He thought while he stared at the silent play of shadows across the ceiling.

What a unique package.

How quickly he pulled himself together!

From what Milson tells me what promise he has as an academic, having completed the last draft of his dissertation literally on the plane ride over.

What a pity that my masters want him dead.

While still weighing and struggling with where his true loyalties lay, the man finally submitted to his nervous exhaustion.

* * *

As the two rose with the sun the following morning, each to his own designs, it was Richards who dutifully arrived at his teacher's quarters inquiring on how his mending leg felt. Piankoff, sitting on the floor with his splinted leg extended, found Richards' expressed concern warming and a subtle reminder not to do something foolish. With his loyal shadow in tow, the guide Thutmose, Richards now casually stood before him with his legs wide and powerful arms crossed as the Russian chewed on a delicious dried date.

"I trust that you slept well, my teacher."

"Yes. Indeed, I did, Mayneken."

"And yourself?"

He thoughtfully added, "Like a rock."

Pause.

"Well then, perhaps we should be off to thank our hosts for their extraordinary hospitality?"

To this direct suggestion, Richards could only raise his right eyebrow in surprise at the Russian's aggressive agenda.

"Would that be wise, my teacher? After all, would not the Master of the Two Lands be far more concerned about the pressing issues of his desired temple's construction than the polite thanks of two subjects? Perhaps a visit to the kindly court physician, Ankhmes, would be more in order."

Listening to Richards' pre-rehearsed lines, said for the benefit of Thutmose's ears, Piankoff just sagely nodded his head.

"Yes, Mayneken, you are right. We should consult with the physician. Please fetch me my walking sticks."

With that direct command, Richards hopped to, an action that was also not missed by Thutmose, who began thinking.

Would that my beloved wife had given me a son only one-third as strong, wise, and attentive as the noble Mayneken. The way he responds to his teacher's every need is truly remarkable. But equally remarkable is Piankhotep's obvious affection for his student.

Their eyes share far more than can be said with mere words. That is clear!

Piankoff, now fully on his feet with his crutches under him, jostled Thutmose to the here and now.

"Well, dear Thutmose, would you please guide us to the physician?"

Bowing slightly deeper at Piankoff's command than usual, this Richards noted, the guide then turned and led the pair off through the warren-like maze that was the royal annex.

Moments later, or so it seemed, Piankoff double-thumped his way into Ankhmes' study where again the physician was found furiously writing before his scribe's desk, the fat fingers of his right hand heavily splattered with black ink.

Looking up in genuine surprise, the court physician said, "My dear Piankhotep! Why do you so insist on moving around so much! Don't you know that you will only slow down, or perhaps even undo, all of my careful work?"

Smiling down on the perpetually sweating head of the overweight court physician, Piankoff could only smile.

Indeed, my fat friend, you did indeed set my ankle just fine. So well, in fact, that my regimental clinician took one look at the x-ray and just shooed me away to the casting room!

"My apologies, most noble Ankhmes, but today my leg feels so good, I was hoping that you might quickly take a look at it. It has been itching quite a lot."

Piankoff slowly lowered himself to the floor before the scribal bench, while extending his bandaged and splinted right leg.

At first annoyed at the disruption to his paperwork, Ankhmes was charmed by Piankoff's emphasis in his use of the term "noble." Sighing, he slowly levered up his mass from his cross-legged position, rose to his full height, staggered slightly, and then gently stepped over and around all the scattered papyrus rolls that littered the floor about him. Reaching where Piankoff now sat, he looked down and remarked.

"These bandages. They are a clever weave, but I did not bind them. Who did?"

Piankoff, blushing, admitted that he had done so.

"Why?" said the now reddening physician.

"So that I could properly bathe." Responded the Russian.

During this slowly heating exchange Thutmose subtly began to hide himself behind Richards, a movement that the young man did not overlook.

So, Ankhmes truly does have a professional and territorial temper? Doesn't like to be second-guessed? Piankoff concluded. *Well, let's just see.*

Now squatting down and looking like a mini-sumo wrestler in a short kilt, the physician gently took the ankle between his two hands and turned it from right to left, examining the tight and neat wrapping. Grunting his satisfaction despite himself, he said, "Itching you say. That is a very good sign. That means that your bones are mending. Now, who rewrapped your ankle?"

"I did." Piankoff quietly stated.

That produced another grunt from the physician.

"Well then, I will unwrap what you have here, examine your ankle, and you can then rewrap it before me."

With considerable care, he began to do just that, but what Ankhmes did not say reveal was his curiosity about how a man with a broken ankle could so cleverly wrap such a painful injury, and so well. He had heard all the tales of this priest's wisdom, that he was a wizard of sorts, but a broken ankle was nonetheless a broken ankle.

Once the ankle was laid bare of its protective bandages and splints, the physician gently lowered it to the floor, knelt down, and sat back on his heels his face blank, focused, and deep in thought.

Oh boy, here it comes. Drum roll please! Richards thought.

For the first time in a long time the court physician, Ankhmes was confused. Still, his analytical and empirical side kicked in.

My dear Ankhmes, we have before us a recently broken ankle, injured in no less than two places that you set only a day and a half ago.

Sigh.

At present, the same ankle is without swelling, is without any sign of bruising or discoloration, and it appears to be in every way normal and healthy.

Why?

Gently placing both of his cool hands on each side of the ankle, the physician, closing his eyes, then with extreme care began to explore the surface topography of the foot. Having not heard any discomfort from his patient, he then ever so gently began to manipulate the foot side to side, and hearing nothing from his patient, even dared to fractionally flex the joint. Opening his eyes, his patient was just sitting there exhibiting no pain whatsoever.

Sitting back again on his heels, he ran through his checklist once more.

No swelling.

No bruising.

Good articulation.

Reasonable movement.

The noble seer Piankhotep's ankle appears to be healed.

But only after a day and a half? That is utter nonsense.

Shaking his head from side to side, the mystified physician could only say to his patient, "Piankhotep, please slowly raise and flex your foot up and down. Good. Good. Now, very carefully, attempt to rotate it in a circle.

"Good. No, remarkable. All right, now just rest your foot down again."

Again silence.

After a few moments and with glazed eyes and a soft awed voice, the physician said, "Noble Piankhotep, I set your ankle that was broken in two places a day and a half ago. Yet today, it appears healthy and normal as if it was never injured. I frankly do not know how this can be. In all of my experience, and that of my ancestors, this has never been before observed."

Looking up into Piankoff's eyes with a steady and strange look in his eye, Ankhmes said, "I am only a physician. I heal the sick when I can. I mend broken bones when I can. I assist in birthing when I can. But Piankhotep, what I see before me now is not the result of my doing. What I see before me could only be a divine healing."

At this point Piankoff decided to throw some fat onto the fire.

"My dear and noble Ankhmes, I disagree. It was you who first set my injured foot. It was you who splinted and wrapped me. It was you who commanded me to drink the raisin wine. Without question, it was your doing."

Now thoroughly confused, the physician shook his head.

"No noble Ankhmes, it is I who wish to thank you for your most excellent care. While your humility is charming, it is also misplaced. How may I thank you?"

Still kneeling and sitting on his heels, the physician quietly asked, "Noble Piankhotep, stand and attempt to walk without your walking sticks. If you can do that, then that is all I require."

With considerable theatrics, Piankoff walked.

Ankhmes gasped in total disbelief.

Thutmose, now pushing himself passed Richards, gaped as well at the medical miracle.

Still kneeling and sitting on his heels, Ankhmes' empirical mind ran now at full bore in an attempt to explain the unexplainable.

"Where were you while Re traveled beneath the earth?"

Caught a bit off-balance by the question, Richards instead spoke for his master.

"We both were praying before the Great God himself."

"Ah," was the physician's only reply. It was also the only answer that his powerfully analytical mind could accept: a miraculous healing.

Now that explains it! It also underscores the power of this priest, or wizard, or seer, or whatever the many rumors say. And as for his assistant, I must watch him as well, for he too will become powerful with time.

Again slowly levering up off the floor, the physician still could only shake his head. Finally, finding his physician's tongue, he said, "Noble Piankhotep, as a precaution, and I do not wish to be disrespectful to the healing of the Great God, for the next few days use at least one of your crutches, until you can again freely walk."

Listening, nodding, and agreeing to this reasonable advice, Piankoff, now only using one crutch, left behind one very flabbergasted court physician, a crutch, two wooden splints, and some bandaging.

Again sitting down behind his scribal desk, Ankhmes crossed his legs and sat back into the soft padding against the wall. He did not take up his pen to continue his editing of the medical corpus. Instead, an intellectual war was being waged in his mind where for the first time the empiricist medical approach of his long dead ancestors was being shaken to its very foundations. Divine intervention had become an option, a shortcut, to nature's own healing way. He had borne witness to it himself!

Thus, the course of Egyptian medical thinking would henceforth be so influenced. Forever lost would be the pristine empiricism that so marked the medical treatises that dated back to the Second Dynasty. From this moment on, the superstitious addition of magical incantations, amulets, and potions would slowly insinuate themselves and eventually outstrip the formerly sound and practical medical advice of their distant ancestors.

And all because of a broken ankle.

Needless to say, the news of Piankoff's recovery rushed through the royal annex in matter of nanoseconds. As such rumors go it was embellished, twisted, and turned around in the most absurd of ways. Piankoff's reputation as a special servant of the Great God was now beyond question. Richards, by his mere association, was similarly held in awe. As for Ankhmes, his reputation as a mender of bones soared. As an inevitable consequence, the target's boundless curiosity eventually would get the better of him.

CHAPTER XLV
Of Dissertations & Publications

It was not often that a dissertation director delivers a copy of his graduate student's approved and signed thesis to the university library's archivist for its microfilming. Nor would it be considered likely that the same dissertation director would then traipse another copy of the dissertation over to the same university press' chief editor. But these two deliveries that Professor John Milson emeritus made were done first with relish, second with pride.

From the library's archivist, he had received a rather strained look that was a mixture of bubbling curiosity and amazement at his presentation of his student's thesis. She was more accustomed to dealing with and intimidating the graduate students themselves. Carefully going over the manuscript and just itching to find flaws in its production and layout, she was then astounded to find that it was—flawless. Such a thing had not happened in the past twenty-two years of her service to the university and its magnificent library. Usually, a thesis such as this went through as many as three or four such grueling reviews. Nonplussed, she began to page through it again.

Surely, she thought, *something must be amiss here. After all, I did edit single-handedly the last edition of* The Chicago Manual of Style.

But to her chagrin, nothing was amiss.

Throughout the entire process, Milson just sat there patiently through the first pass, but through the second, he glared pointedly at the woman. In the end, she finally and grudgingly conceded her imprimatur to the manuscript and off it went to Ann Arbor for its microfilming and archiving.

That godforsaken task accomplished, Milson then hot-footed it over to the university press and his good friend and editor, Dr. Paul Silas. Bounding up the cement steps like a schoolboy instead of a chemotherapy patient desperately fighting for his life, he found himself breathing too hard at the top of the short steps. Pausing for breath, Milson leaned against the railing, while he collected himself in the warm spring sunshine. After a few moments, the old Egyptologist recovered somewhat. Now breathing easier, he entered the building with its familiar ceramic floor of seemingly endless white and black octagon tiles.

Knocking on the milky-glassed doorframe made of old weathered dark oak, Milson heard his friend greet him through the transom. Entering, he took his favorite reading chair on the left. Settling himself with the boxed and photo-ready manuscript on his lap, he took in Silas' impeccably neat office.

As for Silas, he sat behind the desk with his head in his hands, staring at his friend.

John must have lost thirty pounds. Thirty pounds that he could ill afford to lose!

Snapping out of it, he then said, "Well John, what do you have for me?"

The implication being, as with any editor is, will it sell?

"This is it, Paul. It's camera-ready for press, complete with full indices. I checked them myself. In fact, it sent Ms. Palmer over at the library into fits. She went through it twice and found no blemishes."

Raising his eyebrows, Silas replied, "Jesus, John, that's got to be some sort of record! That old bat has been terrorizing graduate students for years. How did she react?"

"She was extremely put out."

"I'll bet. But what's it all about?"

"Well Paul, I believe that this work, and its partner that will follow it, will supplant Alan Gardiner's venerable *Egyptian Grammar*. I know that the institute will adopt it for next fall's classes if it is made available by then."

Milson knew well that every editor needed that initial carrot. But in this case, it was over-kill, for the book and its future twin were indeed the products of genius, but Silas did not know that yet.

"Okay, enough of the hype. Just who is this *Wunderkind*, ah, Joseph Richards, anyway?"

"My prize student."

"Yeah, I kinda' figured that. Where is he anyway? If you say that this work is as potentially hot as you say, we will want to march on this real quick, and to do that we need his signature."

"Well, first of all, he is currently in the field and unavailable. And second, he has granted me power of attorney. I can sign for him."

"Yeah, right. Okay, let's see what it looks like."

Silas carefully opened the boxed manuscript and saw the photo-ready pages. Stopping, he absentmindedly reached into a side drawer and extracted a worn pair of cotton gloves. Now with his gloves on, he removed the manuscript from its box, placed it squarely before him, stared quizzically at the title, and then sat back in thought. The title band was produced in beautiful hieroglyphics and beneath them was its translation in brackets.

The Scribe's Way.

Quite a bold, initial presentation, the editor thought.

Just maybe.

Before he realized it, Silas had paged through the entire work's 176 pages without a pause. Looking up, "You really did royally piss off Ms. Palmer, didn't you?"

"You bet, and it was gratifying, too."

"John, it is a real pleasure to see such clean copy. I can assure you that it will be available for next fall's semester. On that you have my word."

"Paul, I just knew you would say that."

* * *

With the manuscripts safely delivered, Milson now had one more errand to run. After a gentle stroll across the campus, he found himself standing before the main administration building that housed the grand office of Dean Young. Threading his way through its many corridors, Milson stood before the door and paused trying to remember Young's secretary's name. What was it again?

Ah, yes. Andersen. Ms. Andersen.

Now entering with the confidence of knowing one's terrain, Milson found himself stunned to note that the fiery and imperious Ms. Andersen was not occupying the secretary's desk. Instead, he found a stunning doe-eyed co-ed with dark eyes that simply reached out and plucked at his heart. Stumbling over his words, Milson, after a moment of embarrassment, finally got out that he had an appointment with the dean, and oh yes, my name is Professor Milson. For the first time in a long, long time, a glossy sheen of nervous perspiration covered his closely-shaven upper lip. Reaching into his back pocket for his handkerchief, he wiped it dry.

Now John, here is one stunning woman. Such blue-black hair, classic features, and those eyes!

Suddenly finding himself becoming reflective, he thought. *And John, how long has it been that you even thought of yourself, much less another woman, since your dear Alice died? Too long, way too long,* he silently answered.

With those thoughts still fresh before his conscious, a wooden Professor John Milson entered the sacred chambers of the Dean of Humanities. Sitting himself down, the dean rose, pulled over the adjacent chair, sat next to him, and in an infuriated whisper said, "John, you look like hell. What's gotten into you? You should be at home, or better, at the hospital resting. And you know it!"

Milson could just smile, and with a gentle voice said, "You know Paul, if I had not come a-calling, as you have so often said we colonials are want to say, then I would not have seen that absolute angel of a receptionist that you have sitting out there. I can now say that I have something to truly live for. What's her name?"

"John! Shame on you! You horny old goat! I'm shocked.

"But as to your newfound reason to live, I certainly hope that you do, for Ms. Hamady is an Egyptology transfer from the American University in Cairo. In fact, she is now awaiting a reply from your very own graduate department on her admissions application. And if that were not enough, she has been asking all sorts of questions about you as well. It seems that her family is well-connected with the Director of the Cairo National Museum."

Surprised, but also immensely pleased at the news, all that Milson could say was, "Well, I just suppose that it's all in the cologne."

In reply, Young just gave him five seconds of studied silence, which he then broke.

"Now John, what did you really want to talk about besides the erotic allures of Aphrodite?"

"My eventual replacement, Dr. Joseph Richards."

Now leaning back in his chair.

"Ah, the football player, that Dr. Joseph Richards?"

"Precisely."

"What does his *c.v.* look like?"

At those words something just popped within Milson at Young's cavalier remark.

"Paul, I have his power of attorney. I am indeed not here for my health as you have already pointed out. However, what I am here for is to sign his tenured, associate professor's contract with my department. He has already been penciled in to teach a full load during the fall semester and we have the enrollment to more than justify his addition. Now, Paul, as to our previous agreement, where is his paperwork?"

Dr. Paul Young was not used to be being the object of such a blunt and direct command, the exercise of such *auctoritas*, even from a venerable professor emeritus nearly on his last legs. But, calculated as it was, the dean quickly realized that Milson was not to be dickered with, as these colonials are want to say. In short, he found himself squarely placed in a box.

Milson, seeing his flush, sensed the dean's internal turmoil.

"Paul. Please consider the following. First, Richards passed the Annex's quals, did he not? Second, Richards survived his training and Piankoff, did he not? Third, he delivered—big time. Fourth, I delivered his dissertation to our own university press and Paul Silas not only accepted it on the spot, but is pushing it into print so that the department can use it in the fall. Fifth, Richards wrote this dissertation in seven weeks. Seven weeks, man! Sixth, he is currently the best ancient Egyptian philologist in the world. And lastly, you promised."

Pausing to take in a staggered breath, Milson closed his eyes. "Now Paul, do the right thing."

Settling back again into his chair and taking a deep breath, Young privately had to admit, on several counts, that Milson was right and that now was the time to act. Without saying a word he rose and left the office. After about ten minutes, he returned with a manila folder under his arm. Returning to his desk, he sat down and began signing several documents. Looking up he simply said with a sigh, "Now John, if you would be so kind, please sign for Dr. Richards at all the places so indicated."

This process took a good five minutes, for Milson read the contract and all of its particulars. Young, he had to admit to himself, had been more than generous in many of the details. After having signed, initialed, and signed again his student's name, Milson finally sat back and put away his old, tried and true Watermark pen that he had acquired decades ago in old Beirut, while he was a student there at the American University.

"Now, John, only one detail remains—the safe return of your Dr. Richards."

CHAPTER XLVI
The Rape

It began as an innocent enough encounter, one that Piankoff and his handlers had long prepared for, both consciously and unconsciously. Hobbling and getting around on only one crutch, the lean Russian on the one hand was dutifully following his physician's orders, while on the other he was playing out his role as the special servant of the Great God himself. He knew that the rumor mill had gone full circle, for when and wherever he went a hush would fall on any conversation.

Greeted with averted eyes from adults, Piankoff went on the offensive smiling and cheerfully wishing a "Good Day" here, offering a pleasantry there. In reward, he received respectful bows, furtive glances, and even and occasional smile—no doubt of relief. With the many children that scurried throughout the annex hither, thither, and yon, he became known as Piankhotep, the smiling priest with three legs, who told them marvelous stories, who always had time for them and their endless questions, who let them play with his crutch, and even let them touch his magic ankle. Little did the Russian realize, however, that even this well-meaning fun as the smiling priest with three legs would again break the *RUTI*, as his antics would be remembered, retold, embroidered, and eventually provide the core substance for the famous Riddle of the Sphinx.

In many respects the wily Russian sensed that he was more a fisherman trolling for that big strike, all the while he chummed the waters of his wake. Frankly, he was waiting for the well-known curiosity of his target to get the better of him. On the second day following the unofficial announcement of his divine recovery, Piankoff's tactics bore fruit after the mid-day meal.

Fittingly, he was caught unawares, during a quiet moment. Sitting in the cool shade of his bedchamber's porch and half-dozing, half-observing the late afternoon hubbub of the river traffic, Piankoff sensed, rather than heard, the nearby rumble of a powerfully emotional stirring, a presence.

Remaining calm with body relaxed and his eyes closed, he thought in the ancient tongue, *Welcome, oh Mighty One! I have been longing to meet with You again. To share my thoughts with You! Please come, sit in the cool shade, and put Yourself at ease.*

Feeling a gentle stirring in the air, a light scrape of sand from a sandal's sole, and the creak of the adjoining stool as the bulky frame of the target was applied to it, Piankoff slowly opened his eyes. What he immediately beheld were the target's expressive dark eyes and long angular face.

Sensing curiosity and feeling it himself, he mentally asked, *Why have You come to visit me, oh Mighty One?*

With a slight right tilt to his head, the Quimbly first guarded his thoughts before he responded silently in kind, **So this is the man I have sensed so much about. I know his medical situation well from both Meryptah and Ankhmes. In the past he was nothing but a bundle of fear and revulsion at my mere presence. But now, he confidently greets me to converse as if an equal.**

How intriguing. Just who is this man?

With a sigh and disarmingly casual shrug of the shoulders, a gentle reply appeared in Piankoff's mind, **I was most curious about your injury.**

I was curious about your two walking sticks.

I had questioned Ankhmes himself about what he believes to be your miraculous healing.

I had to see this wonder for myself.

And most Noble One, what do you think?

Most interesting, most interesting indeed, that your kind possessed such remarkable regenerative powers, I did not realize.

At this point Piankoff allowed himself to glow an inner smile that he was sure that his guest would sense.

Great One, we do have an expression—mind rules over matter.

This almost chiding statement brought an unconscious chuckle to the visitor's mind and agreement.

Indeed!

And then after a bit of time the Russian restated again his initial question.

Mighty One, again I ask, why have You come to our fair land?

After a mental pause of consideration came a firm and definite answer.

To observe.

To mold.

To encourage.

As you do these wondrous things, Great One, do You intend to judge us as well? Perhaps much the same way that our hearts are weighed against Maat's own feather of truth?

A little taken aback by Piankoff's collective use of the nominative plural "us" juxtaposed with the illusion to an individual's solemn judgment at the entrance to the Egyptian Underworld, the Quimbly granted, ***That is inevitable.***

After another silent pause, Piankoff continued with his probing.

May I ask you another question?

The Quimbly radiated a warm and inquisitive smile.

Ask.

Is it really true that you come from the stars?

This query was again met with silence, but during that time Piankoff clearly sensed a whirlwind of guarded indecision, curiosity, and finally resolve on the part of the target.

Yes.

Where in the sky? Perhaps from the sacred Dog Star, or perhaps even from one of the stars of Orion's Belt?

A mental chuckle again was felt.

Hardly, priest.

My kind hails from far, far away.

In your terms, from a place beyond the stars that you can see in night's sky.

At the Quimbly's frank and unguarded response, Piankoff briefly paused for a mental gasp from which he quickly recovered, but the Russian's reaction was nonetheless not lost on his interlocutor. In fact, the Quimbly was intrigued by the depth of Piankoff's appreciation of the claim and its curiosity became aroused.

But Piankoff persisted.

Great One, then, why are You here from so far, far away? After all, how did You find us? Why do You choose to walk among us? Is the reason really that You intend to assist in the betterment of our kind?

The concatenated string of questions was initially met with silence, but after a bit the Quimbly's answer formed in the Russian's mind.

My discovery of your kind was...accidental.

But yes, to assist, that is as proper a way to express it, but the true measure of any assistance is your kind's ability to grow and assimilate.

I wish only to guide along a path. I am but a shepherd trying to guide an unruly flock of geese.

This response befuddled Piankoff. It wasn't what he expected, but then again, he realized, what really did he expect anyway? Having chewed a bit on the target's reply, he then aggressively asked, *Great One, why?*

More silence, followed by yet another emotional sigh.

Great curiosity.

A desire to gather knowledge.

A desire to seek and perhaps find the first cradle of life.

And, when possible, a deep desire to assist those with promise.

This response stunned Piankoff for the very image of the scout surveyor's dogma, The Survey Institute, what it stood for, and the Quimbly's dedication to it bled through that mental statement, granting that expressed thought a heady texture of commitment that resonated deep within the Russian's psyche, his sense of commitment, his mission.

Several moments passed as the target and Piankoff mutually sipped at that shared nectar.

And so, Great One, are You alone in this quest for this First Source?

The directness of this question about the First Source, the very heart and core of The Survey Institute's ethos and its membership, at first shocked the Quimbly into wondering whether his conversation partner was a latent telepath, or rather he had become sloppy in shielding its own thoughts. While considering this issue Piankoff then bombarded the Quimbly with yet another question.

Great One, do You intend to assist one of our kind over another?

More silence again passed, and then with the forceful impatience of an extremely vexed intellect confronting the incessant buzzing questions of a precocious child.

JUST WHO ARE YOU PRIEST, WHO ASKS OF ME SUCH WEIGHTY QUESTIONS?

Having received this powerful rebuke and curt mental cuff, Piankoff realized that he was now far, far out of his depth. The sheer telepathic resonance and emphasis on the abstraction "Me" was received almost as a physical slap in the face. Quickly recovering, Piankoff nonetheless pressed on.

I am a seer, Great One, nothing more. I too am a creature of curiosity. And You, Great One, meaning no disrespect, are a great curiosity. I am here to observe You and Your children—nothing more, nothing less.

A dull, depthless, and heavily-shielded prolonged silence followed as the Quimbly considered.

A seer . . . Yes, perhaps this one is a latent telepath, but I must see for myself first hand . . .

Still physically relaxed and with an open mind, Piankoff was prepared for now what he and his handlers had feared would happen, and the Quimbly did not disappoint. The mental assault began. At first, it felt like a pleasurable tickling sensation. Next, Piankoff began to rapidly witness portions of his fabricated Egyptian life as it fast-forwarded before his mind's eye. Occasionally, the target seemed to linger here and there over a particularly emotional moment, an intellectual triumph, a tragic loss, the pain of his recent ankle break.

Then the Quimbly went deeper, the sensation now feeling warm as if a heat lamp was being trained on the Russian's bare head. Private, personal, and deeply primal thoughts and memories were rapidly being rifled through as if Piankoff's mind was a mere Rolodex. During this, the Russian noted that the target was comparing and weighing his visceral and physiological reactions to his own, that the target had caught the thread of that observation, and was now tracing it back, and that the Quimbly wanted to know why. Then the target ran into a blank wall, a wall that he could not penetrate. Yet it was a wall that he would penetrate nonetheless, no matter what.

If a casual observer had been watching this conversation, they would have thought that the target and Piankoff were dozing off with their eyes closed, heads slightly tilted toward one another. Only the Russian's steadily growing blush, increased respiration, rapid eye movement, and sheen of perspiration that culminated in a sudden jerking spinal spasm would have indicated that something truly strange was taking place.

Silence. A gentle breeze blew across the pair.

Slowly the Quimbly's languid eyes reopened.

As for Piankoff, he was soaked in sweat, totally drained, confused, nauseous, disoriented, and had a sudden urge to defecate. Opening his now dilated eyes, he found that he could barely lift his hand to cover his face, to shield himself from both the light and a world that seemed to swirl and eddy around him.

What a hangover! Piankoff gasped.

Then he abruptly threw up all over himself and in the process his bowels released as well.

Throughout this entire physiological reaction, including the splatter of spittle and stench of waste, the Quimbly did not move, but just continued to clinically observe. ***These beings are so fragile! Yet this one has a powerfully strong mind. He told the truth.***

He is indeed just an observer, a seer. But many questions, many details, he did not have to give. Even parts of his mind were totally closed to me. I do hope that I have not injured this one's mind, for it is a good one.

If he wishes to continue his observations, well, then, I suppose that I will allow his curiosity no boundaries in repayment for my overzealous curiosity, unintentional violations.

Then with the sad resignation of a child who has just broken a new toy, the Quimbly continued, ***Brave priest. You may continue with your curiosity and observations of Me and My family.***

I find no objection.

As to your question regarding the betterment of your kind, gifts given can only proceed in their own way.

Seeds once sowed must grow and develop on their own.

The true answer to all of your questions is that only time will tell.

With that "said," the Quimbly rose and left the wilted Russian wallowing in his bile and excrement. The entire conversation, which had taken a mere twenty-odd seconds, would remain stored in Piankoff's traumatized mind for the remainder of his life, or until his handlers chose to retrieve and relieve him of its weight.

* * *

While Piankoff was so occupied with the target, Richards that very day had made arrangements through the mediation of Meryptah to observe Queen Nefertiti and her active brood of six daughters and two half-sons. As the two men entered the area of the royal nursery, actually a cluster of several apartments that surrounded and opened to a shared, enclosed courtyard. The tinkling and overlapping sounds of children's giggles, laughs, squeals, and shouts could be clearly heard.

To describe this royal tribe of children is to describe a swarm of bees sometimes teasing, sometimes chasing after one another, sometimes moping and crying, sometimes, but not often, quietly playing. They all knew and loved their mother dearly, wished to please and surprise her at every turn, but they equally enjoyed anticipating her every move, much to her distraction, that of her servants, and the other less gifted children of the royal harem. Today was, as with all days, just such a day.

At the stone threshold of one of the rooms that opened to the bright sunshine of the courtyard, the three youngest girls, the Royals Neferneferuaten II, Neferneferure, and Sotepenre, were all sitting in a circle deeply engrossed in playing with several doll-like figures. Richards judged the three of them as between the ages of four and six years old. Nothing was exceptionally odd about that except that the three dancing dolls were doing so of their own accord, just twirling about in a complex series of gyrations, all the while the three were just chattering away.

Meanwhile, over in an adjoining room, Meryptah and Richards stood quietly to the side and observed the other three royal daughters, all who appeared to be rapidly maturing into adulthood. The eldest, Meketaten, appeared to be already pregnant. Meretaten and Ankhesenpaaten were deeply involved in a competitive board game that Richards recognized as Senet. With one rolling a cube across the board in order to advance their stick marker, the other two sisters would then fight to telekinetically control which side ultimately came to rest. To Richards' way of thinking, these three would wreck havoc at the gaming tables of Las Vegas. As for the boys, Smenkhkare and his younger brother Tutankhamen, they were nowhere to be seen among the constant blur of continuous movement and noise. Noting this, Richards asked, "Meryptah, where are the young princes?"

"Oh, probably out riding their chariots in the desert. In fact, now that you mention it, the two of them have long outgrown the royal nursery. Both are well along toward becoming men. In fact, I suspect that Meketaten is carrying Smenkhkare's child."

As Meryptah confided this interesting tidbit of royal incest with a straight and dignified face, Richards just about choked. *Dr. Milson had not prepared me for this!*

Beginning now to stroll out of the nursery, the pair then practically ran into the queen herself, the beautiful and stunning Nefertiti. At her appearance, Richards tried to become invisible, unobtrusively standing behind the high priest, bowed his head, and studiously stared at the bright and gaily-painted pavement of the nursery with its lotus flowers and papyrus reeds. After the priest had finished with the usual formulaic pleasantries, the queen then rather pointedly inquired as to who Richards was.

"Why, my Queen, Mayneken is the noble assistant of the priest Piankhotep."

Hearing the queen take in a quick, sharp intake of breath, she then said, "Mayneken, you may raise your face to me, despite what you may have been told, I am not a Living God, but a mere noble woman wed to one."

Richards, as commanded, raised his head, beheld the most beautiful and powerful woman of Egypt, and his mind began to unconsciously record as he stood before her.

Five foot even, maybe one hundred pounds. Late twenty's to early thirty's. Exquisite and unblemished golden skin. A remarkably lean frame. Only a slight stomach roll, remarkable, considering her six children. A narrow, almost Arabic-looking face and strong, almost Roman nose. Delicate ears. Graceful neck.

The portrait bust by the artist Thutmose at Berlin's Egyptian Museum and Papyrus Collection by comparison is a poor facsimile, but it does begin to capture the image of the woman, but surely not her essence.

"Why are you here Mayneken?"

"To be the eyes and ears of my teacher, Great One."

"And just what have you seen that your teacher would find of interest?"

"Dolls that move and dance of their own accord. Gaming pieces that roll in the air as if blown by many winds from many directions. Children and young women who are contented, happy, and have only love in their hearts for their mother."

Smiling at his sharp powers of observation and diplomatic tone, the queen replied, "Well said, Mayneken. In comparison to the other children of the royal nursery, what do you think of mine?"

"Your children, Great One, clearly are divinely gifted."

"Divinely gifted!" she said with a quiet snort. "Indeed, they are!" she exclaimed stridently with her hands now on her hips.

"But you try and control them! Only their father can do that. And most of the time, he only encourages them to greater and more creative acts of mischief! Tell that to your teacher!"

Then in a far more tempered and worried voice, she added.

"Tell your teacher that I am also concerned most with Smenkhkare and his younger brother Tutankhaten. They play far, far more dangerous games than their sisters."

With that warning, the queen turned, leaving them to ponder her words. As the pair departed the nursery and began threading their way back toward the royal annex, Meryptah was the first to break the thoughtful silence.

"Mayneken, you have yet to meet the queen's two sons. Take care when you do. What she said about them is unfortunately true. They are absolute demons, who think nothing of invading your mind for its most private thoughts, and when angry, throwing things about without throwing them."

Locking his eyes with the high priest, Richards simply nodded in silent understanding.

This first brood of Wunderkinden is a mixture of fun-loving mischief-makers and holy terrors. Mental control, psychic discipline, call it what you will, are all totally lacking. It's no wonder that the queen approached Piankoff with her list of concerns. Piankoff and I will have much to report this evening!

*　*　*

Lying down comfortably in the cool shade of his bedchamber, Piankoff could only send a silent thanksgiving to the gods for his two maidservants, who had come to his aid.

For despite the fact that they had found me a weak, disgusting, dehydrated, and babbling mess, they had cared for me, washed me, dressed me, and generally cleaned up all the revolting evidence of my encounter with the target.

I must somehow find an appropriate way to thank them.

Pause.

As for my conditioning, he reasoned, *it must have succeeded for I am still alive. For if it hadn't, I harbor few illusions that the target would have quickly snuffed my life's light as would a stiff breeze a candle's flame.*

But the sudden violence of the act, its quickness, I feel inwardly soiled in a way that only a supreme act of revenge could begin to cleanse my injured soul.

What a marvelously curious, yet willful monster! "Time will tell," it had said. *Indeed, and I have seen well enough!*

Sighing deeply just before he fell off into an exhausted slumber, Piankoff's ordered and responsible mind reminded him, Piankoff, dear friend, just last out the day to inform Richards as to what had occurred so that he can report in for you. Then, once rested, you can begin to think of retaliation.

*　*　*

Having returned from the royal nursery, Richards went straight away to his master's quarters, only to find him looking a bit gaunt in the face and dead asleep. What tipped off the American that something was not quite right were the silent and worried expressions on the faces of Piankoff's two handmaidens, who were hovering near his bed frame, not to mention their wringing hands.

Quietly beckoning them outside of the sleeping chamber, he asked, "What is wrong with my master?"

Still wringing their hands and now looking back and forth between each other and Richards, the tears just began to flow down their cheeks to their quivering chins.

"Well?"

Still more hand wringing, tearful silence.

These two are scared out of their wits! Okay, go to alternate plan B.

"My ladies, please follow me."

They dutifully followed Richards back to his quarters, where he sat them down together on stools, offered both cups of water to drink, and then sat down on the floor before them. Having accomplished that, Richards noted that they began to relax, somewhat. The tears had stopped. The quivering and shaking had diminished.

Okay. Now, let's start again.

"My ladies," he said in a quiet and soothing tone.

"How long have you known my master?"

Sobekti, the eldest of the two at fifteen years, spoke first in a halting, clearly fearful whisper.

"We have been noble Piankhotep's servants only for the past several days."

"And has he been a kind visitor?"

"Oh, yes, most noble Mayneken! In fact," looking to her younger partner, Tetisheri for confirmation, "he has been like an older brother to us."

"I see," said Richards. *I just wonder what mine would have said.*

"My ladies, as you know, I am Piankhotep's loyal and faithful assistant. He is my teacher. I, like you, serve him. I, unlike you, treat Piankhotep as if he were my living father. I love and I protect him. Do you understand?"

Richards was answered with two wide pairs of eyes and vigorously nodding heads.

"Now, my ladies, think carefully. What happened to my father?"

Again, looking to each other, it was again the elder Sobekti who spoke, again in a halting and frightened whisper.

"Noble Piankhotep was visited by the Living God. After He left, we were curious but did not wish to disturb your father. But then, then we heard him moan and there was a great stinky smell from where he sat."

"And then what did you do?"

"We, I, peeked around the corner and saw that noble Piankhotep was very ill. So, we, carried him into the bathing chamber, washed his limp body very carefully, perfumed him with his favorite scent, dressed him, and put him to bed, Noble One."

Then Tetisheri blurted out, "But noble Mayneken, your father was mumbling all the time in a very strange tongue, one neither of us as ever heard before!"

Both heads then nodded in confirmation of that fact.

"My ladies, thank you very much for your loving care of my father. Let us now return to him."

With that they made their way back to the deeply snoring Russian. During the way back Richards began to suspect the worst.

It seems that Piankoff got more than he bargained for and really took this one on the chin. Perhaps Doc Allen's concern about the potential for mental invasion was not so far-fetched after all.

Given what I have already seen, individual restraint and discipline in this royal family are totally nonexistent. Given how horrible Piankoff looks, it must have been grueling.

As the sun's angling shadows began to announce the end of yet another day, Richards dismissed the two maidservants and took up his post sitting cross-legged by the side of his teacher's bed frame.

Well, I guess that several hours sleep should do the trick for the Russian and then I will awake him up. Whatever he has to say, coupled with what I saw today in the nursery, what Meryptah told me about the boys, and what Piankoff's servants had related, all have to be reported, even if I have to do it myself. Now is as good a time as any to get out of harm's way and get Piankoff rushed to some expert care. Okay, Joey boy, that's what you'll do. Best to let the suits decide this matter, and soon.

CHAPTER XLVII
The Second Teleconference

Dr. Young, in his self-appointed role as moderator, again began the secured and heavily encrypted satellite videoconference.

"Gentlemen, I wish to thank you for agreeing to participate in this quickly called videoconference. No doubt by now, you have read, reread, and analyzed the startling data that was received eight and a half hours ago after the emergency retrieval of our temporal field agents. May I say on the behalf of the American panel, we all hope for the speedy recovery of Colonel Piankoff, a truly brave and talented man."

At the mention of Piankoff, Karlov grunted and stared back with cold stone eyes.

I should say so, you smug Brit! Right now Piankoff's mind resembles a pot of boiling cabbage! Recovery! Hell's Fire! I just hope that we can get him talking coherently! I would very much hate to lose yet another irreplaceable asset because of this damnable crisis!

"As to the data that we have all recently received, we on our side would like to know what conclusions or recommendations that our Russian colleagues may have."

Momentary silence fell as the three members of the Russian panel briefly looked to one another. Then Vasily Ostrogorsky cleared his throat in preamble.

"Dr. Young, gentlemen, as much as we were initially persuaded by the evolutionary argument of Dr. Philopedes, we now find ourselves irrevocably drawn back to our original position, that being, that the target must be eliminated. Additionally, we recommend that all of the target's children are removed as well. That is our position."

A shocked silence followed.

Then Young nodded to Philopedes indicating that he should address his Russian colleagues.

"Gentlemen, as much as this may be a surprise to you, we are in full and total agreement."

That statement earned three grim nods of approval from the Russian panel. Philopedes then continued.

"The question now is how might we proceed without damaging the present time line, too severely?"

To this open question, Milson, now sporting a truly cadaverous look, decided to speak.

"Gentlemen, allow me to introduce myself, my name is John Milson. I am an historian and Egyptologist. I believe that we can accomplish our goals and not damage the present historical timeline if we carefully take full consideration of the historical record and use it to our best advantage. As I see it, we must move forward in several careful stages.

"To begin, we will first leverage as our ally a convenient circumstance of the time period in question, the outbreak of a regional pestilence that occurred in the sixteenth year of Akhenaten's reign. If successful, and I see absolutely no reason why we wouldn't be, we have an opportunity to eliminate most if not all of the target's progeny. Then, in a subsequent second deployment, we will remove the target vector himself in the summer of his seventeenth year per the present time line.

"Finally, a third deployment will be necessary to ensure that the breeding females do not pass on their extraordinary inheritance. To accomplish this, I foresee our field operatives acting more as advisers, yielding a greater role to be played out by those conservative elements injured and suppressed during the course of the Amarna Revolution. Needless to say, their successful counter-reaction will naturally led to the return of the royal court to Thebes. Beyond that, gentlemen, we will just have to sit back and wait."

Heads bobbed in agreement and understanding from both panels. Then the Russian Karlov mused, *This gaunt Egyptologist Milson I like. He is a man of thoughtful, measured action. Richards is, no was, his student. It shows. Oh, how I have repeatedly underestimated these Americans throughout my life!*

And now I understand better why old Gregori Ivanovich Suvurov had made that papyrologist Latysev a member of his Hourglass Seminar. He and Milson are thinkers much akin to my best field operatives, only craftier and far more dangerous in their subtly.

And then unbidden, the memory of his Sasel came to mind, which caused a noticeable thickening in his throat.

CHAPTER XLVIII
Hippocratic Guilt

"Joseph, I have several bits of good news," said Milson.

"First, if you can make it back in time, God willing, you will walk across the stage and receive your hood during the mid-June commencement.

"Second," he beamed, waving a filled to brimming manila folder in his face, "I have here your signed, sealed, and now delivered contract. You are now a member of the Near Eastern Institute's faculty with the rank of tenured associate professor."

He slapped the manila folder on the Formica lunch table.

"Third," now pointing at another sealed envelope, he continued with pride, "here's your contract from the university press. You are about to become a published scholar."

Bang it went down next to the personnel jacket.

"But fourth," he added somberly, settling himself in a chair opposite Richards.

"I have just finished my last treatment of chemotherapy. The prognosis is very encouraging."

Richards stared in shock at the gleefully seated figure with the haggard face and gauntly filled frame.

"Meaning?"

"Meaning? Meaning, my boy, a celebration! You for all your glorious deeds, and me, for successfully beating the Big C!"

Gulping down a flood of emotions for the elder scholar, all that Richards could say was, "Ya' wanna' beer?"

Slapping again the table top, this time with the palm of his right hand for emphasis.

"You betcha! And come to think of it, I'm quite parched. Let's make it several!"

Richards, never a slow one to respond to the clarion call of party, rose, and fetched two, icy cold aluminum cans from the cafeteria's private stock. Slamming closed the stainless steel cooler door with his hip and plopping a can down before the professor, he returned to his chair. Locking eye to eye, each then ritualistically popped their tops together, raised their cans, and took deep pulls.

Taking a breath, Milson thundered. "Joseph, it's been two years since my last beer. And that tasted just fabulous."

Smiling, Richards sheepishly crushed his already emptied can in his hand.

"You already finished yours!" Milson said with bulging eyes and an accusing finger. "Well then, I shan't be known in these parts to be one to drink alone. Would you be so good and get me another while you're up?"

Still smiling Richards answered, "Sure, anything for you, Doc."

Rising to make another beer run, Richards was back in a proverbial flash.

"Now, Professor Milson, I have a couple of questions . . ."

Finishing his first can and politely burping into the end of his fist, Milson broke in.

"Now, Dr. Richards, burp, if you are going to pull any of that professor crap on me again, and especially during my first beer drunk in what now seems like decades, I'll have you know . . ."

Richards, lifting his beer can, interrupted.

"All right Doc, truce."

With that the pair proceeded to drown themselves, all the while discussing shop, the coming fall semester and what to expect, what Richards had experienced and encountered, figuratively, if not literally, in short, a million things. By the time that the table top had begun to take on the look of a highly refined aluminum deposit, both were now sitting side by side, discussing in the most earnest of terms, several historical issues, and one biological one—pestilence.

*   *   *

"Well now, Dr. Joey, how are you feeling today?"

"With my fingers, Doc."

Grinning with relief through his sterilized surgeon's facemask, Doc Allen snapped.

"All right, smart ass. I'll ask you again. How are you feeling?"

"Fine, Doc. Normal. No temperature that I am aware of yet. Surely no aches and pains."

"Hmmm, good. Okay. Now get dressed. And do me a favor for the next fourteen to twenty-one biological days, do not, repeat, do not breathe, spit, cough, or sneeze on anyone unless you intend to do them serious harm!

"You got that amigo?"

"Roger, Doc."

* * *

"Well, Dr. Allen, how is our prize disease vector doing today?"

"Well, Dr. Borov, if you are referring to Dr. Joey Richards, I would say that he is the luckiest S.O.B. that I have ever met."

"How so?"

"He's young, fit, has the constitution of a battleship, and believe it or not, those Russian-engineered antibodies are keeping him flu free, safe, and sound. And there is no telling how long they'll last either, perhaps indefinitely, which means that Richards could potentially be cold free for the rest of his life."

Several moments of silence. Then Borov broke it and got down to the heart of the matter.

"Doctor. What do you really think his chances are of starting an Asian flu epidemic?"

"Within such a virgin population? Very good, I would suspect. Too damn good."

The two men just shook their heads. Another silence. Again broken by Borov.

"Dr. Allen. I know that you have taken quite a shine to young Richards, and for that matter, so have I. I just wanted you to know that I am not just some sort of cold-hearted monster who is sending a boy out to do a man's job. The fact is this entire situation is eating at me in ways that you just can't imagine."

Allen, for his part looking down at his feet, slowly nodded at the words.

"Ya' know, Dr. Borov, and what I am about to say is nothing personal, but when all of this watershed event nonsense is over, I intend to retire and entirely wash my hands of Horizon Pass. To date, I have seriously messed with that fine young man's mind, inhumanly expanded his recall, and implanted various mental blockades against psychic violation whose long-term effects are totally unknown. Doing so to Colonel Piankoff was one thing, he's a professional and knows what is expected of him. Joey is another matter. Now I am tampering with Joey's physical well being, even if it might be for the better. That goes against everything that I know about 'doing no harm.'"

"But what really eats at me Doc are all the people that I will indirectly harm. I do not relish turning a healthy human being into a biological weapon. Then there is the dicey issue of providing young Joey with that bag of time-release viral crystals that our Russian colleagues cooked up. That sir, as a physician, I am having one hell of a time squaring in my mind."

"I fully understand, Dr. Allen." Borov said, followed with a deep sigh and sagging shoulders.

"Whatever you choose to do Dr. Allen, I will back in full. On that you have my word. But given the rather odd circumstances, well . . . you will be sorely missed.

"As for myself, here I am, fully eighty-four years old, and once only a theoretical engineer. Now I am responsible not only for Horizon Pass and all of its personnel, but I also have a stake in the Philology Annex as well. I too, am frankly tired."

Then looking up at the big and ruddy physician from Oklahoma, Borov asked.

"Where do you plan to retire to Doc?"

"Somewhere up in Colorado where I can get safely lost. Do some fishing, and maybe even do some local doctoring."

"Now that sounds like a plan. I only wish that I had one as promising."

"Well, Dr. Borov, there's no time like the present to start your own."

CHAPTER XLIX

Year 16 of Akhenaten

Once again Richards experienced the curiously sensuous feel of the Soap Bubble as he traversed through to another time. Having landed uninjured, although again a bit woozy, he waited for the feeling to pass while poised like a cat on all fours. He quickly surveyed the darkened sanctuary of the Great God for the presence of another. There was none. Quietly, he moved off from his place of landing to the southern wall, pressing himself up against it, willing himself to blend into it, consciously trying to calm his breathing, checking for and pressing against his chest the small cloth pouch that hung from around his neck. But something was just not right. Looking slowly around in the gloom the light slowly dawned on Richards' conscious.

My God! There's no incense burning. Where are all the lighted oil lamps? The sanctuary—it's empty! Stripped down to its bare walls. And, and where is the golden image of Amen Re? It's all gone!

With this revelation, it took several minutes before Richards would attempt to slip through the massive cedar doors of the sanctuary. As disoriented as he already was, Richards' second thought as he leaned his sweating back against the cool stone was a feeling of total nakedness and isolation, for this was his first drop without his Russian colleague.

Indeed the target had done quite a job to Piankoff's conscious mind, scrambling up his processes the way he had. He was now only able to speak Egyptian fluently and coherently, while his Russian mother tongue came out only in disjointed and broken phrases. As for the Russian's confidence and field craft, well, his superiors were correct in keeping him safely at home, hopeful that he would eventually mend, somehow, somewhen.

What had been done to Piankoff's unconscious mind had told his superiors volumes. How the target had chosen to quickly rifle through this or had decided to minutely investigate that. What had emerged was a truly different perspective on the target, one that was extremely curious, yet curiously impatient, and intolerant. One researcher compared it to a child-savant lacking a measurable attention span. Another to a willfully powerful intellect that was pitting a frog during a biological exercise. Regardless, all agreed that while both characterizations were incomplete and immature, both had framed well the general dimensions of the target's psychological, god-like, and absolutist makeup.

As Richards inched himself ever closer to the great doors, he nonetheless silently prayed that the ropes of the alarm gongs had not been replaced over the intervening thirteen years of his absence.

Now at the central break in the doors, Richards, just as he had in the past, ever so slowly began to ease them apart. As he did so beads of sweat broke out on his smooth head and back. With the doors a mere six inches wide, Richards stopped and thrust his powerful thigh through, blocking and halting the process. Then pausing before squeezing the rest of his body through the narrow slot, he inhaled deeply and successfully did so. Now gripping the two inside edges, he again eased them back into their original positions. Although he was not aware of it, he had only exhaled once the doors had been closed.

Now working his way silently left and using the columns' shadows to his advantage, he found the now familiar, but oddly dusty, black granite statue of Sekhmet and its nearby exit. The cool air of that early morning with its starry sky overhead greeted him like long lost friends. Finally feeling as if his feet were indeed grounded, Richards decided to do some fast and unobtrusive catching up on the local construction of the intervening thirteen years.

He began by first working himself east along the outer wall of the sanctuary itself. His goal was the Eastern Gate of the Great God's temple complex and, once through it, to investigate the Aten temple that should be situated beyond it. Since he was dressed as a priest, he felt relatively safe in doing so.

Richards did not have to go far to see that the brightly painted upper facade of the Aten Sun Temple loomed high above the Eastern Gate. Slipping past and noting the snoring *wab*-priest who so jealously guarded the gate that Richards had just violated, the young scholar's mind briefly wondered whether this was the ancestor of a certain Djehutyhotep, that infamous Chief Doorkeeper of the Karnak Temple, who had organized its plunder in the Twentieth Dynasty. But soon that thought was erased as Richards found himself standing before the Aten Temple itself and remembering the published words of one of temple's twentieth century excavators, "A simple but vast rectangle, about 130 by 200 (?) meters, oriented toward the east."

Known in the vernacular by the name of *Gempaaten*, "The Sun Disk is Found," Richards marveled at the gently sloped, stark, and smooth simplicity of its four-story high limestone outer walls and painted cornices. Its entrance portal, he knew, stood directly opposite from where he now was on the structure's eastern side, facing the sunrise.

Satisfied that he had now located the new Aten temple, Richards retraced his steps and reentered the sacred precincts of the Great God in the hope of locating Meryptah's household, and perhaps even the venerable high priest as well.

Once again through the Eastern Gate and past its sleeping guardian, Richards found himself striding with more authority and confidence, feeling strangely more in tune with this era than ever before. Rounding the last series of whitewashed beehive-shaped granaries that simply glowed in the bright moonlight, he arrived at the low wall that encircled the grounds of the high priest's abode. Wondering what to precisely do next, Richards noticed a stooped figure with an oil lamp slowly moving among the pillars of the colonnaded entrance. With the impetuous confidence of youth and familiarity, he boldly entered the gate of the estate, crossed its grounds, and ascended the steps of the entrance way, only stopping after reaching its top. There he waited.

From the relative darkness of the colonnade, the old man had put out his oil lamp once he had noticed the briskly striding approach of the stranger. Now half-standing behind the shadow of the penultimate pillar, he watched and waited, mildly surprised and thoroughly disgusted at the slight tremor in his left hand that held the lamp, carelessly splashing away some of its precious, scented oil. The stranger stopped at the top of the stairs, waiting as if for an invitation to step forward.

Richards, as he crossed the estate's grounds noticed that the old man had extinguished his lamp and had remained as still as a statue among the colonnades' pillars.

Clearly he had to have seen me coming.

But why is he so shy, or is it fear? But fear of what?

Then, daring to speak to the darkness, Richards, standing in the open and stock still, whispered.

"Have no fear, venerable one. You have nothing to fear from me, for I am certainly not a robber in the night, just a weary traveler. Could you tell me if this is still the household of the noble Meryptah, the first servant of the Great God?"

In response to Richards' query, he heard a distinct gasp at the mention of Meryptah's name. Slowly shuffling forward, the old man approached. Bent over and withered, the smoothly shaved head of a priest emerged from the colonnade's gloom and he too whispered.

"Are my ancient ears and eyes deceiving me, or have I just heard the respectful voice that I remember from my youth, from before the dark times? Mayneken, is that truly you?"

Standing within arm's reach, Richards began to piece together the figure before him, trying to understand, trying to extrapolate what only thirteen years of aging could have done to a once virile and confident high priest the likes of Meryptah.

Forgetting himself and with tears streaming down his cheeks, Richards fell to one knee and exposed the back of his neck before the old priest and choked out.

"Indeed, noble Meryptah, it is I, Mayneken. You may do with me as you wish."

With a dry and raspy chuckle of positive recognition, Richards next felt the feathery soft touch of a gentle pat on the back of his head.

"You may rise, most noble Mayneken. This old man is not about to again knock you senseless. Lend me your strong arm and help me back to my quarters."

Moving deftly to the old priest's right side, Richards easily took on his weight, and the pair wordlessly reentered the shadows of the colonnade, continued on, and then made a left turn into the kitchen. There the glow of a dying cooking fire greeted them. Indicating silently with his right stump of an arm that he wished to sit down on the padded *mastaba* against the wall, Richards did so, and then began looking around for some more dried donkey briquettes for the fire. Finding some, he then bent down over the coals and blew on them until the fire was again raging. Standing and turning around, he found that Meryptah had relighted his lamp and two others. Patting the cushion next to him, Richards walked over and sat down all the while under the intense gaze of his host.

"Meryptah, Piankhotep and I have been away, far away beyond the land of the contrary flowing river. A moment ago, you mentioned something about the coming of the dark times. What in the name of all that is sacred has happened to you and your household?"

Now while he was staring off into space at the vastness of the question asked, Richards noticed the milky-colored evidence of a partial cataract in Meryptah's right eye. Finally rousing himself as if his decision to speak was of considerable physical effort, the priest began.

"My son, clearly you and your teacher Piankhotep have indeed been abroad for a long time. In fact, so much has occurred that I do not rightly know where to begin. But help my old mind, Mayneken, when was the last time we spoke, so that I will not dither on about that which you already know."

Thinking and unconsciously stroking his chin, Richards finally said, "Noble Meryptah, it must have been during the fourth regnal year of the Living Horus Neferkheperure Amenhotep. As I recall, we were your dinner guests, and at that dinner the Great Horus had just told you of his desire to build a new temple, and how that news had greatly upset you."

Silence, a furrowed brow deep in thought, and then.

"Indeed do I remember that evening. And indeed that news did upset me. But now let me answer your question and tell you of these dark times that have fallen like a heavy shadow upon our beloved land."

Sitting back against the now flaking whitewash of the kitchen's mud brick wall, the old priest now took on the relaxed poise of a storyteller, a storyteller squarely on death row who has suddenly been granted an opportunity to bare his entire soul to the world, heedless of self, candid, and without care.

"My noble Mayneken, as with so many things in this world, it all began so innocently."

The old priest said with the expressive sweeping wave of his opened left hand.

"At first, the news of the building of the *Gempaaten* was cause for much celebration. During that inundation, the people were told that they would be cared for, fed, and even entertained if they assisted in its construction, built by the way, on once-cultivated and fertile fields cruelly confiscated from the Great God specifically for this most sacrilegious purpose. Then, as a further lure to the masses, the Living Horus in all of his wisdom caused a vast temple foundation sacrifice of bread, oxen, and beer to occur in the name of his unspeakable deity. So vast was the sacrifice that fully two thirds of the city was reduced to bloated drunkenness. The source of this largess of course came from the stores of the Great God, but never was that ever mentioned. In fact, knowledge of it was flatly prohibited. So in one stroke all of our two-year reserves, should there be a low Nile, were squandered in one voluptuous orgy of food and drink. And throughout it all, Maat was ignored.

"Then, during the time after the laying of that temple's foundation, the Living Horus, with his divine wisdom granted from that unspeakable god-head of his, chose to change the royal artistic canon in such a way as to authentically depict his physical form. In one stroke, gone were the traditional ways of proportion, banished were the traditional themes. To compound this mistaken policy, the Living Horus then decreed that all should be so depicted, that all should enjoy the new royal sense of artistic freedom, that all should be made to physically appear as did the Living Horus himself. Such blasphemy! Such falsehood! So throughout this new structure built to the unmentionable one is paraded the Living Horus' grotesque depiction of physical reality. Nowhere within will you find one sacred image worthy of the name. And throughout it all, Maat was ignored."

As tears began to form in the corners of the old man's eyes, he continued.

"Then, as I best recollect, a year's time passed. Yes, I remember it now, for the Living Horus decided again, in his infinite wisdom, granted by that despicable one, that the sacred name of the Great

God himself was anathema! Can you believe it! But that was not all. The blessed Osiris too was to be ignored, the entire Ennead was cast down! Now, the unspeakable one has to be recognized as supreme above all others. To emphasize this fact, this departure from our most sacred traditions, the Living Horus then turned his back upon his very ancestors and changed his name to one that praised, praised mind you, the unspeakable one. In the process and despite my many arguments that he should not, he did it anyway, and did so maliciously. And throughout it all, Maat was again ignored."

Once watery eyes now became small flowing rivulets of pain and anguish.

"And if that were not sufficient, the Living Horus, although to speak of him as such today is considered heresy suitable for punishment by the cane, announced that his god was not satisfied with *Gempaaten*. That a new structure, no, a series of structures devoted solely to the unmentionable one were required and that they were to be sited far to the north on a desolate sandbar surrounded by mountains.

"On the basis of this divinely inspired command, the Living Horus visited this dead place, surveyed it, and then consecrated it as the new capital of our land. And forthwith the new city's clearing and construction began. After about one year, my eyes witnessed the entire evacuation of the royal court and administration to that leprous and godless place. Almost overnight, or so it now seems, sacred Thebes had been reduced to a backwater village, its most sacred godhead forgotten. Throughout it all, Maat was repeatedly ignored."

A steady stream of tears now coursed down his two weathered cheeks, dripped off of his stubbled chin, and stained the lap of his worn and threadbare kilt.

"With the Great God's name made filth, his blessed name ruthlessly hacked out of any monuments and all inscriptions, our granaries ransacked, now even our sacred temples were ordered closed. Our once multitudinous and bountiful estates now send their hard-earned produce to feed that blasphemous northern city. Only as a royal kindness to the once fond memory of our childhood do I still live here. That I receive a portion of my allotment too is a kindness of the Living Horus. I say only portion, for the overseer of the stores takes a part of my allotment to defray the very burdensome transportation fee of my allotment, transportation from the very grain magazines that are located just beyond my own household's gate! And throughout it all, Maat has been defiled."

The tears had now stopped, for now there was steel in the old man's eyes.

"Then, finally, the Living Horus turned his back on our sacred city totally. He ordered that *Gempaaten* be abandoned and remain unfinished. Its laborers were coldly turned away without their rations of bread, garlic, onions, and beer. Grumbling mouths, spurred on by their grumbling stomachs, were met with harshness by the king's own Medjay troops, for he did not even trust the Theban administration and its own constabulary. And right he shouldn't have, for they were incensed as well. Mayneken, Thebes today is as a broken reed. It is a place of no god and no work. The message has been made manifest. Move to that new northern city and abandon the old of the Great God. And throughout it all, Maat has been treated as filth."

A pause, a deep sigh, and then he said.

"Two last things. The first is a total abomination. I do not remember if you ever met the Living Horus' second daughter, Meketaten, by his queen Nefertiti. She was a beautiful and marvelously mischievous girl, bright of mind with flashing, tempting eyes. She has now gone West and is among the Land of Dead having attempted to give birth to the Living Horus' own seed. He has adulterated Maat."

To this last, Richards then immediately remembered back to the last time that he had seen the young Meketaten in the royal nursery. Then, Meryptah had assumed that Smenkhkare had been her sexual partner, but he was not, it was her own father!

"My second thing, dear and patient Mayneken, despite my now humble station, a god's first servant without a god, a master of a household with no servants, I have now recently learned that the fair and noble Queen Nefertiti has become mysteriously absent from the royal court. Frankly, Mayneken, I fear the worst for her. I fear for her *ka*'s damnation into the abyss, far, far beyond the care of the loving and benevolent Osiris. As close as we once were, I know that she and the Living Horus argued hotly. Even I had argued in the end too hotly with him, the result of which is my present physical state.

"Look closely at me Mayneken. Look hard at this wretched and beaten form. For a time I could not move. My limbs would not obey my commands. I had to be cared for as if I was again an infant, unable to feed myself, unable to wash myself, unable to properly eliminate. It was degrading, humiliating. Mayneken, the Living Horus had reached into my mind with such anger, causing such pain, that I fell to the ground like a wounded sparrow. This is what I fear has befallen my beloved Queen Nefertiti. So much for any final recognition of Maat, for she has been forgotten."

Now silent, and with the lightening of the eastern sky announcing the near arrival of another day, all the old priest now could do was sigh and shake his bristled, unshaven head. During those silent moments, Richards looked around the kitchen, found what he was looking for, gathered the materials together, and began to carefully shave the old man's head and face. It was a small thing, but a thing that bestowed a dignity lost. While Richards pampered the aging man, a plan began to form in his devious mind, a plan that he knew Piankoff would have approved of.

$$* \quad * \quad *$$

Having finished with the old priest's morning toilet, having served him breakfast from what was meagerly available, it was time to leave. That emotion-filled moment would become a heavy, heartfelt burden that Richards knew he would never forget. Standing together again at the threshold of his faded and ill-kept colonnade, the aged Meryptah griped Richards' right forearm, drew him close, and whispered an emotional benediction.

"My dear and noble Mayneken. Today you have answered my prayers for the ultimate redemption of Egypt from these dark times. You have patiently listened to an old man whose time has passed. You have cared for me as if you were my own son. You have fed me. You have overflowed my heart with hope and a private sense of joy. I am now content to face the fair judgment of Osiris, Thoth and his scale, and the righteous feather of Maat. Worry not for me my son. Rather, assist Maat to help Egypt from he who is an abomination, from he who is as filth upon our sacred land."

These quiet words were delivered with an inner strength that Richards did not know Meryptah possessed. Struck by them, by their import, and their relevance, their heady context, he could only bow his head in respect, turn, and attempt to walk away. But, just as suddenly, the old priest reached out and took Richards' right hand, palming within it a small leather pouch with a neck lanyard, again whispering.

"Take this small prayer that your journeys will always be comfortable ones."

* * *

Before Richards began his journey north to the new northern capital of Akhetaten, Aten's Horizon, he thought that he would first make a brief visit to a certain regional overseer of stores. Purposefully passing by the magazine in question and beyond the old priest's sight, Richards then doubled backed to make sure that he had gone back inside. Finding that the good Meryptah had, he then turned and made for the overseer's awning covered office.

Sitting down alone on his portable scissors campstool before a small and similarly portable writing table, the Chief Overseer of Grains, Paser, was struggling with his figures. Although it was still quite early in the day and cool, the overseer was already in a full sweat out of sheer worry. In one day's time the Vizier of Upper Egypt would be present to audit his books, check the granary levels, and Paser knew that his accounts would not match, and that he would not long last under the vizier's withering, hawk-like eye.

He considered his options and realized that he could squeeze past a serious caning if he I withheld a larger portion from that old priest Meryptah's royal allotment. After all, he rationalized, the old one wouldn't miss it, and if he did, what could he do about it?

While this windfall solution began to form in his thievish and conniving mind, a powerful-looking stranger, a priest of all things, appeared before him, just standing there, demanding with his mere silence and crossed arms the overseer's attention. Looking up into the priest's calm face with a deadly glare, Paser right there and then half considered immediately calling out to his Medjay guards to arrest this man.

In truth, he should have, for in the next moment the priest had deftly stepped around his table and with one swift and silent movement crushed Paser's larynx with a slicing blow with the side of his hand. Eyes bulging, unable to scream in pain, and face already turning red, the overseer, gripping his non-functioning throat, fell backwards off of his stool onto the ground.

Looking up, he saw the smiling face of the priest, who now bending over his prone form informed him.

"You miserable wretch of a man. No longer will you steal from Meryptah, the High Priest of the Great God Amen Re. May your miserable *ka* be eaten whole by the monster of chaos Amit at Osiris' judgment, for the rest of the gods have disowned you."

As the man continued to writhe in silent agony and struggled for a breath that would not come, Richards walked away. With his face turning a deep dark blue, Paser simply and quietly passed out. Meanwhile, looking around and finding no witness to his deed, Richards continued to calmly stride off toward the river in search of a boat heading north. Along the way, Richards was quite sure that both Piankoff and that staff sergeant at Fort Benning would have approved whole-heartedly of his actions.

With the modest bag of gold trinkets and jewelry, the parting practical gift from Meryptah, now hung around his neck along with the bag of engineered crystals. Richards knew that he could be underway that morning. Instead, next morning would have to do, for he wished to check in and inform Horizon Pass of all of his plans that could well take several days, if not a week's time.

So, the young, newly hooded and green associate professor of Egyptology began casually strolling through the streets and alleyways of his ancient subject. He took his own sweet time, noting this, recording that, and making it a point to visit the *Gempaaten* temple to see whether or not that Canadian archaeologist and his learned reconstruction team were really that accurate.

Chapter L
AD 2003. Chicago

He had always hated the sterile chemical stench of a hospital. He had always hated visiting those who were its unfortunate guests. Now, unfortunately, Milson was one of those unfortunates, and to top it off, he could swear that he was still hung over from that marvelous time back at Horizon Pass with young Richards.

Just how many cans of Coors did I polish off? The Silver Bullet, you betcha'! That is precisely how my head is feeling!

Just then, a hacking cough convulsed him, the bed, the IV tree to which he was attached, and several assorted monitoring leads and devices.

Damn doctors and nurses! Why don't they just let me die in peace with some dignity, instead of making me a walking and talking pincushion?

Having recovered from yet another bronchial spasm, the struggling Egyptologist took a deep breath and let it slowly out to calm himself.

Now John, just relax one moment. How could you have known that the recycled air on the commercial flight back from New Mexico was nothing more than an overly ripe petri dish of nutrients, chock-full of childhood sneezes and coughs! And to top it off, you were already weakened from the chemo. And to top it off that beer blast certainly didn't help either!

Then the Egyptologist generously concluded.

John. You're a klutz! No! A bloody idiot!

And you're certainly not a kid anymore, either.

Hearing a knock at the door of his private room, Milson brusquely acknowledged it. It turned out to be none other than Dean Young with a smile on his face and suspiciously familiar-looking cardboard mailing tube under his arm.

"Well John, you look like bloody hell! From what I hear, you had yourself a merry old time out west with our young Dr. Richards. So, were we celebrating just a wee bit too much? Just how many beers did you drink before Dr. Allen had to announce that you had reached your toxic limit?"

Trying very hard to hide under the edge of his sheets, Milson replied, "Well, surely and clearly not enough, for I am lying here half-naked in this expensive private hospital room. About the only thing that's a plus are several of the candy-stripers that cruise around here."

Looking down at the old scholar in his best fatherly poise, Young then announced, "Really John, I didn't traipse over here just to hear that your detox recovery was so successful that you're now a rabbit in heat. The reason that I did come over was because I have here the latest from Richards from you know where, or should I say, when."

At this good news, Milson practically levitated off the bed and forgetting his brutal headache, reached over, and snatched the cardboard tube right from out of Young's surprised grasp.

"My, old boy, you really have made a rapid recovery haven't you! Well, go ahead then, and read it yourself."

Now sitting up in his bed, Milson ever so gently extracted the fresh papyrus roll from the tube, noting that it was again weighted with something within. Then with exquisite care he untied the delicate cobalt blue yarn that bound it. Having accomplished that he smiled up at Young and said. "Well, just let's see what's inside!"

And while he unrolled the scroll, out fell its throw weight, this time a beautiful faience scarab about the size of Milson's thumb.

"Well, well. It looks like our museum's collection has just become ever so much richer."

Turning over the scarab to view its flat bottom, Milson could only smile.

"Well Paul, our Dr. Richards has delivered us another rather rare monument that announces the birth of one Tutankhaten no less, of the God's Body, Neferkheperure Amenhotep!"

With a grin on his face, Milson then said.

"So, Richards has delivered his second proof that Tutankhaten's father really was Akhenaten."

Young then added what to him seemed to be obvious. "But John, why are you so surprised? We both read the results of the

Anatol Project and the Norsk Report that our Russian colleagues gave us."

"Yes, I suppose you're right, but then again both of those documents are classified and these two artifacts are not."

Then looking back at the scarab's inscription. "But notice, the mother is again not at all mentioned. Hmmm, that could mean that Tutankhaten was the son of some minor figure of the royal harem. But if that were the case, then what in the devil is the parentage of Smenkhkare?"

After musing for a good fifteen seconds, Milson was wrestled back to reality by a loud clearing of the throat. Looking up he saw Young with his arms impatiently folded across his chest.

"Wonderful news John, now what does our young Dr. Richards have to say?"

Suddenly bug-eyed, Milson had totally forgotten about the papyrus roll that was resting in his lap. Taking it up, he quickly read and then more slowly reread. Having finished it and now with a glazed expression on his face, he said. "Paul, Richards will succeed in this phase of the mission. He will succeed on the basis of his innate sense of religious orthodoxy and strong family background based on a respect for authority, not to mention the inherent structure that it imprinted upon his psyche. But what he now is about to undertake is a profoundly destructive, terrorist act.

"Nonetheless, Richards is not a destroyer nor a terrorist, but a latent visionary, a creative mind and a builder. I just hope to God that he returns and doesn't go native on us! That's totally possible especially if he becomes guilt-ridden. And knowing Joseph, he'll sure as hell attempt to restore all that he is about to destroy."

CHAPTER LI
AD 2003. Moscow

"My dear colleagues," Ostrogorsky began, "before you is a copy of the transcript that Horizon Pass yesterday received from their field operative. Please read it now."

And with that, both Fedorov and Drazinzka bowed their heads before their copies as if in prayer. After a few moments both raised their heads in total astonishment.

Drazinzka breathed. "I didn't know that Americans could be so calculating and cold-blooded. Such qualities in this field agent of theirs I personally find refreshing and a fitting tribute to Colonel Piankoff's tutelage."

Fedorov, ever the suspicious one, stated in an obnoxiously squeaky and imperious tone, "Well now, just how do we know that he will follow through? That he will succeed? That he won't be stopped before all is accomplished? I, for one, am not impressed with the pretty and poetic words of this degenerate, muscle-bound, American gladiator."

Silence.

"What have you to say, dear Vasily?" Drazinzka opined.

"Well, personally, nothing that has not already been said. But I can tell you this. The Americans were shocked at their operative's frankness, his candor. They also believe that he is highly motivated to succeed and believe that he will move 'heaven and earth,' their exact words, to do so. However, their biggest concern is not that Richards will succeed, but that his conscience will compel him to rebuild as well, that he may actually 'go native,' as they put it, and may not return."

Another silence broke out as the importance of the American's read on their own man sank in. Then Ostrogorsky said, "Now Karlov, I have a question. Just how close to operational status is Colonel Piankoff? We need him to assist the American in the assassination of the alien telepath, otherwise our plans will fail."

His smiling colleague answered, "Have no fear, Vasily. Colonel Piankoff will be ready. On that you have my assurance."

A heavy sigh.

"But I truly do hope that this Richards returns. He is formidable. Taking on that telepath will not be an easy assignment for two men, much less one."

"Karlov. I believe that you are going soft on this American," Fedorov teased.

"Hardly. But remember, Academician Fedorov. Milson after all recruited him, and to date that choice has proven to be a wise one. And of course our own Colonel Piankoff trained him.

"No, I am not going soft on him, but his departure from the scene will be a great shame. I only wish that he was one of ours."

"Humph!" The Hungarian grunted in negation.

In immediate response Karlov, with half-slitted eyes and a raised index finger, heatedly stated. "Be careful Academician Fedorov. There exists a code among warriors, something you clearly know nothing about, a well-deserved respect for those who follow orders, no matter how hateful the task. Right now we need Richards to return, so that he can backup Colonel Piankoff. The operational concept is a sound one. It's called the buddy system. Then, once the alien is eliminated, we will deal with Richards."

CHAPTER LII
Year 17 of Akhenaten

He cherished the quiet solitude of these pre-dawn moments just before morning arrival of Re's glorious appearance. To the pharaoh, it seemed as if a sense of expectancy filled the air. The usually noisy riverine fowl remained fast asleep amidst the fragrant lotus and dense papyrus rushes with their heads turned and bills neatly nestled into soft plumage. The many donkeys, cattle, and oxen, heaving in slumber, had not budged from their stalls. Above all, his people were at peace, such as it was on this turbulent world, one of such promise.

Sitting before his favorite scribal desk, itself a breath-taking wonder of delicately carved ivory inlays that glistened in high contrast against its ruddy red cedar wood frame, Akhenaten sighed with satisfaction. He had just finished writing a remarkable tale about the adventures of a most remarkable being—himself.

The sheer fact that he had thought to undertake such a task and so meticulously record the course and observations of his many sojourns among the stars was the direct result of what can be best understood as a remarkably human-like premonition—the absolute certainty of his impending death. This sense of foreboding was really quite odd for this inline telepath, whose alien kind did not even possess a word for fate. Yet, there it was, a nagging sense that all what not well, that forces were afoot beyond even his ken.

Perhaps, the Quimbly reasoned, *the source of this quiet dread is nothing more than my own guilt about that deep and unfortunate mind probe of the* sem-*priest, Piankhotep.*

What a fine mind he had. Such confidence, such disciplined clarity of thought. How he did struggle! How sadly fragile these creatures truly are!

With those thoughts came unbidden other thoughts. Such as never before had he felt so vulnerable, yet curiously at such peace. Its end was at hand. Somehow, just the sheer acknowledgement of such a terminus felt reassuring. After all, the king had calculated that its life form was thousands of years old—at least in relativistic terms. The mere thought of this subject caused the king's long face to break into a gentle smile, with eyes twinkling in pleasure.

Yes, perhaps, it is nothing more than the cumulative effect of this amazing culture's sure sense of birth and rebirth that is influencing me. That mixed with an equal measure of guilt at my recklessness with that priest's mind...and with so many others.

Putting down his personally designed writing quill fashioned from a feather of an ibis, he sighed.

My record is finished.

Noting with some mild annoyance the dried splatter of ink on his fingers, the Quimbly muttered to himself as he carefully rolled up the lengthy papyrus.

Existence. What truly is it? If I can inhabit this form, while my true flesh remains safe and secure within the confines of my surveyor craft, The Hope?

And, it continued silently, *why have I for the first time felt the urgent need to leave behind such a record for the benefit of a developing world? Why do I feel as if I am nothing more than a hunted animal? A quail being stalked by a high-flying falcon?*

During this entire self-examination, the pharaoh could not shake its sense of unease. What it had "seen" in the *sem*-priest's mind had indeed remained unsettling.

Imagine! When I had stated that my origin was from beyond the Dog Star, he had actually grasped the magnitude of that statement! Of the distances implied! How could that be?

What a simply remarkable man!

So concluded the king as it neatly bound the thick papyrus roll in three places with three pieces of brightly colored twine—the center one in red and the flanking pair blue.

And as that thought passed, the papyrus was lovingly placed within a beautifully carved cedar wood box built just for the purpose. As its lid was sealed the first rays of dawn broke across upon the verdant valley, and with their coming, the sleeping world awakened.

* * *

The littlest of things do make their mark. While in the fullness of time the discovery and translation of the Quimbly's own saga undoubtedly would do just that, it would do so only for a very narrow audience as the text of that galactic diary would never see the public light of day. But, perhaps perversely, it was the alien's choice of quill material that would produce a ripple of far greater import.

Previously, a simple riverine reed with a carefully tufted, clipped and shaped end had been the scribal writing implement of choice. But now, perhaps by design, perhaps by sheer serendipity, the being had chosen to write with a trimmed feather of an ibis—an animal that itself was held in close association with the god Thoth, harkened to the divinity who was the inventor of writing itself.

This fortuitous relationship and its significance were not lost upon the subjects of pharaoh. Already well-known for his penchant to cast tradition aside, this was but a small thing. So was engendered a burgeoning ibis quill industry that catered to those who could afford such a minor extravagance. As with all such frivolous fads, this innovation lent itself well to the already well-established papyrus trade and so the use of quills began to spread far and wide throughout the ancient Mediterranean. Eventually, the quill became the writing instrument of choice throughout the later Hellenistic World, in imperial Rome and Byzantine Constantinople, and in the monasteries medieval Europe. Consequently, the feathered quill became the very symbol of literacy, learning, and wisdom—all the while paying quiet and obsequious honor to the totem of a long-forgotten pagan god.

CHAPTER LIII
The Avenging Sword of Amen Re

It had taken one and a half idyllic days by boat, alternately sailing and drifting north with the Nile's current, before Richards laid eyes on Egypt's new capital. Befitting of its name, that event occurred just past dawn's first light. Even from this distance, one could see the wafting plumes of the first meal's cooking fires, and could make out the rising dust of the city's constantly ongoing construction. Along its many quays ant-like activity swarmed over grain transports, while river traffic, foreign merchant traders, and simple passenger boats just like this one edged this way and that for a berth. Without doubt, this was the happening place to be.

Rubbing his chin, Richards then thought of other concerns, the itch of his quickly-deteriorating grooming for one. While in Thebes, he had visited an open air barber for his last head shave. Although serviceable, it just wasn't the same as when Tia and Sia had cared for him. Sighing inwardly, Richards caught himself already yearning for those good old days.

Indeed those days will return. He mused. *After all, am I not the avenging sword of Amen Re? Am I not he who will sow among the godless his deadly viral seeds of destruction?*

Those are dangerous thoughts, Joseph! But true nonetheless.

With his mind returning to the goal of his mission, his right hand unconsciously went to that small cloth pouch, clutching it, making sure for perhaps the one hundredth time that it was still hanging from around his neck. In truth, the action had already become a habit.

Then his stomach grumbled mightily. Yes, he would have to see to that as well upon landing, even though his passage on this water taxi of sorts had included a full meal of half-stale bread, some cheese, warm beer, and a handful of dates.

And all of that for the price of one, small, golden ring! Fortunately, Meryptah had given me many more of the same. How could I have overlooked that issue at Horizon Pass? Just another lost bit of field craft that Piankoff could have passed on. Money sure talks.

As the river craft neared the eastern quays of the city, Richards felt a growing excitement building in his chest.

So much hustle and bustle, so much nervous activity. This is probably what it was like to my European immigrant ancestors when they first arrived at old New York City harbor. A place full of promise, dreams, and wonders to behold.

As the starboard side of the craft silently drifted into an open berth, mooring ropes flew to two young dockhands, and the passengers began to eagerly busy themselves for departure. Just like after a long transatlantic 747 flight, everybody wanted to stretch their legs and get on with it.

Being without any baggage, Richards just jumped off the gunwale onto the dock before the boarding plank had a chance to be lowered. Predictably, several shouts and general curses resulted about self-important priests who thought themselves above common sense. Ignoring them, Richards quickly lost himself within the crowded quay and the many stalls of the daily market. Having first silenced his stomach, he moved on to find a barber. After having himself groomed to his satisfaction, he then moved on to systematically locate each and every well of the city, for in each he had a viral deposit to make.

Needless to say, this portion of the adventure left this young and budding Egyptologist with truly mixed feelings. The sights, sounds, and smells represented such an intoxicating rush of data that he continuously felt the impending threat of sensory overload. On the other hand, it was all and always so exhilarating to actually be walking within the very womb of antiquity itself. But the first and last order of business on this topographical and cultural excursion was and had to be a visit to all the capital's fresh water drinking wells.

Still standing within the market place, Richards asked a kindly-looking fruit vendor where he could get a drink of water and was told. While winding his way in the direction indicated, he had a chance to marvel at all the fresh produce available, the hand goods, knick-knacks, the pottery—some of it clearly imports from as far away as the island of Crete and the Greek mainland, museum pieces all. Over there one could purchase bronze cooking pots, here linen, there spices, over there fresh fish. But it was all the fast food cooking stalls, whose smells readily sent his stomach into spasms of pseudo-hunger pains. The texture of it all was truly dense, overwhelming, and delicious.

At last he found his first well. As he expected, it was a deep, round affair with a rough limestone barrier wall to prevent anyone from accidentally falling in. Instead of a wooden cross-bar, rope, and pulley to raise the dripping pots of water, a twenty-or-so foot counter-weighted boom did the job in one seemingly effortless motion. Seeing this, Richards then remembered seeing this same water-raising contraption during his voyage here, but in that instance it was used for irrigation. He thought. *I believe that John called it a shaduf.*

While waiting his turn, Richards watched how the process was done. Now drinking his fill, and unnoticed by a soul, he dropped a palmed viral crystal into the well's depths and for good measure spat into the drained pot itself. Finished, he stepped away while the next person, in this case a middle-aged woman Richards judged from the sag of her breasts and stomach, who dipped the water pot anew.

And so it all begins, he thought.

Doc Allen had said that the time-release crystals would last up to a day before they were totally dissolved. Before that happened, he estimated that the flu virus would have already been transmitted and begun its typical pattern of mutation as it infected host after host.

Now, let's find another well.

*   *   *

When Richards had first taken possession of the viral crystals, he had been surprised at how many there were contained within it, but no longer. Although Akhetaten was a new city and clearly a growing one, at last count he had already seeded and spit into eighteen community wells, he had yet to get anywhere near the palace or temple areas and now the once substantial little cloth bag was getting light.

It's time, Joey boy, to refocus on the real targets of our mission. We have the background population well seeded. Now let's go for the biggies.

With that thought in mind, Richards began to work his way over toward what he recognized as the central section of the city. There he knew that he could find the stores and magazines of the massively rectangular Aten temple, reportedly some 750 by 300 meters in size, also called *Gempaaten*, as was its smaller Theban twin. Nearby was located the royal palace, conveniently located just to the south, and with it the royal apartments. Getting there was not a problem for the main north-south thoroughfare of the new capital passed between them all. In fact, a bridge had even been built over this busy traffic artery, which connected the royal apartments to the west of the thoroughfare with the royal palace to the east.

As he neared those structures, Richards quickly noted the heightened security of the area for the king's Nubian Medjay troops were practically everywhere. They made quite a show of their presence in such a way that no one could miss them. Standing six foot and taller, these powerfully built and thickly muscled, blue-black warriors simply dwarfed the typical Egyptian's slight build of maybe five foot four. Unlike many of the slightly cowering natives, Richards had long ago become accustomed to such physically dominant figures on the gridiron.

Nearing the main entrance to the sun temple's stores and magazines, Richards decided to see what would happen. Striding confidently up to the biggest and meanest looking of three sentries, he looked up and asked, "Noble Medjay warrior, where can a thirsty priest find some cool water?"

A bit taken aback by the obvious compliment, but more by Richards' unruffled manner in their presence, the large Nubian grunted out and pointed over his right shoulder.

"Within the magazine compound priest."

"And your name, sir?"

With a puffed up chest designed to intimidate and a raised chin of pride, the massive man said gruffly.

"Mahu. I am the Chief-of-Police."

With a slight bow and a kind word of thanks to Mahu for his kindness, Richards then followed precisely the Nubian's directions and entered the compound's entrance without challenge or argument. As for the Nubians, they were a bit stunned by Richards' sense of place, which Mahu immediately noted while shaking his head.

"That is the first time in my life that a priest politely thanked me for anything."

Then, rethinking that remark, the Nubian noted, "Are those indeed the scars of a lion across his back?"

As for his two other colleagues, they merely nodded in acknowledgement that a minor miracle had just occurred and then wondered as well as to their leader's second observation.

Within the magazine compound, it did not take Richards long to find its three wells, all of which he generously seeded in their turn.

Well, so much for the priesthood of the divine Aten. Now, let's go for the palace!

Passing again through the magazine compound's entrance, he made a point of catching Mahu's eye, nodding to him in thanks, and then continued on. In return, the Nubians were very carefully watching the passage of the much-scared priest. So much so that in a prescient moment, with Mahu's suspicions aroused, the three began to meander into the ever-flowing throng following the strangely polite priest.

Now again in the crowd, Richards began to feel a particular tingling sensation on the back of his neck and so decided to use a trick that Piankoff had often mentioned, the old double back move. So he did, beginning by first stopping in the shade of the bridge that connected the royal apartments with the palace. Squatting down and leaning against the cool wall as if resting, Richards just began to idly watch the hectic foot traffic pass by at knee level. And sure enough, his sixth sense had proved to be correct, for the three Nubians, their heads on a swivel, marched right past without seeing him scrunched down as low as he was in the shade.

Well, Joey, it's time for the hunted to become hunter.

Slowly rising with his back against the wall like a submarine's periscope, Richards saw that his prey was about one hundred feet ahead of him. Satisfied with that distance, he then slipped back into the swirling crowd and began to slowly track these easily distinguishable giants. After a few moments even this game got old, and seeing a side alley to the left, Richards took it. Following the passage a bit, it became obvious to the field operative that he was paralleling the north side of the royal apartments and that this alleyway most likely served as a delivery or service corridor for that rambling structure.

Smelling the cooking aromas of heavily spiced foods and coming upon an open doorway, Richards looked in and found a kitchen with two men and a woman busily sorting dates, chopping onions, and struggling with fresh bread dough. Entering he innocently asked, "Would any of you be so kind and direct me to some cool water?"

Again, Richards priestly visage worked in his behalf, for without a thought the woman who had been sweating over the bread dough rose from her knees and said, "For a priest of the Aten, I would be happy to. Besides, I have been working hard on this dough anyway, and could use some refreshment myself. Come."

As they began to leave, grumbling broke out from the two shortly to be abandoned men. Noticing this, Richards took the opportunity to say, "And since when is it beneath a man's labor to work the very dough of the royal house?"

So chastised, the grumbling abruptly ended with ashamed and averted eyes.

Turning back toward the kindly kitchen servant, Richards winked but maintained a straight face. At the wink, she barely could keep from noisily snickering from behind her hand that now covered her mouth. Now Richards knew that he had made an ally.

As it turned out, the private well for the royal apartments was located in the room next to the kitchen. It, unlike the massively built community wells and that of the temple's magazine, was relatively small, being only a plastered hole about three feet in diameter. Here one simply lowered a tightly woven wicker basket by hand on a rope down the shaft to draw the water.

Taking the dipping rope out of the hands of the surprised woman, he himself drew out a basket and then poured its cool and sparkling contents into a large ceramic basin for the purpose. Then taking two drinking cups, he offered the first full one to his kindly guide, who accepted it with wide eyes. Only after gulping down his, did she drink hers. Richards, noting this, then asked.

"Why do you act so strangely? Was it not you who first showed me the kindness of where the water could be found?"

Shocked silence and then.

"Please do not think me rude, most noble priest, but your open and kindly manner is strange, so different from most priests."

"How so?"

"Well, again, I mean no disrespect to your lofty station, but, but it is difficult for me to say. Except only that I am a kitchen servant, while you are a servant of the god."

"Ah, I now understand. And I suppose that you think that a servant of the god is somehow better than a servant who feeds the royal household, even He Himself perhaps?"

It took a moment for the full weight and impact of that thought to register in the young woman's mind, but when it did, her eyes flashed with recognition, and pride, and then something else. Tilting her head, she then said, "Noble priest, you are indeed not like any other priest that I have ever known. Are you married?"

Blushing and looking Richards looked down at his and said, "You do me honor, fair one, but I already am. Now please leave me and return to your bread before your colleagues have good cause to miss your excellent talents."

That said, the kitchen maid grinned, took two steps to leave, stopped, stole a quick peck on his cheek, winked, and hurried off. As soon as she had, Richards quickly seeded the well, twice just for good measure.

Those were the last two crystals, so it's high time that you made your escape. Mission Impossible *accomplished, Mr. Phelps!*

With that thought in mind he exited the well room, walked again through the kitchen, now noting with pleasure that one of the men was hard at work on the dough, received yet another endearing wink, entered the alley, and soon stood before its exit to the crowded main street.

Okay, now just where did those inquisitive Nubians go?

Looking up and down the busy way and not seeing their tall figures, Richards, before he again melted into the crowd, looked up to gauge the time, for his stomach began speaking to him again. On the basis of the high sun and near shadowless conditions, he decided that his stomach must be about right. Instead of heading back toward the marketplace and the quays, along that main north-south street that moderns now know as the Royal Road, his curiosity had gotten the better of him. It had even overruled his constitution, and so he decided to go left and see what he could see of the massive Aten temple, whose outer walls were clearly visible from the main street.

After about a hundred feet, Richards then saw that the crowd had noticeably thickened ahead. Naturally lumping up the way all crowds do when they are somehow impeded, Richards could not help but smile to himself.

Ladies and gentlemen, this is the Channel Seven traffic chopper, and we have a pile up on the Royal Road near the Aten temple during the noon rush hour. Be advised . . .

However that sophomoric ditty never had a shred of chance at completion in Richards' mind, for what he next witnessed simply could not be believed. Standing stock still in the street, with people rushing past him jostling him this way and that, his mind began to furiously record.

The reason why Richards had failed to find his curious Nubian Medjay was because they, and about thirty others, had formed a defensive riot screen before one of the side entrances that led into the sun temple's courtyard. In the press of a massive and building crowd, who were struggling to gain entrance, the Nubians were extremely busy pushing, shoving, and even clubbing as needed. Why such a mad rush on the temple? Because hovering directly above the temple's expansive courtyard was a brightly glowing golden disk about forty feet in diameter!

With his eyes riveted on the flying object, Richards then fought his way over to the side of the avenue and pressed himself tight against the wall of a building, partly to get out of everyone's way, partly for physical support. All the while his mouth was hanging open as if he were a hungry lizard catching passing flies, his mind was analytically recording what he thought he seemed to be seeing.

This is truly amazing. Am I really seeing what I think I am seeing—a hovering UFO! It surely seems to be too solid to be a holographic projection! It isn't wobbling in the air so it can't be a glider or a kite. It's certainly no balloon. Look at the temple's banners fluttering in the breeze. Nope. That's no kite, surely no glider. The winds all wrong. It just sits there stationary, silent as hell. This is just too weird.

This is just like something right out of the X-Files, von Däniken, and hell—even the old Outer Limits*! And yet here it is. Undeniable and tangible proof of high technology present in an extremely low-tech environment.*

Then something happened that again entirely broke the field operative's train of thought. The disk began emitting narrow and continuous rays of light down into the courtyard. With the rays came a great moan of emotion from the crowd already assembled within the courtyard. Again, once the initial shock had passed, Richards' analytical side kicked in.

And a laser light show, too! This is just too much.

Whoever would have believed that all those inscriptions depicting the Aten disk with its rays offering the *ankh* of life was nothing more than an ancient Egyptian's approximation of a hovering UFO and a laser show! Come to think of it, even the word "*aten*" is often left untranslated, as though it were obviously some sort of a name. But in fact is only a common noun that simply means "disk." For us, saucer has done just fine.

Man, this is some really heavy shit! We're talking about some serious paradigm shifts! No wonder the common people follow the Aten religion with such fanatical fervor. What a propaganda tool! What a crowd pleaser!

And then afterwards, all the bread, meat, and beer offerings go directly to feed the crowd. Talk about a blending of religion, bread and circuses!

But now the question is, how does he control that thing? And even more intriguing, where does he keep his toy anyway?

Then the laser show began to end with the individual beams slowly all shutting down one after the other. The crowd's reaction was predictable. Cries, shrieks, and moans of religious rapture could all be distinctly heard. Then, the disk slowly began to ascend straight up and at about five hundred feet, just took off in a blinding streak straight toward the noonday sun—disappearing toward its blinding brilliance.

Still leaning against the wall, but now covered in nervous sweat and with eyeballs that literally hurt from the strain that he had put them through, Richards thought.

That was one really, really, neat trick!

As for the crowded courtyard and its now empty sky overhead, Richards began to hear from that direction much singing, merry making, and laughter.

Bread and circuses indeed! Who would have ever believed it!

Now moving away from the kindly support of the wall, Richards' balance briefly wobbled, but he caught himself. Looking back at the wall, it was soaked with the outline of his back. A returning passerby with a large loaf of bread under his arm noticed Richards heaving chest, his shakiness. He stopped and remarked with the wide eyes of a fanatical believer.

"Ah stranger, I can see that you have never before witnessed the divine rapture of the Aten's presence. Just wait until you have been touched by the warmth of its healing rays! Then, and only then, will you truly know the feeling of divinity!"

Nodding his understanding, Richards then began to hobble his way back toward the market area and its nearby quays, all the while deep in thought as to what to say when he got back. Would they even take him seriously, or, just put him away deep in some secure and secluded funny farm. As is so often said, "The truth is often stranger than fiction."

*   *   *

Not surprisingly, the trip back up river to Thebes, against the prevailing northern current of the Nile, took precisely double the time—three days. By the time that Richards finally reached his destination, he was itching, quite literally, to get off that retched scow because it was teaming with fleas and lice.

Needless to say, finding a shave and a delousing bath was an essential first priority. Sparing no expense, and for the unheard of cost of two tiny golden rings, he got just what the doctor ordered. While sitting in the bath establishment, he suddenly realized that he now required a new, fresh, and thoroughly uninfested kilt in which to wear. For the cost of another golden ring, the proprietor even threw in a pair of wicker papyrus sandals. What a deal!

Now suitably smoothed, oiled, scented, and attired, Richards felt like a human being again and luxuriated in it. In the familiar and far less hectic surroundings of once sacred Thebes, his next priority was to stop and buy some bread, cheese, dates, and beer at the market. Then he would surprise his old friend Meryptah with an early evening meal.

Remarkably, Richards' plan worked out beautifully. Meryptah indeed had been at home. He was delighted to again receive him, practically falling all over himself in the process, and had much gossip to pass on as well. Clearly, Richards noted, the old priest was in far better spirits than when he had left him. Sitting down in the main guest room with all of his purchases arrayed on the low dining table, the priest began, but only after a brief prayer to the Great God in thanksgiving for Mayneken's safe return from that godless place to the north.

Holding a cup of beer before him, Meryptah winked with his partially blind right eye at his guest, and drained the cup straight down. Richards, never to be outdone when it came to the manly art of beer chugging, did the same, which prompted a quick burp.

Smiling broadly, the priest now began.

"My dear friend, noble Mayneken, much has transpired since you departed my house six days ago, much indeed.

"First of all, a remarkable thing occurred on the very morning of your departure for that place of heresy. The now former overseer of the grain magazines, Paser, suddenly and quite shockingly died of what appeared to be a savage blow to his throat that left him breathless. No one before or since had ever seen anything like it.

"What is even more remarkable is that on that very day the Vizier of Upper Egypt had arrived early to inspect the overseer's ledgers and accounts. What the vizier found so infuriated him that he caused the entire staff of Paser, including his Nubian Medjay, to be thoroughly examined. From what I understand, after only a few moments of rigorous caning, one of Paser's subordinates confessed to all the misdeeds that the overseer had himself committed. Consequently, the vizier, by the way a distant family relative, discovered my account, noted what Paser had denied me, and repaid my household in full all those arrears on that very day. Needless to say, the pantry of my household is now nearly awash in beer and overflowing in bread. Praise to the Great God's name!

"My second piece of news has to do with that very godless place from which you have just returned. In fact, you might be able to help explain what I have heard, that a dreadful sickness has befallen that city. Fits of sneezing, coughing, and fever are breaking out everywhere. That the very young and the very old are the most in danger and that many have already gone West. That even the strong are greatly weakened by it if not succumb to it. I have also heard, although I do not know whether it is true, that even the royal household itself has been afflicted. That the noble woman Kiya, the vile one's three youngest daughters: Neferneferure, Nefernefer-uaten, and Satepenre, and his two granddaughters Meretaten and Ankhesenpaaten, all have already fallen to this pestilence. Is this all true, Mayneken?"

With the piercing eyes of experience and the wisdom of age focused squarely upon him, Richards could not lie to the man, after all, was he not the high priest of Amen Re, his protector, his ally, and yes, potentially even his most ancient grandfather. Looking back at him squarely in the eye, Richards frankly said.

"Noble Meryptah. I will not foul the air of your holy presence with falsehoods. While I was in that city, I did not see or hear of any such calamity. But I can assure you, that if any such calamity has occurred since my departure three days ago, it was because I was solely responsible."

Now wide-eyed and slowly sitting back with sudden recognition, the old priest then added.

"And what of the overseer Paser, Mayneken, were you responsible for his death as well?"

"Yes, Noble One."

A stony dark silence fell between the two men. Meryptah looked down into his lap deep in thought, his left hand nervously and unconsciously rubbing his right stump. Richards continued to stare at the priest. The silence extended. Neither man moved a muscle. Finally, Meryptah looked up and said quietly.

"My son, do you regret what you have done?"

With tears streaming running down Richards' cheeks, all he could do was quietly nod.

"My son, you must go and pray this evening in the sanctuary and ask the Great God for his wisdom and understanding. As for that scoundrel Paser, well, he had it coming to him. As for the family of the godless heretic, many were nonetheless innocents. But as for the people of the city itself, that is an abomination.

"My son I have seen and heard many things during my long life. I have faced the cruel brunt of many trials. I have had my body horribly injured, but never have I taken a life."

With a softening to his voice, the old priest then continued.

"Mayneken, I know that you are a warrior, and I can therefore excuse Paser's death, because you did it as a warrior, face to face. I also suspect that you may have done this deed on my account as well. But to cause death while not being present, face-to-face, now that troubles me greatly.

"Now, my son, tell me why you did this terrible deed."

Richards, now practically on the verge of a total emotional breakdown, having finally grasped the true magnitude of what he had done, now was tearless. Absentmindedly rocking to and fro, as he was now before the old priest, all had become a slow-motion reality. All had resolved into a sort of split screen, out-of-body experience, where the magnitude of his crime just could not be grasped or comprehended. When he finally spoke, it was if Richards was sitting in an echo chamber listening to his own words in the third person, and what he said he translated for the old priest for he knew that he would understand.

"My dear father, I have done most grievous wrongs through my thoughts, words, and deeds."

Pause.

"I am the destroyer. I am the cleansing sword of Amen Re. And I will go again to destroy the heretic, and the rest of his foul progeny, if I must, for this blight upon Egypt must be removed."

To these words the priest could only grunt in recognition.

"You are indeed, Mayneken, a most formidable one. You are far more formidable then even your master Piankhotep, who I have personally seen injure three Medjay with his bare hands and feet. But

I must ask you, Mayneken, do you believe yourself to be a divine being, or just a man?"

This question caused Richards to pause and consider what really was on Meryptah's mind, sound psychiatric care or pure superstition.

"Noble One, I am merely a man. And in truth, I am not truly a destroyer. I am a poet, a teacher, a builder of canals, a surveyor of plots. Yet sometimes in order to build, or in the case of sacred Thebes, to rebuild, a cleansing destruction must first take place."

"Hmmm," was Meryptah's only nodding response, and then.

"Mayneken, despite your answer, I suspect an even greater purpose behind your actions. This deed that you have done truly is not your affair, is it? In fact, I can clearly see the troubled turmoil within your *ka* over it. As terrible a deed that it was, you, a warrior, who was told to do this hateful thing, you have remained faithful to he who has commanded you. Is that not true?"

Richards could only nod in affirmation.

"And what of this master? Is he truly worthy of a warrior as brave and as loyal as you?"

"No."

"Then, Mayneken, what will you do?"

"Pray for guidance."

With that issue settled, the pair slowly, silently, finished their evening meal. Richards, just to do something with his hands, cleaned up the debris, placed the remainder of proffered jewelry into his benefactor's hand, closing it with a gentle squeeze, and departed for the silence of the temple of the Great God. As he purposefully strode away beyond the entrance gate and walls of the old man's abode, Meryptah uttered a prayer to Amen Re on his behalf.

"Oh great and powerful Hidden One, be merciful to this strong young one, who does the bidding of others on the behalf of your great house. He seeks your divine wisdom. More, he seeks inner peace as well, because of his terrible deeds."

Having abandoned all pretext of stealth, Richards boldly entered the temple having encountered no one. Now before the doors of the Great God's sanctuary, he carefully and respectfully opened them the prescribed amount and slipped his frame through without fanfare. Within that cool and dark womb, brightened only by the solitary flame of an oil lamp, Richards finally, traumatically, came to terms with the simple fact that he had probably murdered most, if not all, of the royal household that he had come to know. The guide Thutmose and his carpenter brother, Ankhmes the physician, playful Tia and Sia, innocents all. The weight was immense.

As it turned out, that soul-wrenching introspection and resultant catharsis was much needed and therapeutic. Meryptah's softly spoken but pregnant words had unerringly found their mark. As the hours quickly passed, and by the time his extraction had finally arrived, Richards clearly knew who he was and what he had to do.

*　*　*

As the glow of the field above his head began to form and build in intensity, it was almost as if Richards was being bathed in a comforting, soothing, divine light. Once the field was established, he then jumped up with all his might and extended his clenched fist and forearm through the field. This prearranged signal alerted Major Tuna Cartwright and his men on the other side that he was ready. Sure enough, his leaping effort was soon rewarded with the appearance of the now familiar loop of hemp rope.

Cartwright thought, *this kid doesn't screw around! I'll just bet that he was never late for his Momma's dinner, either.*

As the sling went taunt with Richards' weight, and as his men began to reel him in as they liked to say, Cartwright stood outside of the arc of the four portable pylons and just watched as the entire extraction unfolded. It was good that he had, for he witnessed something that he had not seen since he had rescued that downed Air Force zoomie in Bosnia. For as Richards began to spiral out of the field as the burdened rope slowly twisted, the seasoned major saw a tensely coiled human with eyes that possessed the look of either a crazy man or trapped animal.

This man does not look good. Does not look good at all, he told himself, and simultaneously surprised himself with his concern.

What's up with you, Tuna? Have you suddenly decided to adopt this young pup?

As the boom was swung wide of the pylons' enclosure and Richards was lowered to the ground, he made not one attempt to acknowledge anyone around him.

Looks like he's in some sort of trance! Almost like battle fatigue – no shock. The major swiftly diagnosed.

Wisely, the major signaled to his men to give a wide berth, had the Mark V-A shut down, and then dismissed them entirely from the sanctuary. Of that they all were more than glad to oblige, for the vibes that were emanating from Richards, well, didn't seem to be very healthy ones.

Now, with the sanctuary quiet, it was only he and Richards. Standing before and about twenty feet away from the silent form, the major decided that he would just have to wait this one out. It took a good four minutes by his watch before he heard the first shuddering intake of breath, before the knotted rock hard shoulder and back muscles began to relax. Then, slowly uncoiling his whitened knuckles from around the rope, Richards' sweat-streaked and dust-caked head slowly began to rise. When those haunted eyes acknowledged his presence with a subtle dilation, with a straining, tautly tensed neck, a dry and softly dreamy voice emerged in halting and stumbling English with eyes widening with unnecessary emphasis.

"Behold. I am the Destroyer. I am the avenging sword of Amen Re. I have caused the deaths of countless numbers so that the Great God may again return in all of His glory."

A pause, then came a swallow.

"Tell me, Major Charles Abraham Cartwright, Jr. Do you think that you could casually walk through a thriving city, kindly interact with its innocent population, and then calmly sow death wherever you walked?"

Richards could easily register the shock on the major's face at his use of his full Christian name. Could easily see his concerned face over operational security, what have you. He saw maybe even a reaction to what he was saying. Then he continued on in that same tone of voice.

"Well, major, I have. And I can tell you this. Although you pity them, although you grieve for them, although you feel the weight of a mountain crushing down on your heart for what you have done, in the final analysis, what troubles me most is the sheer ability to do such an act, the very intoxicating power of it, made me feel invulnerable, allowed me to take unacceptable risks. Yet, throughout it all, I felt as untouchable as the Angel of Death. I felt like a god. And now, somehow, I know that I must pay for every last bit of it, if I ever want to preserve any shred of my humanity, or at least what's left of it."

With a deep and ragged sigh that sounded like it came from the very bowels of Hades itself, Richards' head drooped.

"My God, I'm beat."

Although Major Charles Abraham Cartwright, Jr. had never before been seen with tears in his eyes, this was the moment. For never before had the major ever seen such abject guilt, such all-consuming self-hatred, for accomplishing something that one was ordered to do.

CHAPTER LIV
The Third Teleconference

One day prior to the agreed satellite videoconference, the members of both panels received the 23-page transcript of Richards' deep hypnotic debriefing that Dr. Allen had conducted and taped at Horizon Pass. To say that the field report made for some interesting reading would have been an understatement. All in attendance were mightily impressed and distressed as well.

After the usual and inane opening pleasantries made by Dr. Young as much by tradition as by default, it was the fast recovering Professor Milson who led the discussion. Both sides easily detected a remarkable amount of control, detachment, and hard calculation in his voice. For both panels, Ostrogorsky probably read it the best, quoting in his mind, perhaps inappropriately, but quoting nonetheless those famous words of the nineteenth century Prussian Prime Minister Otto von Bismarck: *"Blut und Eisen,"* blood and iron.

"Gentlemen, on the basis of the field report before you, which I believe to be an accurate account in all respects, the first phase of our mission has been successfully, and might I add, thoroughly and ruthlessly completed."

On the American side that direct statement was acknowledged with several shifting bodies and a nervous cough. On the Russian side, slightly nodding heads and one softly whispered, *"Da."*

"To date, strangely in our context a most relative term at best, fully one half of the target's eight progeny have died. In addition, all of his grandchildren have succumbed as well. By my count, those that remain to be potentially dealt with include the two males, Smenkhkare and Tutankhaten, and the females Meretaten and Ankhesenpaaten. Of the four, the females hold for us the greatest liability. They must be prevented from producing any offspring. We must make sure that these princesses remain sexually isolated. In all cases, any royal marriages of these siblings must remain sterile, barren unions. As for Ankhesenpaaten, she is the only one who must remain alive, for she will provide the necessary political linkage for the continuation of the dynasty, such as it is.

"On the positive side, thus far, we have not significantly disturbed reality as we know it.

"On the negative side, we have another highly complex mission to execute. Namely, to eliminate, by any means appropriate, the target himself. His children Smenkhkare and Meretaten will later follow as will the containment of the fertile female Ankhesenpaaten. She must be denied any future opportunity to breed.

"Gentlemen, as I had outlined during our previous video conference, I believe that we should next act directly against the target, and not directly against any of his remaining children. That, I believe, will be sufficient for now.

"As for the current status of Dr. Richards, he is undergoing some much needed R & R. To be blunt, he is presently coping with the fact that he is a mass murderer. His sense of guilt is enormous. Yet, his spirit has proven to be remarkably resilient. We remain confident that shortly he will be fit for the next planned deployment.

"In the meantime, it has been recommended that he take a hiatus of several months before he is again redeployed to complete the next phase of this mission. However, he cannot do it alone. He will need assistance."

Now leaning far forward on the table before him and with his eyes locked on Ostrogorsky half a world away, Milson directly queried.

"Academician Ostrogorsky, will Colonel Piankoff be fit for deployment sometime within the next several months?"

Ostrogorsky, looking side to side to his colleagues, received two small nods. In response, he said.

"Da, Dr. Milson. Yes, Colonel Piankoff will be ready."

At that answer, the Russians could clearly see that the tensed shoulders of the Americans had visibly relaxed.

Nikolai Fedorov, the Director of Advanced and Theoretical Technological Research, now chose to speak for what he thought was the first time, since his previous *faux pas* had not been caught. For all the spooks and psychologists who were made privy to these landmark videoconferences, this was like being in a skybox at the fifty-yard line of the Super Bowl—as good as it gets.

Folding his hands before him was his signature habit. The Russian began.

"Excuse me, Dr. Milson, I have a question that has been troubling me and my colleagues greatly, and I suppose your panel as well.

"You have stated earlier that you believed that your field operative's account 'was accurate in all respects.' Do you mean by that statement that you fully accept his eyewitness account of the alleged UFO sighting, his surmise that the target actually commanded it, and then used this hovering craft for religious, propagandistic purposes?"

Those of the American panel and those that had tuned into the satellite link from the various security agencies and organizations had clearly heard the dripping skepticism of Fedorov's voice. But it was the lilt of his body language that had accused far, far more—total incredulity, disbelief, fantasy, if not outright deception.

In response to Fedorov's undisguised challenge, Dr. Jung of the American panel chose to speak for the first time.

"Academician Fedorov, allow me to answer that question on the behalf of our panel and Dr. Milson in particular. First allow me to introduce myself. I am Dr. Ernst Jung, a theoretical physicist by trade. I am sure that we have both had the pleasure to read each other's papers. I, however, Academician Fedorov, have accepted Dr. Richards' eyewitness report verbatim. And here's why. In my chosen specialty, as I am sure in yours, one must always keep an open and receptive mind to new scientific developments, new paradigms. The fact that the target, which by the way is powerfully telepathic, has at his behest a craft and a technology that we presently do not possess does not surprise me in the slightest. If anything, it challenges me, interests me.

"What intrigues me the most about Dr. Richards' report was his immediate desire to locate where such a craft might be based. This, at least to my way of thinking, is not the drooling drivel of an over-imaginative or delusional mind that is suffering from sun stroke, but instead of a lucid, powerfully analytical, and curious one, which is struggling to comprehend what he is witnessing. Consequently, wouldn't it be nice if, during the next deployment, we put some thought into perhaps locating where the target keeps this craft. After all, wouldn't it be nice if it were eventually recoverable?"

Fedorov's reaction to this rebuke could have easily won him an Academy Award in any appropriate venue. Flushing bright red, quivering jaw muscles exercising full rage, bug-eyed, tensed torso, and balled fists. The hidden psychologists in the audience were just going bananas at this emotional display that ran off the cosmic chart.

At the same time, Ostrogorsky began to studiously examine his fingernails as was his habit during embarrassing times such as these. As for Karlov Drazinzka, he merely stifled a grin behind the cover of one of his massive hands. At face value, the Russian panel had become comical. As a result of this exchange, it was clear to all that it was decisively split and that Fedorov was the odd man out. Given the department that Fedorov headed, that too spoke volumes as to why the Russians had never gotten past the theoretical planning stage regarding the Soap Bubble's development.

Ever trying to be the mediator, Dr. Young then jumped into this awkward silence with some more of his patented white noise.

"Well, yes. I thank you both, Academician Fedorov and Dr. Jung, for those stimulating remarks. Now, is there anything else about this report that we should discuss?"

Ostrogorsky then spoke, having first turned to acknowledge his two colleagues.

"Gentlemen, as I speak for our panel, we wish first to thank Dr. Richards for his efforts and personal sacrifice during this crucial phase of our plan. His many observations have provided us with much to consider."

Fedorov, meanwhile, with his head down, had his two hands locked together in an absolute ecclesiastical death grip, the stark and bloodless whiteness of his knuckles clearly apparent to the American panel. By all accounts, he had clearly and totally lost it. Ostrogorsky was then caught peeking over at his distressed colleague's reaction to his words. When apparently satisfied at what he saw, Ostrogorsky smoothly continued.

"We look forward to further discussions regarding the coordination and planning of the next phase of this mission."

With that, Ostrogorsky signaled off camera and the satellite feed abruptly ended.

Young, ever the competitor, whispered under his breath, "I hate it when he does that! That Russian always has to have the last word!"

CHAPTER LV
Exorcism of Inner Demons

To Doc Allen's everlasting surprise, Joey Richards just walked into his office unannounced and asked if they could talk. After about three hours, Allen decided Joey was not going crackers on him. In fact, he judged the young man was well on his way to a full recovery. But as to when he would be fit for his next deployment, only time would tell. In the meantime, Joey could at least get all those infected flea and lice bites healed.

As for Doc Allen himself, this healing "just talk" heart-to-heart between he and his patient caused him to entirely rethink his planned retirement. Without really thinking about it, he too was suffering from a tremendous amount of guilt, from his first programming of Joey for his mission to when he had armed him with those viral crystals. As he now analyzed the situation, they were partners-in-crime, joint accomplices in mass murder. The "just talk" had brought that fact out into the open for all to see. Then it hit him as to how he had been coping—with his jaws. So looking down on his ever-expanding paunch, he decided to put himself on a diet and begin a measured and sustained exercise program.

I think after I lose my first ten pounds, I'll tell Joey I have only him to thank for it.

He cured his own shrink!

*   *   *

Three weeks after Doc Allen and Richards had their little talk, the heat was on to set a firm date for the next deployment and final phase of the mission. As to who was lobbying for a rapid closure remained unclear to the freckled-faced physician. Regardless, it irked Doc Allen fiercely in his gut, which to his pleasure was fast diminishing. Further, he doubted that Richards, or for that matter Piankoff, could be ready in the short term. To those who controlled the company or ran the Russian Academy of Science, these men were just expendable chess pieces to be played.

Of course to Allen, these men, and especially Joey, represented far more. They were temporal pioneers, cultural chameleons, and linguists without peer. To him, the value of such men had no price. Yes, there always lurked the prospect of failure, mishap, and pure bad luck that could, and probably eventually would, catch up, and claim these specialized daredevils. But to send them out poorly prepared or not at their best, well, meant sending them on a fool's errand.

Then, four days later, Piankoff arrived.

At first glance Doc Allen thought the man looked well rested and fit. But occasionally he caught the Russian's eyes drifting off into a classic thousand yard stare that betrayed him. He was still contending with some serious, personal demons. As for his language facility, all seemed up to snuff. Ever an optimist, Allen concluded that perhaps Piankoff and Richards had been kept apart for far too long. The two had become one, and perhaps their reunion would bode well for their mutual healing. On that basis, Allen was all for Piankoff's presence, but the good country doctor from Oklahoma was not naïve. Piankoff was here for one reason and one reason only, preparation for deployment, even though not a word of it had been expressed.

*   *   *

The first time Richards caught Piankoff's vacant look was during a brief water break, while cooling off in the rocky shade of an obliging arroyo. For the past two days he had been watching for it, because Doc Allen had alerted him to what to look for, and if possible, to gently get the secretive Russian to talk, and get his ghosts into the full blinding light of day. So Richards followed Doc Allen's advice and asked in their shared ancient tongue, "My teacher, what troubles you?"

Snapping out of it at the soft sound of Richards' voice, "Why, why, nothing, just nothing."

"It didn't look that way to me. You were actually frowning."

A deep sigh emanated from the Russian.

"Yes. Yes, I probably was."

"Well? Is it anything that you can tell me? Or is it some deep, dark, Russian State secret?"

This question brought a quick smile to Piankoff's face, because his ever-clever and poetic assistant had translated "Russian" into the Egyptian equivalent of big, brown, hairy animal with claws and teeth.

"No, Mayneken, my thoughts are not about other people's secrets. Just my own. And, believe me, they are sufficient. But since you have asked, I will tell you. That at least I owe you. My encounter with the target really messed me up. Flip-flopping my temporal sense of when such and such had occurred, confusing the identities of people that I have known, mixing up entirely the delicate balance between events, the relationships of people, to places, to a given time. And then, of course, there was the sheer surprise at how quickly he had rifled through my mind like an Apis bull in a pottery market."

This obvious attempt on Piankoff's part to mimic in ancient Egyptian the common modern expression brought a broad grin to Richards' face.

Yep, Doc Allen was right. Get him talking, and if he can make a joke of it, all the better.

"But more than anything, Mayneken, I now fear him as I have no other. I fear that he will again force his way into my mind, plunder it, trash it, and then just as suddenly leave me again without any regard as to what he had done."

Silence.

"Those who cared for me back in Russia, three psychiatrists, cannot help me with this fear, which oftentimes visits me in the form of terrifying nightmares. The doctors said that this is a demon that only I can conquer. And every so often, I wonder to myself, 'How can I end all of this?' In truth, I have already considered suicide, several times, several ways, but that is not the honorable way. Somehow, I must beat this thing."

Richards, trying to comprehend such a mental rape, could only imagine what it might be like, not what his colleague was going through. Then he got an idea.

"Noble Piankhotep, do you think that it would help if you could slay the evil one himself, with your own hand?"

"Yes. I think it would. But how?"

"That, my good friend, we will have to discover together!"

With that issue settled and behind them, the pair took off at a quick lope on their way back to Horizon Pass. Piankoff took the lead. Richards, pleased in this case to follow, could have sworn that he could already see an improvement in the Russian in just the way he carried himself.

Doc Allen, maybe I should have gone into psychology.

* * *

After a week's time of re-acquaintance, Piankoff and Richards received the news that their next deployment would be taking place in three days. To them, this came as no surprise, for both had few illusions as to why they were again training together in the New Mexican desert.

From an operational standpoint, the pair knew that they would be on their own with only Richards' brief experience to guide them within the new capital. As for their good friend Meryptah, they both believed that the venerable old priest would be safely among those who had gone West by the time of Akhenaten's seventeenth regnal year. Privately they acknowledged the distinct and distasteful possibility that he may have even been among the thousands who fell victim to the spread of the seeded Asian flu epidemic.

Their list of mission goals was formidable. The primary one being the target himself, whose disappearance from the historical record sometime during the summer of his seventeenth year had to be positively assured.

Secondarily, the groundwork for a totally internal, Egyptian solution for the remaining siblings had to be established. This meant the recruiting of those most likely to benefit from the misfortune of the royal pairs of Smenkhkare and Meretaten and Tutankhaten and Ankhesenpaaten. Fortunately, those opportunistic figures were well known to the historical record. It was just a matter of making sure that their misfortune took place.

Finally, as if the list were not long enough, the pair was tasked to confirm Richards' UFO sighting and then ascertain whether it could be recovered. In all, both Richards and Piankoff agreed that they were up to their eyeballs in details, had much to consider, and chew on. Fortunately, Dr. Milson, the crafty architect of it all, was available to act as a sounding board. Yet, it would be the practical and down-home Doc Allen, who would play his part as well.

* * *

Following their refreshing post-jog shower and a nourishing lunch, Piankoff and Richards next sought out Doc Allen and were told that he could be found in the complex's library. Within the stacks that smelled of ink and slowly deteriorating paper, they found him, sure enough before a computer, evidently trying to keep up with his email. Acknowledging the pair, he cheerfully chirped, "Gentlemen, what can I do for you?"

To this greeting, Richards responded.

"Well, Doc, we'd like to discuss with you some ideas that we have about the upcoming mission. Do you have a moment?"

"Sure, what's on your mind?"

"Well, Doc, how would you go about killing a powerful inline telepath at close range?"

"Why that's a really good question."

Now leaning back in his chair with his hands behind his head in contemplation, the physician took a few moments and then began with several clinical observations.

"Well, my immediate, upfront gut instinct tells me that both of you will have to be heavily blocked. The target must see both of you as totally blank, emotionless slates. In short, totally unreadable minds as if the two of you were wooden puppets.

"Next, the target's own mind must be somehow confused or preoccupied by several diversions, which will play a considerable role if you want any chance of getting in close. So, success will depend on your blocking, diversions—ideally several, and then, yes, some rigorously choreographed assault planning that can be reduced to rote, motor response. Regardless of whatever you plan, it must be swift, deft, sure, and flexible. Otherwise, you both will be, sorry to say, toast.

"You won't get a second chance.

"Not ever."

CHAPTER LVI
The Treasury

Given the current deserted condition of the Great God's temple, the pair anticipated no difficulties whatsoever. But to make sure, Tuna Cartwright decided to test a new reconnaissance toy. By extending and then slowly rotating the probe's arm, the small plastic cobra-like lens attached to its claw sent back a 360 degree low light image through a thin fiber optic cable. What it revealed was a totally empty room. In fact, a room that was in much the same condition as when Richards had last left it. Now satisfied that all was clear, the pair dropped through that slippery feeling field into the past.

Taking the requisite amount of time to reorient themselves after the transit, a period that seemed to be lengthening, Piankoff and Richards deftly slipped themselves through the sanctuary's door leaves. Moments later, they found themselves once again under the bright starlight of the Theban sky. For old time's sake, they made their way over to the old priest's household. Standing outside of its circuit wall, noting its tattered wooden gate and unkempt grounds, the pair had their serious doubts, but still chose to see whether the old man, to whom they both owed so much, was still alive.

Stealthily creeping into the house through its main colonnaded entrance they discovered that the kitchen's ashes were still warm from the evening meal. Next, they dared to light an oil lamp that they had found there. They then moved on to venture deeper into the dwelling in an attempt to find who was sleeping in the old priest's bedchamber. After several wrong turns, several incorrect rooms, and a stray bump in the night, they finally found it. There, snoring ever so quietly was indeed Meryptah, now an extremely old, extremely wizened man.

Piankoff, now looking down on the gently sleeping form, whispered to Richards. "Do you think we should awaken him?"

"If you don't, you will truly regret not having done so."

At this point a dry and raspy third voice entered this almost comedic situation.

"You do not have to awaken me. I ALREADY AM. Now take what you wish. And be quick about it. And please don't awaken my neighbors as you have me on your way out!"

Piankoff and Richards softly chuckled as they both squatted down on the floor next to the old priest's bed frame.

"Now, Meryptah, most noble first servant of the Great God Amen Re, what sort of greeting is that to old friends?"

Piankoff said with a mock-serious voice.

This statement elicited a rather startled snort and then a grunt as the old man levered himself up on one elbow. With two squinting eyes, one now totally white and blind, the other still sharp and clear, he said with a whispered start.

"No, it cannot be!

"Is that you, Piankhotep, and Mayneken too? Is that truly you, or am I having a fanciful old man's dream?"

Piankoff replied in a quiet and soothing voice.

"No, most noble priest, your still good eye and ears are not deceiving you. We are indeed here. My good friend, what do you require of us?"

Now swinging around his old legs to the floor and sitting up on the bed before them he said.

"No. It is I who must offer you two some beer and bread!"

Placing his hands on the old priest's shoulders and gently restraining him back onto the bed frame, Piankhotep calmed his excitement.

"No, no my good friend, now is not the time for beer, but instead for your wisdom. Sit and tell us what news you might have about these darkest of times, as we have been abroad from Egypt for far, far too long."

Beginning to grasp the meaning of Piankoff's words, the old priest settled back into his bed frame, unconsciously pulling his blanket about his knees, wiping off a bit of excited drool from the left corner of his mouth. It was then that Richards noticed that the entire left side of his face had a stiff, expressionless droop to it. Richards thought, *Either that is Bell's Palsy or the tragic aftermath of a stroke.*

"Well, I must say that my health, such as it is, is not the best. As you can see, I am without my right hand, my right eye is now totally blind, and three days ago this side of my face," stroking it with his wrinkled left hand, "has totally lost all feeling to it. As always, the Great God tasks me greatly, but I still secretly pray to him. Apparently my prayers have been heard, for the recent Overseer of the Granary, a young and remarkably honest man by the name of Horemheb, treats this old soul with uncommon kindness."

At the sound of the overseer's name, Richards was startled and the old priest saw it.

"Mayneken, do you know of him? Whatever you do boy, please do not sally out and kill this one, too! I am being truthful when I tell you of his many kindnesses toward me."

At the offhand mention of Richards' killing of an overseer, Piankoff, who had not heard that story, sharply looked at his partner.

"Ah, yes. No. We wish no harm to this Horemheb, noble Meryptah." Richards replied soothingly.

"It's just that we would like to know if you could introduce him to us, or at least, point him out to us, for we wish to speak with him."

"Well, you two certainly picked an odd time to do so!" Came the old priest's sharp reply. "Do you know what time it is?

"But as to these dark times, I am an old man, who is not seen, but who has one good eye, sharp ears, and an even sharper memory. But before I begin, I must first ask Mayneken a question."

"Yes, Meryptah, what is it that your heart wishes?"

"Did you ever find peace my son?"

With suddenly moist eyes, Richards nodded his answer. "Yes, my grandfather, I have found a peace of sorts."

A raspy grunt then preceded Meryptah's terse reply. "Well, by the looks of you, you certainly seemed to."

"As for you Piankhotep, where have you been after so many inundations?"

With an honest smile, Piankoff answered, "Struggling to survive after being attacked by the godless one."

This revelation was met with a quick and strong intake of hissing breath.

"So, you too were so affected. Did you not tell him Mayneken, how the vile one, after I had angered him, struck me down with his eyes alone, and left me like a stunned pigeon? No? Well, for your information, it is believed that the unspeakable one had done the same to his very own Mistress, noble Queen Nefertiti. Since the heretic's fourteen year, she has not been seen or heard of at either the royal palace or the royal apartments. Instead, it is rumored that she has been banished to a northern part of that accursed city, suffering in silence and loneliness in ways that cannot be imagined.

"But as for this once fair city, Thebes has now become a quiet provincial village. Its many temples have been closed and systematically plundered by godless ones without shame. They have even ripped off the bronze sheathing from the temple doors, and in some cases, have even dismantled the massive cedar wood doors themselves. I suspect, if they could, they would have gleefully removed stone as well, if it were not for the piety of young Horemheb, the Overseer of the Granaries. He has prevented any further desecration by that pitiless rabble.

"But as to what I have heard about the strange goings on in that blasphemous city to the north is almost beyond description, beyond reason, and surely beyond all that the beloved goddess Maat stands for. For instance, did you not know that the vile one's oldest son, Smenkhkare, has married his own sister Meretaten? Now, while in times past such a thing was understood for the sake of the royal bloodline, never before has the practice become so perverted."

Now slowly shaking his head from side to side, the old priest continued.

"Did you not know that the vile one then elevated his eldest son as co-ruler and remains so even until today? It is even rumored that the heretic even favors Smenkhkare in ways that normal men do their beloved wives.

"Did you not know that before Queen Meretaten was even betrothed to her brother that the unspeakable one had sired a granddaughter by her? And then later did the same with his other daughter Ankhesenpaaten, producing yet another granddaughter? Simply unspeakable.

"And while all of these distasteful things were occurring in that city of filth, a silent and deadly plague had descended upon it taking countless numbers to the grave, including the two royal granddaughters."

After the mention of the epidemic, the old priest became silent. After a few more moments he reached out with his left hand, gently placed it upon Richards' head, and spoke.

"My son, what you did was an abomination. Of that there can be no doubt. Yet, even I, if I had been given the chance, knowing what I now know, would have done the same. For who could have imagined what adulterous perversions of Maat would have occurred to blight our fair land."

Removing his good hand from Richards' head and returning it to his lap, he then again deeply sighed.

"And now, my guests, what do you wish to tell his old priest of your adventures?"

In a partial answer to this question, Piankoff retold, what he could, of his telepathic encounter with the target. Told of his post-experience confusion and dementia, of his self-doubt and continued recovery. When he had finished, the same question was posed to Richards, who also related, again what he could, of his guilt, his desire to become a teacher of the Egyptian language, his desire to see the dark times end for Egypt. And throughout both of their answers, both had told the truth, at least from a certain point of view. And although the old priest sensed the truth of their words, he also sensed the subtle side stepping of details and the great remove of their words.

"Noble Piankhotep, noble Mayneken, we all have suffered greatly during these dark times, each to his own measure."

The old priest now raised his left hand, as if in a Christian benediction, and continued.

"However, I sense from both of you truths, and half-truths. Certainly no falsehoods to be sure, but half-truths nonetheless. It is as though you both are trying to kindly protect this old priest from the full force of your deeds. Perhaps it is the imagination of an old priest's mind, but I must know who I am truly sitting in congress with."

To this question, both Piankoff and Richards were silent. Then, looking at one another, after a quiet nod, an agreement was struck, Piankoff began, and the rules of the *RUTI* were thrown aside.

"Noble Meryptah, your wisdom and perception has remained undiminished despite the vast passage of time. It is true, I and

Mayneken have been speaking in half-truths, but never have we spoken falsehoods. And yes, our half-truths were spoken to protect you from the full truth, a full truth that both Mayneken and I ourselves can sometimes scarcely believe.

"But allow me to explain the full truth in a way that you will surely understand. First, the unspeakable one is not the true son of the loins of the blessed Osiris Nebmare Amenhotep and the venerable Tiye. Instead, he is the product of a dark magic that even we cannot imagine. This is why his appearance is so odd and his mind can speak to us without the utterance of words.

"Second, our masters, for whom we do their bidding, are fearful of the unspeakable one and his children, whom you well know share the hidden powers of their father. Our masters' fear is that men will no longer be able to possess their own thoughts, which the children of the vile one can read as easily as we can see our hand before a lighted oil lamp. Thus, our masters have sent us as emissaries, as scouts, and yes—sometimes even as assassins, to do their bidding. Our concern is for the preservation of Egypt. Our concern also is for the tens of myriads of yet unborn, who will be directly affected if we are not successful in halting the vile one and his children. Thus, we are here."

Throughout Piankoff's entire dissertation, the old priest listened with a depth of concentration that was formidable and he proved this with his next question.

"Untold 'myriads of yet unborn.' Piankhotep to say such a thing can only mean that you know of the existence of those 'yet unborn.' So Noble Ones, from when do you come, and where are your households?"

Again Piankoff answered.

"We, noble Meryptah, were both born of our mothers and fathers in a time when the land of Egypt and all of its marvels are but a mere memory, a time when only empty ruins stand. We, noble Meryptah, were both born in lands far beyond that of the land of the contrary river. We, noble Meryptah, are travelers, distant travelers, distant time travelers."

To this revelation Meryptah made a thoughtful grunt and then wiped at the corner of his slightly drooling mouth. Following another grunt, he asked for clarification.

"If I understand you, Piankhotep, that you both come from such distant lands, that I can understand, for you both have a spirit and inner manner that is most uncommon, most refreshing. But time, what do you mean by that?"

This time Richards fielded the question.

"Noble Meryptah, in what year were you born?"

After some thought.

"Why, why, I believe it was in the first year of the blessed Osiris Nebmare Amenhotep."

"And Noble One, what was the first year of your station as high priest of the Great One?"

"Why, that is simple, year 20 of the blessed Osiris Nebmare Amenhotep."

"Thus, noble Meryptah, how old are you now?"

"Why, very old, is that not obvious?" The old man stated with exaggerated force.

"Yes, but, how many years old? How many inundations?"

With a puzzled look on his face, the old priest then began to ponder and then started counting furiously on his lone hand and bending over on his toes, several times.

"I calculate fifty-four inundations!" the old priest declared with some shock at the revelation.

"Yes, Meryptah, fifty-four inundations. Now, do you know when your father was born?"

After a moment's reflection.

"No, I do not."

"Do you know how old your father was when he went West to be most fairly judged by Osiris?"

"Well, perhaps fifty-four inundations also, for he was very old indeed when he went West!"

"The men of your family live a long time, Noble One, my congratulations. Now, how old was your grandfather when he went West?"

Richards was met with a totally blank look of befuddled comprehension, wonder, and then the dawning of insight. Richards could have sworn that he saw the old man's lone good eye snap with the fire of enlightenment, when he firmly stated with some irritation.

"I do not know."

"Noble Meryptah, have no fear. I did not think that you would have or even could have known the answer to that question. But the calculation of how old you are, your father, grandfather, and his father and grandfather, is called time. Time is a calculation, nothing more, nothing less. It is something that even a scribe can do. In some ways, time as a calculation is much like the distance between two places. And so, Piankhotep and I are time travelers. If we wished, we could visit your father during his youth and your grandfather during his."

Now with a distressed face, the old priest then whispered, "But why would you do so?"

"Perhaps to prevent a needless broken leg caused by the tread of a heedless ox, or, to make sure that your own mother's water successfully broke to ensure your birth."

"You can actually do such things?"

To these questions both Piankoff and Richards simply nodded their assent.

To this they were greeted with yet another deep intake of breath. Then came the old priest's next question.

"And thus from which time did you come?"

Piankoff answered.

"But I have already said, a distant time, a time when Egypt is a mere memory."

With eyes filled with alarm, the old priest then queried. "You mean, Piankhotep, from a time as far distant as my great-great grandfather?"

Both men tried mightily not to smile and succeeded only by answering spontaneously.

"Yes."

Shaking his head from side to side as if in negation, he then pondered aloud.

"Ah, that is truly wondrous," soon followed by the following observation.

"But you know, Piankhotep, I was often puzzled by your appearance."

"How so?" said the Russian with an inquisitive tilt of the head.

"Well," as the old priest scratched at his scalp, "As I best recall, we first met many inundations ago just before Providence smiled on me, before I became an acolyte to the House of the Great God. I remember that first meeting, now that I think about it, quite well. I was observing the flight of a falcon along the riverbank. I recall thinking how marvelous it would be to fly and soar so, and then you appeared, dressed much as you are now, looking very much the same as you do today. I distinctly remember a conversation on the strength of the wind, the lightness of the falcon, and above all, the shape of the falcon itself. I will never forget how you then demonstrated these facts to me with that folded sheet of papyrus that you caused to fly. Piankhotep, you are as natural a teacher as Thoth the guardian of secrets himself. And I might add that Mayneken here is clear evidence of that as well. But to return to my first thought, even today, as I look upon you and your loyal companion, why is it is that you have not grown old a day. How is that possible?"

"Because noble Meryptah," Richards answered, "we have not."

To these words, only a silent nod was returned. Clearly it was not a nod of understanding, just one of acceptance of something marvelous beyond his ken.

Then the priest asked the ultimate question.

"How then, how do you travel in time? Do you use a sun boat as does Re when he crosses the sky?"

"Oh no noble Meryptah, with a tool, just a simple tool," Richards responded.

And then the Egyptologist thought, boy, would Dr. Borov freak out if he heard that I called the Mark V-A "just a simple tool!"

With that answer, the group noticed that the flickering flame of the oil lamp was no longer throwing the shadows that it once had, for the dawn was fast approaching and its light was beginning to pour through the room's clerestory windows. The old priest announced, "Enough talk, it's time to rise. Besides, all this calculating of inundations has made my head hurt."

* * *

After the first meal, Meryptah decided that it was high time that Piankoff and Richards meet the young Overseer of the Granary, the scribe Horemheb. For reasons that he did not explain, Piankoff begged off, wishing no disrespect, saying that he had to attend to some matters that simply could not wait. Richards was then left alone with Meryptah to meet this future general-of-the-army, this future pharaoh who would restore Thebes to its former glory, who would provide the linkage between the Eighteenth and Nineteenth Dynasties, and then some.

As before, it was a short walk from the gate of Meryptah's household to the awning office of the overseer. For Richards, the taste of *déjà vu* was quite apparent. This time, however, the overseer was not to be found sitting before his portable desk, but evidence of his presence was, for several scrolls and a rough ledger were waiting for his return with several rocks anchoring them in place to foil the sometimes mischievous playfulness of the breeze. So the pair began to wander around and among the large, whitewashed, beehive-shaped granaries in search of their caretaker.

They had not gone far before they heard someone high above them swearing softly, but vehemently. There, perched atop the peak of one of the granaries, Richards was the first to spot a muscularly built man of about his size and proportions. Unlike himself, however, he wore the formal black plaited wig of a bureaucrat. Unlike a bureaucrat, he was getting his hands dirty for he was struggling with a quill, a potsherd for taking notes, the granary's cap stone, and a long measuring stick, not to mention all the while trying to maintain his precarious balance. Richards, forgetting himself, climbed up to the other's position and said to one very surprised face, "Excuse me Noble One, but may I be of some assistance?"

A first startled, the silent face just handed over to Richards the twenty pound or so granary cap. Then, fixed on his task, the man plumbed the granary with the measuring stick, noted the measure indicated, and with the stick still in the silo, quickly and expertly wrote down a cipher on the potsherd. When he was finished, he stuck the quill between his teeth, stuffed the potsherd into the waistband of his kilt and pulled out the stick, after which Richards carefully aligned and then gently dropped the granary's capstone into place.

With his sole-free hand, the bureaucrat removed the wooden quill from his teeth and said, "Well priest, you arrived just in time, for I was just about to either give up or fall off of this accursed magazine! Thank you for your help. I am Horemheb, the overseer of these magazines."

"And I am Mayneken. I wish to thank you as well, for you have been just to my good friend Meryptah."

At that point, Meryptah, not one to miss a good conversation, called up to the two men who were squatting so precariously atop the silo.

"Mayneken, would you please climb down so that I may properly introduce you to the Overseer of the Granaries!"

Richards then whispered quietly under his breath. "You will excuse my venerable friend. He is used to giving orders."

To that shared secret, Horemheb could only chuckle as they both worked their way down to ground level, to where Meryptah proudly stood with his walking stick in his left hand. With Richards in the lead, the overseer then got an eyeful of this helpful priest's well-muscled back and the four long scars that adorned it. Once back on the ground, Richards moved to the old priest's right side, standing slightly behind him out of respect and deference. Now on the ground, Horemheb approached the pair and courteously bowed his head to the old one, offering the traditional respectful greeting of the young to their elders.

"Long life, noble Meryptah."

Then rising to his full height at even eye-level with Richards, he added. "And again, many thanks dear priest."

The old priest then turned slightly to his right and indicated with his right stump in Richards' direction.

"Thank you most noble Overseer Horemheb. Now I wish to introduce you to a remarkable man, warrior, and priest, Mayneken."

Richards produced a curt bow toward the bureaucrat.

"Overseer Horemheb, why were you scampering so atop the granary like Thoth's own baboon with quill in hand?"

Ignoring this witty pun that linked that god of learning and writing with his sometime animal familiar, the overseer responded with a good-natured smile.

"I do not trust my assistant's measurements. In fact, I just may have him examined, and examined severely, for the levels of all of these granaries are much lowered than he reports."

Richards then piped in.

"Noble One, if you need assistance, I would be happy to do so. We, together, could plumb all these silos within moments, I would imagine."

"Thank you, Mayneken, but that will not be necessary, for when my assistant arrives, whenever he arrives, I will have him measure this one here. That should be all I need to discover whether he has been truthful with my accounts or not. After all, one does not have to empty the entire Nile to discover that there are fish in it."

"Most wise," Meryptah added.

"And clever," smirked Richards.

"You really think so?" asked the grinning younger Horemheb.

"Deviously so," Richards embroidered.

Pleased with himself, the young overseer, now even more curious about his early morning visitors, decided to invite them over to his awning "office." He offered his campstool the elderly priest, who graciously accepted it.

"Now Meryptah," the overseer began, "are you receiving your royal allotments on time and in the proper amounts as was decreed by the Master of the Two Lands?"

"Yes, Noble One. I am most thankful."

"Ah, good then."

"As for you, Mayneken, a most interesting name for a priest, especially one so magnificently and nobly scarred, what is it that you require? For I see that you appear nowhere in my accounts."

Before Richards could reply to Horemheb's question, a rather tall, willowy, and lean Egyptian arrived at the overseer's awning. At seeing him, Horemheb's voice whispered a gentle morning greeting to his late-arriving assistant, which was followed with his request for the third granary to be measured. With a sullen attitude, the assistant snatched up the measuring stick, and stormed off stamping his feet, raising clouds of dust, and muttering under his breath something indistinct.

"It would appear Horemheb that you have a morale problem," quipped Meryptah.

"Indeed. He is the spoiled son of a palace official, who resides at that place to the north. This one has no notion of what real work is, or for that matter, any sense of what the truth is. Truly, he is just a nagging thorn in my side that I cannot reach to pluck out.

"Enough of my problems, where was I? Ah yes, as to you Mayneken, why are you not on my granary accounts?"

A young, bright, and quick mind. An honest bureaucrat, now isn't that an oxymoron, Richards thought. *Who cannot be sidetracked, and who has already hinted before two complete strangers his religious affiliation. Guts and conviction. I like him already!*

"Noble Horemheb, I am a visitor from the north, the far north. My household resides in Memphis."

At first the mention of the word north raised the overseer's eyebrows in alarm, but Memphis managed to sufficiently calm them down again.

At this point in the conversation, the assistant returned and boorishly stood between Horemheb and Mayneken, and ignored the sitting old priest as well. He then delivered his measurement directly to Horemheb, who responded with a gentle voice.

"Are you sure of that measure, dear assistant Sekemkhet?"

"Absolutely! Do you dare question the word of a royal official's son?"

Upon hearing the words of this snot-nosed "kid," Richards just couldn't keep his mouth shut.

"Well, if I were the Overseer of the Granary, I surely would. After all, just how intelligent can the son of a royal fan-bearer be, anyway?"

Whirling around and staring down at Richards with true rage in his eyes, Sekemkhet cursed.

"On your knees *wab*-priest, so that I might teach you a lesson!"

"Why? What can the son of a fan-bearer begin to teach me?"

At that verbal needle, Sekemkhet swung broadly with his right arm to strike Richards across the side of the head. The problem was he missed, for the priest had moved. To add salt to the injury, the momentum of the errant swing was caused Sekemkhet to stagger to his left. There a deftly placed foot and a gentle shove placed the enraged teenager sprawled out on his face. Stunned at his fall, Sekemkhet quickly got up covered in dust. As he prepared to spring at Richards, a soothing, but commanding voice froze him in place.

"Enough, Sekemkhet! I have had enough of your behavior, your lateness, your insolent disrespect of your betters, your falsehoods, and your total ignorance of Maat! Mayneken is correct. You are not even fit to be the assistant of a granary overseer!"

Flushed now more in surprise than anger at Horemheb's strong words, Sekemkhet's lower lip began to tremble, his outstretched arms pleading, "What is this Horemheb? What have these, these priests done to your mind? What dark magic have they seduced you with?"

Then his words took on a more threatening aspect.

"Furthermore, how dare you speak to me in such a tone? With such words! My father will have you caned for such impudence!"

Horemheb, a full head plus shorter than Sekemkhet, walked over and stood looking straight up into the sneering face and said with a voice velvet soft.

"No, my dear Sekemkhet, it is you who will be examined today with the cane, for the measurement you just gave me is wildly incorrect, as are all the others that you have so dutifully reported to me. Before I call my Nubian Medjay, now would be a good time to truthfully tell me what is in your heart, and why all the granaries volumes are so low."

Aghast, and with a face rapidly turning as pale as a priest's kilt, Sekemkhet could only sputter out scarcely believable denials, excuses, even that mice were the problem, and such like.

Then, seeing that his excuses were falling on deaf ears, he tried to run. Within twenty feet of the felon's jack-rabbit start, Richards delivered a devastating tackle that would have made the Chicago Bear, Doug Plank, proud. As the youth continued to struggle to get away, Richards had no choice but to kneel on his back, bending the teenager's arm behind him. As he did so, Mayneken whispered into Sekemkhet's right ear.

"*Wab*-priest eh? You scum of a latrine! I will make sure that you never say that again to a second servant and *sem*-priest of the god Ptah!"

Then Meryptah, seeing what Mayneken was up to, croaked out in fear.

"Take care of your strength, Mayneken. Don't harm the boy!"

Now so subdued, Horemheb, taking notice of Meryptah's sharp words of concern, casually walked over and squatted down before the now prone, heavily sweating, and dust-caked face of the youth.

With a voice now as serious as a heart attack, he quietly asked, "Now Sekemkhet. I will ask you one more time. What has been happening to my grain?"

For whatever reason, the strong-willed man-child refused to speak. Faced with this silence, Horemheb now spoke with the words of judgment.

"Sekemkhet, you now leave me with no other choice."

With that courtesy rejected, Horemheb's bandy legs raised him from his squat and he let out a loud call to his Nubian Medjay, who dutifully appeared moments later. Three warriors of massive proportions, Richards noted.

The first to arrive at Horemheb's side queried in confusion.

"Master Overseer of the Granaries, what has occurred here? Why is that priest sitting on your noble assistant Sekemkhet?"

"Pahesy, that dusty jackal upon which that noble priest is sitting is no longer my assistant. In fact, I want you to carefully examine him, beat him like a papyrus reed if you have to, for I believe him to be a thief, and a very big thief. Find out what he has done with my grain. Have a scribe handy as well, for I suspect this jackal is only one of an entire pack."

Sekemkhet was forthwith dragged away, crying and pleading all the way. As for Horemheb, he just looked away and focused squarely upon the now dusty figure, which stood obediently before him.

Just who is this priest, who so casually wears such scars? Who possesses such quickness, such strength, such a cunning mind and tongue? Who speaks his mind as if it were my very own? I like him. But first I must test him.

"Mayneken, do you know what could happen to you once Sekemkhet's father hears what you have done to his son?"

Brushing away the dirt and dust from his eyes, arms, and chest, Richards answered, "Well, I suppose that I do not. But if I were Sekemkhet's father, I would be far more concerned about the consequences of my son's affairs."

Such a frank and honest answer, but also a brave and wise one as well. I like him even more.

Now turning his attention upon Meryptah, the overseer said, "Venerable one, I can now see that I have much to learn from you and from your friend. I sorely need an advisor, someone with a lifetime of experience. Therefore, it is my wish that you are to become a permanent guest within my household. You may hold that place of honor until whenever you wish to leave."

At the sound of these words, true tears of joy began to run down Meryptah's weathered cheeks and his chin trembled with happiness, for Horemheb had just answered a silent prayer of the old priest's. To be so old and unneeded, to be filled with the wisdom that only a full life's experience can bring, and not to be able to share that wisdom with someone of substance, that was the old priest's greatest and last prayer to the Great God. He realized that Mayneken had made that possible. In a truly contrite and humble voice, the former high priest of the Amen Re whispered, "Noble Prince Horemheb, I would be most honored to reside within the walls of your household. What would be my duties, my function?"

Prince? Richards thought. *I didn't know that he was a prince, too!*

"Venerable one, that is a very easy question, for I want you to be none other than my eyes and ears. Never again will you want. Never again will you be in need. I will simply not allow such to again happen to the first servant of the Great God!"

With a bowed head, a sudden, sobbing intake of breath was heard from the old priest.

"As for you, Mayneken," Horemheb continued, "Please consider my household yours as well. In fact, both of you go, now. Clean up from all that dust that you have just wallowed in. Meanwhile, I will alert my household's steward, Meryptah, so that he may bring to you anything needful from your household."

"Now go you two, I have work to do. We will speak again at this evening's meal."

*　　*　　*

While Richards and Meryptah were in the process of ingratiating themselves with Prince Horemheb and his household, Piankoff was busy as well. Before the Russian could arrange passage to Akhetaten, he required the wherewithal to do so. So unknown to Richards, Piankoff possessed what can be best described as a private stash. This little nest egg of highly portable wealth he had managed to squirrel away during his first solo adventures. In actual fact, he had several of them. This tactic of KGB field craft fell under the rubric of something euphemistically called insurance. Whereas Richards witlessly had to depend upon the surprise generosity and foresight of Meryptah, Piankoff had long ago made sure that he was independent of the need or the ties that financial assistance might bring.

Sure enough, there it was intact and unmolested. The "there" was in the foothills of Western Thebes, far beyond the limits of the cultivation, in an area that modern travelers would come to call Deir el-Bahri. There in the cliffs, Piankoff slithered his narrow frame into a crevasse, which surprisingly opened up the deeper one burrowed into it. Deep within, Piankoff had secreted away his emergency funds beneath a heavy rock. Casually picking up and flicking away a noisome black scorpion and taking only what he believed that they would require, the wily Russian methodically removed all trace of his presence. While doing so he thought, *Before today, I never would have thought a bank ATM was so convenient!*

It was almost a full hour before he again reached the Nile, which at this time of year was at its very lowest, meaning that the river's slow and steady rise was less than two weeks away. The sun was almost at its height and after the long walk out and back, Piankoff, now very thirsty, was about to make a serious mistake.

What Piankoff had not at first recognized were the early symptoms. Leaving Thebes in a rush, he had not taken the time to stop and drink his fill. By the time he was half way to his cache, his thirst was noticeable. Upon entering the shade of the crevasse, he had felt chilled by it. Upon exiting once again into the mid-day sun, its heat and glare almost stunned him to his knees. Then the sweating stopped, his heartbeat raced, the chills returned, and his joints had begun to ache. All movement had taken on a surreal, dreamlike quality. Piankoff, belatedly, realized that he was in serious trouble.

So by the time he espied the farmer's well, he had only one semi-delirious thought in his mind—water. At once he drew a reed bucket of the clear water, and drank deeply. Little did the Russian realize, however, that the well was infested with a hateful microscopic river parasite called a *schistosome*, an endemic vector that could eventually perforate his intestines if left untreated. At this single, solitary moment in time, all that he knew was that his thirst had been quenched and his stomach was full. He could now push on and arrange for Richards' and his passage north the next morning. After all, that was all that really mattered.

*　*　*

When Piankoff returned from his errands, he found Richards waiting for him freshly bathed and shaved, sitting on the top stair that led into Meryptah's household. Imagining what he himself must have looked like after his morning's labors and near dehydration, the Russian was not prepared for the almost smug grin on the American's face. So he decided to find out.

"Well Mayneken, you surely look the part of a proper priest who bathes three times daily."

Sitting himself down next to this partner, he queried softly, "And how successful were you today?"

"Beyond imagination, my dear Piankhotep, in fact, I have been waiting here to lead you to Prince Horemheb's own household, where we are his guests for the evening."

Registering the surprised shock on the Russian's face, Richards then continued.

"The very best part of this tale is that the prince has today adopted Meryptah, moved him lock, stock, and barrel into his household, and has tasked him with being his personal advisor. If that were not enough to curl your non-existent hair, then listen to this. The prince is a conservative, closet polytheist, who absolutely despises the present state of the Egyptian affairs."

Piankoff's only comment before allowing himself to be led off was.

"Well Mayneken, I can see that you have everything well in hand."

*　*　*

By the time Piankoff had properly dusted his feet, the evening meal was about to commence. But not so soon that Richards could not go into what he privately called his recording mode. For this ability, he had already thanked Doc Allen, for Allen's deep hypnotic implant had allowed the young Egyptologist to visually perceive, and later remember with practically digital recall, whatever had stimulated his optical nerves.

As Richards exercised this talent, he found that if he ran his eyes over an object as if in a slow video pan, then his memory of that object improved considerably. An unintended residual byproduct of this implant was improved hearing memory as well. To Richards, when he concentrated, the words of a conversation seemed to hang in the air just waiting to be recorded by his visual receptors. Doc Allen had been the first to point out this possibility to him and Richards had never forgotten his words of pure horse sense.

"Joey, my boy, you know better than I that language is like a muscle. The more you exercise it the better it becomes. But guess what? Your brain's memory banks are the same. Focus in on something and try to memorize it on the spot. Be it a word, a conversation, or an object. Then repeat the focusing and create in your mind a three-dimensional image. Then it will stick real good!"

So at first seeing the grounds and rambling household of the prince, Richards had unconsciously gone into recording mode. The first impression that he noted was truly how modest in comparison the dwelling of Meryptah's had been. His second, how on the mark the domestic house plans of the architect and Egyptologist Alexander Badawy truly were. For Horemheb's household was fully four if not five times larger in total area, with a grand colonnaded entrance, massive multi-roomed household, and two separate annexes that he could see, but whose function he could only guess at. If that were not sufficient, four private, whitewashed, conical granary magazines stood in a row along the eastern side of the plot. And this is the house of a prince. *God only knows how extensive his holdings are in cultivated land that supported this dwelling and its household.*

Then it was time for dinner and much as with their first dinner with Meryptah, Horemheb's dinner guests sat on the cool paving of the floor with cushions made available for extra comfort. He arranged his guests according to whim around a low, long, and narrow wooden serving table that afforded easy access to all that was prepared.

420

As for the meal itself and its presentation, well to Richards, it was simply a sumptuous delight for his eyes and nose. Fresh sweet breads, dried dates, cheeses of various kinds, fruits, honey, cooked and spiced pigeon, duck, and quail. All designed to be washed down with either the wine or beer that was produced by the household's own servants. Not to be overlooked was the fragrance of the flower arrangements, predominantly lotus of various shades of white and blue along with several other delicate blooms that Richards did not recognize, but carefully recorded nonetheless.

It was a dizzying blur on his senses. The smells especially dominated as the cooked food, flowers, and scented cedar oils from Minoan oil lamps assaulted his nose. The sights were no less so. However, for as shiny and clean Richards and Piankoff were, so was Meryptah, who had made a terrific transformation. Then there was their host, Horemheb, shiny clean in his kilt, wearing a freshly brushed out wig, and a broad and magnificent pectoral necklace of gold, red garnets, and stunning blue-green lapis lazuli that flowed across the creases of his well-muscled chest. The host's eyes gave him away, however, for they danced with a mixture of excitement at the presence of such distinguished guests at his humble table.

For Horemheb, this was as close to a black-tie dinner gathering as this provincial village had seen in years, so he decided to begin it properly. After everyone, meaning the three priests, had been comfortably seated, he rose up on his knees with a finely-turned ceramic champagne goblet in his hand and toasted to his guests, each in turn, and then made some fitting and pious remarks directly to his new-found mentor, Meryptah.

Richards noted. *Without doubt that goblet is an imported Mycenaean* kylix *from the Greek mainland. This young prince is surely putting on the dog tonight!*

The fine words said and polite replies made, they all began to seriously dig in and plunder the table. When it came time to choose liquid refreshment, Richards decided this time to sample the household's wine, especially since that was what the host was drinking. Richards, not a wine man by any count, found it to be simply a delight with a honey to pinkish color, a very aromatic and spicy bouquet, some bubbles of carbonation, and a rich, clear, and refreshing taste that reminded him somewhat of Cuban sangria.

This stuff just begs to be chugged in mass quantities! I'm such a barbarian!

As for Piankoff and Meryptah, they were heartily enjoying the household's beer, which from what Richards could tell looked and smelled like a fine wheat beer.

And who said that the Germans had the lock on a good Weissbier!

As with any dinner of this sort, an inevitable biological moment of truth finally arrives. Blessedly, Meryptah offered it with a grand and sustained belch, which in the process earned him the everlasting gratitude of Piankoff and Richards, who were clearly in dire need, if not pain, to do so as well. This act earned a glowing, proud smile of satisfaction from Horemheb and brought a funny revelation to Richards.

What a pun! These clever Egyptians' word for wine is written irp, *but is sounded "uurp," as in "burp." That Egyptologist was absolutely right when he wrote that the word is "perhaps derived from the onomatopoeic response to drinking too much or too quickly."*

As the cups were filled, and refilled, and refilled again by the host's attentive and attractive household servants, a discussion naturally enough began. To Richards, it reminded him of an extremely high-level corporate dinner winding down. All that was missing were the cigars. Now it was time to discuss business, and, appropriately, Horemheb, as the host, launched it.

"Noble Piankhotep, Meryptah speaks very highly of you and your assistant Mayneken. I do not wish to be rude, but I am nonetheless a curious provincial, what brings you to Thebes?"

Piankoff, noting his host's self-effacing approach, answered directly.

"Prince Horemheb, as a native of distant Memphis, I have known of you and your noble family for quite some time. The opportunity to share your table is for me and my assistant, a distinct honor and one that will not be forgotten.

"As for why we are in Thebes, we came to do honor to noble Meryptah. We had been abroad for so long that we had frankly feared that this noble priest had already gone West. It brought great happiness to our hearts when we found that this was not so.

"But as for Thebes being a provincial village, instead of what it once was, the first city of a vast empire, it is my belief and hope, as I know that it is of my assistant, that that situation will...in due course...change. In time we wish Thebes to be restored and exceed tenfold its former grandeur."

The table was silent for several moments while all concerned fully digested the implications of what Piankoff had just uttered. Again, the host chose to begin.

"Those are strong words priest, strong and potentially dangerous words if they were heard by the wrong ears."

As Horemheb spoke he cocked his head in the direction of where the servants' galley and the nearby kitchen were located. In one motion, he stood, walked off into that direction, and shooed away the servants for the rest of the evening. Returning, he sat down, and continued.

"Ah, that's better. Now we can speak more freely. As I was saying, strong words, but words that I would expect from a priest of a priesthood that has suffered as greatly as yours. Noble Meryptah, do you have a position on this subject?"

Repositioning his old bones on his cushion, the old priest quietly spoke.

"In truth, such a thing has always been on my lips in prayer to my Great God."

"And you, Mayneken, truly in my eyes more warrior than priest, but priest nonetheless. What does your heart say regarding this matter?"

Looking Horemheb straight in the eye, Richards replied, "Noble prince, have you recently seen what the rabble have done to the once most magnificent temple of Egypt? I am sure that you have. Have you not seen those who have done nothing about it? I am sure that you have. Personally, the entire situation makes my stomach sick. Even more, I care for Egypt. At this dark moment, Egypt is rudderless."

"A most interesting answer from a most interesting priest," the prince replied, deep in thought, now sure of his audience.

Another silence, then Meryptah chose to speak.

"Noble prince, if I may make an observation. Egypt presently is suffering from a sickness that requires a cure that only the Goddess

Maat can provide. To the north, in that accursed city, the unspeakable one uses food, beer, and simple children's toys and tricks to control the mob like a farmer who leads an ox."

With a confused look on his face, Horemheb asked, "What do you mean noble Meryptah, by simple tricks and toys?"

"My prince, in a secret place deep within the Great God's temple, one can find materials that can allow a man to soar far into the heavens. I believe that the unspeakable one is using just such tricks to control and cow his people."

The shock on Horemheb's face, and for that matter on Piankoff's and Richards, was just too great at hearing such news. His face flushed red and in an angry voice hoarsely said, "Meryptah, do you take me for a child to believe such nonsense! I will not . . ."

Raising his left hand for silence, the old priest quietly, but very firmly interrupted.

"Noble prince, I know that what I have just said sounds like childish nonsense, if not an utter falsehood. But it is nonetheless true, for I myself, in my youth, with a strong body much as you possess, many times sailed on the hot rivers of wind that flow over the western desert. As a young child, do you not remember the appearance of the divine Horus as he circled the Osiris Nebmare Amenhotep seven times while he was journeying to the West?"

To the question, the old priest received a wide-eyed, nodding response to that old and deeply cherished childhood memory.

"My prince, on that very day I was standing with several of my priesthood atop the cliffs that overlook the mortuary temples of the beloved Osiris Makare Hatshepsut, the long dead Osiris Nebhepetre Mentuhotep, and that of the Osiris Menkheperre Thutmose. Do you know the place from which I speak?"

Again a nodding response.

"My prince, from that lofty platform one of my acolytes, a very brave and daring one, flew out over the funerary procession and circled it seven times. Afterward, he turned and then flew over the great mountain of the West and disappeared. Did he not?"

Again a nodding response, but now with an ashen face.

"My prince, with your permission, tomorrow we will go to the temple and I will show you the means by which a man can be made to fly."

Just as stunned as their host, both Piankoff and Richards stared at one another. Richards then said quietly.

"So you only showed him how to build a glider model?"

"Mayneken, I had no idea . . ."

Interrupting the pair's private conversation, the prince then asked, "So, Meryptah, you believe that the unspeakable one is using flying men to make the Aten appear over his accursed temple?"

"In a word, yes. Consider my prince, how near the cliffs of the mountains are to that city. As a young man, it would have been an easy glide away."

With heat, the future pharaoh blurted out, "That trickster, that charlatan!"

"Careful my prince," Piankoff whispered, "He is far, far more than that, and Meryptah and I can stand witness to the fact that he and his children, at least those that still survive, can enter your mind and read it like a papyrus scroll. If you doubt my words and my painful experience with the unspeakable one, you have but to ask Meryptah, who had dared to raise his anger and the dreadful price that he had paid for it."

Then Meryptah added this chilling tidbit of gossip.

"My prince, I believe that it is important for you to recognize that the despicable one has committed the same or similar acts upon his own Queen and Great Wife Nefertiti. It has been reported that her absence from the royal apartments and palace since the fourteenth year of his reign is attributed to his angry words toward her. It is also rumored that she, in the wretched condition that he left her, has since resided in the northern portion of the city."

Now fully sober, what had begun as a pleasant evening meal with distinguished guests, had now turned into a living nightmare for the young prince.

What am I to believe? Surely these men cannot all be mad! Can all of this be true? And if it is, what can I do to save Egypt from it?

*   *   *

The next morning, true to his word, Meryptah led the prince and the two other priests into the labyrinthine corridors of the Great God's own temple complex. Moving with confidence and purpose, the old priest took no circuitous routes and took no wrong turns. Having entered directly through the main western pylon that today is now referred to as the Third Pylon of Amenhotep III, they proceeded straight into the depths of the complex.

When they arrived at what we moderns now refer to as the Fourth Pylon of the Pharaoh Thutmose I, upon passing through it they made a left turn. Walking between the niches carved of pure Tura limestone to their left, and the shrine and obelisk of the Pharaoh Thutmose III and massive sixteen papyriform columns to their right, they continued on until they reached a narrow passageway in the northeast corner of the hall. There, they stopped and all four lit their oil lamps. Continuing on through the passageway, they finally entered a long and narrow offering chamber, the goal of their excursion.

Now within the chamber, the old priest handed his lamp to Richards and then turned to face its long left-hand wall that was from floor to ceiling covered with the pious prayers of Pharaoh Thutmose I to his divine father, Amen Re.

Richards observed.

The pristine condition of these inscriptions is just breathtaking, that is if one can overlook all the systematically hacked out instances of Amen's name by the agents of the fanatical Aten cult!

For all appearances, to Richards and the others, the wall that the priest now faced was one continuous wall of beautifully fitted Tura limestone blocks finely cut and exquisitely painted in raised relief. Even the flickering of the oil lamps' flames across their shapes seemed to bring them to life.

Then the old one stepped forward, reached out with his good left hand and pushed mightily against a portion of the wall, which then with a soft grating sigh quietly pivoted inwards! Standing before a pitch dark gap in the wall's inscriptions, about five feet by five feet, the old priest recovered his lamp from an incredulous Richards, motioned all to follow, and disappeared into the darkness. Richards, following on the old priest's heels, thought.

I wonder if this clever architectural feature is still functional back home? If so, I'll bet that the French have been working around it for years and still don't know that it even exists!

Stopping some fifty paces into the secret passage, Meryptah turned, pushed against a stone to his left and the passage closed behind the party with a mild thump, sealing them in. Now raising his lamp above his head, the rest doing likewise, it became apparent that this portion of the Fourth Pylon was hollow. Richards noting the roughness of the pylon's inner core, surmised it as being constructed of sandstone. As to the height of this chamber, he couldn't even guess for its roof was lost somewhere in the gloom above.

Then Meryptah announced, "Dear friends, this passage is known to only a few at any one time. No stranger knows of its contents, its hidden entrances, or exits. Presently, only you know of its existence. Its secret must be maintained. Do you now swear before the Great God to your silence?"

All murmured and nodded in assent.

"Good, for if you had not, we would have all died in this very place. Now, follow me, and be mindful of where you step!"

To Richards' continued amazement, this hollow portion of the pylon was only the beginning. It really was only the entrance to a smoothly walled and sloped passageway some eight feet high and about the same wide. Clearly they were about to descend below the very foundation stones of the pylon and temple complex itself. Looking down, Richards noted that the smooth slope of this descending passageway was a broad ramp next to which were cut regular, but narrow stair steps.

Richards thought. *Where have I seen this combination of steps and ramping before? Yes, in the Great Pyramid's Grand Gallery and again before Seti I's mortuary temple at Abydos! I bet that this passage can accommodate the dragging of really heavy objects!*

As they began to descend, Richards' nose told him that the air was fast becoming stuffy and stale. After slowly working their way down some seventy to eighty steps, they arrived at a landing where all were temporarily blinded by the light of a torch that Meryptah had just set afire.

"Ah, that is better. It is difficult enough for me to see with only one good eye."

Meryptah then continued on with torch in hand along a smooth sided horizontal tunnel of the same dimensions as the descending passage. It then became apparent to Richards from the torch's shadows that this tunnel was actually a central corridor with many adjoining rooms or passageways that led off in all directions. Finally, at a point that only the old priest understood, he stopped, turned around, and announced for Horemheb's benefit.

"My prince, you are probably wondering what is contained within all of these side chambers. I will tell you, the entire treasury of the Great God Amen Re. Before those animals began their plunder and desecration of the temples, I and a handful of selected priests of the second and third rank removed all of value from the temple above. We carefully secreted it all down here, in the Great God's treasury below. We worked only during the darkest hours of the night. It took us one full month to complete our labors. We even preserved the golden statue of the Great God himself, for that was the last to be so hidden. The sudden absence of the Great God's golden image and the rest of the temple's treasures was blamed upon the plundering instincts of the godless ones. When you, great prince, restore the goodly name of Amen Re among the gods and refurbish his temple, now you will know from where to begin."

This statement of responsibility and near-prophecy the young Horemheb proudly bore, even if he was flabbergasted by Meryptah's bold announcement of it. Then continuing, the old priest said, gesturing to the passage on his right.

"As I have said, contained within this chamber are the means by which men can soar in the sky with falcons."

Entering the indicated side chamber with his torch held high, Richards' breath, and for that matter the others as well, stopped. All was silence and wonder, for there in the center of the room, lying as if on display on a light portable framework of sorts, was the narrow and aerodynamic fuselage and tail of a glider. Off to the side, was similarly laid out with care its single, detachable, lifting surface painted as outstretched wings. Off to the other side were arranged a series of leather harnesses and belts and a shockingly authentic, gold and green hawk-headed helmet. While Piankoff and Richards fully understood what they saw, Horemheb did not and said so, demanding an explanation. Meryptah, with an obvious mixture of pride and patience, proceeded to do so.

"As with so very many things, my prince, it is all really quite simple."

While holding court on such topics as aerodynamics, thermals, lift, and the like, the old priest and his folksy analogies proved to be right on the money. It was clear that Horemheb quickly understood, from the questions that he then posed. To Richards, listening to the two of them discuss this design feature, the pilot's harnesses, and above all the hawk helmet itself, was a real treat. He could detect a feeling of regret on the part of the prince, who really wanted to try it all himself, and sadness as the glider was in pieces. Fortunately, Meryptah was extremely firm with the prince indicating the many dangers involved and even dared to point out where his true responsibilities and destiny lay. Then, suddenly realizing that two others were with them, Meryptah asked.

"And do you two have any questions? For I am sure that you have many."

Richards decided to field this one, much to Piankoff's sudden relief.

"Just one, noble Meryptah, you have explained how to soar, but how does one land?"

"Ah, Mayneken, you have put your finger upon the most difficult part of this sport of the gods. In fact, my own body is covered with many such scars from poorly performed landings. At best, and after many experiments, one should approach the earth quickly, and then at the last minute attempt to climb back into the sky. For a brief moment, the hawk frame will slow. At that point, attempt to stop yourself with your feet."

He has just described an induced stall!

Hearing no more questions from his small audience, the old priest then wordlessly began to lead them out. On the way, Richards asked, "Noble Meryptah, before we descended into this passage you said to be mindful of where we stepped. What did you mean by this warning?"

Stopping in the middle of the corridor, the old priest slowly turned around to face his charges and said, "Mayneken. Not all of the entrances to these chambers are as safe as the one I just showed you. In fact, fully two-thirds are protected with a false plaster flooring that will collapse under a man's weight."

Horemheb then asked the question that had to be asked.

"But noble priest, what does the false flooring cover?"

"Pit shafts twenty cubits deep," replied Meryptah. "Pits cut into the bedrock with smoothed walls. Pits deep enough to trap a man. Pits deep enough to break legs, arms, or worse."

And with that said, the old priest turned and continued on.

Eventually they again arrived to the darkened offering chamber of Thutmose I and upon reaching above ground, Richards silently kicked himself for not having noticing how Meryptah had reopened the secret passageway. But glancing back quickly to Piankoff, and seeing his knowing smile, he knew that the wily Russian had not missed that seminal detail.

As for Prince Horemheb, he was silent all the way back to his household, no doubt deep in thought, for he had just been given a cram course not only in aerodynamics, but also in kingly responsibility as well. The prince now knew, better than anyone else, what his true destiny would become. At this evening's meal, Piankoff and Richards wanted to make sure that he did.

CHAPTER LVII
The Progress Report

Sitting before him was the precisely written and bulleted calligraphy of Dr. Richards, written on a freshly minted sheet of ancient papyrus. As had become a sort of tradition, next to the papyrus sat its historically precious throw weight, yet another good sized faience scarab for Dr. Milson to translate, another item to enter into the catalog of the Near Eastern Institute's cultural treasures.

I just love the smell of this stuff, Borov thought. *It so reminded him of his boyhood days on the farm in the Ukraine.*

Day One:

Arrived intact. Meryptah is still alive and has helped immensely – yet again.

Have met and convinced Horemheb of his destiny and responsibilities. Have no doubt that he will carry through.

Have discovered that the Egyptians have developed a sophisticated hang glider technology. They use it for religious propaganda purposes.

Meryptah toured us through a secret, underground treasury beneath the Karnak temple.

Tomorrow we journey 1 1/2 days by boat to Akhetaten. Return should be 3. Time needed there, perhaps as many as 4 or 5 days.

Recovery at Thebes: be prepared to do so from Day 6 onward – at the usual time.

As was his habit, Borov read, and reread the report, and then reread it again for his eyes still could not believe what he had just read the first two times.

Tuna Cartwright was correct again to send the boys, as he so colorfully put it, to hand deliver this package.

*　*　*

Three days later, Milson received the package from Borov and instantly felt that it was Christmas all over again with yet another mystery scarab to translate. Feeling better than he had in recent years, once the package had reached his desk and almost before the fresh papyrus had perfumed his office, he was off to the basement conservatory room with the scarab in hand for some serious work.

Again, as was Milson's habit, the hour was late. Only the Near Eastern Institute's highly cultured family of mice were awake to keep him company. Working in his favorite cotton gloves, over his favorite table, and under its glare-free lighting was a quiet joy for this old and experienced salt of Egypt's antiquities. He carefully took notes on the yellow legal pad at his right elbow.

Okay, let's see what we have here.

One large blue faience scarab, 11.6 centimeters long by 7.8 centimeters wide, let's make it Catalogue Number NEI 734203.

Beautifully formed and of the highest quality, most likely a royal commission, probably a commemorative of some type.

Turning the scarab over to expose its flat-sided base, he mused.

A full inscription, any royal cartouches?

Ah, yes, there is one, hmmm, looks like Neferneferu Nefertiti, Akhenaten's Chief Wife and Queen.

Okay.

So the date is late Eighteenth Dynasty.

Well that's not surprising given where they are now.

At this point, and out of sheer habit, Milson made three columns on his pad with his Number 2 pencil and began to record the six horizontal lines of hieroglyphic text in the far left-hand column and then immediately transliterated them into the Latin alphabet in the center column. The far right-hand column he again reserved for working out the translation itself.

Now let's see, what else do we have here? Well, the text looks like it reads . . . No! That can't be. Can it?

After a half an hour's time of mental gymnastics the meaning of the scarab was clear to Milson, absolutely clear.

Here is the victim

Neferneferu Nefertiti

Who has received the semen of

Him-who-is-in-his-grimness

May his testicles of Set

Be cut off!

If I am correct, Milson thought, *this is hardly a commemorative scarab. Rather, its purpose is more that of a curse than anything else. My guess is that Nefertiti is one, very angry lady at whomever Him-who-is-in-his-grimness may be. But don't deceive yourself, John. You know for a fact that she is talking about Akhenaten for sure.*

But this reference to the testicles of Set, although a traditional one, is new in this context. I just wonder what Richards would have to say about it? I must remember to ask him the next time I see him, when, and if, he returns.

CHAPTER LVIII
Death of a God

The passage to the new northern capital had been uneventful, except for Piankoff's uncommonly growling stomach. As for Richards, he just hoped that the return voyage would be equally free of critters as was this one. What did attract both Piankoff's and Richards' attention was the shrunken and gaunt look of the shallow Nile, the mud of its dried and cracked banks, and the burned out look to the valley during this time of the year. Both knew that the annual inundation would begin on or around the middle to the end of the month. Its occurrence would herald in the much-anticipated five days of New Year's festivities, the mudding of the valley, and the eventual coming of the planting season. It was about high noon as they rounded the final curve in the river from which the new capital could be seen along the right-bank.

Piankoff mentioned quietly under his breath to Richards, who was standing at the bow, how strange it was that the capital's quays, so filled with sailing craft of all sorts and descriptions, and its neighboring market place, looked so deserted. Richards speculated that he thought most of the town's people were at the Aten temple to partake in the daily ritual of beer, bread, and circuses.

Much to his surprise, Richards was right on, for only a few minutes later the pair could make out the arrival of a bright and shining object hovering off in the distance, an arrival that was greeted with the distant sounds of singing and trumpeting.

Richards was right! The Russian's mind screamed. *The Aten is a UFO!*

Before Piankoff could express his surprise to his colleague, others in the boat had also seen the appearance of the Aten disk, heard the nearing cacophony, and fell to their knees whispering the mantra.

"The Aten has appeared.

"The Aten has appeared.

"Grant me life.

"Grant me life eternal."

Seeing this, Piankoff and Richards wisely aped likewise.

By the time the boat had reached the quay, the Aten disk had disappeared and the singing and trumpeting had ended. That did not prevent several fervent individuals from sprinting from the docks toward the temple in the hope, no doubt, of scrounging any leftovers from the daily sacrifice. Piankoff, however, had another idea.

"Mayneken, let's purchase some fruit from the marketplace, fill our stomachs, and hopefully silence mine, find a bath, and then try to establish contact with a certain royal lady."

Richards nodded in approval.

Several hours later, with their bellies sated and bodies fresh and shiny, the pair began to stroll together along the shadows of the almost deserted main street of the city. Most were taking their afternoon siesta during the summer's heat of the day. It would be plain to anyone that whoever was out and about at this hour of the day had to be on some sort of necessary errand. Richards noticed that even the Nubian Medjay, as they passed through the central portion of the town that contained the royal apartments, palace, and Aten temple, were lying low.

As the silent pair made their way beyond the city's center, they entered a domestic neighborhood characterized by its packed and modestly built nature. It too was a ghost town at this time of day.

Then, Piankoff uncharacteristically found himself in distress as his bowels seemed to be in total revolt. Once relieved, they continued on. Ahead, there began to appear several structures to their left that suggested that they were nearing their goal, the northern portion of the city and its so-called Northern Palace. Modern archaeologists discovered that this collection of structures were decorated with lively depictions of bird-life within a papyrus swamp. It was also a place that possessed an aviary and zoo within its walls. It was here that Piankoff and Richards believed that the Chief Wife, the Lady of the Two Lands, Queen Nefertiti, had been sequestered since Year 14 of the pharaoh's reign. Truly he made her a golden bird within a gilded cage.

As they had neared the Northern Palace, they found themselves beyond the outlying suburbs of Akhetaten itself. They knew they were exposed. After all, two lone figures walking in the heat of the day and in this direction just had to have been noticed.

Walking boldly, the two priests stepped unopposed through the palace's main entrance that led directly to a broad courtyard with a small sun shrine to their left. Entering it, they recited the mantra that they had heard on the boat seven times. Finishing, they left the shrine, crossed the courtyard and approached the stairs of the palace's entrance porch.

While climbing its stone steps, a rustling of movement was heard above them. Two solemn Nubian Medjay now stood just inside the shadows of the porch's entrance. The sheer width of their massive shoulders blocked all access.

Taking the lead, Piankoff, stopping atop the last step, announced with a strong voice, "Noble warriors! Announce to Queen Neferneferu Nefertiti that the noble priests Piankhotep and Mayneken have arrived true and faithful to her command!"

A bit taken aback by the strength and volume of the Russian's oratorical delivery, and after a brief glance at one another, one of the Medjay scurried away and into the shadows. Meanwhile the other repositioned himself in the center of the entranceway.

For the next five minutes all proudly held their ground in a dusty, hot, silence. Then, a light woman's voice was heard coming from the interior. To the pair it sounded like an argument. Then with a rush of noisily brushing linen a middle-aged maid servant appeared and squirmed her way around the Nubian as if he had become a black granite statue. Standing at the edge of the sun's glare and porch's shadow, with her head held high and looking down at them from the step above, she demanded, "Just who are you and what do you want?"

Again Piankoff trumpeted. "We are the noble priests Piankhotep and Mayneken. We are here at the Queen Neferneferu Nefertiti's specific request. We have journeyed far on her behalf. We are tired and thirsty. What more are you required to know?"

Again the Russian's authoritative tone took effect and the servant too scuttled off into the shadows of the palace.

Silence.

Five minutes passed.

Then Piankoff asked the Nubian directly.

"Noble warrior, do you know why our rightful entry is being so delayed?"

With a grunt of an apology a deep voice explained, "Because you are the queen's first visitors."

Piankoff and Richards then traded meaningful looks that summed up and confirmed all that they had heard. Yes, the queen was still alive. Yes, she was being held within the Northern Palace. Now the question in their minds was, "Will we be allowed to even see her?"

Another five minutes passed in silence.

And then another.

Then another women's voice was heard, one far stronger in spirit than the first, one that vehemently commanded that the priests be allowed entrance. As to whom she was arguing her point with, Piankoff and Richards could not tell, although it was clear that the Nubian's ears were picking something up from where he stood. With the approaching swishing sound of linen the strong feminine voice said, "Nebka! Stand aside!"

The Nubian then stiffly did so, and there stood Nefertiti, flushed red in anger and frustration, and in a flash she composed herself said with a small bow of the head, "Noble priests, please enter the shade of my household and accept my most heartfelt hospitality in partial payment for the rudeness of my keepers."

The Nubian, fractionally wincing at the queen's barb, stiffly stood erect as the two priests, now quite sweaty and covered with dust from their walk, entered gratefully into the relatively cooling twenty degree difference of the shaded entry. Rapidly passing through its lotus columns and into the palace suites themselves, the queen then quickly turned, inspected both of the priest's faces and said in a low voice.

"Excuse my impertinence, but do I know either of you?"

Again it was Piankoff to lead, and in a similarly quiet voice. "Why yes, my noble queen, the two of us had several meetings in the past regarding the, ah, gifted behavior of your children. I believe that you provided me with several, ah, samples from your husband for me to divine."

Although the reference of her gifted children clearly did not ring a bell, the mention of the samples certainly did for her eyes lit up and eyebrows arched in recognition.

"Ah, yes," she said quietly. "You were the seer with many observations and hints on how I might better manage my gifted children. Yes, I do remember you."

Looking to Richards, she asked. "That must mean that you are his assistant. Am I correct?"

Richards bowed his head in silent confirmation.

"Ah, hah, well then, welcome dear friends to my household. You are my guests until whenever you wish to leave. We have much to discuss, but not now, later during the evening meal."

Looking away, the queen called, "Kia? Where are you?"

Seemingly out of thin air the maidservant Kia appeared, the very same one that had so imperiously interrogated the pair on the porch, but this time with her head submissively bowed.

"Kia, these two priests are my good friends. They will dine with me, alone, at the evening meal. However, they require refreshment for they are parched and require their feet to be dusted. See to these things."

Off the maidservant went to make all the necessary preparations. Once she was out of earshot, the queen confided.

"Kia has been a good and faithful servant. A bit overprotective at times, but she means well and has a good heart. Unfortunately, my husband can also read her thoughts, the thoughts of my Medjay, and the rest of my household quite easily. And I expect that your journey here too did not go unnoticed, but enough of that. Now go, refresh yourselves. We will talk later."

*　　*　　*

Thoroughly refreshed and bathed, Piankoff and Richards presented themselves at the appointed hour as specified by the queen. In Richards' mind, these evening meals were just getting a little out of hand. In retrospect, that first meal with Meryptah had been a relaxed and modest affair. The spread that Horemheb had laid out was light-years beyond that. But this meal, so spontaneous in its preparation, was yet another leap into a totally new gustatory universe.

First of all, the dining area, two stories up, was open on two sides affording a breath-taking view of much of the Nile's northerly course and surrounding agricultural fields. A continuous breeze cooled the scene, while directly below were several well-tended flower garden pools, which perfumed the entire area with the heady scent of lotus.

One sat not on the finely smoothed limestone floor, but on low couch-like, padded furniture without any backs to lean back on. Made of fragrant, imported cedar wood and inlaid with costly ebony from Central Africa and beautifully carved ivory inlays, one was expected here to either sit or recline while dining.

The table itself was raised higher than usual to accommodate the raised seating and it was also constructed, no crafted, of cedar and decorated with ivory, ebony, gold foils, and semiprecious stones. Unfortunately most of this unique *object d' art* could not be seen, for it was covered from edge to edge with floral arrangements and a quantity and variety of foods that staggered the imagination. Try as he might, Richards' eyes were dazzled by the roasted quail, pigeon, and duck, the freshly cooked and smoked perch, and what looked like bullhead, the many daintily proportioned sweet breads, at least three cheeses, several different jars of honeys, other as yet unidentified spicy concoctions—probably sauces, dried dates, grapes, and several other items that simply defied description. In short, a typical, last minute, evening meal at the Northern Palace.

As for the liquid refreshments, Nefertiti's household offered no less than three different types of wine from the Delta, Kharga Oasis, and even as far away as Syria, and four of beer.

As what Piankoff and Richards understood as polite custom, the host began with a toast from a magnificent cup made of beaten silver—a very rare and royal material in a land awash in gold. Sitting regally with an erect back and proud voice she proclaimed, "May the gods again smile upon Egypt. May the temples that lay desolate be restored. May my guests enjoy their stay and have a happy return to their households. May He-who-is-in-his-grimness fall down dead this very day."

With this toast the queen drank deeply from her chalice of hate as did her two lone guests, who barely choked down their sipped libations out of politeness, prompting Piankoff to temporize.

"Noble Queen, those are very strong words. Should one speak so of the Master of the Two Lands before your guests, who in truth, you really do not know?"

"Noble Piankhotep, I am fully aware of what I have just said and he knows it as well. I begin every meal with that prayer of hope and salvation for Egypt."

Silence for a moment, and then Piankoff broke it.

"Noble Queen, when we first arrived, you said that you had much to tell us. You possess our ears."

So the dinner began. While the two field operatives ate and listened to the tale of an embittered wife, a rejected queen, and now that of an ignored, aging, and of an imprisoned royal toy waiting for the blessed release of death, either by her own or that of her husband. Either would do.

Richards was amazed to realize how much he had eaten given the recounted trials and horrors that were laid out before him by this once devastatingly beautiful, but still quite attractive, queen-mother of Egypt. Decisive and graceful, spirited and genteel, intelligent and full of hate, the queen had a great desire for revenge at what had been done to her. How she had been kept so cruelly apart from the rest of mankind for the past three years.

At this point, Piankoff surprised Richards when he asked the following question.

"Noble Queen, I do not wish to ask an improper question, but I must. It has to do with your two sons . . ."

With a smooth voice she said, "I have no sons."

"Then who, Great One, who was their mother?"

After a moments silence, Nefertiti answered.

"Piankhotep, that is a most fair question. They both were sons of the royal harem, both sired by him from two different—females."

The queen again took control of the conversation, such as it was, being more of a meandering monologue, a personal diatribe.

"I have a question for you, noble Piankhotep, why did you and your assistant come?"

"In all truth, noble Queen, we had heard many rumors and we wanted to find out for ourselves as to what the truth really was."

"Mere curiosity, then? Excuse me priest, but I am having difficulty believing that was your only consideration. But putting that issue aside for the moment, has your curiosity been quenched?"

"Yes, yes, it has Noble One. But you are absolutely correct in surmising another purpose. One of the rumors said that He had plundered your mind, leaving you injured. I ask you this personal question only because he had plundered—no raped, both the minds of the High Priest Meryptah and myself. From which, we both still have scars, some of the mind, some of the body."

Shocked at this news, the queen's trembling hand covered her mouth, which quietly released the moan of a tortured soul. She whispered, "You too? And, and the most noble and just Meryptah as well?"

A silent nod.

Tears now flowed freely across her cheeks. She stood up, crossed over to Piankoff's divan, sat, and embraced him. As she did so, she totally broke down in quiet and shaking sobs. After a few moments she calmed herself, stood, and returned to her place of honor. In a strange and detached monotone she again began.

"It is true. He did that hateful thing to me as well. For several months, as I am told by Kia, I was totally incoherent. I was as an infant. I could not feed myself. I soiled myself. I could not wash myself. It was then that He caused me to be moved here. Then, with Kia's care, she slowly taught me how to eat again, walk again, and take care of myself. She even taught me how to speak the words that I share with you. Kia, you see, truly is my second mother, my first being the noble woman Tuya, who bore me."

"Noble Piankhotep, how was it for you?"

With little need of embellishment, if anything that Richards could detect, the Russian told of his rifled memories, scrambled thoughts, and the re-education that he himself had also needed. At the end of which true tears of emotion had flooded his eyes.

Then the queen turned to Richards.

"And what of you, Mayneken? Have you also experienced this exquisite agony?"

"Blessedly no."

"Blessed indeed!"

A quiet, silent, several minutes then broke out as the queen began to graze the table. But her attention to the table was suddenly frozen in time by the slipping sounds of several approaching pairs of sandals that her delicate hearing had picked up. She then breathed and wrinkled her upper lip.

"He-who-is-in-his-grimness has come."

Surprised, but nonetheless long prepared, the pair of field operatives shared a quick, private look, a resigned nod for each other that psychically triggered their next series of actions, full knowing what they had to do within the next ten to fifteen seconds—come what may.

They then stood.

Vaguely out of Richards' peripheral vision he could tell that the queen had already become agitated, enraged, and was ready to strike at the least provocation. That distraction alone, if unleashed, would help immensely. For all the situations that he and his Russian colleague had so arduously choreographed on training mats, and had imagined in their minds, all required a distraction, which was precisely why they were standing at this moment, instead of groveling on the floor.

Doc Allen had been correct. The target was indeed a formidable and powerful, inline telepath, but one who relied on that devastating skill and power to a fault. What the target was not was a physically coordinated being. One quick observation had made that clear. Since he could not physically protect himself except with his mind, that explained his ever-present Nubian Medjay guards. The real question on Richards' mind was would there be a sufficient number of sideline distractions to allow just one of them close enough for a telling blow?

As the two household Medjay rounded the corner to the dining room with their Lord and God in tow, Piankoff and Richards noted, much to their pleasure, that both of them were armed with a bronze, chariot sickle.

They then moved.

What precisely occurred next was such a swift and savage offensive attack that the priests appeared to be nothing more than white-kilted blurs. For this ultimate moment of total savagery, Doc Allen too, had had a hand. The post-hypnotic suggestion for such action had been consciously triggered by first the look and then shared nods of the two priests. From that point onward until their personal death or a positive kill, both field operatives' minds remained heavily shielded. They had consciously become dumb marionettes devoted to pure mayhem. Their unreadable and apparent mindlessness, too, was meant to be a distraction.

The Nubians, a scant one to two steps around the corner of the dining room's entrance, both began to collapse from two well timed and damaging blows to their solar plexi. As they began to bend and fall from the impact of the blows, their sickles began to fall toward the floor as they gasped and began to grasp at their suddenly injured chests and bruised lungs.

At just this moment Piankoff and Richards could not be seen by the target, for the huge Nubians shielded them from his view. In other words, from the target's perspective, they just weren't there. What the target did see, or rather felt, was the assault of his queen's raging and hateful emotions as they flooded out, crested, and impacted upon him, causing him to actually blink and stagger slightly due to their intensity.

While the target's attention was still focused in wide-eyed surprise upon his queen and the strength of her mental attack, it was then, striding only two steps behind his Medjay that he began to notice that there was something wrong with them. All that he could feel from their minds were the sudden mental grunts of excruciating, suffocating pain, which also surprised him in their extreme intensity, staggered him a bit again, distracting him.

At that narrow point in time while the target simultaneously was being immersed in his queen's emotions and the visceral agony of his two Nubian guards, Piankoff emerged from behind the guard to the target's left. With a wide backhanded tennis stroke he slashed out with the guard's sickle and laid open the king's entire distended abdomen.

At first, the Quimbly did not register any pain from the scythe-like blow that had effectively disemboweled him. Instead, he had been further distracted by the sudden appearance of Piankoff, remembering, and casually noting that he was the one who had miraculously healed his ankle, the one who he had felt so guilty about the plundering of his mind, all the time marveling at the man's swiftness of foot. As Piankoff ran past him fully expecting to create another diversion with any Nubians thought to be following up the king, the Quimbly's head turned to follow the Russian's rapid progress past him.

Then Richards struck.

While preoccupied with Piankoff and now his most recent distraction, the lethal gut slash that the Quimbly was just beginning to perceive, Richards rounded his guard to his right. With his acquired sickle in hand, he swung up and across fully catching the target in the throat and neck, while his head was still turned following Piankoff progress in the other direction. Richards, who had swung with all of his might easily passed through that narrow stem of flesh, cartilage and bone and embedded the sickle's point into the doorjamb behind the target with a jarring thud, long before the king's head had even begun to fall from his shoulders.

Piankoff, now realizing the target had only two Medjay in his company, stopped, turned, and deftly reversing the chariot sickle in his hand, began to swing down on the falling head even before it had reached the chamber's limestone paving. The timing of this final blow could not have been more perfect, for both head and sickle reached the floor simultaneously with the weapon's heavily weighed and blunt edge landing across the target's right temple crushing it utterly. The resultant gush of blood from the smashing blow instantly evacuated the head of its otherwise one minute blood supply.

Total attack elapse time, 7.6 seconds.

The Quimbly, headless, disemboweled, and with its torso now kneeling in its own pool of blood and viscera, quivered, jerked, and then finally flopped over silent and unmoving.

The Medjay were on their hands and knees gasping for breath. Immediately following the swift dispatch of their master, both had their necks mercifully broken on the spot.

*　　*　　*

At the very moment of the Quimbly's passing, secreted high in the cliffs above that large and primitive habitation site, several organometallic relays sprang to life within the scout's star craft. Some locked down the scout craft, rendering the pod virtually impervious. Others dropped its onboard internal functions to the barest of minimums, while the passive defensive system went fully and formidably active. Still others passively summarized within the database the strangely truncated impressions of their master's last signals. Finally, one very special bank of relays initiated the commonly understood, universal distress signal of their far-flung scout surveyor community.

This signal passed effortlessly through the planet's dense nitrogen and oxygen atmosphere and reached its sole natural satellite in mere moments, where a powerful relay then boosted the emergency signal across the vast ether of space toward a distant destination. Now with its one-time emergency function completed, the expended relay would lay a dormant, dead, and discarded thing on the lunar surface. With its outward butterfly-shape intact, its internals fused following that tremendous spasm of transmission. The scout craft's message had been brief.

EXTREME EMERGENCY

Scout Craft HOPE
Loss of contact with SURVEYOR 1
Failure of reunification with pod
Scout Craft HOPE recovery needed
Coordinates 3948.4334.3221
Relative Time 585943.001

EXTREME EMERGENCY

Finally, the last group of pod's relays, those faithfully tasked to the maintenance of the Quimbly's native flesh, began an ancient routine designed to preserve its organics on the off chance that the missing Quimbly would reestablish contact with the ship. These last, however, would fail after twelve days, eleven hours and four minutes of waiting for that eventuality to occur.

With that final shut down, the marvelously integrated organics of the First Scout, so long wedded into every fiber and sinew of its craft, would slowly decay. With its vital link broken, the craft husbanded its remaining power at a very low nadir, lay dormant, and defenseless. Eventually, it would be ripe for either salvage or recovery, depending upon whom or what reached it first.

*   *   *

As for the two assassins, blood splattered, looking like butchers, and sky-high on adrenaline, all they could do was just mutely stand, view the carnage, and the ever-expanding pool of royal blood.

As for the queen, she stood in horror, one hand over her mouth, silent, but not shedding a tear. It had all happened so fast. Perhaps too fast for her to comprehend that she was now a free, true queen again. Her private prayers had indeed come true.

Then the much feared, but inevitable, post-battle fatigue descended upon them. With their adrenaline so high, their emotions so peaked, their physiologies so torqued, the pair crashed like lightning-stunned falcons falling out of the sky. Richards, his mind on auto pilot, stumbled over to his divan, flopped down, and passed out from his superhuman burst of destructive effort.

As for Piankoff, now barely standing with sickle still in hand, his day's work was not over as he had a long ago implanted directive to murder the American. While that impulse was indeed strong, his fondness for Richards was far greater.

After all, had not this young whelp cared for him unlike any other? Had not he even saved me twice?

So standing over his helpless victim, Piankoff struggled, successfully resisted, and let go of the instrument of destruction, which noisily clattered against the dining room's pavement.

Perhaps intentionally, the Russian then literally slumped down like an untethered puppet before the lake of royal blood, eventually becoming engulfed by it, bathing quite literally in his own savage revenge, with his mind now very much at peace.

In less than thirty seconds after the target's arrival, all that remained upright was the queen herself, still standing proudly in her place of honor with two passed out priests, three very dead figures, and one bronze chariot sickle embedded a full three inches into the plaster jam of her dining room's entrance.

* * *

All that Richards could remember upon waking that early morning was the terrific headache. Then he had remembered Doc Allen's warning.

"Joey boy, if you survive this all-out ninja assault, you will probably pass out from the effort, and then, buddy boy, fully expect one bitch of an adrenaline hangover. Trust me. They're nothing like an alcohol hangover. Those are easy to get over in comparison."

Keeping his eyes closed, Richards found out in short order that any sort of movement caused pain. Regardless, the American knew that he had to get some fluids into his dehydrated system to begin both the flushing and the replenishment of his overstressed body. So he moved, grunted, sat up, and opened his eyes.

That's nice, I'm still alive, he thought. *But where am I?*

Painfully turning his head and feeling his neck and shoulder muscles rebel, he realized that he was still in the dining room, wondering. *How did I get to my sofa-like chair, whatever it's called?*

Looking around further in the dark twilight of the early morning hours, Richards then saw that the table had been cleared and all evidence of the massacre as well. Standing in disbelief and then stumbling over in the direction of the room's entranceway, he squatted down, regretting that he had for the movement sent his head a spinning, and felt the floor that was once awash in the target's blood.

It's dry and with little or no discoloration.

Standing up just a little too fast his head again reeled. He grabbed the stone entrance jam for support and smelled fresh plaster, but he didn't know why. Now beginning to doubt his own sanity as to what he thought had happened, he wandered back over to his divan, sat down, and then realized that he was naked as a jay bird. Inspecting his hands, arms, and chest, he could find no trace of blood anywhere, whatsoever.

Wow! This is just too weird!

For the moment defeated, hung over, and tired, Richards did the sensible thing. He lay down for what he thought would be a brief nap.

* * *

The next thing Richards felt was a firm hand on his shoulder, gently shaking him awake.

"Huh?"

"Be watchful, noble Mayneken, use the tongue of this land if you wish to keep yours," Piankoff whispered near his ear as he squatted down next to him.

"It is almost midday. You must rise and walk once again amongst the Land of the Living."

Now remembering himself, Richards grabbed the Russian's arm, looked him straight in the eye, and asked quietly.

"Did last night really occur?"

"Indeed."

"How successful were we?"

"Utterly, and we have made a lifelong friend of the Nile god Sobek as well. He has been so well fed."

A deep sigh of relief.

"After awakening this morning, with everything cleaned up, without a trace, I thought perhaps I had imagined it all."

"That's a common, post-stress reaction. However, I do believe that the household staff was quite busy cleaning up last night while we both slept. These servants would like to clean you up so that you look proper for our audience with the queen."

Seeing around Piankoff, Richards caught the eyes of two young servant girls, who immediately began to twitter among themselves at his attentive gaze. Slowly sitting up, greeted again with a dull and pounding headache, Richards managed a brave smile and said, "This is indeed a difficult life," which earned him a knowing smile from his teacher.

*   *   *

"You both have served Egypt well," the queen deeply intoned. "Now, what do you seek in repayment?"

To this question, Piankoff replied.

"We want nothing for ourselves, but desire much the restoration of the Two Lands and the reinstatement of the city of Thebes to a more proud, honorable, and respectful time."

"You say that you want of nothing, but then ask for something that I cannot possibly grant. We have a problem."

Piankoff continued. "May I respectfully suggest Noble One that much as a boatman cannot hope to turn his craft without manning his rudder, so too could you slowly guide Egypt unto its proper path."

"Well said, but why should I do this?"

"Simply because his remaining children are a direct threat to Maat."

Struck by the simplicity of this equation, the queen nodded in understanding and agreement.

"I do see your point, Piankhotep, and it is a wise one. Must I shoulder this task alone?"

"Hardly, Noble One, for there is another of like mind. His name is Horemheb, a prince and nobleman. He too yearns for Egypt's restoration and would make a most suitable ally."

"I will consider it, but what of Smenkhkare and my daughter Meretaten?"

"They must soon go West."

A frigid silence passed, and then.

"Then what of Tutankhaten and my daughter Ankhesenpaaten?"

"He must be isolated, but as for your daughter, she can be spared. However, she must not be allowed to bear a child, to pass on his seed."

"These are harsh pronouncements priest."

"Noble One, think on them. In time you may agree with the wisdom of them, of their necessity."

"Unfortunately, I already do, and, I unfortunately already agree with your arguments."

"In that case, Noble One, we wish to thank you for your hospitality. It is perhaps best for us to depart."

Mildly shocked by the news, the queen then asked with true emotion.

"But, but why? You have only just arrived and there is so much to do, to arrange. To restore Egypt, will . . ."

Piankhotep then dared to raise his hand to stop the queen in mid-sentence.

"Forgive me most Noble One. Those tasks are the happy tasks and price of your newly acquired freedom. Those are not tasks appropriate for mere priests."

"Where are you going?"

"Sacred Thebes, Noble One. Do you wish us to carry a message to Prince Horemheb?"

"Yes! Yes, that is a good thought, but I must think on it."

"Indeed, Noble One, but our passage leaves early this evening, and we do wish to arrive in Thebes before the Inundation begins."

"So soon?"

"Yes, Noble One."

*   *   *

As Richards had hoped, Piankoff indeed had arranged for passage back to Thebes for that evening and best of all there were no critters to be seen. When he had thanked the Russian for the fine accommodations, Piankoff merely replied that it was the queen's doing and as her new royal envoys that we had carte blanche. Then extending his left hand that was wrapped around the thick papyrus scroll to be delivered, Richards saw that the Russian was wearing a truly impressive and massive seal ring of gold and lapis lazuli. Squinting down at its inscription, sure enough, it announced that its bearer was a royal ambassador no less!

Nonetheless, three days on a riverboat, any riverboat, was still three days spent that seemed to endlessly drag on. Midway during that journey south, both Piankoff's stomach and bowels broke in total revolution, but this time with clear evidence of the passing of blood. Clearly some kind of bug had gotten to the Russian, Richards quizzed him.

"My teacher, when did you first notice this illness?"

"Toward the end of our last trip up river to Thebes, three days ago."

"Did you ever drink directly from the river?"

"Great gods never, even I know better than that!"

"But did you ever drink from a well that was near the river?"

To that question, posed as it was, set Piankoff to thinking.

"Yes, Mayneken, you are right, I did. I did so the very morning that you met and befriended Horemheb. I was so thirsty that I just did not think. Come to mention it, you're absolutely right. No one attended that well."

"Well, if you did indeed get a stomach full of river water, then you could have some sickness that will disappear in a week, or be with you for the rest of your life."

"My, aren't we the cheerful one."

"Perhaps on your return, you might want to tell your people about this, just to make sure."

"Have no fear, my good friend, I will do so."

Besides Piankoff's failing health, Richards' chest suddenly tightened with the realization that they had not even attempted to locate the base of the Aten disk and told Piankoff of his concern. But the wily Russian responded with a wicked grin.

"Well, my dear Mayneken, I guess that if they are that interested in its recovery, then they will just have to deploy us again."

* * *

During the early evening hours of their sixth day in country, Piankoff and Richards docked at the quay at Thebes. Just before landing, Piankoff again complained about his stomach and threw up several times and more blood appeared. The rudder man naturally thought that Piankoff's distress was hilarious. Imagine a royal ambassador who got seasick riding the high seas on his Nile riverboat!

Ignoring the usual river front haunts, the pair made their way directly to the household of Horemheb, who, upon their surprise arrival was delighted as was Meryptah, who was already beginning to regain the feeling and function of the left side of his face.

It's indeed remarkable what some care and the feeling of being needed can do for one's recovery, Richards thought.

As Horemheb just finished whipping his household staff into a frenzy of preparation for an instant "welcome home" dinner party, Piankoff showed the prince his ambassadorial signet ring and handed over to him the papyrus scroll from the queen.

With wide eyes and suddenly all business, the prince excused himself, disappeared into his private quarters, and was not seen until all were seated around a truly groaning board of a dinner table.

Horemheb looked like the weight of the entire world had just been placed upon his young shoulders, when he entered the dining room, took his place, and asked for a full measure of beer, instead of wine. Raising the full ceramic cup, he offered his guests the familiar formulaic greetings typical for such an occasion and then continued on with words that were more than just vaguely familiar.

"May the gods again smile upon Egypt. May its temples that lay desolate be restored. May my guests enjoy their stay and have a happy return to their households. This is now possible, because He-who-is-in-his-grimness fell dead four days ago."

Shock at these words filled the room. Meryptah actually swallowed his breath, choked, and began hacking. Only after a quick draught of beer, was he able to regain his composure.

Sitting down, Horemheb then continued. "This evening we have indeed much to discuss. But first let us fill our bellies in celebration!"

Richards a bit dumbfounded asked Piankoff. "Just what are we celebrating?"

"Patience," was his reply.

*   *   *

Never before could Richards remember having drunk so much so quickly and that was saying a lot. In truth, it was Horemheb's fault, for he had midway through the meal began toasting to his guests, toasting the household's cook, the baker, practically all the way down to the candlestick maker. Then of course his guests had to reciprocate with their own toasts to their generous host, his cook, his baker, and, even if he didn't have one, his candlestick maker as well. Richards during a fleeting lucid moment of reflection thought.

Tomorrow is going to be brutal!

Finally, after everyone had eaten their fill, fingers had been wiped off on bits of bread, and the bread then eaten, it was time for the business portion of this soirée. Although thoroughly numbed by beer, the four managed to pull themselves, somehow, together.

As was his habit, Horemheb rose, briefly wandered off, dismissed the servants from the galley and kitchen, and waddled back to his place at the table. Plopping himself down he announced, "Well, my dear friends, it has begun. The full restoration of all the temples and lands to the priesthood of Amen Re will commence tomorrow. As the High Priest Meryptah is sitting here to my right, I wish to assure you, most venerable one, that I, Prince Horemheb, Royal and Chief Overseer of the Granary of Thebes, will proudly hand over the administration of the magazines under my care to you personally. As of tomorrow, your household and servants will be restored to you as is only proper given a noble priest of your high station, unless, of course, you wish to remain my most honored guest within my household. The choice, venerable one, is yours."

Meryptah almost suffered a heart attack on the spot. Tears literally exploded from his eyes. Weeping for joy, all embraced him and congratulated him as was only right and proper. The old priest just kept saying over and over again, "He has truly heard my prayers. The Great God has truly heard my prayers."

"But Prince Horemheb, you have placed before me a most difficult decision. To immediately leave your household after all of your generosity would be an insult. But to stay, especially given all the work that is required of my restored station would be also an unfair imposition upon your household. Therefore, my kind and generous benefactor, I will remain here until my former household has been refurbished, but when it is completed, I must return to my former duties and responsibilities."

And with that pronouncement, the elder priest levered himself up and made the following toast.

"My dear friends, a toast to this feast truly for it is made for laughter, and wine only makes it all the more merry indeed!"

Predictably, the priest's words began yet another round of beverages, which, when poured by the likes of these inebriated men instead of by a sober servant was more like who could spill the most. It was during this latest outburst of energetic drinking that the nagging itch in Richards' mind at Meryptah's words finally was scratched.

Gee, those words sound awfully familiar, but I just can't place them. Where, where oh where did I hear something like them before?

Observing Richards' furrowed brow now deep in thought, Piankoff queried.

"What is it that is so troubling you, Mayneken, that causes your brow to wrinkle up like a series of ravines?"

"I really don't know, but there was something about Meryptah's toast that was very familiar."

Smiling broadly at his young colleague, the Russian was pleasantly surprised by his remark. "Why, my dear Mayneken, those words are a traditional feasting benediction common to this land."

Then leaning over in a shared and hushed tone the cagey Russian continued. "And, I might add, those words were memorialized in *Ecclesiastes*."

Registering Piankoff's words, Richards could only gape in silence and let out a soft whistle.

But the revelation was broken when Horemheb slowly rose put a break on all the caterwauling to make yet another toast, but of a different sort.

"Today, the royal ambassador Piankhotep delivered to me a letter from none other than Queen Neferneferu Nefertiti."

At the mention of her name Meryptah let out a gasp, "She lives!"

Horemheb responded, "Indeed she does! And in the letter she suggested an advantageous and practical alliance based on our common concern for Egypt and our shared love of Maat. Clearly, the queen sees in me a bright future. One that will be sometimes fraught with intrigue and even danger, but one that will be more challenging than an overseer of a provincial granary.

"She suggested, rather strongly, that you Piankhotep, and you Mayneken, become part of my household, as my personal religious and military advisors. Having already seen what you can do alone, Mayneken, with your bare hands, I can only begin to imagine what your teacher Piankhotep can accomplish. So, I am taking the queen's good advice. I am offering to both of you a place within my household. To be my most trusted of advisors. What do you say?"

Stunned silence, but both thought in unison even without looking at one another.

In unison both answered, "We accept."

The beaming broad smile on Meryptah's face lit the room. That of Horemheb's could have lit all of New York City.

Sitting back relaxed, and knowing who his personal advisors were, Horemheb went on.

"The queen mentioned something else as well. She mentioned you, Piankhotep, by name as the author of this strategy, the isolation of the Princess Ankhesenpaaten. I find this strategy most clever, to isolate the seed of the heretic, preventing it from sprouting forth again. I can assure you that I will help the queen in this task until the task is no longer necessary to watch over.

"As for the young boy Tutankhaten, the queen suggests that I befriend him, watch over him, help and guide him. This too is a most wise strategy and one that I will fully accept. Now under the fatherly care of Meryptah, the Noble Nefertiti, and me, Egypt will indeed be slowly and gradually restored. In fact, the queen believes that within two years time the royal family and court will again reside here, at sacred Thebes.

"But one small step at a time."

To which Piankoff said. "Most wisely put."

"As the royal ambassador of the queen, Piankhotep, I request that tomorrow both you and Mayneken return to that accursed northern place and deliver my letter and my thoughts to the queen."

"Absolutely, Noble One, but for one minor issue, my health is declining. May I send Mayneken in my stead?"

"Why, of course, Piankhotep! I did not know that you were ill. Do you wish me to call for a physician?"

"Thank you, noble Horemheb, but that will not be necessary. Instead, I wish to pray this evening before the Great God, and then, very slowly, return home to my beloved Memphis to recuperate. Then, if it is still your wish, when I am strong again, may I return to your service?"

"Wise Piankhotep, return when you are able. I have every confidence in Mayneken as you. But as for now, if you all will excuse me, I have an important letter to write. Sleep well."

Horemheb staggered out of the room. Piankoff and Richards began to rise themselves, but Meryptah with a wave of his hand indicated to them to remain. Curious, Piankoff asked why.

"My dear Piankhotep, our generous host this evening began with a most unusual toast. To all of its points, he provided us with clarification, with the sole exception of one. What became of the unspeakable one? Clearly the two of you were there when he died. I know it in my old bones. Now, what happened? I want no evasions! No half-truths.

"Piankhotep, I know of your warlike powers well. As for you Mayneken, with my own eyes have I too seen things that I thought not possible. Such speed, such strength. Then there is the issue of the pestilence that you caused. Such an abomination it was!

"Now, my friends, am I just becoming too old to reason, or, have far too many things occurred while both of you have been present?"

The pair glancing at one another, Piankoff chose to answer for them both.

"Meryptah, dear friend, we both did Egypt a favor four days ago and you know it. With the spilling of his blood we purchased Egypt's restoration."

That answer deserved, and got, only a grunt of acknowledgement. The old priest then rose, and in passing said, "Remind me the next time that the two of you go to the marketplace. That way, I might bring my ledgers along in order to better count the dead found left in your wake."

And with that acerbic observation made, the priest retired.

Now alone and after several moments of silence, Richards said, "Well, I suppose that we deserved that. We have indeed been busy. But my teacher, we must check in within the hour."

Slapping his forehead with the palm of his right hand, Piankoff exclaimed, "Damnation! We must hurry and prepare our report!"

"No need. Fortunately, I already have written our report and from the sound of your ever grumbling stomach and bowels, you will be able to deliver it in person."

"Indeed," the Russian replied with a nod.

"In fact, despite all the liquids that I have just consumed and my bloated stomach, I am still thirsty and am getting weaker no doubt from blood loss. It is probably for the best that I return and receive some medical attention. By the way, just when did you write it?"

"While on the boat."

"Really? You are to be commended, but didn't anyone see you?"

"Yes indeed, the rudder man. He even asked what I was writing, but I told him it was composed in that barbarian tongue of the Keftiu, and he just shrugged it off."

CHAPTER LIX
Of Bets and Butterfly Nets

Tuna Cartwright and his men, as they stood around the active Mark V-A, knew that they looked funny with their butterfly nets. But no longer did they feel funny, for there was some really active wagering going on as to who would be the next to catch a package. In fact, a lottery had been established to decide who the lucky four butterfly snatchers would be. Even a chalk line was precisely and carefully drawn to indicate whose quadrant was whose. To be a legal catch, one had to properly use the net and not one's hands, as Corporal Charles Flanagan had once done. A former basketball star from Indiana, Flanagan's quick hands had caught the second package barehanded and in the process had thrown the entire pool into the toilet. The fact that the package had flown over another soldier armed with a net that was caught dead-heading it was beside the point. With these guys' reputation for being right on time, or worse even early, another furiously competitive and imaginative pool was centered upon precisely when the package was to arrive. So operates the highly complex military mind.

The field finally formed up and twenty sets of eyes were keenly focused either on their watches or the field itself. They were not disappointed, for as soon as it had gone rigid, plus or minus ten seconds, out flew the package that was then expertly and legally plucked n' snagged by none other than big Chuck Flanagan, this time with a legal butterfly catch. To add further insult to injury, Flanagan had won the lottery on the delivery time as well.

All he could say was, "Read 'em and weep, ladies."

But the biggest surprise of all was when Piankoff's head emerged to announce his needed recovery. Needless to say, all hands dropped what they were doing and scrambled to deploy the old wooden boom.

* * *

With all the hub-bub of Piankoff's emergency recovery over and with the Russian resting easy with the unit's field medic and an intravenous drip, Tuna Cartwright finally had an opportunity to read the field report. Finished with the report he called Dr. Borov using the common encryption, full knowing that the bad guys would be listening in. Waiting for the usual clicks and hisses to stop, Borov answered the line.

"Borov here."

"Howdy, Dr. Borov, this is Mr. Tuna."

"Ah, yes, Mr. Tuna, so how was today's fishing?"

"Quite spec-tac-u-lar."

"How so?"

"Well, it seems that as the high tide came in, there was just a whole bunch of shrimp in our nets. In fact, the fishn' was so good that we figured that you won't mind much if the young'n stays on another couple of more hours, maybe five or six at least, or at least until the tide goes out. Well, sir, whadda' ya think?"

"Well. Mr. Tuna, I think that if the fishing is that good, why not continue?"

"Well, sir, if'n ya say so. By the by, we reeled in one sick old puppy that probably needs fixin' real soon. Nothin' serious tho'. So's how about me flying over to ya'all what we got reeled?

"Why, why by all means Mr. Tuna. We'd be glad to have 'em."

"Yeah, that's what I thought too. Well, good bye, sir."

"And good bye to you, Mr. Tuna. And good fishing!"

Hanging up on Dr. Borov after another one of his Cajun routines always just about broke the major up. The whole thing was just so screwy, off-the-wall, and loony that it must absolutely drive the bad guys crazy. That happy thought alone seemed to make all the weird early morning hours, the sweat, the butterfly nets, the questionable water, the runs, and all the scratching, itching sand fleas go right away.

Meanwhile, half a world away, Borov was enjoying quite a chuckle himself, for he too dearly loved his comical conversations with Mr. Tuna. Looking down at his notes a broad smile came to his lips as he counted off the points on his left fingers.

Let's see here now.

First, the major did go fishing. That means he received a package.

Second, its contents were spectacular. Well, that could only mean that both agents are still safe and sound.

Third, the mention of high tide means that the target has been eliminated. Boy that's marvelous news in its own right!

Fourth, the youngin' wants to stay out fishing for five or six more hours. That could only mean that Richards' extraction has been extended and will occur in either five or six day's time. Apparently, something happened to the Russian. Nothing serious, but something troublesome enough otherwise Piankoff would never have allowed himself to be extracted early. Well, no doubt it was something quite important.

I wonder if they found the UFO?

* * *

From: Karlov Drazinzka
To: Vasily Ostrogorsky; Nikolai Fedorov
CC: Central Archives
Subject: Recent Luxor Sat transmission
Sent: Mon 7/16/2001 3:07 pm
Encryption: 256
Classification: Purple
Attachment:luxor!128!encryptsatmess177200 1.txt123KB)

Gentlemen:

Instead of wasting our time with yet another face-to-face meeting, I wish to report to you that yet another love letter has transpired between a certain Mr. Tuna in Luxor and Dr. Borov at Horizon Pass. Its content is ludicrous crap! It is now abundantly obvious to me that they know about our breaking of their common 128-encryption. Although the content of the attached communication may have meaning, and maybe contain a code, there is no way of knowing and frankly I am not going to task my people on such worthless dreck any longer. My department has already been depleted with the tragic loss of Sasel and I simply will not tolerate any more suicides on my watch!

Karlov Drazinzka
Special Projects Directorate
Russian Academy of Science

CHAPTER LX
A Bittersweet Victory

The shallowness of the river, the danger of suddenly appearing sandbars, and the now totally burned out look of the surrounding landscape made the journey back down river to the northern capital a very depressing one, despite Richards' buoyant attitude. Once ashore however, Richards easily retraced his steps all the way to the entranceway of the Northern Palace, where, just as before, two broad-shouldered Nubians challenged him. These, however, were new ones.

At that point, one very thirsty American addressed them. "Noble warriors, tell the queen that her ambassador Mayneken has just arrived from Thebes."

Apparently these two had already heard of him, and perhaps his handiwork. With wide-eyes they parted and made way for Richards to enter. Once out of the direct sunlight and in the relative coolness of the interior's shade, Richards rapidly recovered.

As the queen made her entrance, Richards fell to one knee and before she had a chance to utter a word. "Forgive me, most Noble One, but my master, your royal ambassador, has become ill and is suffering terribly from sun sickness. He has sent me in his stead. It is his hope that his absence will not displease you."

"Why, why, no Mayneken, I only wish for his speedy recovery."

"In the meantime, most Noble One," extending Horemheb's scroll, "please accept on behalf of my teacher Prince Horemheb's letter of reply. I have been told to act in his behalf and to return to Thebes with your reply."

Looking down at Richards, the queen shook her head in disbelief at the speed of her new ambassador's journeys. No wonder Piankhotep has fallen ill. Thank the gods for his strong and protective assistant.

"As for you Mayneken, Kia here will see to your refreshment after your long journey."

"Thank you, most Noble One."

While she watched the young assistant to her ambassador follow Kia, it was then that the queen for the first time caught sight of the magnificent four scars that decorated Richards heavily muscled back, his powerful arms and legs.

My, she thought, *such a well-formed body. And so bravely decorated! It has been years since my loins have spoken to me so, years.*

*　　*　　*

By the time Richards was resting easy it was nearly the time for the last meal. A mixture of energy-packed date palm juice and water had restored his fluids. As he rose from his quarters, Richards almost ran right into the queen herself!

Flustered, Richards tried to excuse his oxen-like clumsiness, to which the queen only allowed a mirthful, tinkling laugh.

"Noble Mayneken, do not be alarmed. It is a pleasure to have such faithful guests in my household. I find it pleasurable as well the way you have served your teacher almost as if you were his very own son. But that surely cannot be the case. So, tell me, Mayneken. Why do you serve Piankhotep so faithfully?"

Caught for the moment at a loss for words, Richards began to invent. "Most Noble One, it was my father's wish. Piankhotep and he had been life-long friends."

This revelation was received by the queen with widening eyes, but the conversation was suddenly cut short by Richards' stomach that growled loudly. Looking down at it with some amusement, the queen said easily.

"Come my noble and faithful Mayneken, come dine with me or your stomach may well disown you."

The queen led, and Richards followed with the tired and exhausted walk of a full day and one filled with anxiety and worry for his teammate. In truth, Richards was not really paying attention to where he was going. In his exhaustion he just followed the queen by rote. Upon entering a small chamber, the American immediately recognized it for it was—a bathing room with a small open balcony. A very special bathing room it was for it contained a small pool that one could step into. Turning around before him, the queen dropped her diaphanous clothing and stepped into the shallow pool saying over her shoulder, "Join me, Mayneken, so that I may prepare you for your much deserved evening repast."

Realizing that he was in way over his head, Richards momentarily balked at the invitation. The queen, reading this as shyness, merely said, "Do not fear noble warrior, I am not to be feared as the crocodile who lies among the river rushes."

Taking his kilt off, Richards did as he was told and stiffly entered the mildly hot water, most likely warmed so by the sun. Turning him around, the queen began by vigorously scrubbing down his shoulders, back, and arms with a linen mitten, much like a common servant girl. Then, turning him, she did the same for his head, shoulders, chest, and arms. Then she grabbed him by the shoulders and gently dunked him, baptizing him in a sense, in order to rise off all the fine limestone abrasive. For Richards, despite his exhaustion, despite his reservations, the bath felt wonderfully refreshing. Upon surfacing, his stomach growled yet again, this time eliciting from the queen that wonderfully musical laugh that actually tickled his spine. He smiled and Nefertiti said to him with a sly grin, "All right, my young lion, now I will feed you. But later," she warned, "you will feed me."

Now emerging from the pool refreshed and certainly far cleaner than before, the queen grabbed the linen towel from him and began to vigorously dry him off and actually raising a slight blush to the young man's skin. Then she quickly did herself all the while Richards watched. For a woman who has brought into the world six daughters, and who is, I would estimate, about thirty-two years old, she certainly is in fine condition.

As for the queen, she was amused and flattered by Richards' appraising stare. Now both naked, the queen grabbed two dry linen towels, wrapping one around her waist and throwing the other to him to do likewise.

Off they traipsed, leaving a trail of wet and darkened footprints on the smoothed limestone pavement stones all the way to the dining room that Richards remembered so well and for so many reasons. And there, as before, the table literally groaned from all the various types and varieties of delicacies present. Taking her place and indicating where Richards should sit, she commanded, "Sit, eat, and drink your fill my Mayneken. Silence for me forever that ever-rumbling stomach of yours."

Never to be one that had to be called twice to the dinner table, Richards did precisely that, but brandishing some definite table manners so that the queen would not confuse him with a real young lion. While he munched and crunched his way through his dinner, Kia silently and efficiently fluttered about keeping his cup filled with beer and the queen's silver goblet filled with wine.

Finally, and with Richards' siege of the table at end, he sat back and took a long pull on what must have been his fourth or fifth cup of beer. Failing to stifle a burp behind his fist, the queen, who had been watching him throughout, merely smiled with contentment.

"Noble Mayneken, I have read Prince Horemheb's letter that you have brought to me. Now, tell me, what was his reaction to my letter. What did he say?"

Put on the spot, Richards suddenly realized that he could now put Doc Allen's recording mode to a practical test. With that confidence behind him, he sat back, closed his eyes, and began.

"Well most Noble One, you are correct for much indeed was said, but I wish to begin with what the noble and just Meryptah had to say."

"Meryptah you say! He still lives!"

"Oh, yes indeed, very much so, Noble One. In fact, he rejoiced upon hearing that you too were still alive, for he had heard terrible rumors about what had occurred in the Year 14. Frankly, he had feared the worst."

Holding her hands tightly together and with her eyes rimmed with tears, Richards heard her say softly, "Oh, my dear trusted friend! Oh how I miss your wisdom."

A silent moment passed. Then the queen said, "On, Mayneken, what else was said!"

"Well, Horemheb first announced that a full restoration of the all the temples and lands to the priesthood of Amen Re was to begin immediately. He then said that Meryptah was to be reinstated as that priesthood's High Priest, and that he, Horemheb, Royal and Chief Overseer of the Granary of Thebes, was proud to hand over all the magazines under his care to him personally. Horemheb then said that

Meryptah's household and servants were to be restored to him as well."

"He had lost his entire household!"

"Well, no, most Noble One, but it was in such a shabby state of disrepair that it had become practically a ruin. As for Horemheb, he had actually just adopted the old priest into his own household as his personal advisor."

"Horemheb is truly a wise man for one so, so young. Your teacher Piankhotep spoke highly of him and now I can see why.

"Continue."

"Well, as you can probably imagine, Meryptah, at this good news, was practically overcome with joy and had cried openly.

"Then Horemheb mentioned that you had written to him suggesting an alliance based upon unspecified, but common, interests. He mentioned that it was clear that you saw a bright future for him and that this new path would be challenging, certainly far more interesting than being an overseer of some grain magazines."

To this the queen chuckled with that marvelous chuckle of hers.

"Horemheb also mentioned your deep and abiding trust in my teacher and me and that you suggested that we become his personal religious and military advisors. In this he assented and we agreed. The prince also made us members of his household on the spot."

"That was to be expected."

"Then, as I recall, the prince then made mention of a strategy, he called it, of isolating Princess Ankhesenpaaten, which the prince thought was most clever. I believe he said something like being ever vigilant about 'isolating her seed so that it would never sprout again.'

"As for the young Prince Tutankhaten, he will watch over him as would an older brother.

"Finally, the prince concluded that he was most pleased that Egypt would begin to start its restoration under the care of Meryptah, you, most Noble One, and he. His expectations are of a slow and gradual process, one that, in perhaps two years time, will bring the royal family and court back to Thebes. His last words on this subject were, 'But one small step at a time.'"

Now sitting back thinking deep thoughts, comparing the words of Horemheb's letter in her mind with what Mayneken had told her, she began to smile. On the basis of what she had heard about the prince, and now with his letter in hand, and Mayneken's lucid recollections, she now had to entirely reappraise Horemheb as an ally far better, far wiser, than she had ever dreamed.

He would indeed make a most worthy and formidable older brother for young Tutankhaten, especially once that wretch Smenkhkare and my wayward daughter are removed by my hand! What better place to be able to watch over and isolate my third daughter Ankhesenpaaten, that witch!

As for Mayneken, supposedly Piankhotep's mere loyal assistant, well, that too will I have to thoroughly reappraise. Having seen him in action, he is a fierce and devastating warrior. Having heard his words, listened to his measured and clear mind, he now far surpasses that of all the royal ambassadors at the palace, and maybe, maybe even that of his teacher as well! And then there is this other issue . . .

Surfacing quickly from her deep musing, the queen then startled Richards by saying, "Noble Mayneken, now, what do you think of Horemheb? I want to know truly what your heart tells you. I want to know your measure of the man."

Unflinchingly, Richards replied, "Most Noble One, he is young, honest—perhaps to a fault, hard working, possesses a quick mind, has a ready smile, and in some ways seems far older and more mature than his years. Without a doubt, I saw how quickly the prince could take the measure of a man. He is patient, but can be decisive as well. Above all, he has a sense of justice about him. Clearly, he is a defender of Maat."

While Richards spoke, the queen had closed her eyes to better see his spoken words in her mind, and while he did so, a relaxed and confident smile came to her face.

"So well said, Mayneken, so very well said. Do you know that you have a poet's gift for words?"

"My teacher has occasionally teased me about that very thing, most Noble One."

Shifting her weight and now taking on the look of a cat, the queen then looked up to him and complimented him again.

"Noble Mayneken, do you know how long it has been since I have known a man?"

Richards' eyes widened in reaction to the queen's statement. This the queen did not miss.

Joey-boy! Are you prepared for this? This is after all a Queen of Egypt! Now just how are you gonna' handle this situation?

Reading his hesitancy again as shyness, the queen pressed on.

"Do you know how long it has been since I have enjoyed washing a man's back?"

The widening blush that was spreading across Richards cheeks the noble woman found to be titillating and tantalizing.

"And, do you know how much it pleases me that you have eaten your fill at my table?"

Now fully sated and more than slightly drunk, Richards knew where the queen was going with this train of thought and so replied as honestly as he could.

"No most Noble One, I do not. Do you wish to tell me?"

In a distant, almost fragile little girl's voice the queen replied. "Yes, I will my Mayneken. But first you must promise me that in my presence, whenever we are alone as we are now alone, that you will call me Nefer, and Nefer only. Will you promise me this one small thing?"

"But of course most nob . . . Nefer, but of course. For in truth that is the only name that truly becomes you—the beautiful one."

The awkwardly put, yet poetic response of this warrior priest caused the queen herself to blush, smile, and feel as if she were again just a young girl.

I have never before felt so safe, so protected, in the presence of a man, as this truly young lion. He who helped slay the other one, the cruel one, the one who had hurt me in so many, many ways.

"Mayneken, do you have a private name?"

Looking down, Richards' partially numbed brain worked and searched and came up dry. But finally, he said, "Yes, Nefer. It is a strange name with a strange sound, I know, but it is Joey."

"Yo-ee. That is indeed a strange sounding name. What does it mean Mayneken?"

Now reaching back deep, really deep, Richards replied, "Young carpenter."

"How interesting! My Mayneken's private name is Yo-ee. I like it," she replied as if it were a long lost and beautiful jewel that she and she alone had just found in the sand of the desert wastes.

Rising from her seat, the queen then came over to where Richards was sitting, took his hand, pulled him to his feet, and while looking up at him with curious and inquisitive eyes she said simply, "Take me to my bed chamber, my dearest Yo-ee. It has been over six years since my, my . . ."

Richards, instantly recognizing her awkward pain, gently placed his hand over her delicate mouth silencing her. With the gentlest of smiles and laughing eyes, he reached down, picking her up effortlessly, and carried her away.

That night and into the early morning hours, the queen's refrain of "Yo-ee" was heard by Kia and the rest of the queen's household staff. All were delirious with joy, for they knew that their fair queen would soon be whole again.

The next day, and true to his word, Richards announced that he would return to Thebes that evening. In concert with his wishes, the queen marshaled all of the resources at her disposal to make it so and by that very afternoon. Unknown to Richards, however, the queen also had caused a royal messenger to be sent overland to inform Prince Horemheb of his expected arrival.

*   *   *

The return to Thebes went without incident or critters as the queen had arranged for a suitably swift craft for her interim ambassador and now personal confidant. That last job description, however, Richards mulled over repeatedly during the course of the return journey. It was as if a great emotional weight had been placed upon his shoulders, a protective responsibility. And to his surprise, he found that it was a role that he could easily accept. The woman, such a battered victim, was also a supremely powerful queen. Clearly, she had desperately needed his companionship and that experience had been quite a personal education.

In the final analysis, Richards decided that he had somehow, someway returned some missing element to her, something deep and primal, something that had been ruthlessly taken from her very being. He also knew that this new relationship represented a potential liability, one that might cloud his better judgment, something that would require a conscious effort, a search for balance.

Upon his arrival, Richards was surprised at the waiting presence of Prince Horemheb and heartened by his smiling face at the quay.

How did he know when I was arriving? He furiously thought, but then humbly concluded that there was still much about this culture that he needed to grasp.

Once back within the private confines of the prince's household, having had his feet dusted, and now sitting before the prince's evening table, Richards formally made it known that he carried news directly from the queen herself.

Horemheb nodded for Richards to continue and he did so.

"Yes, Noble One, she is very, very impressed with you, and expressed her pleasure many times regarding the tone and contents of your letter, your willingness to be Tutankhaten's older brother, and your decisiveness with the restoration of Thebes, its temples, and granaries. The list just goes on and on. Noble One, I believe that you have found yourself a very influential and powerful ally."

To all of this good news the prince's ego clearly was stroked mightily and he looked it.

Then turning to the venerable Meryptah, "As for you, most venerable one, the queen expressed her joy in genuine and heartfelt tears at learning that you were still among the Land of the Living. She also said that she misses your wisdom."

That news brought a smile to the old priest's face and a gentle bow of his head at the kind words as if they had been delivered by the queen herself, and in retrospect, Richards suddenly realized, they had. Such is the respect and influence of an ancient ambassador.

Then the prince spoke.

"My dear and noble Mayneken, you are truly a remarkable man. Here you have just stepped in for your beloved teacher and it seems as if you were born to the ambassadorial role and its onerous responsibilities. This brings nothing but joy to our hearts."

Sobered somewhat by the prince's observation and realizing that he was correct, Richards said, "Noble prince, my teacher would have wanted it no other way."

"And so shall his fine training of you be noted, Mayneken."

Replied the prince with a quiet strength of conviction that was notable as he raised his earthenware beer mug in salute, which signaled the beginning of what would no doubt be yet another boisterous evening meal. And indeed that evening repast had been a lively one, with much levity and toasting, one that caused all of its participants but one a groaning slowness at the arrival of the next morning's sunrise.

Sadly, only Meryptah failed to greet Re's first appearance, for he had died quietly that very night in his sleep. As the wailing broke out throughout the household at the early morning discovery, Richards quickly found that he was kneeing at the side of the old priest's bed frame feeling cheated. As he slowly and gently stroked the stubble of the man's cold and bluish pate, he was flooded with the fond memory of grooming the old man, a bonding act that created such simple pleasure, and how he already missed his remarkable wisdom.

As tears flooded his eyes and streamed freely down his cheeks and onto the old priest's bedding, the young American did something extremely Egyptian. While under the quiet gaze of Horemheb, Richards leaned forward and whispered into the much beloved high priest's left ear, "Safe journey." He then sealed that heartfelt wish with a gentle kiss to his forehead.

That done and sitting back on his heels, only then did Richards discover that he was not alone. That his act had been witnessed. Abruptly clearing his throat and awkwardly standing, he stated stiffly in the soldiery pose of a parade rest. "Noble Horemheb, I must somehow make burial arrangements for the most venerable Meryptah. Noble One, I seek your wisdom. I do not know whether any of his family still lives. I do not know whether any such arrangements have been arranged and provided for."

With his arms crossed across his chest and feet wide in an appraising, strangely sad, yet approving smile, Horemheb replied, "Indeed, my most noble Mayneken. It is time that we must discuss the soon-to-be Osiris Meryptah's last wishes." Horemheb stated with a somber and serious tone. "Specifically regarding both his burial and you, Mayneken."

To Richards' confused look, the prince continued.

470

"Before the most noble Meryptah went West, we discussed at length these weighty matters, especially given the course of these dark times and his advanced age. So it was agreed that he as part of my household in life, so also will remain for eternity.

"Consequently, it was agreed that he shall rest within and among those of my own kin in my mortuary temple to the north. In fact, I have already sent word weeks ago to my foreman to immediately prepare an appropriately appointed tomb. We together even instructed my scribe to draft his final funerary text that will appear as his testament for eternity. So has already been prepared beloved Meryptah's final house that will guard and embrace his *ka* for all eternity. There he shall rest and await my eventual company and companionship as we journey together throughout the Nether World."

"So have I commanded. So it has been done."

Then the hereditary prince of Memphis paused. Pursed his lips in a deep personal pain and then continued. "It was also Meryptah's wish that you, and not I, accompany him north to Memphis."

Shock was painted across Richards' face.

"Noble One, did the venerable Meryptah say why he chose me for this honor, this noble burden, instead of you?"

Before answering, the disappointment at the high priest's choice was clear on the prince's face, but in all fairness to Meryptah's memory and Richards' request he owed a reply.

"Frankly Mayneken, Meryptah said that you and you alone treated him as the son that he never had. He openly said this, several times. He also greatly admired you both for your strengths and faults. He observed you in times of great mirth and times of deep personal anguish. But most of all, he told me, it was your many unbidden kindnesses to an old man that he had found most endearing.

"Mayneken, I wish to be clear, while I personally chafe at his decision, I know it to be justified. I too have eyes. I too have seen your many concerns toward him. And if you are not fully familiar with all of the responsibilities that will be required of you, I would be more than pleased to assist you with them in any way. In fact, Meryptah even made me swear that his decision would not be a

471

hindrance to our friendship, for he knew that it had stung me mightily.

"He instructed me that I consider you my elder brother and that I listen attentively to your counsel. And that, Mayneken, after some thought, I will do. Not only out of respect to Meryptah's memory, but also because of his vast wisdom and yours. And so from this day forward, if it is your wish, you too will be counted as among one of my kin. I will seek you out for guidance and wisdom as that elder brother that I had never had. While we are of different minds, we are also of the same mind.

"So has Meryptah requested. So it will be done."

*   *   *

After having checked in with his report, and revised extraction estimate, Richards departed for Memphis. Remarkably, it passed swiftly for Richards and his venerable cargo as a team of twelve rowers urged along the funerary bark in concert with the noticeably swifter current of the coming Inundation. Kept cool, tented under fine linen, and out of the sun, the old priest's fine cedar coffin perfumed the vessel with its natural fragrance and managed to effectively mask the inevitable coming of noxious odors. It was as if the Nile itself was in mourning for the aged priest, offering up as tears the rising waters of the annual flood.

For Richards, this northward progress toward Memphis was as if, in his emotionally wracked mind, he was journeying back into the Land of the Dead. Fanciful images of the River Styx flitted briefly into his mind. But that notion was just not appropriate, for Richards began recalling the many illustrations from tombs and funerary papyri, *The Book of the Dead* and *The Book of Gates*. Sitting here now at the bow and watching the river's endless eddies of water ripple around it at its passing, with time to think, consider, and ponder the ways of the world, Richards began to understand in a deep emotional way what few modern minds would ever grasp, much less appreciate. Death was nothing more than a natural transition, part journey, part traverse from one plane to the next. The ancients understood its rightful place in that great cycle that was existence. Moderns intellectualized about it right up to death, all in an attempt either to ignore or run away from it.

How sad we moderns are, Richards mused to himself wearing a sadly ironic smile, *to deny that which is so concrete, so inevitable, and so very human. The Egyptians beat death by embracing it, joining with it.*

Meryptah's last voyage down river ended at the quay of Memphis in the very shadow of the necropolis of nearby Sakkara. The arrival was a moment filled with quiet pageantry and surprise for Richards, while one hundred white-robed *wab*-priests were silently waiting all arrayed along the side of the river's edge. Atop the quay's steps where he could best see, stood an old, saddened, but very proud high priest of the god Ptah, a man named Ptahmesou, a man who Richards was shocked to learn was none other than Meryptah's younger brother. His presence was his way of expressing deep respect for the passing of such an eminent religious colleague, much less his older sibling. Next to him, in his proper place of honor, stood Prince Horemheb, who had also made the journey north, while Richards had taken on the initial burial preparations faithful to the old priest's wishes.

Once the funerary bark glided to its final rest, seven *wab*-priests, all who wore the black cartonnage helmet-masks of the jackal-headed god Anubis, the patron divinity of the embalming community and profession, collected Meryptah's remains. For the next seventy days the inanimate husk of this once kindly being would be in good hands. Richards did then, and only then, end his loyal vigil to guard against any defilement of the corpse, allowed himself to be led from the boat and up to those assembled atop the quay's staircase.

It was Horemheb who greeted him.

"Welcome to Memphis, noble Mayneken, royal ambassador to Queen Neferneferu Nefertiti, son of Meryptah, and my eldest brother. We have much to prepare for."

Impressed by the import of this solemn announcement, Richards, now flanked on either side by the high priest of Ptah and Horemheb, there to support him as if they were his closest of family members, they made their way from the quay toward the prince's Memphite household. As Richards' mind rewound and played back all the events of the recent past, he awaken to the heady meaning of the prince's pronouncement, only then did it all begin to take hold.

I am now considered the son of the high priest of Amen Re, the elder brother to a hereditary prince of Memphis, not to mention an ambassador to Queen Nefertiti. As the consequence of place and luck, such relationships were based power and influence. I must now tread very carefully and most softly so as not to harm history.

The trio were joined by two columns of fifty *wab*-priests each that walked in step, praying softly, beating their breasts loudly in a single-fisted cadence, slapping the foreheads of their freshly shaven heads in time. Before this priestly entourage wailed the professional mourners, who tore at their hair, threw dust upon themselves, and cried crocodile tears.

But among them, Richards saw many from the household of Horemheb itself, who had also traveled north for this event. No, not all of them were hired professionals, but real people whom Meryptah had touched throughout his long life in his own deep and meaningful way.

Upon reaching the prince's household, the procession broke up into a sort of milling crowd that really did not know what to do with itself, but wished to do something. But in time, it eventually dispersed like the smoke of a cooking fire.

*   *   *

"As for myself, after this evening of mirth, good food, drink and fine companionship, I wish to return to Thebes, so that I can be left alone to pray in the sanctuary of the Great God. Then, after the passing of the prescribed days of mummification, I will return to Memphis to participate in the burial of the Osiris Meryptah and complete my filial responsibilities."

The prince, both surprised and pleased at Richards' continued deference toward the high priest's memory, consented to it without remark. He, too, unknown to Richards, also had sent word to the priests of the second and third rank of the Great God that no one on the royal ambassador's return should disturb him during his private search for tranquility and peace.

CHAPTER LXI
Last Retrieval

All bets were off. This was now very, very serious business. Richards had been a no-show on his specified eighth and ninth days. All the lotteries, side bets, and odds-making were a thing of the past. The much-beloved modern mantra, "shit happens," just did for the Mark V-A's recovery crew and its security team, twice. As with all such moments of doubt and foreboding, thirteen collective memories and descriptions of the once young greenie began raising him to veritable sainthood. So it is among the military fraternity. Even Cartwright surprised himself with the level of his own emotional concern. Down deep, he deeply admired Richards.

Once just a kid, well, hell shucks, he was a kid no longer.

He saw him first-hand transform from a puke into a man and a very frightening and formidable one at that, a rite of passage that many troops were far from ever attaining. As for Borov and Milson, they just, flat, freaked during that last satellite conversation.

Now wincing in retrospect, the major realized that yesterday's wide-open chatter over the satellite was probably today's front page headline news for the bad guys.

Fortunately, the Mark V-A's bullet-proof battery pack still had a full eighteen minutes charge left before its needle would drift from the green into the yellow. On the basis of that, the major had argued successfully for staying the course, opening the field every morning at the usual time for a three minute duration, then shutting it down for the next morning's power up. This way, the major concluded, Richards would have an additional five days of extraction time at the minimum. Beyond that, only time would tell.

On the morning of July 26th, at 2:34 am, the third day of quiet desperation, the powering up of the Mark V-A was no longer a mini-Super Bowl Party. It was, as Corporal Flanagan had so colorfully put it in his native southern Indiana twang, "a cause for pause as serious as a heart attack." As the field stabilized, and after that pause of about ten seconds, a lone, defiant fist and forearm materialized from the field and dropped back down through it.

The reaction was immediate. Thirteen lungs began cheering, hooting, woofing, and whistling. The racket was so deafening that the phones at the local Luxor police department began to ring off the hook. No less than three police cars would be dispatched to find out what the source of all the early morning racket was that had awakened so many of the neighborhood's once sleeping inhabitants.

With almost superhuman efficiency the boom was swept in and the hemp sling lowered. Moments later, the familiar tug was felt and thirteen men, including the major, pulled as one, launching Richards out of the field like a shot. The surprise on Richards' face was evident, which incited another round of cheering, whistles, and the like.

Wide-eyed curiosity was apparent among the extraction team and its security squad. The obvious and unanswered question was, "Just what the hell were you doing?"

Cartwright was the first to verbalize it.

"Well Major Cartwright," a serious Richards said, "While I was away, I became a royal ambassador to a queen, became the adopted elder brother to a prince, became the adopted son of a high priest, and then as his son was tasked with his burial preparations. These funerary duties I must complete during another mission. Colonel, to be frank with you, I can assure you that he was a very dear friend and that the duty was no picnic."

Then in an impulse of emotion, Richards turned to the officer, fiercely gripped his shoulders, and said, "Sir, I just want you to know how much I and Piankoff owe you and your men. You guys are just awesome!"

With those words, again the cheering began and again the local police department's phones began to ring off the hook.

CHAPTER LXII
Defenestration of Fedorov

The mood was glum for this trio of men. The American still lived and was now fully capable of acting on his own. In fact, the American had saved their prize temporal field agent for a third time. That fact was bad enough, but now to retrieve him due an unexpectedly fast-acting riverine parasite was beyond their toleration.

Breaking the silence, however, was Nikolai Fedorov.

"That damn American! No, excuse me, that damn Dr. Richards! That son of a bitch attempted to poison our Colonel Piankoff! I want his fucking head on a platter! And I want it now!

"And as for that traitor Borov, no excuse me, that traitor Dr. Borov; I want that jackass to deliver it! And as for . . ."

The insane ranting continued on for another two minutes and thirty-five seconds by Karlov's own watch during which drool dripped and spittle flew from the enraged Russian's mouth.

By Ostrogorsky's count, his esteemed colleague also wanted the entire panel of the Philology Annex either disemboweled or dismembered or some intriguing combination of both.

Finally, having reached his end and gasping for breath, Karlov raised his hand to prevent Fedorov's continuation.

"Nikolai, your logic fails me. You are nothing more than an old, doddering fool who could not engineer himself out of a wet paper bag. Additionally, you are a disgrace, your department is a failure under your watch, and I, for one, am tired of dealing with your senile, infantile mind, and incessant ranting.

"And by the way, the incapacitation of Colonel Piankoff was not Dr. Richards' fault. It was Colonel Piankoff's. He told me himself of his blunder. In fact, Dr. Richards has assisted, now for a third time, in his successful recovery and for that I am most grateful. And by the way, the Colonel is not yours or ours. He is my responsibility."

Fedorov then viciously retorted.

"Fine. *Your* precious temporal agent has returned. *Your* failure. But what now, Karlov? What now of our plans for Piankoff's role in redirecting course of Western Asiatic history?"

As Ostrogorsky looked from one colleague to the other during this exchange, he saw a dangerously cool finality in Karlov's brown eyes as they took on the look of an unblinking viper. Clearly Fedorov was oblivious to it as he was still in full rant, waving his arms, eyes bulging, spittle flying, and his complexion florid.

Then Karlov struck, fully imbedding half of his ballpoint pen into the left temple of Fedorov's skull. With that act, the Russian just stared back at him in silent shock as blood cascaded down and bathed the side of his face and neck. He blinked twice and then fell out of his chair.

Finally, Karlov broke the silence.

"Vasily, I apologize for ruining the carpet. I will personally see to its replacement."

CHAPTER LXIII

The New Recruit

"I want to not only select, but train, my next partner."

"Joseph, you know that is totally out of the question!" Milson said.

"Why? Did not Colonel Piankoff do so with me?"

"No! I selected you. He trained you and reluctantly I might add! But that was different situation. Besides, how can you write him off so casually?"

"I have not written Piankoff off! Far from it."

After cooling down his temper several degrees, Richards continued, "I am just trying to think ahead. That's all."

To which Milson answered with a mumbling, bumbling silence, followed by more of the same, and then a sigh of resignation.

"Well, Joseph. Even I can see that you have already made up your mind." Then Milson went on the offensive.

"And so how would you, if of course Alexander is not able, go about finding such a candidate?"

"Well John, frankly, I'm really not sure. But I have the essential criteria clearly in mind. Has to be someone bright, flexible, imaginative, and fit enough for a start."

"Fair enough, but while that's a sound beginning, what about all the rest? And please don't forget all the screening that you had to go through, the jump school training, and all the examinations. They will have to do the same as well."

A pause of deep consideration.

"Yes, John. I know. I know."

*   *   *

Despite the long trans-Atlantic flight in coach, it was good to be back. The museum was just the same as he had remembered it. But from his new and now rather unique point of view, its contents all seemed so old, so beaten up.

That is what happens when you've been spoiled with the real thing, he mused.

479

Despite all the collected dust, the many fingerprints and nose smudges on the glass cases, it still remained the closest thing to his second existence.

As he slowly made his way through all the cluttered rows and aisles, he found himself stopping here and there, touching a stone, sighing at the oddly familiar meaning of a particular inscription or its remarkably beautiful carving, smiling at the occasional modern misattribution.

Richards realized he had gotten homesick, actually was experiencing a melancholy psychosomatic stab of pain that hit him in the stomach. Finishing his meanderings at the end of a corridor not usually noticed by the myriad hordes of tourists, he finally reached out for that antique brass knob of the dark oak office door with its milky glass.

Wearing his very best suit, tie, and shoes, he opened the door and quietly entered. Dr. Richards then nervously asked the Director's secretary the most important personal question of his still young life.

"Good day, Dr. Moussa. I do not know if you remember me," He said in high-formal Arabic. "But my name is Dr. Joseph Richards."

A broad smile of instant recognition and green eyes looked up, drinking him in.

"I have been told by your father that you might be willing to show me around."

CHAPTER LXIV
The Survey Institute

It was Christmas Eve in the Year of our Lord 321.

In that year, the Emperor Constantine I, recently converted to Christianity, decreed that the day devoted to the ancient god *Sol Invictus*, Sunday, become a day of Christian worship and rest. Luminaries of the period included: the philosopher Iamblichus, St. Eusebius, the Arian heretic Ulfilius, Ephrem the Syrian, and Constantine's advisor, Lactantinus.

Meanwhile, in the Far East, the Eastern Jin Dynasty held a tenuous sway over a politically tumultuous Chinese region and during the brief reign of the Emperor Yuan, the first accurate depiction of a horse stirrup graced the interior of his tomb. A reunited India was thoroughly enjoying its "Classical Age" during the Gupta Empire. With peace came extensive dividends in science, technology, engineering, art, philosophy, religion, astronomy, mathematics, logic, and literature. To the West, the many independent city states of Mesoamerica were experiencing the "Classic Era" of art, architecture, pottery, lapidary, and relief carving.

It was now, on this very date—relatively speaking of course, that the emergency distress signal finally had arrived at The Survey Institute indicating the sudden loss of the link between the first scout surveyor and its craft.

Through the course of millennia others had met their inevitable end. Granted, a certain amount of sentimentality had grown around the adventurous career of that first scout of scouts. In many respects, that fabled career embodied the survey's most endearing qualities of curiosity, patience, and perseverance in the pursuit of knowledge. And now, it too was over.

While a deep sense of loss for that legendary first scout was felt among the rest of the Surveyor community, far greater concerns were voiced about the disposition of the scout's star craft. After a brief discussion, a recovery team was organized and dispatched aboard the ferry craft named The Redemption.

W. J. CHERF

ANCIENT EGYPTIAN CHRONOLOGY

During the third century BC, King Ptolemy I of Egypt commanded Manetho, high priest of the sun god of Heliopolis, to write a history of Egypt. Unfortunately, that work now only exists in the form of tantalizing fragments, which merely list kings, how long they ruled, and their dynastic divisions. Fortunately for Egyptologists, they have at their disposal several papyri and temple inscriptions, which help to fill in the blanks.

But truth be told, king lists are just that, lists, which do not provide us with an absolute chronology. Occasionally, however, hints do appear in the historical record, specifically the recording of exceptional astronomical phenomena, from which can be calculated an absolute date for a given event. Consequently, the absolute dating of precisely when such and such a king ruled has become a sort of scholarly contest between whom can count the most accurately between these astronomical benchmark events.

As if that were not enough to trouble the mind of a conscientious historian, one must contend with the difference between the established Egyptian civil calendar and our own. Unlike our modern calendar that begins on January 1st, the first month of the Egyptian civil calendar began at the Inundation of the Nile River that occurred between June 15th and June 30th. Then there is the tendency among some Egyptian dynasties, and in our case the Eighteenth Dynasty, to employ the use of a regnal calendar as well; meaning that time was recorded in years from the date of a pharaoh's accession to the throne. For example, some have speculated that the Pharaoh Amenhotep IV ascended the throne sometime during the fifth month of the Egyptian civil calendar. Since the start of the civil calendar occurred between June 15th and June 30th, then Amenhotep IV, according to these scholars, was crowned pharaoh sometime between October 15th and the end of that month. Hence, the game.

Whether dealing either with the Egyptian civil calendar or a specific dynasty's regnal calendar, one always must recognize that modern equivalent years often will overlap. For example, the first regnal year of Amenhotep IV lasted from approximately October 15th/30th, 1377 BC, through approximately October 14th/30th, 1376 BC of our modern calendar.

Sadly the debate does not end here, for scholars have over the years argued long and hard on the actual years that should be assigned to a given civil or regnal year. Again, here a game of sorts is played as well as to

482

whether one prefers a so-called high or low chronology. Consequently, as in the example above, the first regnal year of Amenhotep IV could be assigned as 1377/76 by one scholar using the low chronology, while the very same regnal year for this king could be assigned at 1358/57 using the high chronology. This is why this author has tried to avoid attempting to correlate ancient with modern dates. Instead, he has preferred to enlist regnal dating, i.e., Year 16, to date the events that occurred during the sixteenth year of such and such a king.

The recent discussions of the high and low Egyptian chronology are that of K. A. Kitchen ("The Basics of Egyptian Chronology in Relation to the Bronze Age," in P. Åström, ed., *High, Middle or Low*, Gothenburg 1987 I: 40-43, 47, III: 153) and Jürgen von Beckerath (*Chronologie des pharaonischen Ägypten*, 2nd ed., Munich 2001). On the XVIIIth Dynasty the best, although antithetical, English-speaking Egyptologists on the subject are Donald B. Redford (*Akhenaten. The Heretic King*) and Cyril Aldred (*Akhenaten. King of Egypt*).

On the basis of these two scholar's exhaustive research, the following general chronological outline has been constructed. All dates are understood as BC.

Neferkheperru Amenhotep IV (a.k.a. Akhenaten)

Year 1

Amenhotep III dies during the month of January.

Amenhotep IV ascends the throne of Egypt, perhaps in the fifth month of the civil calendar; thus he took the throne on or after October 15th.

First royal daughter, Meretaten, is born.

Year 2

Amenhotep IV orders his artisans to depict him differently than typically done via the traditional Egyptian canon of art.

The second royal daughter, Meketaten, is born.

Year 3

Amenhotep IV celebrates his first jubilee.

The *Gempaaten* temple (The Sun Disk is found) and several other constructions are begun at East Karnak.

The first royal daughter, Meretaten, appears for the first time in an official stone relief.

The third royal daughter, Ankhesenpaaten is born in this regnal year at the very latest.

Year 5

The second eldest royal daughter, Meketaten, appears for the first time with her older sister in stone.

The third royal daughter appears for the first time in stone.

All three daughters appear for the first time together in stone.

Amenhotep IV changes his name to Akhenaten.

All references to the god Amen are declared anathema.

Work is begun on the construction of the new northern capital of Akhetaten.

The new capital's foundation ceremony took place on the 13th day of the eighth month of this regnal year, e.g., approximately late June 1371.

Year 6

Akhenaten revisits the new capital and takes up residence in a temporary tent city called The Aten is Content.

The Amen temple estates are closed and their revenue is funneled to fund the construction of the new capital.

All work on the Aten sun temple at East Karnak is abandoned.

Year 7

The month of April marks the official founding of the city of Akhetaten.

Year 8

Akhetaten's construction continues apace and is now fully functional with its court and royal residences established.

Prince Tutankhaten is born.

Year 9

The three youngest royal daughters Neferneferuaten, Neferneferure, and Satepenre are all probably born by, if not before, this regnal year.

Year 12

This is the last time that the king, queen, and six daughters are depicted together in stone.

The three youngest daughters are never mentioned in the historical record again.

Year 13

Meketaten, the second royal daughter, dies – apparently during childbirth.

Year 14

The eldest daughter Meretaten becomes Royal Consort and bears Akhenaten a daughter, little Meretaten II.

Akhenaten's mother, Tiye, dies in this year.

Nefertiti no longer appears in the art of the central city.

Year 15

Prince Smenkhkare is crowned Smenkhkare Djeser-kheperu (a.k.a. Neferneferuaten) and the eldest daughter Meretaten becomes his wife and queen.

First year of co-regency of Smenkhkare and Akhetaten.

Ankhesenpaaten, the third eldest royal daughter, becomes the new Royal Consort and bears Akhenaten a daughter, little Ankhesenpaaten II.

Epigraphical evidence that Queen Nefertiti now resides in the northern portion of the city.

Year 16

Second year of co-regency of Smenkhkare and Akhenaten.

During the next two regnal years the following family members of Akhenaten died, perhaps due to a pestilence that had struck the entire ancient Near East: Kiya (second wife), Meretaten (first daughter), his three youngest daughters – Neferneferure, Neferneferuaten, and Satepenre, and his two granddaughters Meretaten II and Ankhesenpaaten II.

Year 17

Third year of co-regency of Smenkhkare and Akhenaten.

Tutankhaten and Ankhesenpaaten are married prior to Akhenaten's death.

Akhenaten's dies sometime during the summer of 1359.

Smenkhkare's sole reign lasts but several months.

Both Smenkhkare and his Queen Meretaten disappear near the end of 1359.

A Note on Egyptian Priests & Priesthoods

The duties of Egyptian priests and their many priesthoods, by the time of the New Kingdom (1567 – 1085 BC), were no longer performed on the behalf of the king by secular officials, but instead this burden was taken on by priests devoted to each god. As one might expect due to the formation of so many religious organizations, priestly bureaucracies formed to manage the resources of the god's estate. Just as naturally priestly hierarchies developed in order to apportion and manage the many tasks associated with the care and maintenance of a specific deity. At the top of this priest ranking stood those who served the god, the high priest, literally "the first servant of the god," who in turn was followed by the "second," "third," and "fourth servant of the god" as well.

In opposition to these administrative rankings, the vast majority of Egyptian priests who undertook the day-to-day temple duties were the common priests, the *wab*-priests, literally "the cleaners." This is not to say that specialty priesthoods did not exist, for they did, especially those devoted to mummification and the necropolis. But one class of priests, the *sem*-priests, appears to connote a ranking of importance unto their own. While certainly not as powerful as high priests nor as lowly as *wab*-priests, the *sem*-priests were those associated with cultic activities and even the royal palace itself.

A Note on the Vocalization of Ancient Egyptian

Regarding the vocalization of ancient Egyptian, the fact of the matter is simply this: the language is a very, very dead one – meaning that what it sounded like has been long lost. Its closest linguistic cousin, Coptic, is itself a dead language, but at least one that included vowels within its script. On this shirt-tailed basis, Egyptologists have carefully compared the vocabularies of the two languages and have constructed a scientific vocalization scheme to approximate what the Egyptian tongue might have sounded like. Even if the assigned vowel placements are accurate, their quality remains just as uncertain as is their emphasis or where the accent falls on a particular word – not to mention that there is evidence to suspect several regional dialectics during the course of any given dynasty. To add even more fuel to the fire, different vocalization schemes have been put forward by the dominant Egyptological schools of thought be they American, British, French, Italian or German. As a consequence, the vocalization of ancient Egyptian becomes more a matter of one's cultural preference than anything else. In short, just what the language really sounded like during a given time period and within a given region is up for grabs.

With the above caveats and considerations in mind, the author offers the following possible pronunciations for the ancient Egyptian names and words that appear in this manuscript.

Akhenaten (a.k.a. Amenhotep IV) – King of Egypt: ach-en-a-ten

Akhetaten – capital city built by Akhenaten – aa-khet-a-ten

Amenemhet – high priest of Amen Re: a-men-em-het

Amen Re – chief divinity of Thebes: a-men-ra

Ankhmes – court royal physician: anch-mes

Hapi – Egyptian god of the Nile: haa-pee

Kiya – nurse of Nefertiti: ke-ya

Maat – divine order: maa-haat

Mahu – Chief-of-Police of Akhet-aten – maa-hoo

Mayneken – *sem*-priest of Ptah: may-necken

Meketaten – royal daughter of Akhenaten and Nefertiti: mech-et-a-ten

Meryptah – high priest of Amen Re: mary-p-taah

Nebmare Amenhotep – King of Egypt: neb-maa-ra a-men-ho-tep

Neferkheperure – birth name of Amenhotep IV (a.k.a. Akhenaten): nefer-keper-roo-ra

Neferneferru Nefertiti – Queen of Egypt and Chief Wife of Akhenaten: nefer-nefer-roo nefer-tee-tee

Paser – regional granary official: pa-ser

Piankhotep – seer and *sem*-priest of Ptah: pee-anch-ho-tep

Ptah – chief divinity of Memphis: p-taah

Sekhemkhet – son of the royal fan-bearer: sech-em-chet

Sekhmet – goddess of war: sech-met

Smenkhkare – King of Egypt: ss-menk-ca-ra

Sia – divine understanding: see-ya

Sobek – Egyptian crocodile god: so-beck

Sobekti – royal servant: so-beck-tee

Tetisheri – royal servant: tetty-sherry

Thoth – god of writing and civilization: thoawth

Thutmose – palace functionary: thuut-mose

Tiye – Queen of Egypt and Chief Wife of Amenhotep III: tee

If you enjoyed this book, then look out the next in this series:
Recovery, The Second Manuscript of the Richards' Trust,

ABOUT THE AUTHOR

To craft such a tale takes wit, a love of science fiction, and above all a deep reverence for ancient history and archaeology. All of these qualities are stitched together beautifully in his books, because Cherf has been there, dug that. This is a guy who has even seen the sunrise from atop the Great Pyramid. Cherf likes to tell a story about when he was eleven year old and had become bored with dinosaurs. While exploring the Field Museum along Chicago's water front one Saturday morning he discovered Hall N— the ancient Egyptian collection. From that time forward Cherf was terminally smitten as that truly was his life-changing "ah ha!" moment.

Needless to say Cherf's books have been generously reviewed by his readers, who have eagerly shared their joy. The *Historical Fiction Society* in 2013 rated *Bow Tie* an Editor's Choice. For an author, such sentiments are an embarrassment of riches, precious words like honey deliciously, drizzled.

Cherf has excavated in Israel and Greece and toured and photographed many of Egypt's ancient sites first hand. He is also a big fan of Tom Clancy and Michael Crichton. But Cherf is quick to point out, whenever he can, the four men that professionally shaped him. Rufus J. Fears first lit the fire; Edward W. Kase stoked it; George J. Szemler refined it; and Charles K. Wolfe, Jr. set him free.

With a BA in Anthropology, MA in Egyptian Archaeology, and PhD in Ancient History, Cherf remains current as an elected officer of Denver's Egyptian Studies Society.

Living with his beloved wife Sue, they keep Foxbat 1 out in the garage. They enjoy playing golf, road racing (that's where Foxbat 1 comes in), jawing around a fire pit on a cool evening while sampling craft beers, and rooting for the Cubs – clearly Cherf is a hopeless romantic. Bottom line: Cherf just flat-out makes science fiction, ancient history, and archaeology come alive.

Visit www.wjcherf.com to access free sample chapters to his eighteen works, and follow the temporal adventures of Egyptologist Joseph Richards.

www.ingramcontent.com/pod-product-compliance
Lightning Source LLC
Chambersburg PA
CBHW030539020726
47494CB00005B/1433